ON *in*

cy

Society

CHRISTINE
MERRILL

Published in Great Britain 2014
by Mills & Boon, an imprint of Harlequin (UK) Limited,
Eton House, 18-24 Paradise Road, Richmond, Surrey, TW9 1SR

DECEPTION IN REGENCY SOCIETY
© 2014 Harlequin Books S.A.

A Wicked Liaison © 2007 Christine Merrill
Lady Folbroke's Delicious Deception © 2011 Christine Merrill

ISBN: 978-0-263-24631-5

052-0914

Harlequin (UK) policy is to use papers that are natural, renewable and recyclable products and made from wood grown in sustainable forests. The logging and manufacturing processes conform to the legal environmental regulations of the country of origin.

Printed and bound
by CPI Group (UK) Ltd, Croydon, CR0 4YY

Christine Merrill lives on a farm in Wisconsin, USA, with her husband, two sons, and too many pets—all of whom would like her to get off the computer so they can check their e-mail. She has worked by turns in theatre costuming, where she was paid to play with period ball gowns, and as a librarian, where she spent the day surrounded by books. Writing historical romance combines her love of good stories and fancy dress with her ability to stare out of the window and make stuff up.

A Wicked Liaison

CHRISTINE MERRILL

To Maddie Rowe, editor extraordinaire.
You make this so much fun
that I forget I'm working.

Chapter One

Anthony de Portnay Smythe sat at his regular table in the darkest corner of the Blade and Scabbard pub. The grey wool of his coat blended with the shadows around him, rendering him almost invisible to the rest of the room. Without appearing to—for to stare at his fellows might prove suicidally rude—he could observe the other patrons. Cutpurses, thieves, petty criminals and transporters of stolen goods. Rogues to a man. And, for all he knew, killers.

Of course, he took great care not to know.

The usual feelings of being comfortable and in his element were unusually disconcerting. He dropped a good week's work on to the table and pushed them towards his old friend, Edgar.

Business associate, he reminded himself. Although they had known each other for many years, it would be a mistake to call his relationship with Edgar a friendship.

'Rubies.' Tony sorted through the gems with his finger, making them sparkle in the light of the candle guttering on the table. 'Loose stones. Easy to fence. You need not even pry them from the settings. The work has been done for you.'

'Dross,' Edgar countered. 'I can see from here the stones are flawed. Fifty for the lot.'

This was where Tony was supposed to point out that they were investment-grade stones, stolen from the study of a marquis. The man had been a poor judge of character, but an excellent judge of jewellery. Then Tony would counter with a hundred and Edgar would try to talk him down.

But suddenly, he was tired of the whole thing. He pushed the stones further across the table. 'Fifty it is.'

Edgar looked at him in suspicion. 'Fifty? What do you know that I do not?'

'More than I can tell you in an evening, Edgar. Far more. But I know nothing about the stones that need concern you. Now give me the money.'

This was not how the game was to be played. And thus, Edgar refused to acknowledge that he had won. 'Sixty, then.'

'Very well. Sixty.' Tony smiled and held out his hand for the money.

Edgar narrowed his eyes and stared at Tony, trying to read the truth. 'You surrender too easily.'

It felt like a long hard fight on Tony's side of the table. Tonight's dealings were just a skirmish at the end of the war. He sighed. 'Must I bargain? Very well, then. Seventy-five and not a penny less.'

'I could not offer more than seventy.'

'Done.' Before the fence could speak again, he forced the stones into Edgar's hand and held his other hand out for the purse.

Edgar seemed satisfied, if not exactly happy. He accepted the stones and moved away from the table, disappearing into the haze of tobacco smoke and shadows around them, and Tony went back to his drink.

As he sipped his whisky, he reached into his pocket to remove the letter and his reading glasses. He absently polished the spectacles on his lapel before putting them on, then settled his chin in his hands to read.

> *Dear Uncle Anthony,*
> *We are so sorry that you were unable to attend the wedding. Your gift was more than generous, but it does not make up in my heart for your absence on my most happy of days. I hardly know what to say in thanks for this and so many other things you have done for my mother and me over the years. Since Father's death, you have been like a second father to me, and my cousins say the same.*

*It was good to see Mother finally marry again,
and I am happy that Mr Wilson could be there to
walk me down the aisle, but I cannot help but
think you deserved the position more than he. I do
not wish my marriage or my mother's to estrange
me from your company, for I will always value
your wise counsel and your friendship.*

*My husband and I will welcome your visit, as
soon as you are able.*

Your loving niece, Jane

Tony stopped to offer a prayer of thanks for the
presence of Mr Wilson. His sister-in-law's discovery
of Mr Wilson, and marriage to same, had stopped in
its tracks any design she might have had to see Tony
standing at the altar in a capacity other than loving
brother or proud uncle.

Marriage to one of his brothers' widows might have
been expedient, since he had wished to involve himself
financially and emotionally in the raising of their children, but the idea always left him feeling squeamish.
Not an emotion he sought, when viewing matrimony.
Seeing the widows of his two elder brothers well married, in a way that did not leave him legshackled to either of them, had been a load off his troubled brow.

And the wedding of young Jane was another happy
incident, whether he could be there to attend or no.
With the two widows and only niece comfortably re-

married, all to gentlemen that met his approval, he had but to worry about the boys.

And, truth be told, there was little to worry about from either of his nephews, the young earl or his brother. Both were settled at Oxford, with their tuitions paid in full for the duration of their stay. The boys were sensible and intelligent, and appeared to be growing into just the sort of men that he could wish for.

And it left Tony—he looked at the letter in front of him. It left him extraneous. He had hoped, when at last he saw the family set to rights, to feel a rush of elation. He was free of responsibility and the sole master of his own life. Now that the time had come, it was without joy.

With no one to watch over, just what was he to do with his time? Over the years, he had invested wisely for the family as well as for himself, and his forays into crime had been less and less necessary and more a relief from the boredom of respectability.

Now that he lacked the excuse that there were mouths to feed and no money in the bank, he must examine his motivations and face the fact that he was no better than the common criminals around him. He had no reason to steal, save the need to feel the life coursing through him when he hung by drainpipes and window sills, fearing detection, disgrace or, worst of all, incarceration, and knowing every move could be his last.

No reason save one, he reminded himself. There

was a slight movement in the heavy air as the door to the tavern opened and St John Radwell, Earl of Stanton, entered and strode purposefully towards the table.

Tony slipped the letter back into his pocket and tried not to appear too eager to have employment. 'You are late.' He raised his glass to the earl in a mocking salute.

'Correction. You are early. I am on time.' Stanton clapped Tony on the shoulder, took the seat that Edgar had vacated, and signalled the barman for a whisky. St John's smile was mocking, but held the warmth of friendship that was absent from others Tony typically met while doing business.

'How are things in the War Department?'

'Not so messy as they were on the battlefield, thank the Lord,' responded St John. 'But still not as well as they could be.'

'You have need of my services?' Tony had no wish to let the man see how much he needed the work, but he itched to do something to take away the feeling of unease he experienced as he read the letter. Anything which might make him feel needed again.

'I do indeed. Lucky for you, and most unlucky for England. We have another bad one. Lord Barton, known to his companions as Jack. He's been a naughty boy, has Jack. He has friends in high places, and is not afraid to use those connections to get ahead.'

'Dealing with the French?' Anthony tried not to yawn.

St John grinned. 'Better than that. Jack is no garden-variety traitor. He prefers to keep his crimes within the country. Recently, a young gentleman from the Treasury Department, while in his cups and gaming in the company of Lord Barton, managed to lose a surprising amount of money very quickly. Young men often do, when playing with Barton.'

'Does he cheat?' Tony asked.

'I doubt he would balk at it, but that is not why the Treasury Department needs your help. The clerk's efforts to win back what he had lost went as well as could be expected. He continued to gamble and lost even more. Soon he was facing utter ruin. Lord Barton applied pressure and convinced the man to debase himself further still, to clear his debt. He delivered to Barton a set of engraving plates for the ten-pound note. They were flawed and going to be destroyed, but they are near enough to perfect to make the notes almost undetectable.'

'Counterfeiting?' Tony could not but help admire the audacity of the man, even as he longed to ruin his plans.

St John nodded. 'The clerk regretted his act almost immediately, but it was too late. Barton is now in a perfect position to destabilise the currency for his own benefit.'

'And you need me to steal your plates back.'

'You will be searching his home for an excessive number of ten-pound notes, paper, inks and, most especially, those plates. Use your discretion. Your utmost discretion, actually. This must not become a public scandal, but it must end immediately, before he begins circulating the money. We wish to break him quickly and quietly, so as not to upset the banks or the exchange.'

The earl dropped a full purse on the table. 'As usual, half in advance and half when the job is completed. Feel free to take an additional payment from the personal wealth of Barton and any associates you might need to search. He has homes in London and Essex. But it has been less than a week since the theft. I doubt he has had time to get the plates out of the city.' As an afterthought, Stanton added, 'You had best search his mistress's home, as well.'

'A criminal's mistress?' Tony grinned. 'You are sending me off to search the perfumed boudoir of some notorious courtesan? And paying me for the privilege.' He rolled his eyes. 'I fear what may become of me, if I am discovered by her. I had no idea that government service would hold such hardship.'

St John sighed with mock-aggravation. 'I doubt there will be any such threat to your dubious virtue, Smythe. The lady is of good character, or was until Barton got his hooks into her. The widow of a peer. It is a shame to see such an attractive young thing consort with the likes of Jack. But one never knows.' He scrawled an address down on a scrap of paper. 'Her Grace, the Dowager Duchess of Wellford. Constance Townley.'

Tony felt the earth lurch under him, as it always did when her name rose unexpectedly in a conversation. But this time, it was compounded by a thrill of horror at hearing it in the current context.

Oh, my God, Connie. What has become of you?

He took a careful swallow of the whisky before speaking. Any hoarseness in his voice could be attributed to the harsh spirit in his glass. 'The loveliest woman in London.'

'So they say,' St John responded. 'The second-loveliest, perhaps. She is a particular friend of my wife and I've often had the opportunity to compare them.'

'Night and day,' remarked Tony, thinking of Constance's shining black hair, her huge dark eyes, her pale skin, next to the fair beauty of Esme Radwell. In his mind, there was no comparison. But to be polite he said, 'You are a fortunate man.'

'As well I know.'

'And you say the duchess has become Barton's mistress.'

'So I have been told. It is likely to become most awkward in my home, for I cannot very well encourage Esme to associate with her, if the rumours are true. But Constance is often seen in Barton's company and he is most adamant about his intentions towards her in conversation with others. Either she is his, or soon will be.'

Tony shook his head in pretended sympathy, along

with Stanton, and said, 'A shame, indeed. But at least that part of the search will be of no difficulty. If the duchess is naïve enough to involve herself with Barton, then she might be unprepared to prevent my search and careless in hiding her part in the crime. When would you like results?'

'As soon as can be managed safely.'

Tony nodded. 'I will begin tonight. With Constance Townley, for she will be the weak link, if there is one. And you will hear from me as soon as I have something to tell.'

Stanton nodded in return. 'I will leave you to it, then. As usual, do not fail me, and do not get caught. My wife expects you to dinner on Thursday and it will be damned difficult explaining to her if you cannot attend because I have got you arrested.' He stood then, and took his leave, disappearing into the crowd and out the door.

Tony stared down into his glass and ignored the pounding blood in his ears. What was he to do about Constance? He had imagined her lying alone in the year following her husband's death, and expected she would be quietly remarried to some honourable man soon after her period of mourning ended.

But to take up with Barton, instead? The thought was repellent. The man was a cad as well as a criminal. Handsome, of course. And well mannered to ladies. He appeared most personable, if you did not know the truth of his character.

But at thirty, Constance was no green girl to be dazzled by good looks and false charm. She might appear to be nothing more than a beautiful ornament, but Tony remembered the sharp mind behind the beauty. Even when she was a girl, she would never have been so foolish as to fall for the likes of Jack Barton. And the thought that she would willingly betray her own country...

He shook his head. He could not bring himself to believe it. If he must search her for Stanton, best to do it quickly and know the truth. And to do so, he must put the past behind him and clear his mind for the night's work ahead of him. He finished the whisky, dropped a sovereign on the table for the barman, and went off into the night, to satisfy his curiosity as to the morals of the Dowager Duchess of Wellford.

Chapter Two

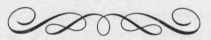

Tony did not need to refer to Stanton's directions—he knew well the location of the house in London where the dowager resided. He'd walked by it often enough in daylight for the twelve months that she'd been in residence. Without intending to observe the place, he'd given himself a good idea of the layout of rooms by watching the activities in the windows as he passed.

Her bedroom would be at the back of the house, facing a small garden. And there would be an alleyway for tradesmen somewhere about. He'd never seen a delivery to the front door.

He worked his way down the row of townhouses, to a cross street and a back alley, counting in reverse until he could see the yellow brick of the Wellford house. As he went, he pulled a dark scarf from his pocket and wrapped it around his neck to hide the white of his shirtfront. His coat and breeches were dark, and needed no cover. Greys, blacks, and dark blues suited him well and blended with the shadows as he needed them to.

The wrought-iron gate was locked, but he found an easy toe-hold in the garden wall beside it. He swung himself to the top with no difficulty, crouching in the protection of a tree. Then, he gauged the distance of open ground to the house. Four paces to the rose-bush, another two to the edge of the terrace and up the ivy trellis at the corner of the house. And, please God, let it hold his weight, for the three storeys to the bedroom window would be no problem to climb, but damned tricky should he fall.

He was across the yard and up the ivy in a flash, happy to find the trellis anchored to the brickwork with stout bolts, and a narrow ledge beneath the third-storey window sill. He walked along it in the darkness, feet sure as though he was walking down a city street.

He stopped when he reached the window he suspected was hers. If it had been his house, he would have chosen another room for solitude, but this one had the best view of the garden. When he had known her, she had enjoyed flowers and he'd been told that the gardens at the Wellford manor had been most splendid because of the duchess's attentions. If she wished to see the rose-bushes, she would choose this room.

He slipped a penknife under the frame, feeling along until he found the latch and felt it slide open with the pressure of the blade. Then he raised the sash a few inches, and listened at the gap.

There were no candles lit. The room was dark and quiet. He threw the window the rest of the way open, and listened again for an oath, an exclamation, anything that might indicate he had been heard. When nothing came, he stepped through the window and stood for a moment behind the curtain, letting his eyes adjust to the dim glow from the banked coals in the grate.

He was alone. He stepped further into the room, and was shocked to feel a wave of sadness and longing overtake him.

So it was not to be as easy as he'd hoped. The irrational jealousy he'd felt, when he'd heard she had found a protector so soon after leaving off her mourning, was burning away. He had hoped he could keep the anger fresh, and use it to protect his resolve when the time came to search her rooms. If she was no longer the innocent girl he remembered, but instead a traitorous whore, then she deserved punishment.

But he probed his heart and knew vengeance would be impossible, as would justice. If there was something to find in the room, he would find it.

And he would destroy it before St John Radwell and the government could ever see. He could not let Barton continue, but he would not let Constance be punished for her lover's crimes. If there was a way to bring her out of it with a whole skin, he would do it, no matter the cost to his own reputation.

He scanned the room. He had chosen well. It was definitely a lady's bedroom: large and high-ceilinged, decorated in rose with delicate furniture. Along the far wall, there was a soft and spacious bed.

Where the Duchess of Wellford entertained Jack Barton.

He turned away from it, looking anywhere but towards the bed.

He had expected to find a well-appointed boudoir, but this room was strangely empty. It was pretty enough, but almost monastic in its simplicity. On the walls there was no decoration. He ran his hands along the floral paper and felt for empty hooks. There should be sconces, there and there. And in the centre? A painting, perhaps, or a mirror with a gilt frame.

He strode across the room, to the wardrobe, threw open the doors, and was momentarily stunned by the scent of her. He closed his eyes and inhaled. Lavender. Had she always smelled this sweet? It had been so many years...

Eyes still shut, he navigated by touch through the dark wardrobe, his fingers playing along the back panels and feeling no spaces, no concealed latches. He patted the gowns and cloaks, feeling for lumps in pockets and finding none.

He opened his eyes again and went through the draw-ers, one at a time, feeling no false bottoms, nothing concealed between the dainties folded there. Silk and linen and fine Indian cotton. Things that had touched her body more intimately than he ever would. His fingers closed on a handkerchief, edged in lace and embroi-dered with a C. Impulsively, he took it and thrust it into his pocket, moving to the dresser to continue his search.

The Dowager Duchess of Wellford perched on the edge of her seat in her parlour, staring hopefully at the man on the couch next to her.

He was about to speak.

It was about time. He had been hinting for weeks.

She did her best to drum up a thrill of anticipation.

'Constance, there is something I wish to speak to you about.'

'Yes, Jeremy.' Jeremy Manders was not her ideal, of course, but neither had her late husband been, and they had suited well enough.

'We have known each other for a long time, since well before your husband passed. And I have always held you in high esteem.'

She smiled and nodded encouragement. 'And I you. You were Robert's good friend, and mine.'

'But I will admit, even while Robert was alive, feel-ing the occasional touch of envy at his good fortune in having you, Constance.'

She blushed and averted her eyes.

'I would never have dared say anything, of course, for Robert was my friend.'

She looked up again, still smiling. 'Of course not.' Her late husband, Robert, was far too much in the conversation for her taste.

'But you were quite the loveliest…still are, I mean, the loveliest woman of my acquaintance.'

'Thank you, Jeremy.' This was much better. She accepted the compliment graciously. But she wished that, just once, a man could comment on something other than her appearance.

'I hesitated to say anything, while you were still in mourning. It would hardly have been respectful.'

'Of course not.' He was hesitating to say it now, as well. Why could he not just go down on a knee and speak the words?

'But I think sufficient time has passed. And you do not appear to be otherwise engaged. I mean, you are not, are you?'

'No. My affections are not held by another, and I am quite out of my widow's weeds.' And growing older by the minute. Was it too much to expect him to seize and kiss her? That would make the point clear enough.

And it might be most romantic. But it would be too much to ask, and she forced herself not to wish for it.

'So there is no one else? Well, that is good to know.' He sagged with relief. 'I thought, if you were free, that we might do well together. You find me attractive, I hope.'

'Oh, yes, Jeremy.' She hoped it was not too obvious to a casual observer that she was reaching the point where she would find any man kind enough to offer marriage to be of surpassing handsomeness.

'And I assure you, I will be able to meet your expenses. I have ample resources, although I am not a duke, as your late husband was.'

Robert again. But Jeremy could afford to pay her bills, so let him talk. 'That is a great comfort to me.'

'And I would want you to get whatever gowns and frippery you might wish, as soon as possible. It must be most tiring to you to have to wear black for a year, and then to make do with what you had before.'

Shopping for things she did not need. She had quite forgotten what it was like. She smiled, but assured him, 'Really, it is only foolishness. It does not matter so much.'

'Oh, but it does to me. I wish to see you as bright and happy as ever you were.'

Relief flooded through her.

'I will provide a house, of course. Near Vauxhall, so that we might go there of an evening. And a generous allowance.'

'House?' The flood of relief became tainted with a trickle of doubt.

'Yes. And the dresses, of course. You could keep a staff, of…' he calculated '…three.'

'Three?'

'And your maid as well,' he amended. 'Which would really be four.'

'Jeremy, we are not negotiating my living arrangements.'

'Of course not. Any number you choose. I want you to be comfortable. And I brought with me a token of my esteem.' He reached into his pocket, and produced not a small square box, but one that was thin and slender.

She took it from him and snapped it open. 'You got me a bracelet?'

It was his turn to blush. 'There were matching earbobs. I could have got those as well, but perhaps after you say yes…'

'Jeremy, it sounds almost as though you are offering me a *carte blanche*.' She laughed a trifle too loudly at the ridiculousness of the idea.

She waited for him to laugh in return and say she was mistaken.

And he was silent.

She snapped the box shut again and thrust it back to him. 'Take it.'

'You do not like it? Because I can get another.'

'I do not want another. I do not want this one.' She could feel the colour in her face turning to an angry

flush as her voice rose. 'You come here, talking of esteem, and your great fondness for me, then you offer
to put me up and pay my expenses?'

Jeremy stiffened, a picture of offended dignity.
'Well, someone must, Constance. You cannot go on
much longer living on your own. And surely, after
twelve years of marriage, and over a year alone, you
must miss the affections of a man.'

'Oh, must I?' she said through clenched teeth. 'I do
not miss them so much that I seek to dishonour myself
outside of marriage just to pay my bills. I thought, if
you held me in such high esteem…'

'Well…' he swallowed '…here's the rub. Father
will be wanting me to guarantee the inheritance. Now
it's a long time before I need to worry about such. But
when it comes time for me to marry, I will have to pick
someone—' he searched for the correct words and finished '—that my father approves of.'

'And he will not approve of a thirty-year-old childless widow. That's what you're saying, isn't it, but
you lack the spine to say it out loud? You wish to
bounce me between the sheets and parade me around
Vauxhall in shiny new clothes. But when it is time for
you to marry, you will go to Almack's for a wide-
hipped virgin.'

Jeremy squirmed in his chair. 'When you say it that
way, it sounds so—'

'Accurate? Candid? Cruel? It sounds cruel because

it is, Jeremy. Now take your compliments and your jewellery and your offers of help and get them from my house.'

Jeremy drew himself up and gathered what righteousness he could. 'Your house? For how long, Constance? It is apparent to those who know you well that you are in over your head, even if you do not wish to admit it. I only meant to help you in a way that might be advantageous to both of us. And I am sure there are women who will not find what I'm suggesting so repugnant.'

There was that tone again. She had heard it before, when she'd refused such offers in the past. Reminding her not to be too particular, or to expect more than she deserved, but to settle for what was offered and be glad of it. She glared at him in silence and pointed to the door.

He rose. 'Very well. If you change your mind on the subject, send a message to my rooms. I will wait, for a time. But not for long, Constance. Do not think on it overlong. And if you expect a better offer from Barton, then you are sadly mistaken. You'll find soon enough that his friendship is no truer than mine. Good evening.'

He strode from the room, then she heard him in the hall calling for his hat and stick, and the adamant snap as the front door closed behind him.

She sat, staring into the fire, her mind racing. Jeremy was to have been the answer to all her problems.

She had been so sure of it. She had been willing to overlook a certain weakness of chin and of character. She had laughed at his boring stories. She had listened to him talk politics, and nodded, even though she could not find it in herself to agree. And she had found him foolish, sober or in mirth. She had been more than willing to marry a buffoon, and smile and nod through the rest of her life, in exchange for a little security and consistent companionship.

Maybe Jeremy had been a fool, but an honest and good-hearted one, despite his offer. And he had been right when he'd hinted that anything was better than what Lord Barton might suggest, if she allowed him to speak to her again. Jeremy could at least pretend that what he was doing would be best for both of them. There had never been any indication, when she'd looked into Jack Barton's eyes, that he cared in the slightest about anyone but himself.

'Your Grace, can I get you anything?' It was her maid, Susan, come downstairs to see what was the matter.

Constance glanced up at the clock. An hour had passed since Jeremy had gone, and she had let it, without moving from the spot. 'No, I am all right. I think I will put myself to bed this evening, Susan. Rest yourself. I will see you in the morning.'

The girl looked worried, but left her in peace.

When Constance went to stand, it felt as if she had to gather strength from deep within for the minor effort of rising from the chair. She climbed the stairs with difficulty, glad that the maid was so easily persuaded. It would be better to crawl up the stairs alone on her hands and knees than to admit how hard a blow Jeremy had struck with his non-proposal.

Susan knew the trouble she faced. The girl had found her before when she'd come to wake her, still dressed and dozing in a bedroom chair. Constance had been poring over the accounts in the wee hours, finding no way to make the expenses match the meagre allowance she received from her husband's nephew, Freddy. If only her husband had taken him in hand and taught him what would be expected, Freddy might have made a decent peer.

But Robert had been so set on the idea that they would have a child. There would be an heir, if not this year, then certainly the next. And if his own son were to inherit the title, he might never need bother with his tiresome nephew.

And now Robert was gone, and the new duke was heedless of anything but his own pleasure. He knew little of what it took to run his own estates and even less what Robert might have expected of him in regards to the welfare of the dowager.

Dowager. How she loathed the word. It always brought to mind a particularly unattractive piece of furniture. The sort of thing one put in a seldom-used room, allowing the upholstery to become faded and moth-eaten, until it was totally forgotten.

An accurate enough description, when one thought of it. Her own upholstery was sadly in need of replacement, but with the butcher's bill and the greengrocer, and the cost of coal, she dare not spend foolishly.

Of course, she could always sell the house and move to smaller accommodations, if she had the deed in hand. She had seen it, the day her husband had drawn it up. The house and its contents were clearly in her name, and he had assured her that she would not want, when his time came.

Then he had locked it in his safe and forgotten it. And now, the new duke could not be troubled to give it to her. When she asked, it was always tomorrow, or soon. She felt her lip quaver and bit it to stop the trembling. She had been a fool not to remove the keys from her husband's pocket, while his body was barely cold. She could have gone to the safe and got the deed herself and no one need have been the wiser. Now the keys and the safe belonged to Freddy and she must wait upon him to do the right thing.

Which was easier than waiting upon her suitors to offer something other than their false protection. She had been angry the first time someone had suggested that she solve her financial problems on her back. When it had happened again, anger had faded to dread. And now, it had happened so many times that she wanted nothing more than to hide in her rooms and weep.

Was this the true measure of her worth? Men admired her face and wanted her body, there was no question of that. And they seemed to enjoy her company. But never so much that they could overlook a barren womb when it came time to wed. They wanted the best of both worlds: a wife at home, great with child, and an infertile mistress tucked away for entertainment so that they could remain conveniently bastardless.

Damn Jeremy and his empty promises. She had been so sure that his hints about the future were honourable.

What was she to do now, other than to take the offer, of course? It would solve all her worries if she was willing to bend the last little bit, and give up on the idea that she could ever succeed in finding another husband. She shut the door behind her and snuffed her candle, letting the tears flow down her cheeks in the dark.

And in a corner of the room there was movement.

She caught her breath and held it. It was not a settling of the house, or a mouse in the wainscoting. That had been the scrape of a boot on the wood floor near the dresser. And then something fell from the dresser top. Her jewellery box. She could hear the meagre contents landing like hailstones on the rug.

A thief. Come to take what little she had left.

Her fatigue fled. A scream would be useless. With all the servants safely below stairs, no one would hear her. To get to the bell pull, she would need to go closer to the thief, and he would never allow her to reach it. She turned to run.

The stranger was across the room and caught her before she could move, and a hand clamped down over her mouth.

Chapter Three

'Remain silent, your Grace, and I will do what I came for and be gone. You are in no danger from me, as long as you are quiet.'

His hand eased away from her lips, but he held her close in a most familiar way, one hand at the back of her neck, the other cupping her hip, and his legs bumping against the length of her.

And suddenly, she was sick and tired of men trying to sample the merchandise without buying, or wanting to rob her, or dying and leaving her penniless and alone. She fought to free her arms and stuck him hard in the face. 'I'll give you silence, you thieving bastard.' She hit him again, in the shoulder, but his hands did not move. 'Is that quiet enough for you, you dirty sneak?' And she beat upon him with her closed fists, as silently as possible, shoulders shaking with effort, gasping out tears of rage.

He took the rain of blows in silence as well, except for the occasional grunt when a well-landed punch caused him to expel a puff of air. And when her blows began to weaken he effortlessly caught her wrists and pinned them behind her. 'Stop it, now, before you hurt yourself. You'll bruise your hands, and do more damage to them than you might to me.'

She struggled in his grip, but he held firm until the last of the fight was gone from her and there was nothing left but tears.

'Finished? Good. Now, tell me what is the trouble.' He produced a handkerchief from his pocket and offered it to her, and she was appalled to recognise it as her own.

'Trouble? Are you daft in the head? There is a man in my room, holding me against my will. And going through my lingerie.' She crushed the linen square in her hand and tossed it at his feet.

'Before that.' She could barely make out his face in the embers from the banked fire, but there was sympathy in his voice. 'You were crying before you ever knew I was here. Truth, now. What was the matter?'

'Why do you care?'

'Is it not enough to know that I do?'

'No. You have a reason for it, and as a common thief, you must wish the knowledge to use against me in some way.'

He laughed, soft in her ear. 'I am a most uncommon

thief then, for I have your interests in mind. Does it help you to trust me, if I assure you that I am a gentleman? If you met me under better circumstances, you'd find me a picture of moral fortitude. I do not drink to excess, I do not gamble, I am kind to children and animals, and I have loved only one woman the whole of my life.'

She struggled in his arms. 'And yet you do not shirk at sneaking into other women's bedrooms and taking their things.'

He sighed, but did not let her go. 'Sometimes, perhaps. But I cannot bear to see a woman in distress, and I do not steal from those that cannot afford to lose. In the box on your dresser there is a single strand of pearls and a pair of gold earrings. The rest is paste. Where is the real jewellery, your Grace?'

'Gone. Sold to pay my bills, as was much of the household furniture. You see what is there. Take it. Would you like the candlesticks from the mantel as well? They are all I have left of value. Take them and finish me.'

His grip upon her loosened, and he took her hand and bowed over it. 'I beg your pardon, your Grace. I mistook the situation. Things are not as they appear to the outside, are they? The world assumes that your husband's wealth left you financially secure.'

She gathered her dignity around her. 'I make sure of that.'

'Can you not appeal to friends for help?'

She tossed her head. 'I find, when one has no husband to defend one's honour, or family to return to, that there are not as many true friends as one might think. There are many who would prey upon a woman alone, if she shows weakness.'

'But I am not one of them.' He was still holding her hand in his and his grip was sure and warm. She thought, in the dimness, she could see a smile playing at the corners of his lips. 'I have taken nothing from your jewel case. I swear on it. And the handkerchief?' He shook his head. 'I do not know what possessed me. I am not in the habit of rifling through women's linens and taking trophies. It was a momentary aberration. I apologise and assure you that you will find nothing else missing from your personal items.'

She thought, for just a moment, how nice it would be to believe him and to think there was one man on the planet who did not mean to take more than she wished to give. 'So you have broken into my rooms and mean to take nothing, then?' she asked suspiciously.

Now she was sure she could hear the smile in his voice. 'A trifle, perhaps. Only this.' And he pulled her close again to bring her mouth to his.

The thief did not bother with the niceties. There was no gentle caress, no hesitation, no request for permission. He opened her mouth and he took.

She steeled herself against the violation, deciding,

if it was a choice of the two, she had much rather he took a kiss than the candlesticks. It was foolish of her to have mentioned them, for she needed the money their sale would bring.

In any case, at least the kiss would be over soon and she did not need to spare his feelings and pretend passion where she felt none, as she had with Jeremy. But unlike Jeremy, this man was most expert at kissing.

Her mind drifted. His hand was on her shoulder and her head rested in the crook of his elbow, as he tipped her back in the cradle of his arms. It felt strangely comforting to be held by the stranger. She need barely support herself, for he was doing a most effective job of bearing her weight. She tilted her head slightly, and he adjusted, tasting her lips and her tongue as though he wanted to have every last bit of sweetness from them before letting her go.

She relaxed and gave it up to him. And was shocked to find herself willing to give him more. It had been a long time since she had felt so well and truly kissed. Her husband's kisses, in recent years, had been warm and comfortable, but not particularly passionate. The kisses she'd received from suitors since his death were more ardent, but could not seem to melt the frozen places in her heart, or ease the loneliness.

But this man kissed as if he were savouring a fine wine. He was dallying with her, barely touching her lips and then sealing their mouths to steal the breath from her lungs.

His hands were gentle on her body, taking no further liberty than to support her as he kissed, and she knew she had but to offer the slightest resistance and he would set her free.

But she was so tired of being free, if freedom meant loneliness and worry. And suddenly, the kiss could not be long enough or deep enough to satisfy the craving inside of her. His hands stayed still on her body, but she wished to feel them do more than just hold her. She wanted to be touched.

Her own hands were clenched in fists on his shirt-front, and she realised that she'd planned to push him away before now. Instead she opened them, palms flat and fingers spread on his chest, before running them up his body to wrap her arms around his neck. The hair at the back of his head was soft, and curled around her fingers as she tangled them in it, pulling herself closer to kiss him back. He smelled of wood smoke and soap, and he tasted like whisky. And when she moved her tongue against his, he tensed and his hands went hard against her body, his thumb massaging circles deep into the flesh of her shoulder. His other hand tightened on the soft flesh of her hip to hold her tight to him. She could feel his smile, tingling against her lips.

And then, as quickly the kiss had begun, it was

over. He set her back on her feet again and for a moment they leaned against each other, as though neither were steady enough to stand without support of the other. When he pulled away from her, he shook his head and sighed in satisfaction. He was breathless, as he said, 'That is quite the richest reward I've taken in ages. So much more valuable than mere jewels. I will live on the memory of it for a very long time.' He traced the outline of her lips with the tip of his finger. 'I am sorry for frightening you and I thank you for not crying out. Know that your secrets are as safe with me as mine are with you. And now, if you will excuse me?' He bowed. 'Do not light the candle just yet. Count ten and I will be gone.'

And he turned from her and went to the window, stepping over the sill and out into the darkness.

She rushed to the window after him, and looked out to see him climb down the side of the house and slip across the garden as noiselessly as a shadow, before scaling the stone wall that surrounded it.

He paused as he reached the top and turned back to look towards her. Could he see her there, watching him go, or did he merely suspect?

But she could see him, silhouetted on the top of the garden wall. He was neither dark nor fair. Brown hair, she thought, although it was hard to tell in the moonlight, and dark clothes. A nice build, but she'd felt that when he'd held her. Not a person she recognised.

He blew a kiss in the direction of her open window, swung his legs over the side and dropped from view.

She hurried back into the room and fumbled with a lucifer and a taper, trying to still the beating of her heart. She might not know him, but he knew her. He knew the house and had called her by her title.

And now he knew her secret: she was helpless and alone and nearing the end of her resources. She found this not nearly as threatening as if Lord Barton had known the depth of her poverty. If he had, he'd have used that to his advantage against her.

But the thief had apologised, and taken his leave. And the kiss, of course. But he'd left everything of value, so it was a fair trade. She knelt to pick up the contents of the spilled jewel box, and her foot brushed a black velvet bag on the floor at the side of the dresser.

He must have brought it, meaning to hold the things he took. And it was not empty. As she picked it up, she felt the weight of it shift in her hands.

Dear God, what was she to do now? She could not very well call the man back. He was no longer in the street and she did not know his address.

She did not want to know his address, she reminded herself. He was a criminal. She would look more than forward to seek him out, after the way she had responded to the kiss. And the contents were not his, anyway, so why should they be returned? If the bag contained jewellery, perhaps she could put an ad in *The*

Times, describing the pieces. The rightful owners would step forward, and she might never have to explain how she got them.

She poured the contents of the bag out into her hand. Gold. Guineas filled her hand, and spilled on to the floor.

She tried to imagine the ad she must post, to account for that. 'Will the person who lost a large sum of money on my bedroom floor please identify it…?'

It was madness. There was no way she could return it.

She gathered the money into stacks, counting as she went. This was enough to pay the servants what she owed them, and settle the grocer's bill and next month's expenses as well.

If she kept her tongue and kept the money, she could hold off the inevitable for another month.

But what if the thief came back and demanded to know what had become of his money? She shivered. Then she must hope that he was as understanding as he had been this evening. It would not be so terrible if she must part with another kiss.

Tony arrived at his townhouse in fine spirits, ignored the door before him and smiled at the façade. He rubbed his palms together once, and took a running start at it, jumping to catch the first handhold above the window of the front room. He climbed the next flight easily, his fingers and toes fitting into the familiar places worn into the bricks, then leaned to grasp the edge of the balcony, chinning himself, swinging a leg up and rolling his body lightly over the railing to land on his feet in front of the open doors to his bedroom. He parted the curtains and stepped through. 'Good evening, Patrick.'

His valet had responded with an oath and seized the fireplace poker to defend himself, before recognising his master and trying to turn his movement into an innocuous attempt to adjust the logs in the grate. 'Sir. I believe we have discussed this before. It is a very bad habit, and you have promised to use the front door in the future, just as I have promised to leave it unlocked on nights when you are working.'

Tony grinned back at him. 'I am sorry. I could not help myself. I am—'

Deliriously happy.

'—full of the devil, after this evening's outing. You will never guess who Stanton sent me out to spy on.'

Patrick said nothing, waiting expectantly.

'The Dowager Duchess of Wellford.'

This was worthy of another oath from Patrick. 'And you informed him that you could not.'

'I did no such thing. He was under the impression that she was consorting with Lord John Barton, that they were in league in some sort of nefarious doings involving stolen printing plates. If he had not sent me, it would be someone else. I went post-haste to her rooms for a search. The climb to her bedroom window was—'

As easy as I've always dreamed it to be...

'—no problem. Thank the Lord, there was no sign of anything illegal hidden in her rooms. Although there is evidence that she is in dire straits and in a position to be forced to do things against her nature, by Barton or someone else. And then—and here is the best part, Patrick—while I was searching, she caught me at it.'

'Sir.' Patrick's tone implied that the word 'caught' was not under any circumstances the best part of a story.

'She caught me,' Tony repeated. 'And so I was forced to hold her tight, and question her. And because I wished to be every bit the rogue I appeared to be, I kissed her.'

'And then?' Patrick leaned forward with a certain amount of interest.

Tony sighed. 'And then she kissed me back.'

'And then?' Patrick prompted again.

'And then I climbed out the window and came home. But not before leaving her the purse that Stanton had given me to cover the night's work. I dare say she will not be required to sell the last of her jewellery for quite some time. St John was most generous. It was quite the most perfect evening I've ever had. What say you to that?'

Patrick dropped any attempt at servitude. 'I say, some day, when you are old enough to be shaved, you will be quite a man with the ladies. Ah, but wait. You are thirty, are you not? Then it is quite another matter.'

'And what would you have had me do?'

Patrick was working very hard not to make any of the more obvious suggestions, which might get him sacked. 'You might, at least, have told her the truth.'

'Just what part of it?'

'That you have been pining for her like a moon calf, low these long years.'

'I did tell her. Well, not the truth, as such. Not that truth, at any rate. I told her that she needn't be afraid, which is true. And that I was a most unexceptional fellow. And that I have loved one woman my entire life.' Tony frowned. 'I did not tell her it was her, as such. You might think a woman would be glad to hear that? But trust me, Patrick, when she is hearing it from a stranger who is hiding in her bedroom, it will not be well received.'

'But you are not a stranger to her.'

'But she does not know that. I did not have time to explain the full story. An abbreviated version of the truth, one which omitted my identity, was definitely the order of the day. And despite what you may think of my romantic abilities, I've told the story before and found that omitting the identity of my beloved works in my favour. Nothing softens the heart of a woman quite so much as the story of my hopeless love for another. And how can I resist when they wish to comfort me in my misery?'

'Sir,' said Patrick, in a way that always seemed to mean 'idiot'. 'If you are with the object of the hopeless passion, and you wish the passion to cease being a hopeless one, then the unvarnished truth is usually the best course.'

No longer hopeless...

Tony shook his head. A single kiss was a long way from the fulfilment of his life's romantic fantasies, and it would be foolish to set his heart upon it. 'Nothing will come from this night's meeting. Even if the whole truth is revealed. Think sensibly for a moment, Patrick. Much time has passed since I knew her. She barely knew me then. I doubt she even remembers me. She is a duchess, even if she is a dowager. And while I am her most humble servant, I am most decidedly not, nor ever will be, a duke. Or, for that matter, a marquis, an earl or even a baron. With me, she could live quite comfortably to a ripe old age.' He dismissed his own dreams on that subject with a wave of his hand.

'But should she attach herself to me, it would mean that many doors, which were once opened, would be closed to her. She would go from her Grace the Duchess to plain old Mrs Smythe. In the face of that, an offer of undying devotion is no equal. And the whole town knows her as the most beautiful woman in London. She will not want for suitors, and need not settle for the likes of me. She will aim higher, when she seeks another husband. Man is not meant to have all that he dreams possible. Not in this life, at any rate.'

Patrick applauded with mock-courtesy. 'Most humble, sir. I had forgotten that you studied for the ministry. You have done a most effective job of talking yourself out of the attempt. In winning the hand of a lady, it would be better if you had studied the Romans. *Carpe diem*, sir.'

'I *carpe*-d the situation to the best of my ability, thank you very much.' Tony closed his eyes and remembered the kiss. 'And perhaps there will be other opportunities. I must see her again, in any case, to settle the business with Barton and to make sure she is all right.'

He remembered the missing ornaments and the empty jewel box. 'Stanton is wrong. I am sure of it. He told me she was Barton's mistress. But if Barton is keeping her, he is doing it on the cheap. If she were mine, her jewel box would be full to overflowing.'

If she were mine...

'But it is almost empty. And there is evidence that she is selling off the furnishings of the house to make ends meet. I had assumed that that old ninny Wellford would make provision for her after his death. Surely he did not think taking a young wife would somehow extend his own time on this mortal coil. He must have known she'd outlive him.'

He sat in his favourite armchair and stared into the

fire. 'She is putting up a brave front, Patrick, but things are not right, above stairs. The least I can do, as an old friend of the family, is see to it that she comes through this safely.'

Patrick snorted, and poured him his brandy. 'What utter nonsense. Yes, that is the least you could do. And I do not see why you feel it necessary to pretend that you wish to do as little as possible. It astounds me that someone who has no trouble taking things which do not belong to him balks when there is a chance to take the thing he most wants.'

Tony took the proffered glass and gestured with it. 'She is not some inanimate object, Patrick. I cannot just go and take her. She has a say in the matter.'

Patrick shook his head, giving his master up as hopeless, and, totally forgetting his station, poured a brandy for himself. 'Not the woman, sir. Happiness. You are so accustomed to thinking in terms of what you might do for others that you forget to do what might be in your own best interests. By all means, empty your purse and risk your fool neck helping the woman, if it pleases you to do so.

'But when the moment comes to collect a reward for it, do not stand upon your honour and deny yourself what pleasure you can gain from the moment. Do not think twice about your inability to rival her late husband in rank or pocketbook. If, in the end, the woman cares only for those, you must admit you have been wrong about her, and the girl you loved no longer exists. No matter how beautiful she may be, if she is a fortune hunter, then she is not worth saving and you are best off to forget her.'

Chapter Four

Constance sat in her morning room, paging through the small stack of receipts in front of her. It was ever so much more satisfying than the stack of overdue bills that had been there just a few days before. She was a long way from safe. But neither was she standing on the edge of financial disaster, staring down into total ruin.

She would need to visit the new duke, to remind him of his promised allowance, which would cover the incoming bills. And while there, she could retrieve the deed. With that in hand, she might secure a loan against the house, or arrange its sale. With money of her own in her pocket, she might protect herself against the vagaries of Freddy's payments for many months to come. For the first time in ages, she felt the stirrings of hope for the future, and cautious optimism.

And her salvation had come from a strange source,

indeed. She offered a silent prayer of thanks for the timely intervention of the thief, whoever he might be, and hoped that the loss of his little bag had not forced him to do other crimes. She would hate to think herself the cause of misfortune in others, or the further ruination of the man that had climbed out of her window.

But, somehow, she suspected it was not the case. Perhaps she was romanticising a criminal, and most foolish for it. She might be creating a Robin Hood out of a common scoundrel. But the situation had been so fortuitous, it almost seemed that he had meant to leave the money behind for her use.

It was a ludicrous notion. What reason would he have had to help her? But he had offered, had he not? And if he had not meant to leave it, he must have missed the bag by now. Surely he would have returned to take it from her? After she was sure he was gone, she had gathered the money back into the sack, and placed it under her pillow. And then she had lain awake in dread most of the night, convinced that at any moment, she would feel a breeze at the window and hear a light step on the carpet, approaching her bed in the darkness…

And at last she had forced herself to admit that it was not dread she was feeling at the reappearance of the strange man. The idea that he would return and she might open her eyes to find him bending over her bed and reaching to touch her, held no terror, just a rush of passionate emotion fuelled by the memory of a stolen kiss.

Which was utterly ridiculous. It had been a very nice kiss. And best to leave it at that. He was a thief, and she would be a fool to trust him with her heart or her reputation, despite what he had said to her the previous night.

And even if he were a gentleman, as he claimed, what could they possibly have in common other than a single moment of weakness? Could she have a conversation with him, in the light of day? Would he even wish to see her? He had said something about being in love. Did he care for her at all? Kisses meant very little to most men. He had probably forgotten it already.

But it had been a most extraordinary kiss.

Her mind had circled back again, to replay the kiss, as it seemed to do whenever she tried to talk herself out of the fantasy. She was fast creating a paragon out of nothing. A man both dashing and kind, but more than a bit of a rogue. When the candles were lit, he would be passably good-looking, and as innocuous in appearance and behaviour as he had claimed. But at night, he was a burglar, living off his wits. And a single kiss from her would make him forsake all others and risk capture by returning to her rooms.

She closed her eyes and smiled, imagining his arms about her again. He would confess that he was unable to resist the attraction, and assure her that, if she could find it in her heart to forgive his criminal misdeeds, he would love and cherish her 'til the end of her days.

'Your Grace, there is a gentleman here to see you.'

Susan was standing in the door, hesitating to interrupt. And for a moment, Constance thought that her dream had come to life. She looked enquiringly to her maid.

'Lord Barton.'

Damn.

'Tell him I am not at home, Susan.'

'He is most insistent, your Grace.'

'As am I. I am not now, nor ever shall be, at home to Lord Barton.'

'I thought you might say that.' The voice came from the hall, just beyond Susan's head. 'So I took the liberty of letting myself in. I hope you don't mind.' Jack Barton's tone made it clear that he didn't care one way or the other whether she minded—he intended to do as he pleased in the matter.

Constance swept the papers she'd been holding under the desk blotter to hide them, and stood to face him.

'I mind very much, Lord Barton.'

'I believe I requested, when last we talked, that you call me Jack.' He was smiling, as though he had totally forgotten her response to their last conversation.

'And then you insulted me.'

'I meant the offer as a compliment, your Grace. I do not make it lightly, nor do I make such generous offers to all the women of my acquaintance.'

'You suggested that I become your mistress,' she reminded him, coldly.

'Because I wish to surround myself with beauty, and can afford to do so. You are quite the most beautiful woman I have ever seen, and I mean to have you.'

'I am not some item, to be added to your collection,' she replied. 'You are mistaken, if you think you can purchase a woman as easily as a painting.'

He was unaffected by her answer. 'I have not been so in the past. For the most part, it is only a matter of finding the correct price. Once you do, you can purchase anything.'

'Let me make myself clear: you cannot buy me, Lord Barton. No amount of money would induce me to submit to you. Now, get out of my house.' She pointed towards the door.

'No.'

This presented a problem. She could not put him out herself, and such male servants as she had were either too young or too old to do the job for her. To a gentleman, her demand that he leave should have been enough. But if she was forced to rely on Barton's honour as a gentleman, she was left with nothing at all to defend herself. 'Very well, then,' she said, resigned. 'State your business and then be gone.'

He smiled and took a seat in the chair near her desk, as though he were a welcome guest. 'I expected you would see it my way, once you had thought about it. I came about the ball I am hosting, tomorrow evening.'

'I sent regrets.'

'Yes, you did. You are the picture of courtesy, if a trifle stubborn. I must break you of that, if we are to manage well together.'

'Do not think you need to manage me, Lord Barton,' she snapped back at him. 'I thought I made it clear, when I refused your contemptible offer, that we would not be doing anything further together. I do not wish to dance with you. I doubt I can eat in your presence, since the thought of you sickens me. And thus, I sent regrets for your ball.'

Her word seemed to have no effect on his continued good humour. He was still smiling as he said, 'That is not acceptable.'

'It is most acceptable to me,' she insisted. 'And that is all that matters. I doubt that you have any tender feelings that I might have offended. I do not believe you capable of them.'

'Let me speak plainly,' he said.

'I have been unable to stop you.'

'You will be in attendance at the ball, because I wish it to be so.'

'And why would I care what you wish?'

Without another word, he reached into his pocket, and withdrew an object, wrapped in a linen handkerchief. His eyes widened and his mouth made an 'Oh', like a conjuror performing a trick. Then he dipped his fingers into the bundle and withdrew a ruby-and-diamond necklace. He dangled it in front of her.

And without thinking, she reached for it, and cursed her hand for acting faster than her wits.

'I knew you would not be bribed with pretty words or baubles like a sensible woman, since I've tried that and failed. But then I thought, perhaps I was using the wrong bait.'

She watched the necklace, glittering in his hand, and tried to conceal her desire for it.

'You were most foolish to sell the whole thing. You needn't have made a complete copy you know. Just pried out the stones and let the jeweller fit paste ones into the old setting.'

She had learned that herself, after selling the rubies. The cost of even the cheapest copy ate almost all of the additional profit from selling the gold setting.

She said nothing.

He turned the necklace to let the jewels sparkle in the sunlight. 'And you made the copy, once you realised that the necklace was not technically yours, did you not? It is part of your husband's entail. It belongs to the new duke, and not to you. It was very wrong of you to sell it. What do you suppose the new duke would say, if he knew you were selling a necklace that has been in his family for generations?'

The new duke would likely go many months before noticing its absence. When he did, she'd hoped to stall him with the copy until she could afford to buy back the real necklace. But she kept her foolish mouth shut over the secret since Barton had enough power over her without her full confession.

'I trust you have seen the error of your ways, and do not wish to continue stealing from your nephew.'

She thought to argue that it was not really stealing, if one was only trying to get money that one was owed, and continued to hold silent.

He nodded as though she had spoken. 'Fortunately for you, I am an understanding man. I will give you back your necklace. Once you have done something for me.'

She closed her eyes. Now she must decide. Lie with Barton, or let him go to Freddy with the necklace. The choice was easy. Let him tell Freddy the truth. Perhaps it would move the duke to loosen his purse strings.

When she opened her eyes again, Barton was watching her with amusement. 'You are not asking what it is I wish.'

'I know what it is that you want. The answer is still no.'

He laughed. 'You think I demand unconditional surrender, for a single strand of rubies? While it is a lovely necklace, I suspect you hold your honour to be worth more. A price above rubies, perhaps?' He laughed. 'Listen carefully to my offer, and then give me your answer.

'First, what will happen to you, if you deny me: I will let the necklace fall from my pocket somewhere public. Everyone knows it is yours. Someone will ask me how I came by it. I will explain how you left it in my rooms. The world will draw its own conclusions, and you will be ruined.

'Or you can attend the ball tomorrow. You will stand beside me as hostess, and dance with me as I wish. At the end of the evening, I will return the jewels to you, and you may go home.'

'And if I stand up with you, the world will draw much the same conclusions that they did, if I do not obey you,' she said.

'They might wonder, but they will not be sure.'

She weighed the possibilities. The ruby necklace was clear proof of her perfidy. If she could retrieve it without much cost to her honour, it would be worth the attempt. Of course, there was a chance that he would deny her.

He saw the suspicion in her eyes. 'You needn't fear. I swear that you shall have the thing back before the clock strikes twelve. And I do not expect physical intimacy. Not yet, at any rate. But if you think you can toy with me, or trick me in some way, the price for the necklace may be much higher the next time I offer it.'

What was she to do? It was not really such a great sacrifice to go to a ball. Although she hated Barton, it would do her reputation no real harm. 'Very well. I will attend.'

He laughed, again. It was a cold sound, short and

brittle like cracking ice. 'Excellent. I shall have the pleasure of your company, and you shall have your necklace.'

He leaned closer, the laughter gone from his voice. 'And you will have learned a valuable lesson. When things go my way, I am happy and reward those around me. Rewards are so much better than punishment, are they not? I find that training a woman is not much different than training a hound. It all begins with the smallest act of obedience. Once a man has achieved that, he is well on the road to becoming a master.' There was a half-smile of satisfaction on his face, as though his eventual victory was a foregone conclusion.

'You will find, Lord Barton, that I am not some lapdog to be easily brought to heel. You have won in this. But that is all. Now, if you will excuse me, I must prepare for your ball tomorrow. I wish to look my best, so that you may remember me well, for it will be the last time that you see me. If you please.' She gestured to the door.

He rose, indolently, and proceeded out of the room, leaving the air around her bitterly cold.

Constance waited in the drawing room of the London townhouse of the current Duke of Wellford. She had no right to feel the wave of possessiveness that she was feeling towards the house and its contents.

It did not belong to her, after all. It had been her husband's home long before she married him, but never truly hers. She had seen to the care and cleaning of it, of course. She had entertained guests in this very room. She had chosen the furnishings, and the food. She had hired and fired the servants.

And now, after twelve years in residence, and only a year away, she was a visitor. The butler who had greeted her was not familiar. When crossing the entrance hall, she caught sight of a footman she had hired herself. He had almost smiled when he'd seen her. Almost. And then there had been a flash of pity, before he went back to his duties, and treated her with the excessive formality due a ranking guest, and not a member of the family.

And to add to the discomfort, Freddy left her to wait. She had informed him that morning that she'd planned to visit, but when she arrived he was not in attendance, having decided to go riding in Hyde Park with his friends.

Robert had often railed against the folly of keeping horses in town. To keep the beasts fed, groomed and stabled was disproportionately expensive, when compared to the amount of time he had to ride while residing in the city. Apparently, the new duke had no such concerns.

Constance drummed her fingers against the small gilt table beside the settee, then folded her hands in her lap, willing them to be still. It was best to marshal her patience before Freddy arrived, if she wished to greet him pleasantly and keep him in good humour. She would make no ground in securing money or deed if she angered him by censuring his behaviour.

Especially if she must admit to him that she'd pawned the family jewels to pay the butcher's bill. He would see such behaviour as a weakness in her own character, and not his own for denying her funds and leaving her in need. She had learned from past discussions that, although Freddy was nearly useless at his best, if she angered him or questioned his judgement he could be even worse.

She had refused a servant's offer of refreshment for the third time before Freddy deigned to grace her with his presence, still in his riding coat. The smell of horses followed him into the room, and she noticed, with distaste, that there was mud from the stable still on his boot. He was tracking it on the Aubusson.

Not her Aubusson, she reminded herself. And not her problem. Someone would clean it. It did not matter.

'Aunt Constance, to what do I owe the pleasure?' There was a moment's awkwardness as he greeted her, and remembered that he was her better, and not a guest in her house.

'I wish it were only for pleasure that I am visiting, your Grace.' She rose to greet him, dropping a respectful curtsy.

'Please, Constance. Call me Freddy.' There was still

the touch of a little boy's pleading as he said it. 'You can, you know. I want you to treat this as though it were your home. It can be your home in truth, if you wish. Lord knows, I could use a woman with a level head to run the household for me.'

And how could she tell him that she could not bear to? The memories of Robert were still fresh in her mind. The knowledge that the servants were no longer hers to command, and that she could, and should be, displaced when Freddy took a wife of his own—she tried not to shudder at the thought.

'You know I must not, Freddy. It is no longer my place. It would be far better were you to find a wife to take the house in hand.'

He scoffed. 'Settle down so soon? Surely there is time for that later. I am just learning to enjoy the advantages of the title. A wife would spoil it all.'

She dreaded to think what advantages he had discovered that would be so hindered by a wife. 'It is your duty, you know,' she reminded, as gently as possible.

Freddy shook his head like a stubborn child. 'All you ever talk of is duty, Aunt Constance. There is more to life than doing one's duty.'

'Duty is much a part of your position, Freddy. You have a responsibility to your King, to your tenants, to your servants.' She hoped that the responsibility to herself was implied, and that he would not make her beg for her allowance.

'Well, yes. I suppose. But Parliament is not currently in session. So there is one thing I needn't worry about. And the tenants take care of themselves, for the most part.'

She resisted the urge to point out that they never seemed to manage it, when her husband was alive. 'But there is still the matter of the collecting of rents, and the paying of bills, and making sure that all your financial obligations are met.' And there was a broad enough hint, if he cared to take it.

'But it is a tiresome business to worry over every little detail, when the sun is shining and one is aching for a gallop.' Although Freddy's dirty boots had come home, his mind was still on horseback in the park.

'An estate manager, or man of business, can take care of such things. It would leave you with less to worry about.'

'But, Aunt Constance, I am not worried now.' As Freddy smiled, it was evident that her financial problems had in no way touched him. 'And being duke is not so hard as all that, I'm sure. With a little practice, I can manage the estates on my own, just as Uncle Robert did.'

Constance fought the urge to inform Freddy how distant his abilities were from those of his uncle. She took a deep breath, and tried a different way. 'I am sure you are right, Freddy. Once you have held the title for a while, you will have everything set to rights.

But I must admit, right now, that I was rather hoping we could deal with the part of the estate that concerns my allowance. It worries me greatly, that I have not received this month's cheque, and in the past, the amount—' she took another breath and rushed through the next words '—has not been sufficient to cover expenses.'

'You know,' said Freddy, as though the thought had just occurred to him, 'that if you were to live in the dower house of the manor, your expenses would not be so very great.'

'They are not great now, I assure you. I have made what economies I can.' A year of mutton instead of lamb, and no shopping, and cuts in staff had done nothing to make the income match the outflow.

'But really, Aunt Constance. Be sensible. If you were to leave London and return to the country, I need not give you any allowance at all.' He was smiling as though he had found the perfect solution.

'That is not technically true, Freddy,' she said. 'I still must eat. And pay my maid. And there are dresses to buy, carriages to hire, small entertainments... The only way you will be free of the expense of me is when I re-marry and my upkeep falls upon my husband.'

He stared at her as though the idea had never oc-curred to him. 'Surely you do not mean to remarry so soon, Aunt Constance.'

'On the contrary, Freddy, I find it a most respectable

choice. I am sure that Robert would have had no problem with it. He said as much to me, when he was alive. And he always meant me to set up housekeeping in town, in hopes that I might meet someone suitable, and not be too much alone. For that reason, he deeded me the house in Grosvenor Square. Speaking of which…' she eased the conversation towards her next request '…if possible, I would like to take the deed away with me today, to give to my bankers.'

Freddy's brow furrowed. 'I never saw the logic in Uncle Robert's deeding the house to you, Aunt Constance. It is too much responsibility for a woman, in my opinion. As I told you before, you are welcome here, or in the dower house, in Sussex. It is very nice.'

She had to hide her annoyance before continuing. 'I have no doubt it is a nice house, Freddy. I decorated it myself, for Robert's mother. And I have no problem staying in it. When I visit,' she said, slowly and clearly. 'But I have no wish to move back to Sussex. Robert meant for me to be out in London, after he died, mixing freely with society.'

'But why must it be London? Society in the country was quite good enough for you before.'

'Although the country life is most pleasant, I know the gentlemen in the neighbourhood, and can assure you there is no one to suit me, in regards to matrimony. I am not likely to meet a husband if I cloister myself in the dower house.'

'If you are there, where I can keep an eye on you, I can advise you, if and when it comes to the matter of your marriage.'

If and when she married? 'Freddy,' she said, struggling to maintain her temper, 'I am not a child that needs advice in this matter. I am a full six years older than you, and will know a good match when I see it. I do not need your advice, or your permission.'

'But you do need my money,' he pointed out, petulantly.

'Not for so very much longer, I hope. I am endeavouring to be out of your hair and your pocketbook with as much expedience as I can manage. But you need to help me in this, Freddy.' She softened. 'Please. If you will give me my allowance, I can pay my bills and will not bother you again for quite some time. Perhaps never. If you give me the deed, I can dispense with the house, and move to simpler accommodations. It will mean less expense for both of us.'

Freddy looked uncomfortable. 'The deed is fine where it is. I really do not see the need to bother you with the care of it.'

'Oh, it is no bother, Freddy,' she assured him. 'It makes sense, does it not, to keep it with the rest of my papers? And it will be one less thing you need to keep track of.'

His eyes darted around the room, as though looking for some excuse to escape the conversation. 'I mean…really, Constance, you cannot expect me to lay hands on the thing, on such short notice.'

'Freddy, it is not short notice at all. I have asked you for it for the better part of a year. Please can you not go into the study and bring it to me? Then I will be gone and you need not hear me ask again.'

'Well, the truth is, Constance…' Freddy looked more than uncomfortable, now, and had to struggle to meet her gaze '…the truth is, I have lost it.'

'Do not be ridiculous, Freddy. I know it lies in the safe, in my husband's—I mean, in your study. You could get it for me now, if you wished.'

'Constance, you do not understand.'

'Clearly I don't, Freddy. Let us go to the study, now. I will show you where it is.'

His voice was lower, almost hard to hear, and he was looking at the ground. 'It is no longer in the safe, Constance. As I told you, I lost it.'

'Well, then let us go and search for it. It is probably among the papers in your desk.' She could not resist a reproof. 'Although it might have been wiser to never have removed it from the safe. It would have saved the bother now.'

'At cards, Constance.' He said it loud and looked her straight in the eye. 'It is not on the desk, or anywhere else in the house. I lost it at cards. I was in my cups, and in deep play. And I am a little short of cash, until the next rents are collected.'

'And so you paid your debt with a thing that does not belong to you.' She looked at him in horror, as she realised just how bad things had become.

She no longer bothered to contain her temper. 'I come here at my wits' end, without a penny in my pocket, and you berate me for the high price of my keeping. You tell me I only want your money. As I see it, Freddy, I do not need your money nearly so much as you needed mine. You took the only thing I had that truly belonged to me and you gambled it away. And you did it because you are too busy drinking and gaming and whoring to be bothered to collect the rents on your properties, which you need to do to keep the coffers full. And now you think you can force me back to the country to play housekeeper to you, while you destroy everything my husband worked so hard to build.'

'I am the duke now,' he shouted back, although he sounded more like a spoiled child than a peer of the realm. 'Not your husband. I do not have to take advice or listen to you criticise my methods. I can do as I please.'

'Then you do not understand what it means to be a duke. Not a good one, at any rate,' she snapped.

'Good or bad, Aunt Constance, it would serve you to do as I say, for I am head of your family now. Uncle Robert was a fool to give you as much freedom as he did, for you seem to think that you can do just as you please, and answer to no one. I am glad that the deed is gone, and I no longer need hear you whine for it. It is time that this stupidity of maintaining an expensive residence in London is brought to a halt, and you are brought to your senses.

'And with regard to your allowance—you will have no more money from me, not another groat, until you come to your senses and move to the dower house at Wellford, where you belong.'

Chapter Five

At the door of the ballroom in Barton's home, Constance greeted her guests with a frozen smile. If she could manage to control nothing else around her, she could at least control her temper for the few hours necessary to earn back her necklace.

She had pleaded with Freddy to see reason, and he had all but thrown her from his house. He would not even tell her who held the deed to her own home, and she was left to wait for a knock at the door, politely explaining that she must pay rent or vacate the premises.

And tonight she must dance to Barton's tune, if only to retrieve the necklace and sell the stones again. The rubies would mean another month's income, perhaps two. Or even more if she was forced to reduce her staff and move to a smaller place.

But it did no good to think about what might come,

if there was a more immediate problem to deal with. Until she had the rubies in hand, she must keep a tight rein on her emotions, and give Barton what he wanted. To that end, she made sure that she looked her best, and was ready when the carriage he'd sent for her arrived. Her gown was not new, but she had not worn it in over a year. Susan had retrimmed the deep blue satin with silver lace, and dressed her dark hair with silver ribbons.

Constance was afraid to wear the necklace that best suited the gown lest someone recognise the sapphires as paste, and settled for the pearls. And she made sure that there was enough empty space in her reticule to carry away the rubies, should Barton be true to his word and return them to her.

Of course, if he did not, she would feel most foolish for being rooked into attending the evening's affair. But it would be a small loss, and the trick would not work twice. If she did not have the rubies at the end of the evening, she would reconcile herself to whatever might result from Barton's revelation.

But at the moment she was trapped in the receiving line next to a man she detested, and forced to entertain his guests as if they were her own. She smiled politely at the man bent over her hand, smiled at his wife as well, and responded to their greetings by rote, as she had to hundreds of guests at parties she had thrown for Robert. Her smile brightened as she noticed them to be strangers. Barton was not privy to the first circle of the *ton*. Many of her closest friends recognised the man for what he was and declined the invitation, or cut him outright. Constance wholeheartedly regretted that she had been slow to see his true character, but she was not alone, for the ballroom was full of people willing to befriend him.

She looked past the next man in line, barely hearing Barton's introduction of him, and scanned the crowd. Of course, a fair portion of the guests were social climbers, cits and hangers-on. But after this evening, she need never see them again, and they certainly would not be in a position to go gossiping to her friends about seeing her here.

'Mr Smythe, the Dowager Duchess of Wellford.' She winced. Barton insisted on using her title to his friends, as though he wished to make sure that everyone knew the value of his new possession.

The man before her bowed low over her hand. 'Your Grace.'

Although his face was unfamiliar, his voice struck a chord of memory. There was laughter in it. And the touch of his hand on hers was at the same time, ordinary and intimately familiar.

It was the thief from her bedroom.

He rose from his bow and looked into her eyes for a fraction of a second too long, as though daring her to speak and knowing she could not. His eyes were hazel and sparkling from the shared conspiracy, his smile was broad and a trifle too intense for a common introduction. If it were another man, she might think he had arrived half-foxed and up to mischief. But this man had already proven to be more than he appeared. If he meant to cause trouble, she doubted he would blame an excess of wine.

'Mr Smythe?' That was what Barton had said, had he not? She could not very well ask him to repeat himself, or demand to know how he knew Smythe. To express too much interest in a male guest was not the quickest way back to her necklace.

Of course, she could wipe the familiar grin from Smythe's face, and prove to him that she recognised him. A casual word could ruin him just as quickly as it could her. She opened her mouth.

And perhaps he would ask about the money she'd stolen from him or the kiss he'd stolen in her bedroom.

She closed her mouth again, and pasted on a delighted smile. 'How do you do, Mr Smythe.'

'Quite well, thank you.' She could swear he winked at her.

And then, he was gone.

If Barton had noticed anything pass between them, he said nothing. And soon the guests were through the line and Barton led her out in the first dance of the evening.

She moved through the patterns as if sleepwalking, speaking to her partner only when she could not avoid it. He danced with her several more times, when she could not manage to dodge his attention, and she maintained the same demeanour: polite, cordial and distant. Nothing that might make the guests assume there was anything of a more intimate nature likely to happen between them in the future.

And while she held Barton at a distance, she also managed to avoid contact with the curious Mr Smythe. It was possible that she had imagined recognising him. Perhaps she had been wrong. She could not very well ask him about it in a crowded ballroom.

But she was sure she was not mistaken. He was the thief. She had seen the recognition in his eyes. And she was somewhat frustrated to realise that it was not to be the least like she had fantasised, with him carrying some burning desire to see her again. She thought she could feel him, observing her from across the room, but this might be her imagination as well. He made no attempt to contact her; when she looked in his direction, he was always looking elsewhere. He seemed to care very little that she was in the room at all.

She was relieved when it finally came time for supper. Barton led her into the dining room, and her position as hostess meant that she was seated at the far end of the table from him. But nowhere near Smythe, either. The people around her were unexceptional, and she relaxed for a time, chatting amiably with them before the meal ended and she had to gather her wits and return to the dance floor.

When she reached the ballroom, she took care to get lost in the crowd and separated from her host. The next dance was a waltz, far more intimate than she liked, if she should have to dance with Barton. If she could find another partner quickly, it would be several minutes before she need speak with him again. She searched the room. Quickly, someone. Anyone.

'Your Grace, may I have this dance?'

She'd said yes to the man before even turning to face him. And when she looked up, it was into the smiling eyes of Mr Smythe.

He saw her discomposure and said nothing, taking her hand and leading her out on to the floor.

As the music began, any doubt that he was the man from her bedroom disappeared. He held her as he had held her that night, in a grasp that managed to be both relaxed and intimate. It felt good to be in his arms again, and to be able to admire him in the candlelight.

And there was much about him that was admirable. His hair was brown, and had an appealing softness to it. She remembered how it had felt when she'd touched it, and wanted to touch it again. He had pleasant, even features, and the smile on his lips gave every indication of breaking into a grin, given the slightest provocation. His eyes were bright with suppressed mirth. If his profession left him racked with guilt, there was no indication of it, for he seemed a most happy fellow.

They danced in silence, until at last he leaned a trifle closer and whispered, 'How long do you suppose we can pretend a lack of recognition to each other? We have managed quite well so far, I think. Longer than I expected. But one of us has to break eventually. I surrender. You have won.'

'I don't know what you are talking about.'

'And now you are taking the game to extra innings. Not necessary. I am conquered. Vanquished. You nearly had me in the receiving line, you know. Finding you there, next to Barton, was a nasty surprise.'

'You will survive it,' she responded tartly. 'Seeing an acquaintance unexpectedly in a public place is not nearly so shocking as finding a total stranger in one's private rooms.'

'*Touché*. But I had hoped you had forgiven me for that. Why so cold to me now?'

'Perhaps I don't approve of people who take things that don't belong to them.'

'Oh, really? But I notice, when you were in need, that you had no problem keeping the money I left for you.'

So he had left it for her. But did he expect thanks for involving her in a theft? 'That was different. What else was I to do with it? I had no idea—'

'Where to find me and who the money belonged to. And you were in desperate need, so you took it. Believe me, I understand completely.'

'I will pay you back when I am able,' she said.

'You will pay me back tonight,' he replied.

Her heart sank. He had seemed so nice. And he had promised not to compromise her. Now he would become just another man with a hold over her, and he would use it to his advantage like all the rest. She stumbled as they turned.

He caught her, incorporating the misstep gracefully into the movement of the dance. 'Oh, do not give me that melodramatic look. We are in a ballroom, not Drury Lane. I have no intention of asking you to whore yourself to me. I merely need you to keep your lover, Barton, occupied while I go to search his study.'

'He is not my lover,' she retorted.

'Really? But you stand as hostess, at his side.'

'It was not my desire to do so.'

'And you have been seen often in his company.'

'For a time,' she corrected, 'but no more after tonight. He is nothing singular. I have been seen in the company of many men.'

His eyebrow arched suggestively.

'I am in your company now. But that does not mean I would invite you to my bed.'

Of course, if he wished to be there, he would hardly require an invitation. She would be quite helpless to stop him, and perhaps next time he would wish to steal more than a kiss. Once the thought was formed, it showed no intention of fading.

He was staring at her again, noticing the gap in the conversation. And his smile was definitely a grin. She wished she had not mentioned the bed at all, for if he did not have the idea before, he must surely be thinking of it now.

She cleared her throat. 'What I meant to say was, I hope to marry again, and that means I am likely to be seen in the company of gentleman who I think might be of a mind to take a wife.'

'And you chose Barton as a possible husband?' Smythe's tone was incredulous and the smile disappeared from his face.

'I sometimes find that the interests of gentlemen are less than worthy. It is a tribute to my naïveté and not my lowered standards.'

'So you and Barton are not…?' He spoke a trifle too hastily and his hand tightened on her waist.

'He made an offer that had nothing to do with matrimony, and I gave him a set-down. More than once.' She frowned. 'At the end of the evening I will probably have to give him another, since he ignored the others. And he tricked me into coming here, for reasons I'd rather not discuss.'

He blinked down at her and his hand relaxed. He was holding her in the same loose grip as before, as though he was confident that she would stay with him, even if he had no hold on her. 'Well, then. Perhaps I was misinformed.'

'Most definitely you were.'

He looked bemused. 'Then I hope you will not think

it too rude when I will ask you to keep the man who is not your lover, though he seems to think he will be, occupied while I pay an unaccompanied visit to his study.'

'And how do you expect me to do that?'

'Use your imagination. A quarter of an hour is all I need and easily worth the hundred guineas I left in your room.'

The dance came to an end and he led her from the floor. 'Your Grace, it was an unexpected pleasure. Now, if you will excuse me?' There was the slightest inclination of his head, which seemed to hint that he had business to attend to, and that the clock was ticking.

She glanced across the room, and somewhere in the distance a clock chimed the three-quarter hour. Very well, then. She would give him fifteen minutes. It was a small price for the money he had given her. She glanced around the room, searching for Barton, and saw him too close to the stairs that must lead to the study. 'My lord?' She had hoped to ask him to dance, and out of the corner of her eye, noticed that the orchestra had chosen that inopportune moment to take refreshment. Very well, then. It was near enough the end of the evening. Now was as good a time as any to retrieve the necklace. 'If I might speak to you?'

'Certainly, my dear.' He bowed low over her hand. 'What is it?'

She resisted the urge to inform him that she was not now, nor ever wished to be, his dear. 'In private.'

'My study, then.' He turned to lead her to the exact place that she did not wish to be.

'Not so private as all that, I think. The garden, perhaps? It is quiet enough there.'

'And most romantic in the moonlight.'

She bit back another retort. There would be time enough in fifteen minutes to set him straight.

He took her hand and led her to the balcony doors, and, at the back of her mind, she felt a minute pass. And another, as he led her outside, and down the stone steps to the garden. When they were in the darkness and a distance from the house, he turned to her and smiled. 'To what do I owe this sudden desire to be alone with me? Have you reconsidered my offer?'

'You know very well the reason. Have I performed to your satisfaction in this little farce?'

'Most admirably. We can make it a regular occurrence, if you wish.'

'But I do not wish,' she said firmly. 'I have told you over and over again.'

'And yet, you agreed to do it tonight. And it was a delightful evening. Not so terrible as you made it out to be, I'm sure.'

'There was only one reason I agreed to come, and you know it full well.'

'Ah, the necklace.' He reached into his pocket, and produced the rubies, holding them in front of her.

She snatched the thing from his hand and secreted it in her reticule, turning to go back to the house, no longer caring about Smythe and his fifteen minutes.

Barton's fingers closed on her upper arm, holding her in place. She attempted to pull away, and he tightened his grip, ever so slightly. To struggle further might leave bruises on her skin. She imagined the shame of going back into the ballroom, the red marks of a man's fingers already blossoming on her arm.

She stayed still.

'Willing to stay with me, after all?'

'I do not wish my behaviour to create gossip.'

He smiled, realising that he'd won again. 'And why would a rumour frighten you? If I am in the wrong, and you do not wish to be with me, then surely you could appeal to one of the many gentlemen of your acquaintance for assistance?' He snapped his fingers. 'But that is right. Many of the gentlemen here have received setdowns from you, have they not? They are likely to be more sympathetic to my plight. Over and over again, you allow men to lead you to the fence, and then you do not jump.'

'That is not the way it has been at all,' she argued. 'I had no idea that the gentlemen in question did not intend marriage. Or you, for that matter. I never sought anything less.'

Barton smiled. 'How refreshingly naïve you are. I think it is the combination of experience and naïveté that attracts me to you. You believe it is possible to go back to the way things were, before you married, and to have a second chance at a husband and a family. But you will never again be that young and innocent. When men look at you, they know that you are too old to guarantee a first child, but fully ripe for all the pleasures that a man might wish to experience with a woman. When we look at you, my dear, we know that you know precisely what will happen when you are alone with us.'

He smiled and drew closer. 'I can see it, even now. The lust sizzles in your eyes. You fear scandal, more than you fear my touch. I can steal a kiss, perhaps a caress in the darkness. These things do not alarm you so much as the thought that someone might catch us at it. I suspect that you would have no problem giving yourself freely, if you could be assured of the discretion of your partner. Take this instance. If you do not submit, you must walk away from me, and I have but to call out and draw attention to the fact that you are with me, or squeeze your arm, ever so slightly.' He tightened his grip, and then relaxed it again, as he felt her submit. 'Then people will notice that we were alone together, and there will be even more talk than there already is.'

'People will think you a brute for forcing yourself on a woman.'

'Since the woman is yourself, and you just spent the evening at my side as hostess, I doubt that anyone will assume force. It is far more likely that they will assume you were a willing participant in anything that might have occurred. The assumptions of a curious society will be confirmed, the minute you complain. Or you can allow me to kiss you, here in the dark, and we can return to the ballroom separately. No one will be the wiser.'

Damn her for her foolishness in thinking she could win against Barton in his own house. She had gained the necklace, only to lose more ground. And damn Mr Smythe for using her as well. He had been gone more than fifteen minutes, she was sure of it. And he thought nothing of leaving her in the clutches of Barton. Now that Smythe had what he wanted, he had forgotten her.

It would do no good to fight Barton now. If she gave in, perhaps the incident would pass quickly, and she might escape. She closed her eyes and tipped her head up to meet him as he leaned in and kissed her.

And she did nothing to stop him, because he was right. The last thing she needed was more gossip. When he wished for her to open her mouth, she did that as well. She could but hope that he would not take things too far in so public a place. And after tonight, scandal or no, she would not be alone with him again.

He was doing his best to arouse feelings in her, and she took great pleasure in ignoring the attempt. If he wished to make love to her, then let him. But eventually, when she did not respond, he would lose interest and let her go. In the meantime, she would see to it that the experience was not so pleasurable as he imagined.

He was working industriously on her mouth, and his hands were on her shoulders. It was only a matter of time before they strayed lower.

She was disappointed to find that she felt neither desire nor outrage at the fact. Her mind felt strangely detached from her body, uninterested in the proceedings and wishing only to go home and put the experience behind her. Let him do what he wished and be done with it. It had been so long since she'd felt anything at all, she doubted that Barton could move her with his fumblings.

As though he'd heard her thoughts, Barton's hand began a slow descent towards the swell of her breast.

And then he pulled away from her with an oath. There was the sound of someone crashing clumsily through the ornamental shrubbery, soft, tuneless whistling growing louder as the intruder approached.

Barton took off in the direction of the sound. 'Here, you. What do you think you're doing?'

'Trying to find my way out of this damn briar patch.'

Constance strangled a laugh. It was Mr Smythe, making it clear to all within earshot that he was done with whatever business he'd been up to.

'I only wanted a breath of air. Two steps from the house and I was lost in the wilderness. I've a good mind to complain to the host.'

'I am the host, you drunken idiot. And you're stepping on my rose-bushes.' Jack was furious.

Constance stepped off the path and disappeared into the darkness, leaning against a tree and giving way to silent giggles.

There was a pause as an apparently drunken Smythe took stock of the situation. 'Roses? So I am. Oh, well. No harm done. The spindly little things were half-dead, anyway. Could have used more water.'

'They are in perfect health. And they are imported from France.'

'Well, that's your problem. Get yourself some proper English flowers. Just as pretty and not so delicate.'

'Get off of my yard, you drunken buffoon! I invited you here, Smythe, on the recommendation of a friend. I can see I was mistaken in the courtesy and it will not be repeated. Kindly take yourself from the premises, before I have you forcibly removed.'

'I was going. Going. Know where I'm not wanted.' She could hear more crashing, as Smythe wandered noisily away in the direction of the street, trampling more expensive landscaping as he went.

There was more swearing from Barton as he came back in her direction, and softly called her name.

She stepped behind a tree, scarcely daring to breathe.

He walked within an arm's length of her, but she stayed still in the shadows and let him pass.

Barton released another quiet oath, and turned in the direction of the house, probably hoping to find her there.

She smiled in satisfaction. Let him look. She had the necklace again. There was no reason to stay a moment longer. It was not a chill night, she had no wrap. She could find her own way to the street through the garden, without taking leave of the host.

She turned into the darkness. At least she thought she could find her way to the street. If the house was behind her, then surely…

'Allow me.' A hand reached out of the darkness, and caught her arm.

She gasped. 'Smythe.'

'The same.'

'I thought you had gone.'

'And leave you alone in the dark? I think not. Do you have a carriage back at the house?'

'Barton sent a coach for me. I assumed that I would find a friend to escort me home.'

'And so you have. I will see you home, if you can leave immediately. I suspect I am no longer welcome in Barton's home.' She could see his grin in the darkness.

She smiled in return. 'And I have no wish to return. It suits me well.'

'Excellent.' It was impossible to tell, but he sounded sincerely pleased to have her company. He slipped his arm through hers and lead her in the direction of the street.

A thrill shot through her at the idea of being alone in the dark with him again, far from the safety of the house. Anything could happen and no one would be the wiser.

'You should not be so careless with your reputation, your Grace.'

'I beg your pardon?'

His voice was gentle, but held a hint of disapproval. 'You were alone in the garden. With Barton, I mean.'

'Only because you wished me to distract him,' she said acerbically. 'You left the method to me.'

'And I did not expect you to choose that one, after what you said to me as we danced. Did you wish for him to kiss you?'

'Not particularly.'

There was a hesitation. 'Did you enjoy it?'

'That is a very impertinent question.'

'And that is a very evasive answer.'

'But it is all you will get from me,' she said. 'Did you at least get what you were searching for?'

'No, I did not. And what makes you think I was searching for anything?'

She tipped her head to the side, considering. 'I am not sure. But I hope, if you merely intended burglary, you would not want or need to involve me in it.'

He nodded. 'That is true. And do not worry. It will not happen again. I have involved you too much already.'

'That is all right,' she said hurriedly. 'It was not too great a burden.'

'Allowing Barton to kiss you in the moonlight.' There was a cynical bite to his words that did not escape her.

'It was only a kiss,' she responded.

'Oh, really? But a kiss can be a dangerous thing, if done correctly.' He swung her body into his and wrapped his arms around her. 'Allow me to demonstrate.' And then he brought his mouth down upon hers.

It was as it had been on the night in her room. His kiss was as heady and romantic as the smell of the roses in the garden, and she relaxed into it, letting it awaken her senses.

She slipped her arms inside his coat, and felt the muscles of his back and shoulders tense as her fingers touched him. His arms strained to pull her closer to him, and he stroked her tongue with his, varying the pressure of his lips against hers from punishing firmness to a featherlight touch. When he released her mouth, she caught him about the waist and arched her body away from him, baring her throat and willing him to kiss her there, and lower.

He accepted the invitation and his lips trailed fire down her neck to rest on her shoulder. 'Do you enjoy it when *I* kiss you?' he murmured into her skin.

'Yes.' She shuddered against him.

He ran a finger inside the neckline of her gown and

pulled the dress away from her body, pushing to slide it down her arm. He planted a kiss just under the place where her dress should end, and she gasped.

He laughed and his finger traced her collarbone. 'I am going to kiss you there again. Hard enough to mark you. No one will know it but we two, because your gown will hide all. Would you like that?'

'Yes.' She shocked herself by saying it, knowing that it was true. 'Oh, yes.'

'I thought you might.' And he lowered his head again, and she felt him suck on the flesh, felt the feeling run through her all the way to her toes.

It was the work of a moment. And then it was over. He leaned his head against her ear and whispered, 'If you would kiss, then do not give them cheaply to one such as Barton. Choose someone worthy of your affection.' He walked her the last few steps through the trees and they came out at the bend of the drive. He whistled once and a carriage appeared from out of the darkness. Black and unmarked, with black horses and a driver muffled beyond recognition.

Smythe gave instructions to the driver and then he handed her up into the carriage, shutting the door behind her.

She leaned out of the window to where he stood in the road. 'Are you not coming as well?'

'My man will see you home.' There was hunger in

his eyes as he stared up into her face. 'You are safer with him tonight than alone in a carriage with me.'

'But how will you get home?' *And where is home? And are you alone there?* She was bursting with unasked questions.

He smiled at her, his face dim in the light from the carriage lamps. 'Never worry about me, your Grace. I have ways. Until we meet again.' He bowed to her as the carriage pulled away and he disappeared into the darkness behind her.

She leaned back into the squabs, her heart hammering in her chest. He had been right about the danger in a kiss. His were as intoxicating as anything served at the party, and as compelling as Barton's were not.

Perhaps what Barton accused her of was true. She was more than willing to bend the rules if she felt she would not be caught. And Mr Smythe would see to it that what they did was safe and in secret.

Perhaps it was no more than that. He was passionate, but solicitous of her reputation. Where other men wished to parade her fallen virtue as a trophy to their skills at seduction, with Smythe no one would know that they had been together. When he was done with her he would leave as quietly as he had come, moving through her life like a fish through water.

And when they parted tonight, he had not said goodbye. She could scarce control herself at the thought of seeing him again. She could still feel the kiss, hot and sinful, a brand on her shoulder to remind her of all the ways and places he might kiss her, should she allow it.

And why had she been so quick to agree? Was it because he had not asked at all?

Not at first, perhaps. But once he had started, he had asked her what would make her happy. He had not tried to negotiate her out of her honour, or worried that he was being outbid by some other man. He had not given her an ultimatum, or threatened her with shame or discovery.

He'd given her the first kiss as a sample of what was to come, and pointed out that he could give her even more pleasure, this instant, if she would allow him to. There had been no talk of bracelets or houses, or paying off her grocer and cutting back her staff. Or even what he wanted from her. He had kissed her again because he had wanted to, and because he had known she would like it more than she had when kissing Barton. Just a moment of shared bliss, and then he was gone.

She slipped her own fingers under the shoulder of her dress, imagining that his lips were still on her. He had said that she wouldn't be safe with him, and she imagined him climbing in beside her and pulling her close in the darkness of the cab. She would be alone and completely at his mercy. And his hands would roam freely over her body, taking everything he wanted from her.

As though it mattered. She never wanted to be safe again.

She shook her head to clear the fantasy and leaned her face to the open window, feeling the breeze in her hair. She glanced at the passing streets. The direction seemed right, but how would the driver be able to find her house? She had not heard Smythe tell him the address.

She turned and knelt on the seat, opening the connecting window between the carriage and the driver. 'I live on Grosvenor Square, just past—'

'I know the way, your Grace. Do not concern yourself.'

He had used her title. And over the sound of the horses, she thought she heard a trace of amusement in his voice. He knew of her. And he knew other things as well.

'Your master, Mr Smythe—have you known him long?'

There was no answer. And the driver tickled the horses with the tassel of his whip so that their speed increased.

He was loyal. Enough so as not to speak. And Smythe trusted him more than he did himself.

Then that answered the question. The man was no casual hire, but a trusted associate. A partner in crime, perhaps?

They were nearing her house, and she bit her lip in frustration. She knew nothing about Mr Smythe. He was not one of Barton's familiars. And she had been too careless when he had been introduced to her and had not paid attention. She had not even heard his Christian name.

The carriage pulled smoothly to a stop in front of her home. The driver hopped down from the seat and opened the door for her, taking her hand and guiding her to the ground.

She looked at him, not sure what to expect. His face was no longer shielded from her, and she found it plain and honest. Surprisingly friendly. He was gazing back at her with a frank curiosity that she should have found inappropriate in a servant, had she not wanted words with him.

She tried again. 'Please. About Mr Smythe. I know very little. Not his address. Or even his first name. If I should need to contact him…' It was all horribly bold of her. The words died away in her throat.

The driver stared at her for a long moment, in a way that was totally devoid of subservience. And then his shoulders rose and fell once in a way that was part shrug and part silent laugh. He rummaged in his pocket, and came out with a white pasteboard, glancing at it before handing it to her. 'His card, your Grace.'

She swallowed. 'Thank you.' She tried not to appear too eager, but snatched the card from his hand, and turned from him, concealing it in the bodice of her dress. And then she ran up the walk and into her house.

Once inside, she fled up the steps and into her room, shutting the door and reaching down the front of her dress to find the card, nestled close between her breasts.

'Anthony de Portnay Smythe. Anthony Smythe. Tony. Anthony.' She tried various versions of the name, tasting them, and enjoying the way they felt on her tongue.

Before Susan came to help her undress for bed, she looked for a place to secrete the card, finally slipping it under her pillow. She could not help smiling at the foolishness of it, as her maid undid the hooks of her gown. As a token of affection, a calling card was not much to speak of. And the man had not given it to her, after all. Perhaps he did not mean for her to know more of him.

Susan was undoing her stays and as she turned the maid gave the slightest gasp. The mark was there on her shoulder. 'Did you have a pleasant evening, your Grace? At Lord Barton's party?' The remark was offhand, as though nothing unusual had sparked it.

'Most pleasant,' Constance answered, unable to resist a small sigh of pleasure.

'So I suspected.' Susan was faintly disapproving.

'Despite the presence of Lord Barton,' Constance corrected. 'The man continues to be quite odious. I do not plan to see him again.'

'I should hope not, your Grace.' This seemed to put the maid's fears to rest.

'Although there is another gentleman…' She hid her smile behind her hand.

Susan grinned back at her. 'If he puts such a sparkle in your eye, then he must be a most singular person.'

'But how is one to know, Susan,' she asked impulsively, 'what the intentions of a gentleman are? I have been wrong so many times in the past.'

'If he makes you happy, your Grace, perhaps it is time to think with your heart and not your head.'

The thrill of it ran through her. If she were to think with her heart, the choice would be easy. She wanted Anthony Smythe, and she could have him.

For now. Her mind brought it all crashing back down to earth. It was seductively pleasurable to think of Mr Smythe. And surely there was no harm in dreaming. But it would be a temporary solution at best. If she accepted any more purses from him, while allowing him to toy with her affections and use her body for his own pleasure, then she was little better than what she feared she would become.

But suppose he offered marriage?

The thought was as fascinating as it was horrifying. And not something that needed reckoning with. She would be a fool to trust him, or read too much into a few kisses. The first night, he had sworn that he loved another. He might be faithless to the other woman, and willing to dally with Constance for a while, if she encouraged him to. But in the end, his intentions to her would prove the same as all the others.

Although it might be more pleasurable with him,

than with others, for he was as passionate as he was considerate.

But he was a thief, she reminded herself. Even should she wish for an honourable union, there would be no way to overlook her lover's chosen occupation. A breath of the truth would destroy her reputation along with his. Eventually, he would be caught, and hanged, and she would be ruined in the bargain. Worse than she was now, alone, unloved and disgraced as well.

She shook her head sadly at Susan. 'Alas, I think I cannot afford to allow my heart to lead in this. The answer is not Barton, certainly. But it cannot be the other, no matter how much I might wish it so.' She allowed Susan to help her into bed and to blow out the candle, leaving her in the dim light of the fire, alone between the cold sheets.

And almost without thinking, her hand stole beneath the pillows and sought the calling card, running her fingers along the edge, feeling the smoothness of the pasteboard, and stroking the engraving as sleep took her.

Chapter Six

Patrick opened the bed curtains with more vehemence than necessary. Tony squinted as the late-morning sunlight hit him. And now his servant was rattling the plates on the breakfast tray. 'And a good morning to you too, Patrick,' he grumbled, reaching a hand out for his coffee. Patrick did not approve of the hour his master had gotten in, did he? Then he could go to the devil.

After sending his carriage away, Tony had enjoyed the excellent hospitality of the Earl of Stanton, given his regards to Lady Esme, and assured St John that he had been quite mistaken about the Duchess of Wellford. The woman was innocent.

In all the ways that mattered to the State. He smiled in satisfaction as he remembered the way she'd bitten her lip when he'd sucked on her shoulder, and dug her fingers into his sides to pull him closer. A certain lack of innocence in other areas might not be the worst thing.

But it had been embarrassing to stand before Stanton and admit his lack of success, when it came to the rest of the Barton matter. He could report on the location of the printing press in the basement, along with the inks and the paper. There was no evidence that printing of any false bills had occurred, but all the components needed were easily accessible. It would do him no good to destroy the supplies, other than to demonstrate to Barton that someone had tumbled to his plan. Tony needed to get the plates, and they were most likely locked tight in the safe in the study, behind a Bramah lock where he could not get to them.

St John had been most unimpressed with the gravity of the situation.

'Try again,' St John had said, pouring another whisky for his guest.

The fact that the Bramah lock was reported to be unpickable had little impact on his host. Had he never seen the challenge lock that Bramah displayed in their shop window, to taunt thieves and lockpicks? The company offered two hundred guineas to the first man who could open it. It had stood for more than twenty years so far, with no one able to claim the prize.

Stanton was too kind to suggest the return of the down payment, but Tony suspected it might enter the conversation if he belaboured the impossibility of the task before him.

He could afford to return the money and walk away, of course. But it stung his pride to think that such a thing might be necessary. It went against his grain to admit defeat, and although the impregnability of the lock was common knowledge, common knowledge was frequently wrong. It might take more time than was available to a burglar, but perhaps with practice…

He looked at Patrick, who was laying out his clothes for the day, and turned his mind to more pleasant matters. Willing his face to give nothing away, he said, 'The return trip to the Wellford house was uneventful, I trust.'

Patrick finished brushing his coat before responding. 'A stray cat almost met an unfortunate end beneath the carriage wheels, but I was able to prevent disaster.'

'And the duchess arrived home safely?'

'To her very door. She was a most grateful, and, you will forgive me for noticing, sir, a most attractive passenger.'

Patrick approved. It was strangely pleasing to have his opinion of Constance confirmed by his valet.

'Although strangely talkative, for nobility,' Patrick continued. 'Most of the peerage can't be bothered…'

'Talkative?'

'Yes, sir.' Patrick returned to the choosing of shirts as if nothing important had been said.

When Tony could stand it no longer, he asked, 'And what did she say?'

'She asked after you, sir.'

'After me.' Tony sat up, almost spilling his coffee in the process.

'Indeed, sir.' Patrick set the rest of the breakfast tray in front of him, refilled the coffee cup and stepped away.

'And what did you tell her?'

'I didn't think it my place, sir.'

The man picked the damnedest times to remember his station and to behave as a servant.

'I assumed you must have had a reason for neglecting to mention your Christian name, or to give her your direction. Perhaps you had no wish to be troubled by the lady again.'

Tony groaned, and wiped his face with his hands. She did not know who he was? He'd been formally introduced to her, for God's sake.

And she had had eyes only for Barton. Tony stabbed his kipper with more force than necessary.

Patrick brightened. 'And then I realised what a great ninny you are around women, and more so with a certain woman in particular. And I suspected that you had merely forgotten the importance of the information. So I gave her one of your cards.'

Tony slumped in relief. 'And how did she receive it?'

Patrick mimed putting a calling card down the front

of an imaginary dress. 'I dare say your good name has got further with the lady than you have yourself.'

Later, as Patrick shaved him, Tony could feel his face, set in a ridiculous grin. She'd wanted to know his name. And carried it next to her…heart.

The image of the card nestling against her body, warmed by her skin, made him almost dizzy with desire. Patrick was right, he should capitalise on the situation immediately. He rubbed a finger experimentally along his jaw line. Smooth. Not that she had complained the night before. But it would not do to let her think he took her interest for granted. 'Patrick, my best suit, please, I am going out. And extra care with the cravat, please.'

'Yes, sir.'

'And while I am gone, Patrick, I have a task that needs doing. Please go down to the Bramah Locks Company. I wish a safe installed in my study. Fitted with one of their fine locks. The job must be rushed, for I have valuables to store, and am most afraid of thieves.'

'Yes, sir.'

Two hours later, Tony had to admit that the day was not going to plan. He had imagined a quiet chat with Constance, in her sitting room. Kissing in the moonlight was all well and good. Much better than good, to be truthful. But he must make some attempt to assure her that in daylight he was not without the manners of a common gentleman, if their association was to go any further.

He ignored the novelty of it, and called at the front door, but was disappointed to find her Grace was not at home. He left a card and enquired of the butler, as politely as possible, where she might be on such a fine day.

And now he found himself frequenting the lending library in Bond Street, hoping to catch sight of her as she ran her errands. When she entered, he was paging though a volume of poems that he had read a hundred times, trying to appear the least bit interested in contents that he could barely see, since his reading glasses were at home in his desk.

And she was not alone, damn the luck. There was a man at her side who gave every indication of solicitous interest, and two young ladies as well.

What was he to do? In the scenario he'd imagined, she'd been shopping alone, or perhaps with her maid to carry packages. It would be easy to approach her and he would make some offhand remark that might make reference to the evening before without mentioning it directly.

She would laugh, and respond. He would offer to carry her books. She would graciously accept. Conversation would ensue. He would let slip certain facts, recognition would dawn in her eyes, and he would be spared the embarrassment of having to reintroduce himself to a woman who had known him since they were both three.

Nowhere in his plan had he considered that the position of book carrier and witty conversationalist might already be occupied. Tony could not very well pretend not to see her, and she could not help but notice him, for he'd positioned himself in such a way as to be unavoidable.

Damn it to hell, but he must speak to her.

He turned and took a step towards her, just as she made to go past. And in the second before he spoke, he caught her eye as it tried to slide past without meeting his. There was alarm, followed by embarrassment, and finally resignation, before she managed to choose an expression to suit the situation—a friendly smile that said to the people around her, I think I know this man, but am unsure.

It was too late. The words were already out of his mouth. 'Your Grace. A most lovely day, is it not?'

'Why, yes. Yes, it is. Mr…'

'Smythe, ma'am. We met at Lord Barton's party last evening.' The words sounded false, but she leapt on them as salvation.

'Why, of course. How foolish of me. Mr Smythe, may I introduce Viscount Endsted and his sisters, Catherine and Susanne.'

'Ladies. Your lordship.' He made his best bow, and was dismayed to hear the ladies giggle in appreciation.

When his eyes rose to Constance, he saw fresh

alarm there at the young ladies' reaction. He was not suitable for them, either. Once he had gone, she would have to warn them off.

'Mr Smythe.' There was a slight emphasis on the mister, and the Viscount took a step forward to head off the interested sisters and gripped his hand.

His handshake was firm to an almost painful degree. Tony considered, for a moment, the advantage to responding in kind, then discarded it as infantile.

As the viscount sensed him yield, he released his grip as well. Endsted glanced at the book in Tony's hand. 'Byron?'

'Yes. I find it—' How did he find it? He did not wish to give the wrong answer and further jeopardise his position with Constance. 'Most edifying.'

Endsted's sisters giggled, and Endsted glared at them. 'The man's scandalous. I do not hold with him. Not in the least.'

'I have no real opinion of the man,' Tony responded, 'for I have never met him. But his poetry is in no way morally exceptionable.' He glanced to Constance.

She looked as though she would rather cut out her tongue than have an opinion. Endsted was glaring at her, waiting for her to agree.

'He is rather fast,' she managed. She flashed a brief, hopeless look in Tony's direction, before looking to Endsted for approval.

Endsted nodded. 'His works are not fit for a lady.'

Which showed how little the man knew of ladies or of poetry, Tony suspected. 'I do not know, sir. I find his skill with words to be an excellent tribute for certain ladies.'

Constance pretended to ignore the compliment, but he could see a faint flush at the neck of her gown.

'But not something one might wish to speak of in a lending library.'

Tony chose to ignore the man's disapproval and answered innocently, 'For myself, I should think there would be no better place to discuss books.'

'I suppose it is a way to pass the time for one who has nothing better to do than read poetry.' He said the last words as if reading were one step from taking opium with Lord Byron himself. 'And now, sir, if you will excuse us.' He took Constance by the arm and led her past.

She did not look back, although the Endsted sisters cast a backward glance in his direction, giggling again.

Tony debated calling the man back to argue poetry, morality and general manners, or planting him a facer and reading works by the scandalous Lord Byron over his prone body, then thought the better of it. He doubted demonstrating Endsted's ignorance would win him points in the eyes of Constance, and might endear him further to the man's sisters, which was a fate to be avoided.

And he had no evidence that there was any behaviour that might find favour with Constance. At least, in the light of day. There was no question that she responded to him in the dark. And she did so in a way that made it very hard for him to wish to remove himself totally from her company.

But it appeared likely that, should he continue to meet with her, he would spend evenings losing all reason in her passionate embrace, only to be replaced at the breakfast table by a viscount and his giggling sisters. And really, if she wanted to marry another peer, then who was he to stand in her way? She had her own future to attend to, and, if he loved her, he must accept the fact that it was not in her best interest to associate with him.

All in all, his life had been much easier before he'd climbed in her window. His nights had been lonely and his passion had been hopeless. But he had made peace with that years ago. Now, the only hope he had of a return to peace was to put all thoughts of Constance Townley aside, and spend evenings in quiet communion with his lockpicks and his new safe.

He set the book back on a nearby shelf, and yielded the field to the better man.

Chapter Seven

'Lemon?' Constance arranged the tea things, for the hundredth time, trying to ignore Endsted's growing irritation with her.

'No, thank you.' Looking at the sour expression on the viscount's face, she suspected he had no need of any additional bitterness. She offered the sugar, instead.

She offered each, in turn, to his two sisters, and they helped themselves, casting sidelong glances at her last, uninvited tea guest.

When there was no one else to serve, she turned to him, and repeated her offer in a tone that she hoped would tell him to take his tea and go to the devil.

'Thank you.' Jack Barton smiled as though there was nothing unusual in her voice, took the lemon she offered, and set it at the side of his saucer.

She felt his fingers brush hers, and silently cursed.

She had been too slow to move, and he had managed to arrange the accidental touch.

And Endsted had noticed. He was an annoyingly observant man. He was also upright, noble and extremely respectable, if a bit of a prig. But he was the first man whose company she had shared who was clear in his willingness to introduce her to his family. His intentions were honourable, or he'd never have allowed her to meet his sisters.

And she had managed to disappoint him, first with Mr Smythe, now with Barton, who had been waiting in her sitting room when they'd returned from the library, uninvited and unmoving.

And Susan had made her day even more of a disaster, by whispering that, while Lord Barton had taken up residence despite her encouragement that waiting would not be welcome or convenient, Mr Smythe had been most co-operative and departed after enquiring of her whereabouts.

So Smythe had been hoping to see her when they'd met in the library. She had feared as much. From a distance, he'd appeared to be the poised and confident man that she'd seen at the ball the previous evening.

But as she'd approached him, she'd seen an eagerness in his manner that she had not seen in a man in… How long had it been? Since she'd had suitors, well before Robert. Long ago, when those who sought her affections had had hopes of success and fears of disappointment. There had been none of the sly looks and innuendos that accompanied all interactions with men now that she was a widow.

Tony Smythe had looked at her as though the years had meant nothing, and she was a fresh young girl with more future than responsibilities. And she had crushed him by her indifference.

She had feared, last night, that there would be nothing to speak of, should she see him in daylight. But today she had found him reading Byron.

She adored Byron.

She looked across the table at Endsted, and remembered that he found Byron most unsuitable. If she succeeded with him, there would be no more poetry in her life. She could spend her evenings reading educational and enlightening tracts to Endsted's rather foolish sisters.

She looked to her other side, at Lord Barton. Surely a boring life with Endsted would be preferable to some fates.

Of course, Mr Smythe would read Byron to her. In bed, if she asked him to. Or would have done, had she not set him down in public to secure her position with Endsted. She doubted she would be seeing him again.

And why was she thinking of him at all, when she needed to keep her mind on her guests? She dragged her attention back to managing the men in front of her. Silence between them was long and cold on Endsted's side. It appeared he had heard the rumours of Barton's character and was only suffering contact with him out of straining courtesy to Constance.

Barton did not seem to mind the frigid reception. He ignored Endsted and smiled at the ladies. 'Might I remark, Lord Endsted, on the attractiveness of your sisters.'

Endsted glared and the girls giggled.

'I cannot remember a day when I have been so fortunate as to find myself in the company of so many charming young ladies.' He focused his gaze for more than a little too long on the eldest, Catherine, until she coloured and looked away.

'Are you a friend of Constance's?' the girl asked timidly.

'Oh, a most particular friend,' Barton answered.

Constance could not very well deny it while the man was in her parlour, sipping her tea. She dare not explain, in front of her other guests, that she allowed him there only because of the things he might say to them about her, should she try to have him removed.

'Yes,' Barton repeated, 'I am a friend of her Grace, and would like to be your friend as well, should your brother allow it. Might I have permission to call upon you tomorrow?'

'Most certainly not.' Endsted's composure snapped, and he rose from the table. 'Catherine, Susanne. We are leaving.'

The girls did not like the command, but they responded quickly, and rose as well. He shepherded them towards the door, and turned back to Barton and Constance. 'I know your measure, sir, as does the rest of decent society. And I'll thank you to give my family a wide berth in the future. If I catch you dangling after my sisters again, we will settle this on the field of honour and not in a drawing room.'

And then he turned to Constance, and there was disappointment, mingling with his anger. 'I cannot know what you were thinking, to allow him here. If you will not be careful of your guests, Constance, at least have a care for yourself.' And with a final warning glance, he left the room.

She turned back to the tea table, where Barton had returned to his seat, and his cup. She stood above him, hands planted on hips, and he had not even the courtesy to rise for her. The insults and the threats from Endsted had had no effect on his composure, either. He had the same serene smile as when she'd returned home to find him waiting.

'There,' Constance snapped. 'Endsted has gone, and I doubt he will return. I hope you are satisfied.'

Barton looked at her, and his gaze was so possessive and familiar that she wished she could strike him. He stared as if he could see through her clothes. 'Not totally. But I expect I soon will be.'

'If that was some pitiful attempt at a *double entendre*, you needn't bother.'

'Oh, really, it is no bother. In fact, I quite enjoy it.'

She shuddered in revulsion. 'You horrible, horrible man. I do not care how you feel about it. I do not enjoy it. I find it offensive. It is vile. I cannot make it any plainer than that. I do not want you, or your rude comments. If you persist in your pursuit of me, my response will be the same as it was the last time: I do not want you. I will not want you. I never want to see you again. Now get out of my house.' By the time she was finished, she was shouting.

'Your house?' He smiled and his tone never wavered.

And, suddenly, she knew that he knew about the loss of the deed and she also had a horrible suspicion about its current ownership.

'I believe you are mistaken,' he continued, 'about this being your house. If it were yours, you would be able to show me the deed, would you not?'

He knew. He had to. But if there was even the smallest chance that she was wrong, she would keep up the pretence. 'I do not have it here. It is in the bank, where it can be kept safe.'

'Is it, now?' He wagged a finger at her. 'I think, Constance, that you are not telling me the whole truth. It is far more likely that your nephew had the deed in his keeping, not wishing to give up his power over you so easily. He is not the best card player, even when sober. And he is rarely sober, Constance. Quite likely to gamble away his estate.' He smiled coldly. 'Not his estate, perhaps. When one loses enough in a night to equal the cost of one's townhouse…well, one might as well lose the cost of another house instead.'

'He didn't.'

'I'm afraid he did. The deed is safe enough. I have it in my possession. Would you like to give me a tour of my property? We could begin upstairs.'

'I do not believe you,' she stalled.

'Then you must go to the duke and ask him. It must be very trying for you to have your future in the hands of such an idiot.'

She grasped at her last hope. 'Freddy cannot legally give away what is not his. I will appeal to the courts. It is my house. My name is on the deed.'

Barton shrugged. 'Now, perhaps. But it does not take much talent to change a few lines of ink. By the time anyone sees the paper, I will be sure it says what I wish it to say. You will find, Constance, that the courts will want proof. You will have your word, of course. But I will have evidence. If you have any doubts, you can ask Freddy what he has to say on the matter.'

Too late to pretend, then. 'Lord Barton…' she began hesitantly. 'I have already been to see the duke, and he has explained to me what has become of the house.'

Barton nodded, still smiling.

She swallowed. 'And I assume that there will be a rent set, now that I am your tenant.'

He was enjoying her discomposure. 'You know that it is not money that I want from you.'

She closed her eyes in defeat. 'Then I will be out of the house by morning.'

He grabbed her wrist and her eyes snapped open at the shock of the unwelcome contact. 'Not so fast, my dear. I understand it is fully furnished. There is an attached inventory. If you can assure me that everything is in its proper place, we can dispense with the tour.'

She wet her lips. He knew that her furniture had gone the way of her jewels. There was no point in pretending it had not.

'There is an easier way, you know. You stay in the house. You keep the servants and I give you enough money to replace all that you have taken, even the stones in the rest of your jewellery. But you accept the fact that it is my house that you live in, and I will come and go, and do as I please when here. And no door will be barred to me.'

The hand on her wrist relaxed into a gentle grip. 'It is not an unpleasant proposition I am making, I assure you. I am not a cruel man. My mistresses have always found me to be generous and they assure me I am good company. But I do not like to be opposed.'

'And I do not like to be forced.'

'You are not being forced. You have options. You can leave the house and its contents intact. Then there will be no reason for me to call the law to retrieve my property. Or you can accept that you are my guest here, and treat me with the gratitude I deserve for solving so many of your problems. I will give you two days to consider the matter. That should be enough time to put your house in order.'

He snapped his fingers. 'Correction. My house in order. I will return on Monday, Constance. At that time, you will give me the keys. Whether you stay or go is completely up to you. Until then.' And he bent his head to hers and kissed her.

She wished that it had been a repellent kiss, and that she had fought it, as one would fight untimely death. But instead, she closed her eyes and leaned into him, opening her mouth and trying to remember what it had been like to kiss Robert so.

She had to admit the truth to herself: Barton was not unskilled at kissing. If it were not Barton holding her, the experience would not be unpleasant. He did a creditable job of trying to arouse her passions.

She imagined she was in Tony's arms, and she did a creditable job of pretending to be aroused. And so it was likely to be from now on.

'That was not so very bad, was it?'

Her voice quavered as she spoke, and she could feel a flush of shame on her face. 'We are not finished here, Jack. Do not think that you have won.'

'We can discuss my chances of victory on Monday, Constance. Until then.'

And he left her there, trembling with rage. It was one thing to sell one's dreams to get a husband. If there was no promise of love, then at least there was a guarantee of security until such time as the fool man had to go and die, leaving one's future in the hands of his idiot nephew…

She shook her head. She would not let Barton use her at his will, and cast her off when he tired of her. There had to be another way. If she had the deed and the inventory, then the house would be hers. She would put it somewhere safe, out of the hands of Freddy and all others, as she should have done from the first. There would be no further discussion.

But Barton was not likely to give it to her just because she wanted it. He would make her earn it. If she wanted it, then she must find a way to take it from him. She imagined sneaking into his house in the night, and rifling his desk. He would keep it somewhere he could look at it and admire his cleverness, much as he planned to keep her on display in her own house.

All she need do was go to his house under cover of darkness, find the deed, and steal away with it without anyone noticing. An impossibility. Even if she could get past the locked door, she doubted she would have the nerve necessary to take the thing.

But she knew someone with nerve enough for both of them. Her heart skipped at the memory of him climbing boldly out of her window and down to the ground as silently as a shadow. And he had been in the study before. He might even know where to look.

If she could make him do it for her. She had done what he wished at the previous night's ball. He had said that would clear any debt she might owe, with regards to the money he had left her. And she had allowed him to kiss her in the garden. But she had hurt him, too, in the circulating library. What reason could he possibly have to help her, after that?

The same reason everyone else had to offer her assistance. He, at least, had made a more interesting proposition when he'd made her pay him back. And he'd left her with hard currency to trade.

And, she had to admit it, a certain willingness to barter. Did she seriously plan to sell her honour so cheaply?

She thought of the single kiss in the moonlight, and the way her body had responded as they'd danced. She was hardly selling herself cheap if it was a house she gained. And it was not as if she would need feign too hard, when the moment came to give all. It might be quite pleasant to lie back and let him have his way.

She flushed. Her current fantasy of what might happen when next she was alone with Anthony Smythe had very little to do with passive submission to his advances. She must take care or her response, when the moment came, was likely to be aggressive to an unladylike degree.

But to the matter at hand, how did one go about offering oneself in exchange for services?

She shuddered. That was what she was planning to do. And it did no good to paint the act in romantic fantasies, even if the experience proved as pleasant as it was likely to. Any relationship they might have after tonight would be in fulfilment of a transaction and not the passionate idyll she'd created in her imagination.

She sighed. If life were dreams, it would not be as it had been in the library, today. She would have come upon Mr Smythe when she was alone, and he would ply her with poetry and promises of discretion. They would meet in secret, and he would grow bolder with each meeting. She would put up a token display of resistance before succumbing to his considerable romantic skills. Their inevitable parting would be bittersweet, but she would have a memory that she could carry into whatever cold future awaited her.

But now, she must forgo romance and throw herself on the mercy of the thief, or she would be spending her immediate future in the company of Lord John Barton. Nothing was lost, she reminded herself. Neither path led to a likelihood of slow seduction by Anthony Smythe, but one was infinitely more pleasant, once she got over the initial distaste of being so forward as to make the first move.

And if she was to move, there was no time to waste. She hurried up the stairs to her room and called for her maid. 'Susan?'

'Yes, your Grace.'

'I am going out. The gold dress, I think.' It was attractive on her, she thought. And she wished to look her best. Susan helped her into the gown and Constance appraised herself in the pier glass.

She had always thought this her most lovely gown, but now she was not so sure. It was grand, certainly. The gold threads caught the candlelight, and tiny beads glittered in the poufs of white satin that trimmed it, and weighted the skirt. But it seemed too stiff and formal for what she had in mind this particular evening.

She wanted to be beautiful for him. A prize worthy of any risk he might take to achieve it. But she did not want to seem unapproachable. How best to make the point clear? She took a deep breath to steady herself, and then she said, 'Susan, help me out of these stays.'

Her maid's eyes widened in alarm. 'You are not going to see Lord Barton again, are you, your Grace?'

'I should think not, Susan. I know someone who might be willing to help on that account, if I ask him nicely.' And with no stays, she would not have to ask aloud.

The maid nodded. 'Very good, ma'am.' Susan removed the dress, helped her out of her corset and tossed the dress back over her head.

The effect was startling. While the fabric was not sheer, it clung to her body, heavy with the weight of the beads. She could almost see the outline of her breasts inside the dress.

And if she could see them, so could he.

She swallowed. Very well. At least there would be no misunderstanding. It needed but one thing to complete the effect. She closed her eyes in embarrassment. 'Susan? How does one damp one's skirts?'

'Your Grace?' Her maid gave an incredulous giggle.

'I've heard of it's being done, but I don't think I've ever actually seen it…'

Chapter Eight

The evening found her shivering inside her cloak, waiting for Mr Smythe to enter his study. Constance had discovered the reason, firsthand, why the practice of dampened petticoats had never caught on. She had thought it was the extreme immodesty that prevented popularity. But now that she had tried it, she suspected it had as much to do with the discomfort involved. The fabric was cold and wet against her body, and she thought she was as likely to catch her death as catch a man because of it.

But the image presented when she saw herself in the mirror might be most effective, if the object of the evening was seduction. The thin fabric of the skirt clung to her legs and outlined her hips and belly. Without the troublesome stays, her breasts rested soft and full in the bodice of her dress, and tightened in response to the chill of the skirts. The rouge on her cheeks and lips was subtle, but made her mouth look kissable in the candlelight. There was no trace left of the aloof duchess to obscure the vulnerable and desirable woman she saw there.

When she'd arrived at Smythe's rooms, she'd almost lost her nerve, and had clung to the cloak as her last line of protection when the servant had offered to take it. It would be hard enough to shed, once the object of her mission was in sight, and she meant to keep it as long as she could.

At last, Smythe stepped into the room, and she turned to greet him.

He smiled politely. 'Your Grace? To what do I owe the honour of this visit?'

She let the cloak slip from her shoulders and drop to the floor around her.

There was a long pause, as he took in her appearance. And then, he said, 'Oh.' And his face went blank.

She waited, but no response was forthcoming. He stood, rooted to the spot, silent and staring at her as though he did not quite understand what he was seeing.

Dear God, what had she done? She had assumed that she recognised his interest. And he had kissed her. Twice. But perhaps he was thus with all women when he was alone with them.

It had been the servant who had given her the direction to this place, not Mr Smythe. She had not thought, before coming here, to question whether he wished to entertain her in his home. He had certainly never invited her to it. After the afternoon in the library, he might not wish to see her at all, much less see her nearly naked in his study.

He might have other plans for the evening. He might not be alone. Worse yet, he might be married, although there was nothing about the rooms to indicate the fact. And she had blundered forward, dressed like a courtesan and expecting a warm greeting.

She stared down at the cloak on the floor, willing it to jump back into place around her shoulders, and then she looked back at Mr Smythe.

He was still staring at her, taking in every detail. He forgot himself and sat down. And then sprang from his chair, and motioned to her. 'Please, sit. May I offer you a drink? Tea?'

She sank gratefully on to a nearby settee. 'Sherry?'

'Of course.' She noted the speed with which he summoned a servant, and the eagerness of his voice. He did not let his man come fully into the room, blocking the entrance with his body and taking the tray from him at the door. Then he returned to her, busying himself with the pouring of wine as though he did not know what to do with his hands.

Did this mean he was still interested in her? Or had she embarrassed him in some way? Until he spoke, it was difficult to tell. But whatever he felt, it wasn't anger, for he showed no sign of turning her out, and he'd have done it by now, surely.

He offered her a glass, but still said nothing. She took her sherry and sipped, crossing her legs, and watching as he watched the movement of her skirt and swallowed some of his own wine.

At last she could stand the silence no longer. All the witty conversational gambits she'd imagined had involved two people who were capable of speech. There would be no clever sparring around the truth, or coy avoidance if she could not get Tony to respond beyond a monosyllable. Finally she gave up and went directly to the reason for her visit, without preamble. 'I need your help.'

'Anything,' he breathed. And then he remembered to look into her eyes. He cleared his throat, and his face went blank again, as he pretended that he had not just been trying to stare through her clothes. When he spoke, his voice had returned to its normal tone. 'How may I assist you? I am at your service.'

Very well. He wished to pretend that there was nothing unusual about her appearance? Then so would she. She stared unflinchingly into his eyes. 'I need something taken. Stolen, from another person.' Her nerve began to falter. 'It was mine to begin with, so in a sense, it is not stealing at all.'

His voice hardened, as he responded. 'Do not justify. I trust that you would never ask this of me if the reason were not a good one. You need something taken? Then I am your man. Direct me to it.'

'Jack Barton has the deed to my house. My house, mind you. Not my husband's or my nephew's. It was promised to me.' She heard the whine in her voice, and took a deep breath. 'I assume you can guess the reason why he might wish to keep it. It is very economical on his part to allow me to remain in my own house, in exchange for my hospitality when he visits me there. He needn't even let some rooms.'

She was pleased to see the murderous look on the face of Mr Smythe as the situation sunk in.

'And I would like to have it back. But I am not sure where he might be keeping it.'

'That is all right,' he said hurriedly. 'I have a pretty good idea of its location. It was a rum trick to play on you, and I have no objection to settling the score. I'll fix the bastard so that he's ill inclined to try it again.' He seemed almost relieved not to have to think about her, and his eyes lost focus as he began to plan the job. 'The thing will take several days, but you must be patient and allow me to know what is best in this matter. I will bring the deed to you as soon as I have it safely away.'

'I need it before Monday. That is when he means to…take occupancy.'

His attention snapped back to the present, and he was aware of her again. There was a long pause, and for a moment, she feared that he was about to retract his offer of help. Then he said, 'Monday? This is not an easy thing you are asking. But I understand that your need is urgent. I will adjust my own plans so that I may help you. You will have it by Monday.'

'Thank you.'

There was another long silence. She had expected that this was where he would explain to her the cost of the service, and she took another sip of the sherry, wetting her lips to agree, when he asked.

But he said nothing. He just continued to gaze at her, watching her lips as she drank the sherry, scanning slowly down to admire her breasts, making no effort to clarify her position. She could feel her skin grow warm under his gaze, and her nipples tightening.

At last she could no longer stand the silence. She stared down into her wine glass and said, 'If you were to do this for me, I would be very grateful. Once it is done, of course. Once the item is returned to me, there is nothing that you would ask that I would refuse.'

'Nothing,' he said flatly.

'Nothing,' she affirmed.

'Anything I might think to ask in payment, any request I might make, you would be willing to comply?'

She ignored the heat rising in her. 'Yes.'

His voice dropped to a sensuous murmur, and she could feel the words dancing along her nerves. 'Be warned, I have an extremely vivid imagination.'

Suddenly, so did she. She closed her eyes tight and

the fantasies that rose at the sound of his voice became more intense. Her blood sizzled as she imagined what it might be like to submit to the whims of a man who was little more than a stranger—a hardened criminal, accustomed to taking what he wanted. 'Anything you wish.'

'But what will you say in the morning, I wonder?' His voice had returned to normal again.

'I have no idea what you mean,' she responded, a little too easily.

'I should think it's obvious. It was to me, at least. I am not good enough to be seen with, when you are in the presence of your friends. It is much safer here, is it not, where there is no one you know?'

The words stung her. 'And how could I have introduced you to Endsted?' she retorted. 'This is Mr Smythe. We met in my bedroom, when he was stealing my jewellery. Really, Tony, you ask the impossible of me.'

'Tony, is it, now? I had no idea, your Grace, that we had progressed to that level of familiarity. I suppose I should be flattered. When you meet me in the future, you may call me whatever you choose. You need not mention knowing me in my professional capacity at all. We have been introduced at a formal gathering, although you did not pay a great deal of attention at the time. You have danced with me. We have made polite conversation. I had hoped that you might be able to treat me as you treat others. And as I have treated you: with courtesy and respect.'

'Courtesy and respect? That is beyond enough. You have taken liberties with my person.'

'I apologise,' he responded stiffly. 'I rather thought, at the time, that you enjoyed them. And if I do not miss my guess, you just invited to do as I pleased with you. But if I was mistaken, and have been taking unwelcome liberties, then I humbly apologise. It will not happen again.'

Her anger faded, as she remembered how he'd looked in the library. She had hurt him with her snub. And now she had come to his rooms to hurt him again. She could feel the cool air passing through her gown, fighting back the heat in her skin. She was being utterly shameless, trying to trap Tony into helping her. And yet she was berating him for his behaviour. She looked down at the designs her toe was tracing in the rug. 'I mis-spoke. You have not taken anything from me that was not freely offered. But Barton came to my rooms after we spoke this afternoon. And in my panic, I could not think where else to turn. I thought, after the kiss in the garden, you would not be averse to my offer tonight.'

He laughed. 'Oh, your Grace, I'm not averse. Not in the slightest. Especially with you dressed like that.' He stared at her body, making no effort to hide his interest. Finally, he gave a deep sigh of satisfaction. 'Say the word and I'll have you on the hearthrug, right now, and make sure you don't regret the offer. But understand, if I wished to be compensated for my services, I would request payment in full, up front of the job.' He stared into her eyes and his smile faded. 'With the risks I'm taking, I never withhold pleasure or payment for tomorrow. One can not guarantee the outcome. If they catch me and hang me, your gratitude is worthless.'

'Very well, then.' Here and now? He would not even lead her to his bed? She felt her knees turn to water and a tremor of excitement go through her at the thought of what was about to happen. She reached to undo her bodice, trying not to rush in her eagerness.

'I did not request payment.'

Her hand stopped.

'When did I ever demand anything of you?' he asked softly. 'I said I would do this for you, and I shall. I do not wish to—how did you put it?—"take liberties". From you, I do not wish to take anything at all. I will take care of your problem.' He waved his hand as though dealing with Barton were no more difficult than shooing a fly. 'Tonight, all you needed to do was ask and I would have offered to do all in my power to aid you. And as a gentleman, I do not require your gratitude afterwards. Do not mention it again.'

'Thank you.' But she did not feel like thanking him. She felt like shouting at him. And the flush in her cheeks was from shame, not excitement.

There was another long pause. And his eyes remained focused on her face, studiously ignoring the rest of her. 'Is there anything else you wished of me?'

There were many things, none of which she could very well ask for. To begin with, she wanted him to gaze at her as he had done, when she had entered the room, and not with the coldness and disdain he was showing now. 'No, I think that is all.'

He nodded, and said nothing more. His expression did not change. The silence stretched between them.

'I should probably be going, then.'

He nodded. 'I think that's best. Do you wish me to escort you home?' And now he showed the same level of concern that any gentleman might show to a lady.

'No. I am all right. It was not far to walk.' She could not stand the embarrassment of his respect a moment longer.

'You walked?' His voice held disapproval. 'It is not seemly or safe for a woman to travel alone at night. I will tell Patrick to get you a hackney.'

'No.' She had shocked him, by her behaviour, by coming alone to his home, and by her dress, or lack thereof. This was not how the night was to end at all.

'I insist.' His voice was emphatic, so she nodded and rose. He reached for her cloak and dropped it on to her shoulders, concealing her body from view before opening the door. She reached to pull it closed in front of her.

He escorted her to the door of his study and out into

the hall. He directed his servant to find her transportation. Then he turned his back upon her and returned to his room.

The servant whom she had met the previous night led her down the stairs and left her standing at the front door, as he hailed a cab for her, and she sensed pity in his smile as he helped her into the coach.

Anthony returned to his chair and waited until the door closed behind her, and then waited a little longer. He imagined her progress through the house and out of the front door. Then he drained his wine in a gulp, and called for his valet.

The man appeared like a ghost behind him. 'Sir?'

'Patrick, bring me brandy. And plenty of it.'

'Yes, sir.' Patrick was resigned to his master's behaviour, even if he did not approve of it. He left the room and reappeared a short time later, carrying a tray laden with a full bottle of the best brandy in the cellars.

Patrick poured the first glass, and when he seemed to be finished, his master signalled him with a raising of the hand. 'Eh, eh, eh, a little more, still.' Tony watched the level rise in the glass. He held up a hand. 'Stop. That's the ticket. And keep them coming, Patrick.' He drank half the brandy and blurted, 'That woman. I swear, Patrick, she will be the death of me. I cannot countenance what she did, just now.' He finished the glass, and held it out to be refilled.

'First she snubs me in public, and makes it known to me that she prefers another. Then she comes to me, soft and willing, just as I've always dreamed she would. She is finally here, and wants my help. And at any time, does she recognise me? No.'

'It has been a long time, sir. Both you and she have changed significantly.'

'One thing has not changed. She did not want me then, and she does not want me now. Did you see her? Dear God.' He allowed himself a moment of carnal pleasure at the memory. 'No stays, thin silk gown, and I swear she'd damped the skirts.' He shook his head. 'Like a French woman. Nothing left to imagination, not that my imagination needs any help when it comes to her. But she should not have been out in the streets in that condition. She'd catch her death. She made it quite clear, in the library today, that she wanted no part of me, and that our association was an embarrassment.

'Very well. I do not need to be told twice. I meant to avoid her in the future. If she does not want me, then there is no point in making an even greater fool of myself than I have been.' He stared down into his second brandy. He was already feeling the effects of the first, and thought the better of the second drink, tossing the contents of the glass into the fire, listening to the spirits hissing in the flames.

'A few hours pass, and she comes to my room dressed to seduce me. Very well, thinks I. She has no trouble acknowledging me when we are alone. If I had any pride, I would refuse her. Which would prove I'm an even bigger fool than I thought, for how can I turn down an offer like this? She's been married long enough to know what's what and widowed long enough to miss it. She might ignore me tomorrow, but the morning is a long way off, and we'll have a time of it tonight.'

He stared down into his empty glass, and Patrick shook his head and poured again.

'And why did she come to me? She wants me to steal for her. Not a problem, of course. I'd die for her, if she but asked. Burglary is not a sticking point. And if I did, she would deign to lie with me. Afterwards. In gratitude.' He closed his eyes and drank more slowly this time.

'She looked at me with those sherry-coloured eyes, and hung her head as though the path to my bed was a passage to Botany Bay.' He finished the brandy and said sadly, 'It was not the way I'd imagined it.'

Patrick looked at him in disappointment. 'What you have wanted for half your life was here, within your grasp. And you choose instead to send it away and call for a brandy bottle.'

'It wasn't what I wanted,' he argued. 'Her gratitude, indeed.'

'What, exactly, do you want from her, then, if not to lie with her?'

'I want her to see me for who I am, even if she cannot see me for who I was. All she sees is the thief, Patrick. And to catch him, she was willing to be the whore that a thief deserved.' He thought back to the sight of her, her breasts swaying beneath her gown, her legs outlined by the cloth. 'Not that I minded, seeing her. But I wager she does not dress thusly when she is trying to impress Endsted.'

'Would you wish her to, sir?'

'No. Of course not. If it were my choice, she would not see Endsted, again, under any circumstances. And I would make damn sure that he never got to see what I saw tonight. The man is an utter prig. I doubt he'd have known what to do with her, in any case.'

'Unlike you, sir, Endsted would have sat there like a lecher, staring at her charms while making it clear that he disapproved of her behaviour. And then he would have insulted her by sending her away. She would have gone home, with head hung low and near tears, convinced that she was in some way morally repellent or deformed in body. I am sure she will think twice in the future before exposing to the gentleman in question any sign of interest or vulnerability that might lead to further ridicule.'

Tony ignored the dark look that Patrick was giving him, to drive the point home. 'You're saying I should go to her, then. Apologise.'

Patrick nodded. 'Because there is nothing that will

make amends better than appearing on her doorstep after half a bottle of brandy, and trying to say the things in your heart that you cannot manage to say when you are sober.'

'Damn it, Patrick. Other men's valets will at least lie to them when they have made fools of themselves.'

'If it is any consolation, sir, Lord Endsted's valet often has cause to lie to his master on that score. We have discussed it.'

Tony held up a hand. 'Let us hear no more of Viscount Endsted. My night is quite grim enough, without thinking of him, or knowing that valets trade stories when they are gathered together. It chills the blood. Instead, tell me, Patrick, since you are so full of honesty, what am I to do to make amends with the Duchess of Wellford?'

'Perhaps, sir, it would go a long way to restoring her good humour, if you did the thing that she wished you to do in the first place.'

'You have returned early, your Grace.' Susan was looking at her with curiosity, no doubt trying to spy some evidence of carnal activity. 'Was the gentleman you wished to visit not at home?'

'On the contrary, he was in, and willing to see me.'

'That was quick.' Susan's face moued in disapproval. 'But I suppose it's the same with all men. The more time we takes on our appearance, the less time they needs. It don't seem right, somehow.'

Constance started at the familiarity, then admitted the truth. 'He sent me home. He took one good look at me, and he sent me away.' She looked at her maid, hoping that Susan could provide some explanation.

'He did not find you attractive?'

She sat on the end of the bed, shivering in the damp gown. 'He as much as said he did. He made comment on my appearance. He knew how I expected the evening to end. And he turned me down. I fear I have insulted him. Or lessened his opinion of me.'

'Then your friend left you to settle with Lord Barton yourself?' Susan looked more than a little dismayed at the thought.

'No. There was no problem about that. Mr Smythe said he was most willing to help, but that my gratitude was not necessary. Then he covered me up and sent me away.'

Susan sat on the end of the bed as well, clearly baffled. 'Forgive me for saying it, your Grace, but he must be a most unusual gentleman.'

Constance frowned. 'I think so as well, Susan.'

Anthony stared at the locked door of Barton's safe, and felt the sweat forming on his palms. He wiped his hands on his trouser legs and removed the picks from his coat pocket. Now was not the time for a display of weak nerves or a distaste for the work at hand. He could fulfil his promise to Stanton and destroy the plates by burning the house down if he could not manage to open the safe.

But for the promise to Constance? A fire would do him no good, for it would destroy the thing he searched for. And she wanted immediate action.

Patrick had been right. It had been stupid of him to give way to temper, and waste the better part of the evening with drink. When reason had begun to return, he had realised that he might need every spare moment between now and Monday, working on the lock, if he wished to deliver the deed to Constance and forestall Barton. He had been forced to spend several more hours becoming sober enough to do the job at all, and still might not be unaffected enough to do it well.

Now, it was past three and he had but a few hours before dawn. It was the quietest part of the night, when all good men were asleep, leaving the bad ones the freedom to work in peace.

Entry to the study was as uneventful as it had been the night of Barton's ball, even though he'd climbed up a drainpipe and into the window instead of using the stairs. Would that the results with the safe would be more successful than the last attempt.

The thing was still there, taunting him from its place on the wall behind the desk. Barton had not even bothered to conceal it, leaving its obvious presence as a sign of its impregnability.

If the man had anything of value, it was most assuredly behind the locked safe door. Tony had found the printing press in the basement along with the rest of the supplies, hidden under a Holland cloth, with little effort made to conceal them.

But there was no law against owning a press. To rid Barton of the paper would require one lucifer and the work of a moment, perhaps doused with the ink. Tony did not know if ink was particularly flammable, but, since so many things were, it was quite possible.

The engraved plates had to be somewhere in the house or the press would be useless. He fitted his pick into the lock and felt for the sliders, working one, and then another before feeling the pick slip. And now he must start over.

How many were there supposed to be? As many as eighteen, and any mistake meant a new beginning and more time wasted. He tried again, progressed slightly further and felt the pick slip in his sweaty hands.

Damn it. Damn it all to hell. He swore silently and repeatedly. Then he took a deep breath and began again.

It would have to work, because he would not return to Constance empty handed. He imagined her as she had been when she visited him. Huge, dark eyes, smooth skin, red lips, body soft and willing.

And he had sent her away. He must have been mad.

Of course, what was one night of gratitude against a lifetime of devotion, if there was some way she could be persuaded to see his intentions towards her ran deeper than the physical? In the end, she would think him no better than Barton, if he took advantage of her need. There would be time, later, if he could wait.

He felt his pick catch another slider and move it into position. And he focused on the touch of the lock and the vision in his mind of her leaning close to whisper softly in his ear.

There was a click of the room's door handle, which seemed as loud as a rifle shot in the dead silence of the house. Tony withdrew his pick and darted behind a curtain, praying that the velvet was not swaying to mark the passage of his body.

He could see the light at the edge of the curtain; the glow was faint, as though someone had entered the room, bearing a single candle.

A man, by the stride. Long, and with the click of a boot heel.

Barton.

Pace, pace, pace. Tony counted out enough steps for a man of nearly six foot to reach the desk.

He held his breath.

There was a faint rattle as a drawer was unlocked. The rustle of paper. A pause. A sigh. The sound of retreating footsteps, along with the retreating light. And the click of a door latch again.

Tony grinned to himself. Where best to keep a deed? In a safe? Hardly necessary, since no one would be seeking it. Best to keep it close, where one could admire it. Touch it when one wanted to reassure oneself of victory and fantasise over the conquered in the dark of night.

All in all, he was lucky that Barton was not keeping the document at his bedside. Perhaps with the prospect of Constance so firmly in his grasp, the deed was not necessary.

Tony stepped from behind the curtain and produced a penknife, then slid it along the space in the desk drawer until he heard a satisfying click. He opened the drawer and found the deed, face up in plain view.

Too easy, really, once one left common sense behind and entered the realm of obsession. He could almost feel sorry for Barton, had the man chosen a different object for his passion.

Tony folded the paper and tucked it into a pocket. He went to the window and was gone.

Chapter Nine

Music played softly in the background and Constance sipped her champagne and pretended to enjoy herself. Sunday night's ball at the townhouse of the Earl of Stanton was to have been a night of pure pleasure in the company of friends. She had been looking forward to it for weeks. And now Barton had ruined everything. The music made no impact and the drink held no flavour. All she could think about was the impending doom of Monday morning and the cold look on Tony's face as he had sent her away.

Her friend, the countess, had hugged her when she had seen the expression on Constance's face, and enquired after her health.

She had pretended that nothing was wrong, but even the earl had noticed the change in her and remarked on it. And Esme had clasped her hand again and assured her that, whatever the problem might be, she had but to ask, and they would find a way to resolve it. She could treat the Stanton home as her own, if need be. Stay the night or longer, if she wished. And take pleasure in the entertainment at hand, for it was expected to be most fine.

Constance had insisted that she was in no dire need, and that her friend needn't worry, although the earl's look at her as she passed through the receiving line was too shrewd and it was clear that he was not fooled.

It had been a mistake to lie at all. For it would look even worse to her hosts when she needed to swallow her pride and beg Esme for refuge at the end of the evening, if it was to be a choice between her house and her honour.

There was some comfort, at least, in knowing that only the best company was invited through these particular doors. She had no reason to fear a run in with Barton before the morning, for such as he would never gain entrance to a ball held by the Stantons.

Which made it all the more surprising to see Anthony Smythe in close conversation with the host. The earl could not possibly know the man's true occupation, or St John would throw him bodily from the room. And Constance could not very well inform them of what she knew. Certainly not when she had gone to Mr Smythe, requesting the very service she pretended to abhor.

He was across the room from her, and she tried to resist the urge to look in his direction. How utterly mortifying it had been to go to him, practically bare and obviously willing, only to be patted on the head and put from the room. If she had behaved in a similar manner, with any of the other men of her acquaintance…

Then she need not have gone to Mr Smythe at all. Upon seeing how she had costumed herself, and hearing of her willingness to co-operate, they'd have given her any sum she required to clear her debts. The ink would scarcely be dry on the cheque before they'd have taken her up on her offer.

Then why, for the sake of her already-battered spirit, had she gone to the only man unwilling to take her body as payment? Was it because she had known in her heart that he would be too honourable to accept?

Or simply because she wanted a reason, any reason at all, to see him again, tempt him in a way that would make him forget her behaviour in the library, and offer him no resistance when he pulled her close, laid her down, and took from her what she wanted to give him?

It had been so easy to restrain herself through the last year, as the suggestions she'd received had become bolder and bolder. And, on some level, she'd known that if there was no one to offer her marriage, there might be one whose offer was not quite so insulting as the rest. She had no desire to be a mistress. That would be no better than marrying for money.

But if there were a man who valued her, and whose company she enjoyed, and if he was willing to be discreet? She would gladly yield just to feel arms around her again, and lips on her temple, and to sleep secure in the knowledge that someone cared about her, even if it was for only a night.

She glanced into a mirror at the far end of the room, catching a glimpse of the image of Tony Smythe reflected back to her. His dark blue coat fit smoothly over the muscles she felt when he'd held her. His legs, as well, were straight and strong from climbing, and graceful as he walked. She thought she could hear his distant laugh, and could imagine the light in his eyes, and the way his smile curved a little higher on one side than the other.

It was a face not so much beautiful as it was interesting. There was energy in it, and enthusiasm. One could look at it for a lifetime and always see something different. And when he had a passion for something, or someone, his excitement would be impossible to resist.

Constance averted her gaze from the mirror, casting her eyes downward, focusing on the trails of bubbles arising from her champagne. It did no good to watch him now. She might see the one thing she most feared, a look of pity in the eyes for her pathetic behaviour of the night before, and confirmation of his lack of success in getting the thing she needed. How had she expected him to manage in a night what might take days of planning? She was a fool to even ask him.

And she would look an even bigger fool, if he caught her spying on him in public.

'Would you stand up with me, your Grace?'

She was startled. He was close to her now, standing beside her, and she'd never heard him approach. Her heart was pounding in response to his nearness, and it was not because of fright.

He gestured to the dance floor. There was polite interest on his face now. Neither more nor less than she would expect from any of the other men attending.

'I would be delighted, Mr Smythe.' She tried to read his face, but it gave no clue. Did he have news for her? She was dying to ask it, but what was the point in swearing him to secrecy if she blurted out the whole truth in a crowded ballroom?

They took their place in the set and he bowed to her, and the music began.

He was an excellent dancer. His steps were sure and his touch light as he guided her down the row. She tried to relax and enjoy herself, but his steady gaze was both pleasant and unnerving. He wanted to tell her something, she was sure.

And found herself wishing that that was not the reason for the intensity when he looked at her. Robert had not cared much for dancing, and was most relieved when other men had been willing to stand up with her in his place. But none of them would dare gaze at her so, with the duke in the room.

She had watched other young ladies, and watched their beaus watching them. She had thought it sweet and tried not to lament on it. Men had looked at her thus once, very long ago, but so long ago that she could hardly remember how it felt.

They had looked as Anthony Smythe was looking at her now. His hand took hers again and he smiled. When it was their turn to wait at the bottom of the set, he leaned closer to her, and said, 'You are very lovely tonight.'

'Thank you.' She wondered if that was the case.

He must have seen the doubt in her eyes. 'You were lovely last night, as well.'

'You did not seem to think it at the time.'

'On the contrary. You were inordinately tempting. But speed was of the essence, was it not? If I had accepted your offer, we would be there still, on the floor of my parlour, too exhausted to move.'

She stared around her, to make sure no one had heard him speak. And, as always, he had taken care that the other guests would know nothing of his scandalous comments, but her delighted blush might make them stare.

'I am just as diligent and careful in taking pleasure as I am in doing business, and I take care not to mix the two. In the future, there will be ample time to spend together, if you still wish it. But if I had lost myself in you last night, I would have quite forgotten to go to Barton and get the thing that you wished me to retrieve.'

She opened her mouth to speak, and he smiled placidly.

'Please act as though nothing has happened. Remember where we are, your Grace.'

He was right. Throwing her arms around his neck and begging to see it this instant was sure to incite comment. But she could not help the joy that showed upon her face.

He looked at her, smiled back and said, 'The look on your face right now is payment enough for me. Have you forgiven me for last night?'

'There is nothing to forgive. It was I—'

'Shh. Let us hear none of that. May I visit you, later? With your permission, I will come to your house, to return the thing that concerned you so.'

She whispered, 'I shall leave here immediately and tell my servants to expect you.'

'You shall do nothing of the kind. No one need know of what has transpired between us. Enjoy your time here, for Esme is a particular friend of yours, is she not? And this is a delightful ball. It would be a shame to go so soon. Return home after midnight, send your maid to bed and wait for me at one.'

She nodded, wondering how he knew of her friendships, for she had not told him.

And he nodded back to acknowledge her assent and led her through the rest of the dance as though nothing unusual had happened, with an occasional comment about the music, the fine quality of the food, and the fact that summer had been uncommonly warm.

But he continued to fix her with the same intense gaze that had unsettled her before.

He was coming to her rooms later, and in secret. She found the prospect quite exciting. And with the way he was looking at her, perhaps he had decided to mix business and pleasure after all. It was not so surprising, she reminded herself. Despite what they might claim to put one off one's guard, men had needs and would act on them, given the opportunity.

He might say that he was honoured to help and needed no reward, but he had taken great risk to do what she had asked. She doubted that he would deny her or himself, once they were alone. And try as she might, she could not bring herself to be bothered. Why, if Lord Barton's offer had been so distasteful to her, was she not offended now?

Because she did not want to lie with Barton, as she did with Anthony Smythe.

The thought of them together warmed her blood. She wanted to feel his hands upon her and see that crooked smile in the firelight as he took her. Her stomach gave a lurch at the thought and her steps faltered.

And he caught her hand and led her on, smiling in curiosity at the look that must be on her face, but making no comment.

Very well, then. Her virtue was not as steadfast as she had once thought. And she did miss the touch of a man, just as everyone kept reminding her.

Everyone except Tony.

Perhaps that was why she wanted him so.

The dance ended and she moved through the rest of the evening as if on a cloud. Her home was safe. Barton had no hold on her. And when she retired, she would have Tony.

When Esme saw her again, as she said her goodbyes, she proclaimed her looking better. The food and the dancing must have done her good, for she was in fine colour. Almost blushing.

Constance smiled the secret back to herself and agreed that she was feeling worlds better, and that she intended to retire early. Then she returned home, prepared for bed and sent the maid away. The lawn of her nightdress was crisp and cool against her fevered skin as she unlatched the window and waited for the clock to strike one.

As the bell was chiming, he stepped over the sill, smiling back at the window she had left open for him. 'Thank you for the small courtesy, your Grace. It is rare to enter in this way and find evidence that I am welcome. Most refreshing.'

'Did you find the deed?' She hurried to his side.

'What? No "Hello, Tony. So good to see you.

Lovely dancing this evening…" No preamble. Small talk? Chit-chat?' He grinned. 'I supposed not.' He reached into his pocket and brought out a document, which he laid upon her night table. 'It is exactly as you said. In your husband's hand, the house is deeded to you. And here is the attached inventory. Put it somewhere safe. Your bank, perhaps. But do not trust it to that young jackanapes that holds your husband's title. And do not mention it to Barton until you have to. He will know that someone has got into his study and taken it, and you do not want to be associated with other thefts that might occur there. I will be visiting him again, before my business with him is done, and he will be on guard against me.

'If you can just stall him for a time, he will forget his plans for you, for I dare say he will have troubles enough soon and little time to pursue you.'

She wondered if this might have something to do with the theft at the ball, but was afraid to ask. Instead she looked down at the deed, which need be her only concern. She swallowed. 'It is such a relief to know that, no matter what, the house is mine.'

Then she looked at him significantly. 'And I am so very grateful. How can I ever repay you?' And she leaned close to him in the moonlight and waited for the obvious suggestion.

He smiled. 'No thanks are necessary. It is enough to know that I have helped a woman in distress.'

'No thanks. At all.' She hoped her disappointment was not too plain.

'I know something of hardship, and of being forced to make decisions that might compromise myself, for the sake of stability. I would not wish it on another.'

'Many men would take advantage, given the circumstances. You held the deed yourself and could just has easily have used it against me.'

'But I would not.'

'I am sorry to create more work for you, when I can do nothing in return for you.'

He sighed. 'Some day, quite without even thinking, you might do a thing that seems like a trifle to you, but will make all my efforts on your part seem as nothing. Until then, do not trouble yourself. While it would be easy to accept what you are trying to give me, I fear you might live to regret it. If I succumb, in the end you will think me no better than Barton. You are safe now, but if Barton, or any other, should prove difficult, please feel free to call upon me.' He started towards the window.

She followed him, searching for something that might stay him a little longer. 'Will I see you again?'

He smiled. 'It is likely. You have seen me many times before, you know. I certainly knew of you. But we have not been introduced until just recently. Now you know me, I suspect you will not be able to help but run into me again.'

'I should like that.' She touched his sleeve.

He had reached the window and then turned back when he felt her touch. 'I should like that as well. Under better circumstances.' He put his hand on the sill, ready to lift himself over the edge.

And she remembered the first night, when he had assured her of his character, and hazarded a bolt. 'Your wife is very fortunate to have such an honest thief for a husband.'

He pushed away from the sill and turned back to her. 'Wife?' He looked puzzled. 'I have none.'

'But when we first met—'

'When I was robbing your jewel case,' he reminded her.

'You said that you had loved but once, and I thought perhaps…'

He shook his head and stepped back into the room. He opened his mouth to speak, closed it again, and paused to take a deep breath. Then he said, 'And this is where I admit the truth, and you think me a fool. I've loved but once. But she has never loved me. It has been years… We were childhood friends.' He shook his head again and muttered, 'That puts too fine a gloss on it.' And then he admitted, 'We were acquaintances. I was too terrified to speak to her.'

'You, afraid to speak to a woman?' She stared at him incredulously.

He looked into her eyes and nodded. 'I was then. And I still am, when it comes to her.'

'Because she rejected you, all those years ago.'

He shook his head. 'She did not give that much thought to me, I'm afraid. I doubt she said three words to me in the time we knew each other. She married young and well.' He looked up at her. 'She is as high above me as you are. And as beautiful. But I doubt she would know me if we passed in the street. She has forgotten all about me. There can never be anything between us, of course. How can there be, if but one of us loves?'

She took a step towards him. 'But that is so sad. And you have kept yourself for her, all these years?'

'Not as such. I have known the company of women, of course. But my heart is elsewhere. I do not wish to marry, if I cannot have her.'

'But if you do not marry, you will not have children.' The next question mocked her, but she forced herself to ask it. 'Do you not wish for a son?'

He looked genuinely puzzled. 'I had not honestly given it much thought.'

'You did not think on it?' It was her turn to look puzzled. So many hours of her life and her husband's had been consumed with the subject of children. And here was a man who did not think about it at all. 'But you will have no heir.'

'Of course I will have an heir. I am quite well stocked with nephews. I have two of them, and a niece as well. I have been "dear Uncle Tony" for so long I can hardly remember a time when I wasn't. And I have done my share to raise them up. I always assumed that what was mine now would some day be theirs.' He smiled fondly, as he thought of children that had been fathered by others.

'But they are not *yours*,' she insisted.

'As much mine as anyone's. Their fathers are long dead. They have stepfathers now, at last. So the burden is no longer solely mine.'

'You do not care for children,' she surmised.

He shook his head. 'You misunderstand. The raising of them was not so much of a burden, even at its worst. I like children. And I would welcome my own, should any appear through design or carelessness. But it has always seemed to me to be a frivolous thing to insist on raising the fruit of one's loins when one is surrounded by windfalls.'

He would not care, even if he has already guessed the truth. Her legs almost collapsed under her, her knees trembled so. 'Then, if your wife could not give you children?'

'If the wife of my choosing could not give me children?' He sighed. 'If I could but get her to give herself to me, it would be more than I ever expected. What kind of fool would I be to win my heart's desire and then find fault with her for a thing that was not under our control?'

What kind of fool would he be? A fool like her husband and all the other men of her acquaintance. Children did not matter to Tony. If he wanted her, he would have her, and not think twice about her infertility. There would be no snide offer of fun and games, followed by a pitying smile when the talk came to marriage.

'It would not matter to me in the slightest. There is but one woman for me, Constance. And I will not love another, as long as there is life left in us, and even the smallest chance.' He looked into her eyes and it was as if he were looking into her very soul and making the vow to her.

He shook his head again and looked down, unable to meet her gaze. 'I do not expect you to understand. It really sounds quite mad, when I explain it thus.'

'Oh, no. I understand perfectly.' And, suddenly, she did. It was possible to fall hopelessly in love with someone who was totally wrong for you, and even worse, could never love you back, because of a foolish fantasy of perfection that he'd been carrying with him for his entire life. How could one compete with that?

He was smiling at her again. 'That is most kind of you to say so. Because...' He appeared to be about to speak. But he said nothing. There was a pause that seemed ready to become long and awkward.

So there was nothing wrong with her. He did not wish to raise false hopes by a casual seduction that would lead nowhere. He respected her. She should feel more relief than frustration. She broke the silence. 'Do not feel you need to explain yourself further. I think it is very noble of you. I have often wondered what it might be like to be as brave as you and to not care for reputation or stability, hazarding all for the sake of love. But I fear I am disappointingly practical, far too concerned with my own security in the distant future to risk following my heart on the moment. Still, I very much enjoy seeing others do so, and will pray fervently for your good fortune. I fear some of us are not destined to feel that kind of grand passion.'

If possible, he looked even more mortified than he had the night she came to him to ask for the deed. He coloured again, and his eyes fell. And when he looked up, his expression was earnest, as it had been when she had seen him in the library. 'Do not say that. Do not ever say that. You deserve all that love can give, and you should settle for nothing else.' And when he pulled her to him, it was shockingly sudden and she had just enough time to lift her face to his kiss.

It wasn't the same kiss that he had taken from her on the night they met. This one was hard and demanding. A soul-deep kiss, full of desire. And she kissed him back, hoping that the night might last just a little longer, that he might forget himself and stay.

He devoured her mouth and she took his tongue, thrusting into his mouth in return. And she felt his hand opening the buttons on her nightdress, cupping a breast and pinching the nipple between his fingers until she moaned.

She pushed her leg between his, and rocked her body against him. There was no question that he wanted her as she wanted him and she reached to pull him even closer so that he might know how well their bodies would fit together.

He pulled away from her, then, shaking his head. And he said, 'I must go.' He laughed, and it was unsteady. 'Although you do make it most difficult to leave. Especially since I need my body to obey me as I climb down from your window, and it is making it almost painfully clear to me that it would much rather stay here with you.'

But his eyes were bright with excitement as he said, 'I promise you, soon. But alas, I must not stay tonight. I have other work I must do before the sun rises. I cannot spend it in play with you. Besides, I have no desire to rush what I will do with you, the next time we are alone.' He traced the line of her throat downwards with his finger to massage her breast again. 'Are we in agreement?'

She nodded, dazed at the idea.

'Very good, then.' She looked into his eyes, and her body trembled at the suggestions in them. 'And remember, if you need anything at all before I come to you again, you know my direction. Feel free to call on me, or send a message and I will come to you. But do not think that you ever need walk through life alone, or that you must be practical instead of happy.'

And he was gone again, taking her heart with him.

'What do you mean, you did not tell her?'

Tony stared down into the glass in his hand, and willed himself not to throw it. But with Patrick standing between him and the fire, the temptation presented itself.

'I mean,' he responded to his valet, 'that it is a damned tricky thing, when you have been speaking to a woman as one person, to suddenly come out and admit that you are not who you seem to be. I thought, once Barton was gotten out of the way, and there was nothing standing between us, it would be easier.

'And in a way it was. She was not the false jade she played in my sitting room last night. She was much more herself, grateful, but not brazen. She cared enough to make conversation. She asked about me. She made it plain that she wanted to know me better.'

He remembered the feel of her body against his and her breast in his hand. 'She was willing to know me even better, by the end, I dare say. And I did declare my continued and unwavering devotion.' He shrugged. 'Not technically to her, but I believe she was responding well, even though I did not specifically say I was speaking of her.

'But then she declared me too noble and showed

signs of giving me up entirely, for my own good, so that I could continue to worship her from afar. And so I kissed her again, and then everything got fuzzy and I quite forgot how it was I meant to go on. But I had to get back to Stanton's damn ball since he wanted to speak to me in private, after. I could not very well drop anchor for the night.' He grinned. 'Although I got the distinct impression, there at the last, that I would have been a welcome guest, had I decided to do so.'

Patrick smacked his forehead with the palm of his hand. 'But now she has the deed, and you have no reason to see her again.'

'On the contrary, I have every reason. She might pretend uninterest during the day, but she has kissed me again. That is the third time and it is not often enough.

'Now that she has noticed me, I plan to be very much under foot. She cannot ignore me for ever. Perhaps next time we meet, I will not need to climb through her bedroom window. If I am not conversing with her in her bedroom, it will be much easier to keep my head.'

And perhaps, in good light, she will recognise me. He did not want to think it. He did not want it to matter. And yet, it mattered so very much.

Patrick replied with confidence, 'Once you tell her the truth, there will be no problem at all.'

Other than accepting that, if I am not attempting to

rob her, I am utterly forgettable. 'It is rather embarrassing, not to have told her from the first.' He tried to toss the comment out in a way that made it unimportant.

'It will only grow more embarrassing as time passes.' Damn Patrick and his reasonable advice.

'I gathered that. But it is vexing to have my true nature go unrecognised by one who has known me my whole life.' There. The truth would out, somewhere, if not where he needed it.

'Your true nature?' Patrick snorted. 'And by true nature, you mean the nice young cleric who pulled me out of Newgate, pretending charity, but really wanting me to help him dispose of his ill-gotten gains?'

Tony bristled. 'That is most unfair.'

'But it is the truth. You were only too happy to learn all I could teach you, and assume all the risks, while sensible men such as myself preferred to retire from crime and devote themselves to pressing milord's coat and perfecting the knot for a Mathematical cravat.'

Patrick was staring at him in disbelief. 'You insist on seeing yourself as no different than you were when you were children. But you are both changed by the past thirteen years. Your true nature, as you put it, was not in evidence when she saw you last. She paid you no heed then because there was no reason to. You were shy, bookish and painfully honest. It was easy enough to cure you of the honesty, and now that you are putting your education to use, you are not so quiet as you once were. Once you rid yourself of the shyness, there will be nothing left at all of the old you, not even the name. And you have her complete attention, do you not? She does not love another?'

'There is Endsted,' Tony admitted.

Patrick snorted. 'Then you have nothing to fear. The results are guaranteed, once you declare yourself to her.'

Perhaps Patrick was right. 'Very well, then. I shall call on her tomorrow. At her home this time, so she has no reason to be distracted by a rival. I have no doubt she will welcome me, since she said as much last night. In daylight with the servants about and a respectable distance between us, it will be much easier to part with the truth. And then we shall see how things go.' And he knew the path was right because of the sudden flare of hope that sprang beside the banked fires of desire in his heart.

Chapter Ten

The next morning, Constance paced her rooms, uneasily, looking at the deed on the night table. And the note beside it: *We must talk. Barton.*

The note had arrived with the morning's post, even before she could get the deed to the bank. And now she was afraid to leave the house with it, lest he be waiting outside to take it from her again. He knew. That had to be the truth of it. If he thought he was still in possession of the deed, he would have marched boldly into the house this morning, as he had threatened to do. Instead, he had missed the thing, and guessed her involvement in the theft. He meant to harass her about it. Perhaps he would go to the Runners.

But what could he do? He could not very well claim the deed was his and she had taken it, since it clearly stated that she was the owner of the house. Tony was right. She had but to avoid him, until he lost interest, and her life would return to normal and the already-long string of problems that she must deal with. But the sale of the house, along with the last of Mr Smythe's purse, would lend some time in which she could think.

And what was she to do about Anthony Smythe? It was all so much more complicated in daylight than in moonlight. She wanted to see him again. As soon as possible. The pull on her heart was undeniable.

And he could help her against Barton. She pushed the note to the side, hiding it under her copy of *The Times*. Tony had helped her before, and proven a powerful ally. She needed help again. He was attracted to her, and knew she was attracted to him, but he showed no intention of forcing her to take action.

She knew what action she wished to take. But in the morning, she could remember why it was wrong of her to want him as she did.

She listed the reasons against it. She knew nothing of his family or his life. He was a criminal, albeit a charming one. And he loved elsewhere.

And on her side, if she took one lover, it would be easier to take a second, once the first lost interest. And then a third. And some day, she would awake to find she had no lover, no husband and no reputation. If she wished for marriage, she must not begin by settling for less.

Yet it was hard to think beyond the moment. She

could have his help and his affection, should she but ask. He might leave some day. But she remembered the feel of his hands upon her, and the rushing in her that was unlike anything she had ever felt for Robert. He might leave and she might find another. But who was to say that her next husband could arouse such passion in her? If she did not give in to him now, she might never know that feeling again.

Her teacup trembled in her hand. Very well, then. She would ask him to be careful of her reputation, but she would yield to him as soon as he asked. And no one need ever know of it, but the two of them.

And then she stared down at the front page of her paper. A hanging. She stared down at the article, reading with horrible fascination. The man had been a burglar, stealing purses from a rooming house. The gallows mechanism had failed, and his body had dropped scant inches, leaving him to dance out the last of his life for nearly an hour. And the whole time his wife and children had stood, at the foot of the gibbet, pleading for leniency, or at least a quick death. The crowd had not wanted their fun spoiled and had mocked them, laughing and pelting them with offal until they had run from the scene. And the woman had lacked even the money necessary to retrieve the body for burial.

She imagined the man, spasming out the last of his life in front of a cheering throng while his family stood by, helpless. And then she imagined Tony, dancing for the hangman, and standing below him, crying her heart out and unable to help.

But if she kept to her current plan, it would be even worse. Then, she would hide in her house, afraid for her precious reputation, leaving him to die alone and friendless. And she could read in *The Times*, the next day, how he had suffered for the amusement of the crowd. She would hate herself, to her last breath, knowing that the man she loved had suffered, and she had done nothing to help.

Her hand jerked as a shudder racked her, and the tea spilled on to the paper, blurring the words.

'Your Grace, there is a gentleman come to call.' Her maid was holding a salver.

'I am not at home to Lord Barton.'

'Not Barton, your Grace. Mr Smythe.' Susan had guessed the identity of her visitor, and was grinning in anticipation.

Constance stared in fascination at the card upon the tray. She wanted to go to the parlour, grab the man by the hand and pull him upstairs with her. If she asked him, he could help her forget Barton, Freddy and the horrible thing she had just read. For a few hours. And then she would have to come downstairs and face reality again. A tryst with Mr Smythe would be lovely while it lasted. But what future could there be in it?

Only the one she had just seen.

'I am not at home. Not to anyone. If you need me, I shall be in the garden, but whoever else may call, I am not at home.'

She tried not to rush as she took the back stairs, far away from where anyone at the front of the house might see or hear her. Stopping in the tiny still room by the kitchen, she found a bonnet and basket, and her pruning scissors. It would all be easier in the garden, surrounded by her flowers and herbs. The sights, the smells, the taste. Everything made more sense there.

She stepped out into the sunlight, feeling the protection of the high brick walls on all sides that muffled the sound of the city. Here, there was only birdsong, the faint trickle of a fountain, and the fragrances of the plants. She ran down the path that led to the wrought-iron gate and the street, to the small bench hidden in the shade of a tree.

She sank down upon it, and let the tears slide down her cheeks again, now that she was safe where no one could see her. Her shoulders shook with the effort of containing the sobs. She did not want to be alone any more, and there was a man willing and full of life who could take the loneliness away. It was so unfair, that the one thing she wanted could lead to a pain and loneliness greater than anything she had felt before.

It had been hard to watch Robert die, but he had been older, and they had known the time would come. But Tony was likely to die a young man, suddenly and violently. And despite it all, she wanted him beyond all reason, aching with it.

And she heard a sigh and a faint rattle of the gate. She looked up to see Smythe, hands wrapped around the bars of the gate, observing her.

She wiped her face dry on the back of her sleeve. 'Mr Smythe! What are you doing here?'

He was nonplussed to be discovered. 'I beg your pardon, your Grace. I...I...I did not mean to spy on you.'

The stutter surprised her. When he came to her at night, there was no hesitation, only resolute action. But now, he seemed almost shy when talking to her. He was a different person in daylight. But then, so was she, or she would have opened the door for him when he had come calling.

She tried a false smile, hoping it did not look too wet around the edges. 'You did not mean to spy, or you did not mean to be caught spying?'

He released the gate and held out open hands, and there was a flash of the smile she recognised. 'I did not expect to find you here. I was told that you were not at home.' There was the barest hint of censure there.

'And yet you came to the back of my house. Were you looking for something?'

He leaned his forehead against the iron of the gate. 'I often walk by on this street. And you must admit, the view of the garden is most restful. I greatly admire it.' He stared wistfully in at her.

She gave up. At least, if he were near, she could touch him and reassure herself that the fancy she'd been spinning was not yet reality. She rose. 'You might as well come in, then, and have a better look.'

Without further invitation, he took a few steps back, and ran at the gate, catching a bar easily and swinging his body over the spikes at the top with inches to spare, landing on his feet on the other side.

There was an awkward pause.

'I meant to open that for you, you know.' She hoped the reproof in her voice hid the thrill of excitement that she felt in watching him move. He was still very much alive, and it did her heart good to see it. She sat back down, arranging her skirts to hide her confusion.

'I am sorry. It was most foolish of me. I am sometimes moved to rash actions. Rather like spying on you in your garden a moment ago, and then lying about my fondness of flowers to gain entrance.'

There was another awkward pause.

'Not that I am not fond of flowers,' he amended. 'And yours are most charmingly arranged.'

'Thank you.' She patted the seat on the bench beside her, and he came towards her. His stride had the same easy grace she saw in the ballroom and in the bedroom, and she tried not to appear too observant of it. 'Do you know much of flowers?'

He smiled. 'Not a thing. I can recognise a rose, of course. I'm not a total idiot. But I tend to take most notice of the plants that provide cover when I am gaining entrance to a house.' He touched the bush he was standing beside.

'Rosemary,' she prompted.

'Eh?'

'The shrub you are touching is rosemary.'

He plucked a sprig and crushed it between his fingers, and the air around them was full of the scent. 'For remembrance.' He held it out to her.

'You know your Shakespeare.'

'If you knew me, you would find me surprisingly well read.'

'Is that important? In your line of work, I mean.'

He dropped the rosemary and looked away. 'I am more than my work, you know.'

'I didn't mean to imply…'

His eyes were sad when he looked back to her. 'There was a time when I intended something other than the life I chose. I was the third son, and there was not very much money. I knew that there would be even less, once I was of age and my brothers had families to support. I would need to fend for myself.'

She felt a rush of sympathy. He had been lonely, even in a large family.

He continued. 'What I wanted did not matter, in any case. My oldest brother was killed duelling, and the second took a bullet to the brain at Talavera. And suddenly, there was only me, two widows, two nephews and a niece. My brothers were older, but not necessarily wiser. Their estates were in shambles and they had made no provisions for their deaths. The whole family was bound for the poorhouse, unless I took drastic action.' He shrugged. 'There are many who have more than they need.'

'But surely, an honest profession. You could have read for divinity.' She looked at his politely incredulous expression and tried to imagine him a vicar. 'Perhaps not.'

He sat down at her side. 'It was my plan, once. And I went to interview for a living, hoping that I would be able to send some small monies home. But the lord met me at a public house to tell me that it had gone to another.

'And when he got up to leave, he forgot his purse. I was halfway out the door to return it, when it occurred to me that he had money enough to fill many such purses, and my family had no food on the table and no prospects for the future. I put the purse in my pocket, and brought the money home to my family. And that was the end of that.' He smiled, obviously happier thinking of theft than he had been thinking of life as a clergyman. 'And what of you? Did you always plan on the life you got?'

She frowned. 'Yes. I suppose I did. My mother raised me so that I might be an asset to any man that might offer for me. And she encouraged me, when offers were made, to choose carefully in return so that I might never want. Until Robert died, things had gone very much as I would have hoped. I would have liked children, of course.'

'It is not too late,' Smythe responded.

She resisted the urge to explain matters to him plainly. 'I fear it is not on the cards for me. But beside that one small thing, my life was everything I might have hoped for. I made a most advantageous marriage.'

'You were happy, then?'

She answered as if by rote, 'I had money, social position and a husband who treated me well. I had no right to complain.'

'That did not answer the question.'

'Of course I was happy,' she said in frustration.

'And yet, when you say it thus, I wonder if you were.'

She sighed. 'It is different for men than for women. If you have a talent for something, you can proceed in a way that will develop it and find a career that will make the best use of your abilities. There are options open. You might study law, or go into the military, or become a vicar.'

'Or a thief,' he reminded her.

She nodded. 'But because I was born female, it was my fate to marry. It is not as if I could expect another future. Fortunately, I had no talent to speak of, or any other natural ability than to be beautiful, or I might have felt some disappointment about that fact.'

He looked at her in surprise. 'No natural talent? I'll

grant you, you are a beauty, a nonpareil. But you are wrong to think you have no other virtues. You are intelligent, well read, and you have a sharp and agile wit.'

She laughed. 'You base these fine compliments on an acquaintance of several days. My dear Mr Smythe, I would be a fool to be flattered by one with such a shallow understanding of me. There was nothing about my character, my wealth or my family that would have led Robert to want me, had I not been a beauty. I assure you, it was a great weight off my parents to know, before they died, that I was to be well taken care of.'

Tony shook his head. 'That sounds as if you were a burden to your family. But your parents spoke often of your fine character, although your mother was most proud of her only child being so well placed.'

She glanced at him sharply. 'You speak as if you knew her.'

'We were acquainted,' he replied. 'I knew your father, as well. I sympathise with your loss of them.'

'You knew them both?' She started. 'They never mentioned you.'

'It was a long time ago. You had been gone from the house for several years when last I met them. And they never knew of this.' He made a vague gesture, meant to encompass his life. 'Believe me, I never visited them in my professional capacity.'

'I never suspected that you would.' And it was strange, but she trusted his word on the matter.

'You are being unfair to yourself, if you think you are without talent, or suspect that you might have no value to a husband other than to beautify his home.'

But the one thing that Robert had most wanted from her, she had been unable to give him, and she held her tongue.

'I know for a fact that you are much more intelligent than you appear, even if you pretend it is not so in the presence of the Endsteds of the world. I saw the books he was carrying for you, and the ones you keep in your room. Philosophy, Latin, French. Not the reading of a simple mind.'

'It is a pity, then, that I could not have put all that learning to use, and saved myself from the financial predicament I find myself in.'

He gazed at her with surprising intensity. 'You have managed most cleverly with little money or help, where a foolish woman could not have gone on at all. It is not your fault that you put your trust in people who should have protected you, only to have them fail you.'

She found his comments both flattering and embarrassing, and sought to turn the conversation back to familiar ground. She summoned her most flirtatious look, fixed him with it and said, 'How strange you are to say so. Most men content themselves, when I am alone with them, to comment on the fineness of my skin or the softness of my hand.'

He was having none of it, and responded matter of

factly, 'You know as well as I do the quality of your complexion. But I will comment on it, if you insist. Your skin is almost luminous in its clarity. Chinese porcelain cannot compare. But I also know that the skin is nothing to the brightness of the spirit it contains. I know you, your Grace, although you do not believe it. I do.'

She smiled, overwhelmed by his obvious sincerity. 'And I do not really know you at all.'

'You know my greatest secret: that I am a thief. It was embarrassing to be caught. But I was glad, when it happened, to find myself in the hands of such a charming captor.'

She blushed at the notion that she had taken him prisoner, and not the other way around. 'You really shouldn't steal, you know. It is wrong.'

'I am familiar with the commandments,' he said with asperity. 'And follow nine out of ten to the best of my ability. It is a better average, I think, than the people I steal from, who have no thought to any but themselves. They are greedy, indolent and licentious.'

'Is that why you came to my rooms? To punish me for my sins? Because I am guilty.' She hung her head. 'Of pride, and of lust.'

'Serious, of course, but the seven deadly sins are not in the Bible, *per se*,' he remarked. 'But what makes you think you are guilty of them?'

'Barton has been able to manipulate me easily, because he knows how carefully I guard my reputation. If I were willing to admit that I am poor, and that he has gulled me…'

'Then you might ruin any chance to marry well. You are not guilty of anything, other than being forced to place your trust in one who proved unworthy. Why should you suffer, while the Bartons of the world live in comfort? You could don a cap and remain a poor widow, I suppose. Take in sewing. Do good works. Live off the charity of the church, since your wastrel nephew cannot be bothered to live up to his obligations to you.' He made a face. 'It does not sound very pleasant. And it would be a waste of one as young and lovely as yourself, if there is any other alternative.'

He paused, and then added as an afterthought, 'You could marry below your station. No one would think you proud, then.'

'I will consider it, if someone asks. But none has. No one offers marriage at all. Men below my station avoid me as unattainable. And men who would be fine catches want nothing more than…' She shook her head. 'Barton says that he, and the others, can see that I secretly desire what they offer. That I am too willing, too interested in their company. That I allow too many small liberties, and they are surprised when I refuse to follow through.'

Smythe sniffed. 'Men have ever used this, when

trying to persuade a woman to do more than she wishes. It is no reflection on you. Ignore them.'

'But look how I behave, when I am alone with you.' She blurted the words and stopped, embarrassed to have told him the truth. 'I…I am wanton.'

He was grinning again. 'Yes. I noticed. It is most flattering. Tell me, is this how you behave with all the other men of your acquaintance?'

'Of course not. How dare you even think—?'

He laid a finger on her lips to silence her. 'I did not think so. But it is even more flattering to hear you admit that I am the only one to move you so.' He looked down at his feet, and she thought for a moment that she could see a faint blush in his check. Then he said, 'It is not so bad a thing, to take pleasure in the company of the opposite gender. Of course, I am bi-ased, since I am the man in question. I would have to be made of stone to wish you less willing when in my embrace. And I would have been most put out to find you sighing over Barton's embrace, and behaving thus with him. But I would not expect that, just because you have lain with one man, that you are game to lie with any that might ask.

'And because you allow me a degree of intimacy, for which I am most grateful…' he looked up and smiled at her and there was a wicked glint in his eye that made her heart beat faster '…I do not assume that I can do as I please with you. If ever I make a suggestion that offends you, you have but to tell me to stop. I am yours to command.'

And thoughts appeared of what she wished to command him to do. They had nothing to do with stopping his current behaviour or being any less wicked in her presence. Quite the contrary. She blushed. 'No. It is quite all right. You have done nothing to offend me. I am…' She whispered the next words, 'I fear I am enjoying it too much.'

He whispered back to her. 'You have nothing to fear. As I told you the first night, your secrets are safe with me. All of your secrets. But if you enjoy my company so much, why were you not at home, when I called?'

'What we spoke of last night… I do not know if I can go through with it. It seemed so right, at the time. But it is foolish of me to make promises in the moonlight that I am afraid to keep in daylight.'

'I see.' He reached out and gently touched her arm. 'And why were you crying? This is the second time that I have come upon you and found you in tears. I do not believe you gave me a clear indication of the problem on that night, either. What is it that distresses you so?'

'I thought I informed you then that it was none of your concern.'

'But we hardly knew each other, then. I dare say we are much closer now. One might say, thick as thieves.' He considered. 'Although for the most part, I have not found thieves to be much in each other's confidence.'

'Then why should I trust you?'

'Because I care enough to ask, and sincerely hope that the problem will be something I can aid you in. You must admit, I have helped you before.'

She laughed through her tears. 'It is not so easy, this time, I fear. You tempt me. And it is hard to resist you. But the gentleman you discovered me with in the library? I had hopes…' She left the sentence unfinished.

Tony stiffened next to her. 'I see. And does the gentleman reciprocate your feelings?'

She blinked away the tears. 'I did not claim to have feelings. It would be most insensible of me, at my age, to base everything on "feelings." Instead, I had hopes.'

'Oh,' he said, clearly not understanding at all.

'He is a gentleman, his income is not as great as my late husband's nor his estates as fine, nor his title as prestigious. But, truly, I do not expect to find the equal of Robert. My first marriage was extremely fortunate in that regard. Lord Endsted was more than rich enough. And he seemed interested. Of course, they all seem interested, at first.'

'I should think that they would be. You are a charming and attractive woman, your Grace. Any man would be honoured to have your attention.' He opened his mouth, ready to say more, then stopped and looked at her. 'But I take it, the man of your choosing is not among them?'

She shook her head. 'As I said before, this is not

so much about what I choose, or what I feel. I would have been more than willing, should he have offered, or any of the others. It would have been most foolish of me to say nay if he'd have offered matrimony. But he saw me with you, and then Barton was here, when we returned. And he now thinks me inappropriate company.'

Anthony exploded with an oath. 'He does not want you because other men find you attractive? Then the man is a jealous fool. Or blind. I will find him and call him out.'

'Don't be absurd.' She laid a hand on his arm. 'He offended me, not you. And if you wish to call out every gentleman who has disappointed me, then I would have to make you a rather long list. I expect it to grow even longer, ere I find a man who will do otherwise. You came upon me in a low mood, that is all. I had not expected, at thirty, to be so thoroughly on the shelf with regard to matrimony. And I am not yet to the point where I find the other suggestions to be flattering.'

'I should think not,' he responded indignantly. 'The cheek of these men. I had thought that one such as yourself, fair as any of the young ladies of the *ton*, but with grace and poise, with wit as well as intelligence…' He showed signs of continuing, and then looked down. 'I would have thought that one such as you would have no end of suitors.'

'I have had suitors enough.' She smiled sadly. 'But

they are rarely seeking a wife. I suppose it is a comfort to know that men still find me desirable.'

'Oh, I must say yes, you are very much that. But that they would be so coarse as to suggest…'

She stared at him. 'You yourself had admitted that you would have me, should I be so inclined. I fail to see the source of your indignation on my behalf.'

'But that is before I realised that you would settle for nothing less than marriage.' He dropped to his knees before her. 'I am ever your servant, your Grace. You would do me a great honour, should you give me your hand, and I would endeavour to keep you in comfort and safety for the rest of your days.'

She pulled her hand from his grasp. 'And now you are taunting me with my foolishness.'

'I assure you, I am not. If you cannot find another who suits you, and do not wish to accept any of the other base offers made to you, then have me.'

'Most certainly not.' She had blurted out the words before she could stop to think how they might sound.

He looked up at her, eyes glazed with shock, and skin white, but with a streak of colour on each cheek as though she had slapped him hard. 'May I ask why?'

'I should think that would be obvious.'

His voice was steady, but strangely distant. 'Not to me.'

She ducked her head so that he might not see the fear in her eyes. 'We hardly know each other.'

'I doubt you knew the other gentlemen so well as you thought, if you were surprised when none of them offered. So that is not the real reason, is it?'

'All right. If you insist.' She steeled herself and said the words, 'You are a criminal. How could you expect me to accept that fact, and bind myself to you? You would ask me to live in comfort off ill-gotten gains and feel no guilt about it?'

He rose from his knees and dropped back into the seat beside her. There was a flash of pain in his eyes, but when he spoke, his colour was returning to normal and his voice was light, albeit with a slight edge of sarcasm. 'Women I have supported in the past took care not to know where the money came from. They assumed, correctly, that someone would take care of them, and shield them from the unpleasantness of finances.' He looked at her. 'Just as I assumed that, since you took the first money, and had no problem with the theft of the deed, you would not be bothered with the rest.'

'You assumed incorrectly. I take pride in knowing the details of my finances, although I cannot say I've done a very good job with them. And I am tired of men who promise to be a shield against unpleasantness, since unpleasantness has managed to find me in any case.'

'You would not have the details of it rubbed under your nose. I do not entertain my fence at my rooms. I keep my private life very much removed from my professional one.'

'Or you will until such time as you are caught and hanged. Then you will drag those around you to disgrace as well.'

The words pained him, and his voice was quiet when he responded. 'It is not as if I have never considered the fact. And I have taken great care not to be caught. Another reason I never married, I think.'

'It was probably wise of you. I cannot imagine a crueller fate for a woman than to know such a thing about her husband and to live in fear of his discovery. I could not bear it.'

A shadow passed over his face again. 'Thank you for making your opinions clear on the matter. I intended no disrespect. I only wished to offer you a solution to a problem that seems to weigh most heavily upon you. The offer stands, of course, for I doubt that my attraction for you will wane. But I will not break my heart over your refusal, since I suspect there is nothing to be done to change your low opinion of me.' His tone was light, and he seemed to have returned to normal, but she could tell he did not speak the whole truth.

'Thank you for your understanding.'

'And thank you for your honesty.' There was more than a touch of bitterness in the word. 'And tell me, does your refusal of my more noble offer extend to my friendship as well?'

'No.' Her voice was small and unsteady.

'Because I will not trouble you with my presence

again, if you find my criminality so offensive.' She had hurt him again, and she felt her resolve wavering. But she could not very well marry him, just to spare his feelings. Why could he not understand that one of them must hurt, no matter what path she chose?

She reached out to take his hand again. 'No. Please, do not forsake me. I cannot help the way I feel. I wish I could, in so many ways, and yet, I cannot. I know I cannot marry you. But neither am I able to let you go. And I do not know what I am to do, in either case. It hurts me to think of it, just as it hurt to say it aloud. And that is why I was crying.'

He laid his other hand over hers and squeezed it tightly. And his smile was sad, but it was a real smile. 'That is all right. I did not think you would say yes, and yet I felt moved to ask. I do not wish to make you cry, and am sorry to have done so. And truly, I have no desire to leave you and will not unless you send me away.'

He sighed. 'So let us not think overlong on the details of this, since they pain us both. Until such time as you say otherwise, I am yours to command, your Grace, and that should be more than enough to be happy on, I think.' And he pulled her close to him, so that she could lay her head on his shoulder, and rocked her in his arms until she dozed.

When she awoke, he was gone.

Chapter Eleven

She returned to the house, lightheaded from her nap in the sunlight and unsure of her emotions. The crying had left her with a megrim that the nap had only partly soothed.

But it had been so restful, leaning against Tony, that she had quite forgotten what a bad idea it was to do so. And strange that he'd even allowed it. He had offered. She had refused. Afterwards, one of them should have slunk away in embarrassment, to nurse their wounds in private.

But he had been very accepting of her refusal, even though she could tell he was hurt. It would have been much easier if he had raged and stormed and then left her in peace. If he had abandoned her, she might have begun the difficult process of forgetting him, rather than closing her eyes and leaning into his shoulder, losing herself in a dream of what it might be like if they were two different people and she could say yes to him.

It could not have hurt him too deeply, then. It was a blow to the ego, of course. No man wanted to be told that he was not good enough to be marriage material. But it must not have been a blow to the heart. If it had been a mortal wound, he would not have recovered so quickly. It might actually have been the answer he wanted to hear, since he had done his best to help her, but had been able to keep his heart free, in case he ever managed to succeed with his dream woman.

All the more reason not to marry him. Although he might want her, he did not truly love her. Their marriage might have been a very workable relationship, if she had had the sense not to fall in love with him before he had asked. But if she had agreed to marry him because she loved him, she could see a grim future ahead. Once he had her, his ardour would cool and he would lose interest. And she would sit like the fool she was, suffering with every small indifference and worrying the night away that he would be captured and killed, or, worse yet, unfaithful.

He would be baffled by her behaviour, since he had given her no reason for it. He had made no grand promises of undying faithfulness before the marriage. Why should she expect them after?

So, it was all for the best. As long as she ignored the emptiness she felt, after denying him.

'Your Grace.' Susan rushed to her side, as she entered the house, trying to stop her as she walked down the corridor. 'I am sorry. I tried. But his foot was in the door. And when I tried to close it, he pushed me and I fell. And I told him you were not at home, but he would not go away.'

The words were overwhelming, and made no sense, but Constance knew, before she opened the door to her sitting room, who she would find there.

Barton was smiling the same placid smile he always did when dealing with her, as though common sense and reason would eventually lead her to do the unspeakable. He did not rise as she entered, remaining relaxed and in control. 'You ignored my note to you.'

'Yes, I did,' she responded. 'And my servants were instructed not to open the door for you. You cannot continue to force your way into my home, Lord Barton.'

'Your home.' When he said it, it was no longer a question. He must know that she'd got the deed.

She pretended to ignore the fact. 'I will have no more of these nonsensical threats of yours. I have no intention of becoming your mistress. And I do not acknowledge your ownership of my home. If you think you have a case, then take me to court, and prove that you own this house.'

He laughed. 'You are beautiful, Constance, and more clever than I gave you credit for. I know you have taken the deed. I don't suppose you would care to enlighten me on how that might have happened. I suspect that the one who helped you might have another motive to gain entry to my house. And I would like a word with him.'

'I do not know what you are talking about.'

'Of course you don't, darling. To hear you, I am almost convinced. I doubt that you have the necessary skills to achieve this yourself. I know you had help. So I will watch you closely, and watch the men who watch you, until I see who your favourite shall be. And when I have discovered him, I will deal with him as he deserves.'

'My favourite? I have no favourite.'

'Not that I have noticed. But if you do not, you soon shall. The man that got the deed to your house made you work for it, I'll wager, just as I intend to.'

She almost responded that Tony had been different, before she could help herself.

He smiled as he saw the look in her eyes. 'You almost told me. But no matter. You will slip eventually. With a word. A glance. A chance meeting that is no chance. I will find him, and punish him. If it matters to you, you might warn him that I wish him to stay out of my business and that if he thinks he can take you from me, he is sadly mistaken.' He looked up at her and reached into his pocket, producing a packet of papers. 'I took the liberty of going up to your room as you slept in the garden, and retrieving what he took from me. And thus, we are back to where we started. You owed me then, and you owe me now.'

'You lie.' She reached to snatch it from his hand, and it disappeared again, inside his coat.

'It was in the drawer of the night table, in your room. It is no trouble, getting by your servants, Constance. Freddy has kept anyone of value in his service. And you, with your soft heart, have employed his castoffs. You are left with foolish girls and old men. It did not take more than a single blow to dispense with the few that stood in my way.'

'You struck my servants?' she said, with horror.

'I taught them who the master of this house is to be. I doubt I will have to teach them twice.'

'You had no right. They were doing their duty to me. You were trying to enter my room without permission.'

'Then you had best give them permission to obey me, or next time I will strike them harder.'

'If you must hit anyone, then hit the person who gave them the command.' She stood in front of him, daring him to raise his hand to her.

'And what good would that do, other than to mark that which I wish to remain unblemished? You are much more likely to obey me to save others, than you would to save yourself. Allow me to demonstrate. Call your maid into the room.'

'I most certainly will not.'

He got up, stepped out into the hall and said, 'Susan, come here, please. Your mistress needs you.'

'I do not!' But even as she said it, the girl had obeyed the first command, and come to the door of the sitting room. Barton seized her by the wrist and hauled her into the room, closing the door behind her.

Susan struggled, but was no match for him and he pulled her arm until her hand was held high above the flame of a candle. 'At this height, she barely feels the heat.' He pulled her arm lower, and the maid closed her eyes. 'At this height, she is beginning to feel some discomfort. It is very warm on the skin, is it not? Answer me, Susan.'

The girl nodded.

He looked again at Constance. 'Any lower, and the flesh will burn. Would you like me to demonstrate, or are you willing to see the value of co-operation?'

'You cannot do this. I will call the Runners.'

'Afterwards, perhaps. And what good will it do poor Susan then? If you try to leave the room, I will have cooked the flesh of her hand before you can return with help.'

'Let her go.'

'Give me the key to this house.'

Constance saw the resolve in his eyes and hurried to her desk, fumbling in the drawer for a spare key. Her hand trembled as she handed it to him.

He released the maid. 'Very good. We have an

understanding. And if you have a notion to bar the door against me or change the locks, know that the next time I come, I shall bring servants of my own, and it will go worse for all inside.'

He smiled thoughtfully. 'And now, let us return to the matter of your lover, the thief. He is your lover, is he not? I suspect you traded that lovely body of yours for his assistance. You should not have done that, for you knew to whom you belonged when you went to him.'

He sighed. 'And so, I will find him. And I will punish him for taking something that belongs to me. But how I punish him might well depend on how co-operative you are. I could be moved to leniency, if you treat me well and give me no more trouble. A light beating, perhaps, just as a warning. Or would you like to refuse me again, and see the consequences of your actions?' He leaned close and whispered, 'I will make him suffer. He will die screaming, and I will make sure that you hear it. Does that move you?'

'You would not dare.'

'Oh, I think so. The man is meddling in things far more important than the fate of your honour. I do not like my privacy invaded. And I do not like one to stand between me and that which I most desire. If you have any feeling at all for the man, you will warn him off, and submit to me. Or do as you please and let him feel the consequence of it. What is your decision?'

She felt her stomach drop, and she trembled. She

looked at Barton's eyes, willing them to be less heart-less than they were, to give her any indication that he was not as dangerous as he appeared.

He was still smiling. 'I'm waiting. Is your contin-ued freedom worth the cost?'

By denying Barton, she had stumbled into a situa-tion that was well over her head and now she was drag-ging others down with her. 'If I agree to what you want, you will not harm him?'

'When next you see him, tell him that you are fin-ished with him, that you belong to me, now. And that he must cease meddling in my affairs. If he leaves me alone, he will escape unharmed. If he continues to interfere, I offer no guarantees. I suggest you be very persuasive, if you have the opportunity.'

She swallowed. 'All right.'

He smiled again. 'You will find you have made a wise decision. We will dine out this evening. Vauxhall Gardens. Wear something festive. I do not wish to see you in mourning. Red, I think. And the rubies.'

A scarlet woman, she thought.

'When we have had supper, I will return here, to spend the rest of the night. Tell your maid that we are not to be disturbed.'

He rose, reaching for his hat. 'And, Constance…?'

'Yes, Lord Barton?'

'From now on, you will call me Jack. And when I take my leave, you will kiss me as if you mean it.'

He stood in the doorway, waiting.

And she stepped close to him, put her arms around his neck, and kissed him as if a life depended on it.

Chapter Twelve

Tony dropped into the wing chair in his study, staring pensively into the fire before him. He was not moved to work on the lock, though he knew he must. He wanted nothing more than to sit in the gathering darkness, alone, for the rest of his life, if need be. Would that the end were not too distant.

Patrick, sensing his mood, brought the tray with the brandy.

Tony poured a snifter for himself and waved the rest away. 'It is over,' he said.

'How so?'

'I have proposed to her, and she has refused.'

'This is most sudden.'

'It seemed like the right thing to do at the time. She hid from me, when I tried to visit her. And when I found her in the garden, she was crying. Patrick, I was defenceless. It seems that other men are offering for her in ways that are less than honourable, and she longs for matrimony. I offered my services in that department, and they were firmly declined.'

'Even after she knew who you were?'

'The matter of my identity did not come up,' Tony muttered.

'Did not…' Patrick sank into the wing chair on the opposite side of the fire, and poured himself a glass of his master's brandy. 'You expected her to take you, sight unseen, on a very limited acquaintance, and are surprised that she turned you down.'

'She seemed willing to accept many other gentlemen, with little previous acquaintance, as long as they had money or position. And before I offered, I gave her a fair description of our childhood together. There were enough clues that, had she cared to, she could have seen the truth.

'But it does not matter, whether she knows me or not. It is the reason she gave, not the denial itself that creates the problem. She said she could not marry a thief.'

Patrick shrugged and sipped his brandy. 'Then the answer is simple. If you want the girl, stop stealing.'

'There is the little detail of ten years of crime.'

Patrick waved his hand. 'Immaterial to the discussion. How much have you personally profited from it?'

Tony considered. 'Very little. When I began I had a

small inheritance, and I invested it well. But it was in no way enough to support the family. So I stole. And since I enjoyed stealing, I continued. But my own money is still there, should I choose to retire.'

'So you did not steal for yourself. You stole for others. And when you steal now?'

'There is really no cause for it, other than to cover the activities I perform for Stanton.'

'So you are, in effect, stealing for the Crown,' Patrick reasoned.

'I cannot very well tell her that, though, can I? It defeats the purpose of covert activities, if one goes trumpeting them about the neighbourhood.'

'But you are not exactly trumpeting about the neighbourhood, if you reveal the truth to one person. Or do you not trust her to keep a confidence?'

He glared at Patrick. 'I would trust her with my life. I already have. For she knows the truth about me, and has had the power to ruin me for several weeks. If she wished me ill, she had but to say something before now, to see me carted off to Newgate.'

'Then reveal the better part of your occupation, since you have revealed the worst and not come to ill. Along with your true name and history, of course,' Patrick added.

There was an annoying emphasis on the last bit of advice, and Tony chose to ignore it. 'Perhaps when I have run Barton to ground... There are risks involved. He is a dangerous man, if Stanton is to be believed.'

'All the more reason to tell her the whole truth, since she was involved with him before you entered the picture. It is the curate in you speaking again, sir. Humility does you no credit when you are using it to mask cowardice. And that is what it is. While you think nothing of staring death in the face while attempting a burglary, you stick at speaking the truth to Constance Townley since you are convinced that, once she knows who you are, she will reject you. But since she has already done that, sir, the worst is over.'

Tony readied a response, and then checked himself. What did he have to lose, after all, in telling her everything? 'Much as it pains me to have a valet who continually points out my stupidity, you are right again, Patrick. It can be no more dangerous to her than it was at the beginning, when Stanton believed her an accomplice in treason. And whatever she thinks of me, I cannot let her go blundering about, where she might thwart my schemes, or put her own freedom at risk by inadvertently aiding Barton in his plans.'

And if revealing his reason for robbing Barton raised her estimation of him? He could not help smiling at the thought.

Tony knocked firmly on the front door of Constance's house, hoping for better results in the evening than he had achieved in the afternoon. He had spent an embarrassingly long time on his toilet. His boots were polished to mirror brightness, his coat was fresh from Weston. His cravat was sublime. He had forced Patrick to shave him so close that he suspected he was missing a layer of skin, but his cheek was soft.

He hoped to be able to demonstrate the fact to Constance later in the evening.

She would be home, of course. He knew for a fact that there were no balls, soirées, or *musicales* of any value that evening—if there had been, he'd have been invited to them. His original plan had been for a quiet evening at home with a glass of port and his new safe, until he realised that Constance would be having a quiet evening at home as well. He had rehearsed his speech in his head, willing himself to stick to the plan and not be dazzled by the fineness of her eyes or the nearness of her lips. He would find her, and beg an audience. She would entertain him in the sitting room and they would chat casually of things that had nothing to do with Barton or her financial state.

He would make it clear over the course of the evening that his interest had nothing to do with the business of the deed, and everything to do with the high esteem in which he held her. In which any sane and decent man could not help but hold her.

He would explain his current interest in Barton, his present occupation and the relative safety of it, compared with his life of a year ago, when he had been stealing full time. Should he ever be caught now, Stanton would manage to free his neck from the noose and explain all. While it was not without scandal, and not so honourable as a title and land, it was not such a horrible thing as she imagined and she would not be embarrassed, should the whole truth of it come to light.

And then he would explain to her that they were not the strangers she might think them, and that it would make him the happiest man on earth if only she would consent to marry him.

But he remembered the kisses and the way she'd responded to them and changed his plan.

He would tell her that it would make him the happiest man on the planet if she might consent to marry him tomorrow, and consent tonight to everything else. Because he was quite mad with desire for her, and had been so for as long as he could remember. And there was little hope of him progressing with the Barton matter or anything else until he'd had her.

He grinned at the thought. Doubts presented themselves, of course. He had lacked the nerve to strike when the iron was hottest, the woman in his arms, and the bed scant paces away.

But he remembered the previous night, the way she had clung to him, when he had turned to go, and asked if she would see him again with such sweet hope in her eyes. That must have been more than gratitude. She might deny him in daylight, but the sun was down and his luck was about to change.

The maid, Susan, opened the door, and he was surprised to see fear in her eyes before she recognised him. And then, as she always did, she told him her mistress was not at home.

'Susan, let us have no more of that tonight. Be honest with me. Is she not at home, truly, or is she not at home to me?'

Susan was looking at him as though she expected him to eat her. 'Not at home, sir.'

'Because I will hear no more nonsense on the subject, from you, or from her. If she is hiding in her bedroom, or the garden, or any other room in the house, you are to go to her immediately and tell her I wish to speak to her, just for once, in the parlour over a cup of tea, like a civilised gentleman. Tell her, if you would, that I have fallen off the ivy and twisted my ankle, and will not leave her sitting room until it is healed.'

Susan now looked both baffled and terrified.

'It is a lie, of course,' he assured her. 'My ankle is fine, as is the ivy. But say anything you need to, to get her down out of her room.'

'I cannot, sir.'

'Can you say it for a crown, then?'

'Sir!'

'A guinea?'

'I cannot…'

'A five-pound note, Susan. Name your price, and I will pay, but you will not put me off.'

She ignored the money in his hand, closed her eyes and said, 'Mr Smythe. I will not take your money, for it will mean disobeying my mistress. And she said I am, under no circumstances, to tell you that she has gone out this evening, to Vauxhall, with Lord Barton. If you arrive, I am to do whatever is necessary to get you to leave this house so that you are not here when they return for the evening.' Susan seemed no happier saying the words than he was in hearing them.

He could feel the muscles of his smile tightening to a rictus. 'Thank you, Susan. I will not seek her here, then. I feel the need of some night air. Perhaps a trip to the Gardens.'

'Thank you, sir,' Susan whispered. 'And be careful. He's a bad 'un.' And she closed the door to him.

The glitter of Vauxhall at night was lost on Tony, as he paid his admission to enter. Acres of land, much of it secluded walkways. How was he to find her in the throng of revellers present? He must trust that Barton meant to keep her where she could be seen, since there was little point in stepping out with her if he did not intend for them to be noticed.

Tony scanned the crowds in the avenues, and the people gathered around the tightrope walker, and worked his way around the dance floor near the orchestra until a flash of crimson caught his eye. She was there, on Barton's arm.

She was stunning, as only she could be. He had grown quite used to seeing her about town in mourning, or half-mourning, but even after her recent return to fashion, he had not seen her looking so splendid as this. The deep red of her gown made her skin glow luminous in the lantern light, her dark hair was dressed with tiny red roses, and her throat and ears were adorned with pigeon's-blood rubies that would have left the thief in him quivering with excitement, had the man in him not been more interested in seeing the bare skin beneath.

The image of her as she had been when she came to his rooms was still burning in his mind: the true outline of the body hidden just under the satin. There was the swell of her breast and the place where the nipple would raise the fabric of the gown, and there was the curve of her stomach, and the place where the gown would pool where her legs met. Her cruelty knew no bounds if she had revealed herself to him in that way only to give herself to another.

But now Barton was escorting her along the dim pathways, deeper and deeper into the dark walks of Vauxhall Gardens.

Tony knew the reason that a gentleman might escort a lady into the grounds, for he had done it himself. But the ladies were rarely ladies, nor did the gentlemen have any intention of keeping to manners.

Her dark eyes were unreadable and her face revealed neither joy nor sadness. She was as cool and aloof as any of the statues adorning the garden walkways. After all the fine talk of marriage and reputation earlier in the day, she showed no sign of caring how her behaviour must look to any who saw it tonight.

The couple disappeared around a bend on the darkened path, and Tony hopped the nearest hedge and cut across the grass, staying out of the glow of the lanterns to keep pace with them as they proceeded. Around him, on other paths in the darkness, he could hear the sounds of other couples: giggles, sighs and the occasional moan.

And a few yards away from him, Barton had stopped, and pulled Constance close to speak into her ear.

She was leaning into him and looking up into his face, and when he whispered to her, she did not pull away. She glanced around, to see if there was anyone following.

Tony stepped further into the darkness to be sure that he was hidden.

When she was sure they were alone, she kissed Barton quickly on the lips.

The bastard tilted his head and spoke again.

And again she kissed, more slowly this time, with her sweet mouth open to his. It was nothing like the kisses Tony had seen between them, in Barton's own garden. That night, she had been awkward and it had appeared that she could barely tolerate the man she was with.

Tonight, she was kissing him with her whole spirit, her body tight against his, her arms clutching his shoulders.

Tony's heart sank. Had anyone noticed the pair together, other than him? Most probably not. It was Vauxhall, after all, and the other couples walking these paths had secrets of their own to keep and no time to pry.

But Constance must have known what would happen if she came here. Why would she let Barton take such a liberty, after the way she had acted in her rooms, and his?

She had said that Barton had the deed to her house. And she had offered her body in trade to Tony if he could get it back.

But had she truly said that Barton's attentions were unwelcome? Tony swallowed. Perhaps he had misunderstood. It was only the theft of the deed that was unwelcome. If she owned the house, she could invite who she chose to share her bed: him, or Barton or anyone else.

So perhaps what Stanton had first claimed was the truth. She was a faithless traitor, with no more loyalty to Barton than to anyone else.

The thought made him ache.

And yet, he could not stop wanting her. He had wanted her all the time she was married, he had wanted her before that, he had wanted her when they were children, before he even knew what he wanted her for. And because he was a fool, he would continue to want her, if she belonged to Barton or married another. It was lucky that he had not told her when he'd had the chance, or she'd have known the strength of her hold over him and left him with even less dignity than he already possessed.

But if he could not have her, the least he could do was get her clear of Barton before the man's inevitable destruction.

The garden was as it ever was, gay and enchanting in the darkness. Robert had disapproved of Vauxhall, saying it attracted too common a crowd, but the few times she had gone, she had found it strangely exciting to be able to mingle with royalty and courtesans, watching the entertainments, and listening to the orchestra while eating overpriced ham sandwiches and drinking cheap wine. The pavilions glittered with gilt and mirrors. There was dancing and laughter all around her. And later, there would be fireworks.

She doubted she would be there to see them, for she would be home, in bed. With Barton. He had already led her down one of the dark walks so that they might kiss. She tried not to think of it as a preamble to what was coming. At least it had not been quite so horrible as when she had admitted defeat and kissed him in the sitting room, earlier that day.

This time, she had been able to close her mind to who she was with, imagining that she had been lured down a walk by another who wished to pull her into the darkness, a few steps away from the familiar world, and kiss her to insensibility.

And she had gone willingly, for after a few glasses of wine, the familiar world had seemed intolerably dull, and wickedness in the darkness of Vauxhall excited her.

When she was sure they were alone, she had kissed Barton once, and asked to go back to the dancing. But he had told her that she would need to try much harder. So she had closed her eyes and thought of how different it might be if she were here with Tony. And a few minutes later, Barton had pulled away and declared himself pleased with her response and led her back towards the light.

When they neared the orchestra pavilion, she requested another glass of wine, and he left her alone in the crowd to go find her refreshment. She suspected it would take many more glasses to get through the evening, but it would be worth any price to settle Barton's vicious temper until she could think of a better plan.

The music began again. It was to be a waltz. She looked around her with resignation. Barton would return and claim her for a dance. She had been lucky so far, and seen no one familiar. But if any who knew her were present, there would be talk. It could not be helped.

A hand from the crowd seized hers and pulled her

out on to the floor. And she found herself not in the arms of Barton, but staring into the face of Anthony Smythe, inches from her own.

'There, now. Did I not promise you that you would run into me at many gatherings, now that you know me? And here the truth is proved, for you are waltzing with me.'

She looked over her shoulder, in panic. 'I had promised this dance to another.'

'I suspect it is Barton, for he is coming towards us and looks most furious.'

She struggled to escape from Tony's grasp. 'He must not see us together.'

Tony's grip held tight and he pulled her closer. 'I do not see how he can help it, for we are together before his very eyes.'

She stared into the crowd, looking for Barton, sick with dread of what was to come.

'Do not search after other men, when you are in my arms. I find it most damaging to the spirit to think I cannot hold your attention for the space of a single dance.' His tone hardened. 'Particularly if you must look at Barton. I had hoped, after what I needed to do for you last week, and all the fine talk in the garden about wanting an honourable marriage, that you would have the sense to stay away from him.'

'I could not help myself,' she admitted with honesty.

'Nor could you the last time. You needed *my* help,

as I remember it. And were willing to go to surprising lengths to get it.'

She lifted her chin. 'And I do not need you any more.'

'You are done with me, then?'

'Yes,' she insisted. 'I wish you to leave me alone. And leave Barton alone, as well.'

'And what happened to all the pretty words about preferring my attentions to those of Barton's?'

'The situation has changed.'

'I see.' He could see exactly what she wanted him to see. He was angry. Angry enough to leave, she hoped, since she did not know how much longer she could stand to lie to him.

'I do not need your help or your company, and wish you to stay far from me in the future.'

Instead he pulled her even closer, so that her body brushed his coat front and his lips were near her ear. His voice was rough as he said, 'I will leave you, then. But before I go, let me help you one last time with a word of advice. Stay away from Barton. His star is no longer on the rise. When things come crashing down about him, I would hate to see you caught in the result.'

She felt sick and frightened and angry, all at the same time. She could go to Barton because he forced her to, only to have Smythe destroy her along with Barton. Or she could not go to Barton, and he would destroy Smythe and everyone else around her. Either way, she was trapped.

'And that is your idea of help, is it?' She slapped him on the shoulder hard enough to knock him out of step. 'And now, Mr Smythe, I will tell you what I think of your help. You have been breaking into Barton's home for reasons of your own, and only pretending to help me. But it does not really have much to do with me, does it? For you have been spying on Barton since that first day, when I caught you spying on me. You claim you want to help, and you pretend to be different. But you are no different than Barton is. First you flatter, then you steal, and if you are not successful, you try blackmail. And at last, you resort to threats to make me do as you wish.'

'Threats?' He pushed her away so that he could look down into her eyes, trying to read the truth in them until she was forced to look away to hide it. 'He is threatening you still?' The hand that held hers squeezed her fingers and he pulled her close again. 'Why did you not just tell me? When I saw you together, I thought… Well, never mind what I thought. I was a fool.' He glanced at the musicians. 'The dance will be ending soon. Tell Barton whatever you like, that I forced you to dance or that you went willingly to spite him. Then, the first chance you get, lose yourself in the crowd. Do not go to him tonight, no matter what he is holding over your head. And I will be sure he does not come to you. You needn't be afraid of him or do anything that you do not wish to do. I can still help you, if you will let me. Why did you not ask?'

She thought of Barton's threats, and what might happen to Tony if she involved him again. 'The last time, what I asked you to do was wrong. I can not ask it again. It is too dangerous.'

He leaned forward and laughed in her ear. 'It is in my nature to do wrong. There is very little you can do to redeem my character other than to allow me to use my more improper talents in a good cause. What you asked was no imposition, and a chance to see some much-needed justice done in the world. I do not care a fig for the dangers that concern you. I will bring down Barton in any case, but I do not want my actions to injure you, for you are innocent of his villainy. If he is doing something to thwart that, then will you do me the great honour of allowing me to help you again?'

She hesitated, and he spun her around the floor so that Barton could not see them speak.

'Say the word, your Grace. I will not impose on you further, if you truly do not wish it. But if you but nod, I will come to your rooms later, and you can tell me all. Then, if you do not wish my help, send me away.'

She was almost weak with relief at the thought of talking to him, and leaned against him and let him feel the change in her body as she gave herself up to his protection.

He squeezed her hand again. 'Very well, then. Go home and unlock your window.' He smiled at her. As the music ended, he spun her back to the place she had been, to stand by the irate Barton. 'Delightful, your Grace, and so sorry to impose, but I could not resist the temptation to steal the dance.'

She watched the light of recognition flare in Barton's eyes at his choice of words.

Barton glared at him. 'You should be careful what you steal, sir. For you know what happens to thieves.'

Tony laughed. 'I have but to read *The Times* to see that, sir. Hanging. But at least it is not so bad as the thing that happens to traitors. While the courts might show leniency to a thief, counterfeiting is high treason. To be hanged, drawn and quartered for acting against your own country?' Tony shuddered theatrically. 'A nasty end, is it not, Jack?'

Barton's normal composure broke, and he grew even angrier than he had been; his cold smile turned to a grimace of fury and his colouring was mottled red. 'Then a traitor need have no reason to fear doing murder, Smythe. The slow and painful death of another will add nothing to the severity of the punishment, should one be caught.'

She reached out and tugged Barton's sleeve to distract him, and he shook her off.

Tony tipped his head to one side, considering. 'I suppose it would not, if one could manage such a feat. But in your case, I have my doubts. Shall we see?' And he turned and started towards the dark walks.

And Barton cursed once, and made to follow. Then

he turned back to her. 'You are to return home immediately, go to your room, and wait for me there.'

She grabbed his arm. 'I will do nothing of the kind.
I know what you mean to do. And you promised you
would not.'

Tony turned back and looked at her curiously. 'Do
as he says, Constance. Go home. Whatever occurs, I
do not wish you to be a part of it. Do you understand?'

She looked between the two men, both implacable.
'Go.' Barton pointed towards the exit as though order-
ing a dog to its kennel.

'Please, your Grace,' Tony added.

And then he walked away, in the direction of the most
secluded paths, disappearing into the nearest crowd.

Barton followed.

Chapter Thirteen

Constance sat on the end of her bed, knotting and un-
knotting her handkerchief in quaking hands. Why had
she listened to either of them? She should have thrown
herself onto Barton and held him back.

But Tony had gone so quickly and left Barton to
push and shove his way through a group of people.
When she had gone after him, she had been swept
along with the group, and was near to the exit before she got clear, having seen no sign of Tony or
Barton.

She had searched for a while, but been afraid to ven-
ture into the darkness alone, and finally had hired a
hackney and hurried back to her house, shooed the
maid away, locked the door and unlocked the window.
Please, dear Lord, let it be Tony who arrived and not
Barton. She did not think she could bear the sight of

him, much less his touch, if she knew that he had come to her rooms with Tony's blood on his hands.

'By your leave, your Grace?' Tony stood framed in the open window, awaiting her permission to enter.

'Oh, do not be such a fool. Come in before someone sees you.' She rushed to the window and reached to pull him in herself, patting at his chest with her hands, searching for some sign of injury.

He stepped into her room as easily as if he'd entered it from the hall, laughing as her hands touched him, catching them and bringing them to his lips. 'You thought I would come to harm from Barton?'

She looked at him incredulously. 'I was terrified. You must have known what I would think.'

'That I would go into the darkness and let him brawl with me, in a public park? Not knowing who he might have brought with him for aid or what trap might await me? I'm sorry to disappoint you, darling, but I ran like a rabbit until I was quite sure he was lost on the paths, and then I came here. And I can assure you; I am quite unharmed.' He placed her hands against his chest again. 'But you may touch me as much as you like. I find it most pleasant.'

She snatched her hands away and turned from him. 'I was a fool to agree to this. I should never have allowed you to come. I put you at risk for helping me, and you treat it as if it were a joke. But I thought you deserved a warning. Barton knows I had help getting the deed. And yesterday he forced his way into my home and took it back. After tonight, he must know it was you who helped me. He wants revenge. He means to hurt you.'

Anthony laughed. 'I gathered that. I wish him luck in it.'

'Do not talk that way. You do not understand what he is capable of.'

He smiled. 'I am sorry, but so many men have threatened me over the years. I am still here, and quite whole.' He stood before her, hands outspread, inviting another examination. When she did not reach for him, he became serious again. 'I thank you for the warning, although I am not particularly concerned by Barton's threats. And what might all that have to do with your kissing him in a public place?'

'You saw?'

'Indeed. You were not enjoying it? Because you appeared most enthusiastic.' His smile was gone, and his tone demanded an explanation.

'What choice do I have? He gave me a demonstration yesterday of the depths he is willing to stoop to ensure my obedience. He beat my servants. He tortured my maid before my very eyes, until I gave him the key to my house. And threatened to do the same to you if I did not submit to him.

'He has everything, and yet he wants more from me. I have no money, no power in this. But I cannot allow him to hurt you. And he would, since he knows how it might hurt me.' Her hands had begun to shake and her breathing was becoming unsteady. If she did not get hold of herself, she would be gasping, and the gasps would turn to sobs. And she feared the crying would never stop.

'And why did you not come to me when I asked you to?' His voice was gentle.

'He is watching me. Every move I make. He was waiting for me to go to you, so that… He said…' She closed her eyes. 'That he would know who helped me, because I would go to him, or he would come to me, just as you did tonight. And when he found you out, he would get back at you. It would go hard for you, but it would go harder still if I did not co-operate. He said that I must tell you he knows what you are seeking more than the deed. He will kill you, if you try again. There might be clemency, if I do as he says. But if I resist, he will take pleasure in hurting you, and that I should know that it would be all my fault.' She stared at him, willing him to understand enough to be worried.

But he laughed. 'That is all, then?'

'Tonight, when we danced, he suspected. And then you taunted him and removed all doubt. How could you be so foolish?'

'I could not help it. He stood there, all puffed up like an angry red balloon. It was too tempting to deflate him.'

'You called him traitor.'

'Because he is one,' Tony replied simply.

'And so you know he has nothing to lose. He is angrier still and will be watching us both. For all I know he has followed you here tonight.'

'He did not follow me,' he reassured her. 'No one knows I am here. You need have no fear of it.'

She smiled in relief. 'If he does not know where to find you, then you are safe for now. But he must know your direction. He will try to find you there. He may be waiting for you at your home, even now.'

'Very astute of you. That is exactly where he is. I followed him to my home and have seen him, watching my house. I left him catching a chill on the street corner, waiting for me to return, so that he could do me mischief. And I have set a man of my own to watch the watcher. If Barton moves from the spot, he will not get far.'

She reached out to clasp his hand. 'Then you can get away. Leave from here. Leave tonight. Get out of the country. Go to the Continent, or perhaps the Americas. I do not care. But swear to me that you will be far away from here by morning, so that I need have no fear for you.'

He smiled and shook his head. 'And what will become of you, if I leave?'

'He does not mean to hurt me. He has assured me of that.'

'He will be quite public about keeping you, and everyone will know it. Think of what you will lose, Constance. Your friends. The prospects you held so dear, even this morning. All of it will be gone.'

'Honour is only an idea. It will not hurt to lose it. I am no innocent, Tony. I know what must be done, and it means nothing, compared to your life. It does not matter to me, as long as I know you are safe.'

'You would be willing to ruin yourself, to preserve my miserable hide?' His eyes were serious. Then his face spread in a lazy grin, but he showed no sign of taking his leave. 'On the contrary, I think it matters a great deal.'

'Not to me. Not any more. I will go to him if I must. If that is what it takes to keep you safe. But you must leave him alone. Whatever you are after, do not seek it in his house. Has no one told you that it is wrong to steal? It was only a matter of time before you met someone like Barton, who was worse than you and could punish you for your crimes.'

He waved the argument aside, his grin wide and without care. 'Leave off with your begging, for I am not moving from this spot until I am good and ready. But tell me again, because I love to hear you say it— you do not go to him by choice?'

'Of course not. The man is horrid.'

'And you are only tolerating his attentions to protect me?' he prompted.

'I cannot let this go any further. He will not have you, if there is anything I can do to prevent it.'

Anthony sighed and fixed her with his smile. 'I cannot tell you how relieved I am to hear that. I thought your problem was something serious, or difficult. Or that you secretly fancied Barton and were using me to control him. But you are trying to save me?' He laughed. 'And that is all? Do not worry. You need do nothing. I will take care of everything.'

She paced the room, wringing her handkerchief in her hands. 'You will go back out the window to search his rooms, and I am to stay here and wait for a report of your death? I vow, your offer of assistance is most welcome, but there is nothing you can do that will not put you in greater jeopardy.'

Tony replied, with gentle insistence. 'You need have no fear. Relax. Let everything to me.'

'That is what my late husband said. Do not worry, Constance. Do not be such a goose. Everything will be fine. I trusted him in all things, and look what I have come to. Barton means to have me and kill you. It is too late for me. But you can still escape him. Run, Tony. Run far away. If you come to harm because of me, I swear I shall go mad.'

He moved as silently as a cat and was upon her before she realised, taking her by the shoulders and pinning her to the wall to stop her pacing. He looked down into her face with his wild smile and dream-filled eyes, and said, 'I shall go mad, if I must watch you make another circuit of the room.' He reached behind her and caught the tie of her bodice, tugging to undo the bow. 'Although it is rather pleasant to see you so overwrought for my sake.'

'But he is a villain, Tony, and he knows about you. What are we to do? I—'

His lips came down on hers, stopping her words. The kiss was forceful, almost brutal in its intensity, and he held her tight against him, so that she could feel his body responding to her. She could feel his hands on her back, dealing, one by one, with the hooks of her dress. Then he pushed away from her, placing his hands on her shoulders, holding her tight in place. 'You shall do nothing tonight. Not with Barton, at any rate.' He trailed his fingers forward, along the gaping neckline of her dress.

'Stop it,' she muttered. 'We mustn't. There isn't time. He will come for me tonight. And if he finds you here…'

'I said—' he pushed at the fabric, and the dress slipped off her shoulders '—I would take care—' he reached behind her to undo her stays '—of everything. But if you are sure you want me to run away, then you need merely say the word, and I shall go.'

'He said—'

'Never mind Barton, for a moment. What is it that you want, your Grace?' He was trailing his fingers over the bare skin of her back and she shuddered with the shock of it.

And then his hands slipped beneath her chemise, stroking her sides, grazing her breasts. 'All things being equal, do you wish me to stay?'

She closed her eyes and tried not to think of what his touch was doing to her, and spoke. 'Of course I do not want you to go. But—'

'Stop right there.' He laid a finger on her lips. 'Do not spoil it with more talking. You have said enough. Now let me help.'

Oh, dear. She stayed very still as he worked the rest of the laces free.

It was not as if she objected. But it all would have been easier a night ago, when she was not so frightened. Tonight, passion was the last thing on her mind. But if she could be still and give herself up to Tony, she could keep him away from Barton for the rest of the night. He had been working on her behalf for quite some time and she had done nothing for him but cause him trouble. And if this was to be goodbye, she could not send him away without something.

It would be better for him if he ran, as she had told him to. She would be alone again, but he would be safe.

But she did quite miss the comfort of a man's arms around her, the soft words and gentle kisses.

He freed the corset and in one smooth move pulled it forward and away from her body and pushed her bodice and chemise to her waist. She was bare before him.

She closed her eyes, afraid of what she might see

in his eyes. She was not old, certainly, but well past her prime. Suppose it was not what he had expected? She opened her eyes to look at him.

And he did not notice, for he was gazing at her breasts in hungry fascination. He reached up to cup them in his hands, closed his eyes and sighed, and when he looked at her again his smile widened.

All right. He seemed satisfied in that. And she had to admit that even though her nerves were jangling with dread, the feel of his hands as they caressed her was more than pleasant. There was a low humming in her blood as he looked at her. She was lying to herself to pretend that it would be a hardship to submit to him. And if they did it quickly, he would still be away before Barton tumbled to his whereabouts.

She reached up and pulled his hand away, ready to lead him to her bed.

And he shook off her touch and pushed her firmly back against the wall.

Dear Lord. Did he mean to take her standing up? The humming was a singing in her at the thought. It would not take very long at all, then. Or so she thought. She had never tried it. It would be something that required more co-ordination, more balance, more stamina than she was used to in a partner. It was not something she had experience in. And was unlikely to be gen—

His lips came down on hers, stopping thought as he

took her tongue. His hands grasped her waist and found the strings of her petticoat, undid them and pushed the fabric to the floor, leaving her naked before him.

He stepped away to admire her.

She regained her thought. Gentle. He was not likely to be gentle, but she doubted that he would be so rough as to hurt her. She must need remember to relax, when the moment came, to make it easy for him to enter, and perhaps afterwards she could ask him to lie in her bed and hold her for a few minutes, before he had to go.

Did one ask for such things? She was not sure.

He was staring at her naked body, and she remembered too late that she should be embarrassed. At the very least, she should do something to help him out of his clothing, since the situation was highly unequal. She reached for the buttons of his waistcoat.

He seized her by the wrists and pinned them against the wall, and said, his face close to hers, 'I said I would take care of everything, your Grace.'

And before she could suggest that under the circumstances he might call her Constance, his mouth was on hers again. She tried to pull her hands free, but he was too strong for her and held her pinned as he took her mouth. His grip on her hands was relaxed but unmovable, and she found she quite liked the feeling of struggling against his hold, the wool of his coat rubbing against her nakedness. And the way her movements seemed to inflame his ki—

He was kissing her mouth with savage ferocity, and she writhed in his grasp, and with a shudder, she gave herself up to him, going weak and pliant in his arms. Only then did his lips move to her throat, and she could feel his tongue licking and his teeth biting at her pulse and making it jump in response. He released her hands and imprisoned her body between his and the wall, stroking down her back to cup her bottom before taking her by the shoulders and steadying himself as he lowered his mouth to her breasts.

She tried to catch her breath, now that her mouth was free, but found it impossible. His mouth was greedy and hard against her and his hands slipped to her waist and squeezed, holding her steady as he su—

Oh, dear Lord. His mouth was on her nipple, pulling hard and his hand slipped between her legs and…

She pressed her back into the wall to keep from collapsing with the shock of it. He was making love to her with his hands, caressing her legs, spreading her sex and slipping those agile fingers in and out of her. She grabbed at her own hair, and it fell in a shower of pins and rose petals, the curls forming a curtain around him as he kissed her breasts. Then she ran her fingers through the waves in his hair, clutching at the back of his neck to hold his mouth to her and urge him on. Her breath was coming faster, sensations piling on top of sensation. And then subsiding as he pulled his mouth away to…

He cupped his hand over her sex and slid to his knees before her, trailing kisses down her belly until he came to her navel, setting up a rhythm with his tongue and his hand, until she was rocking against him and pressing herself down on his hand to push his fingers more deeply into her, clutching his shoulders as though he were the only solid thing in the world.

And he stopped. He lifted his head to look up into her face, dominating her even as he knelt at her feet. And again he smiled, and this time it was in triumph as he thrust into her with one hand, grabbed her hip with the other, and pulled her to his mou...

And she lost herself, her cares, her body, and her mind, and yet the kiss did not end. She begged him to stop and in the same breath begged him for more, and he laughed against her and began it all again until her legs shook under her and she writhed against him as the feelings rolled through her again and again.

'Your Grace?'

He pulled away from her at last and laid his head against her thigh, idly kissing the soft flesh.

'Your Grace, is anything the matter?'

She shook her head, trying to understand what she was hearing.

'Because I heard you cry out.' Oh, dear, she had forgotten the maid. 'Your Grace? The door is locked. Do you need assistance?'

She leaned her head back against the wall, wondering if she could stand any more help for the evening without dying of happiness.

When Tony smiled up at her, the lazy, carefree grin was back. He bit her hip, and let his fingertips play over the back of her knees.

'Your Grace?' There was a trace of laughter in her maid's voice. It had been obvious to Susan what she had been doing. And, Constance suspected, quite loud.

'No, Susan. Do not trouble yourself. I am fine.' The maid retreated.

'You are fine. Very fine indeed,' Tony whispered against her belly. 'And I must go.'

'But you haven't—'

'But you have. Twice, at least.' He smiled with pride and rose to take her hands. 'I told you I would make it all better. I must go and take care of Barton and retrieve your deed and your keys. I suspect he is quite cold and stiff after all this time standing in the street. Whereas I feel most refreshed.' He let go of her hands and scooped her up in his arms, and she squealed in delight as he carried her to her bed and tossed her under the covers, pulling them over her naked body. 'You need not fear a visit from him tonight. Now, go to sleep, and if you would...' he kissed her '...dream of me.'

'Sleep?' How could he even suggest it?

'I have work yet to do. It is a shame, isn't it, that in my chosen profession the work begins when the sun goes down, for it leaves me less time to spend with you.'

'But you will come again,' she whispered. 'Soon. When you can stay with me.'

And he grinned. 'As your Grace pleases.'

There, he thought with some satisfaction as he climbed out of the window and gained the street. She had left off the notion that he need run for his life. In fact, he was quite sure that she would be most vehemently opposed to his going anywhere without her. And she had forgotten all about sleeping with Barton as well. Although the notion that she would make the ultimate sacrifice for him was flattering, under no circumstances would he allow her to do so.

But it gave him proof enough that he need no longer worry about Constance's feelings towards him. She might think that marriage was an impossibility. But there were many other things she seemed ready to agree to, and he would soon teach her that the advantages of becoming his wife might outweigh the negatives of birth and career.

As he approached his rooms, he saw the shadowy figure concealed in the bushes long before it saw him, which was highly amusing.

'Barton.' He smiled his most unctuous smile, and strode up to the man, clapping him on the back.

Barton started at the unexpected contact, and then straightened and failed miserably at hiding his confusion.

'Forgotten me so soon? My name is de Portnay

Smythe. I believe we spoke this evening, when I was rescuing Constance Townley from the tedium of having to waltz with you.' Tony smiled. 'I was most disappointed to lose you in the crowd at the Gardens, for I rather thought that you meant to teach me a lesson.'

Barton's eyes narrowed. 'Someone must, Smythe. It is well past time you learned that sticking your nose where it doesn't belong can be very bad for your health.'

Tony shrugged. 'Perhaps. But I doubt you will be the one to teach me, for you have not learned that lesson yourself. Your continued harassment of the Dowager Duchess of Wellford, for example, is about to prove extremely unhealthy.'

Barton smiled. 'I beg to differ. I was there first, Smythe. She did not seem the least bit harassed, when last we were alone, and I have no desire to part with her. I assure you, the lady's services are already engaged.'

Tony ignored the red haze of rage that formed at the idea of Barton alone with Constance, and sneered. 'Her services are engaged? You talk of her as though you are hiring a coach. If she were in agreement on that point, then we would have nothing to speak of here. But in talking to her, I gather she is somewhat distressed by your attentions. And so, you will cease them, immediately.'

It was Barton's turn to sneer. 'You believe that she prefers you, a low-born thief?'

Tony ignored the insult. 'Whether she might prefer me is immaterial to this discussion. We are talking of that which she docs not prefer. And that would be you. Noble birth does not erase the fact that you are a criminal as well, *Lord* Barton. Perhaps, in respect to your fine blood, I should offer you the chance to settle our differences on the field of honour.' Tony laughed to himself at the idea. 'But I am just a common man. I am no fencer, sir, and not much of a shot. I will not give you a chance to stick me when the sun rises, any more than I will allow you to knife me in the back on a street corner this evening. If you think you deserve Constance Townley's affections, then prove to me that you arc the better man. Try and take them from me.' He raised his hands, prepared to fight.

Barton took the stance of so many fine gentlemen, fists up to protect his noble profile.

Tony ignored it and punched him once in the stomach, watching him fold and drop to the ground. He looked down at the man who lay gasping at his feet. 'And this is why, if you wish to fight, it is better to learn it in the street, than from Gentleman Jim. You may find, Barton, that much of the prancing and preening you've been taught is quite useless against a rogue such as myself. And while you are quite terrifying to old men and ladies' maids, I find you to be a bit of a joke.'

Tony reached down, grabbed Barton by a lapel and ran a hand efficiently through the pockets of the coat, until he came upon the deed. 'Carrying it with you to prevent me from stealing it? I thought as much. And you see how well that succeeded.' He continued his search, removing more papers and a key ring. He flipped through the papers. 'Let us see what else we have. IOUs. And here is one from Constance's idiot nephew.' He stared down in disgust at Barton. 'No one is this lucky at cards, Jack. Therefore, I will surmise you cheated and will take the lot. I suspect it will be like early Christmas for the owners to get them back.'

He examined the ring of keys, removing one that fit the lock he had noticed on Constance's front door. 'You will not be needing this, and so I will return it to its owner as well.' He glared at Barton. 'A true gentleman would never accept something that was not freely given.'

He made to return the keys, and then hesitated. 'I don't suppose, while we are here together, that you would like to tell me the location of the key to your safe. I do not see it, on the ring here. It would be round, with a notched end. With a little cap to keep the dust out of the grooves.'

Barton glared up at him with murder in his eyes.

'Didn't think so.' Tony smiled. 'Never mind. I didn't really want it. I will open the lock on my own, soon enough. I enjoy the challenge, and having the key would spoil my fun. But do not think for a moment that you can succeed in your plans to mint your own money. The government is on to you, and has set me to stop you to prevent scandal. But they will have you, no matter what you do. My advice to you, as a fellow criminal, is to admit defeat, turn over the plates and run while they will still allow it.'

He tossed the other keys back into the muck of the street.

'Do you understand?'

Barton had left off gasping, and he struggled up on one hand and spat on the ground at Tony's feet.

Tony kicked the hand out from under him, rolled Barton over with the toe of his boot and planted his foot across the man's throat. 'I said, do you understand? I am concerned, predominantly, about the Duchess of Wellford. It stops here, Barton. You will leave her alone. Are we clear on that?' He increased his pressure on the man's throat.

Barton nodded with difficulty.

He removed his foot from Barton's neck, allowing the man to sit up. 'You are no doubt having thoughts right now about what you will do to me, once you get your wind back. If you mean to call me out, you will be unsuccessful, for I will laugh in your face. I am proud to be a live coward in a family of dead heroes and I do not need to duel to prove my worth. If you accost me in public, I will make it clear to all within earshot what I think of the sort of man who needs to use blackmail to gain the affections of a lady.

'And if you think, as you did tonight, that it will be possible to waylay me, alone or with the help of friends, or that it will be possible to send servants or lackeys to give me a taste of what's coming to me, then I suggest you think again. Better men than you have tried it, but none has been successful. Should you manage it, know that when I am not dealing with the likes of you, I am a likeable fellow with many friends in high places and in low. They should be unhappy, should anything happen to me, and have been warned from whom the attack is most likely to come. They will take action on my behalf should I be unable to do so.'

He smiled down at the prone man. 'Likewise, do not attempt to harass the duchess further, or seek retribution for my actions. I will take a wrong against her as a wrong committed against my own person. I believe the Italians have a word for what I intend. Vendetta. It is much what you intended for me.'

He looked down at the beaten man. 'You may consider this your last warning on the matter. I mean to finish you in any case, and will have those plates. I suggest you drop what you are planning and run, as far and as fast as you can. I will not follow, and the state is willing to let you go. But if I ever hear that you have interfered with the duchess or her household, justice will be swift and no distance great enough to protect you. Do you understand?'

Barton glared.

Anthony dug a toe into his ribs. 'Yes or no, Barton. Do you understand?'

'Yes.'

Tony smiled down at him. 'Very good. We have an understanding. Good night to you, sir. And don't make me have to do this again.'

Chapter Fourteen

Constance stretched under the sheet and enjoyed the feel of the linen on her bare body. She felt a *frisson* of desire and the memories came flooding back. In spite of herself, she smiled.

He had told her not to worry, and then he'd taken off her clothes, and pleasured her until she could bear it no more.

And then he'd put her to bed and taken his leave. She'd dreamed all night of him, lying next to her on the pillow, and it was sweet disappointment to wake and find that he wasn't there.

There was a quiet knock on the door.

It was still locked, and her maid could not get in. She wrapped the sheet around herself, then hurried to the door in bare feet and turned the key in the lock, grabbed the clothing from off the floor and tossed it over the nearest chair, trying to give the illusion that she had found her own way to bed.

Susan came in smiling, and doing her best to pretend that there was nothing unusual about her mistress's behaviour. There was an envelope, set beside the morning's hot chocolate.

Constance looked to her enquiringly.

'It was delivered this morning, your Grace, with the first post.'

She glanced down at the seal. An S, unfamiliar in its design. She slit the wax and unfolded the note. Her deed and inventory slid on to the tray.

So soon?

Obviously. She felt the last of the tension leaving her body. A short note slid from the envelope as well, and she laid it against her heart before reading.

I am safe as houses, as are you. If you would welcome a visit from one who will always be your humble servant, so that you might have return of your house key, send your maid to bed early and leave your window unlocked.

There was no signature.

She sank back into the pillows, and closed her eyes, holding the note to her lips. He had the key to her front door, and yet he asked her permission to enter. If she had not loved him before now, she would have been unable to resist him, just for that fact. And he still wished to use the window. Which was both discreet, and arousing. And he was coming to her tonight.

Susan gave a quiet cough to remind Constance of her continued presence.

She smiled up at the maid.

Susan smiled back. 'Have you decided to listen to your heart after all, your Grace?'

'It beats so loudly when I think of him that I have been unable to do otherwise.' She allowed the maid to help her into her morning dress. 'I think, Susan, that there is no hope for me. It is not wise of me to want Mr Smythe. It would be much better could I bring myself to feel this towards Lord Endsted. But my mind will not obey reason. When I think of Tony, the sun shines brighter, the air smells sweeter, and I feel as if I could fly, rather than walk.'

Susan nodded. 'You are in love.'

Constance looked back at her, sadly. 'I never meant to be. I never have been, before. And I am not sure, when it ends, that I will like it very much.'

'It will be worth it,' Susan assured her. 'For you will always remember this morning.'

That night, supper was barely cold when she called for Susan to ready her for bed. It was foolish of her, she supposed, for it was far too early to expect a visit. But he had given no indication of the time he would come. And when he did arrive, she did not wish to waste a moment of his company in preparation. Susan had laid out her best night rail, and she allowed it to be put on, only to toss the thing aside as soon as her maid had left the room. Then she crawled naked between the sheets.

It was almost midnight when, at last, he climbed in the window, silhouetted in the light from the street. She leaned on her elbow and watched him, admiring his movements. How strange that he should be able to climb in and out as easily as going through the front door. And how accustomed she'd become to his habits.

'Good evening.' She could see his grin in the darkness, when he saw her already in bed. 'I hope I am not disturbing you.'

'Not at all.' She stretched and let the sheet slip down her body so that he could see she was bare beneath the linen.

He caught his breath at the sight. 'Not disturbed? Give me fifteen minutes and you shall be.' He slipped off his coat and tossed it over a chair. 'You received the deed?'

'Yes. Thank you.'

He undid his cravat and tossed it and his shirt after the coat. 'Did you send your maid away this evening so that we might not be interrupted?'

'Yes,' she breathed. He was slim, unlike her husband. His belly was flat and his shoulders broad and she could watch the muscles move under the skin as he undressed.

He sat on the end of the bed and pried off his boots.

'I hope that she is on the other side of the house.' He looked over his shoulder at her. 'You were quite vocal last night. It is most gratifying to get such an enthusiastic response.'

She blushed. 'It was very... I don't think I... Thank you.'

He turned to look at her with a fond smile. 'You're very welcome.' He sighed and shook his head in amazement. 'And very, very beautiful. Especially as you are now, naked in bed, and waiting for me.' He stood and unfastened his breeches and let them drop to the floor. He was large, and already growing hard. But then, his whole body was well muscled and firm, and she longed to touch every inch of it. He stretched out on the bed beside her, with only the sheet separating their bodies.

He took her in his arms and cradled her against his body, and she felt the hair of his chest rubbing against her breasts and bringing every nerve alive in her.

In response, she kissed him.

There was nothing gentle in his answer as he kissed her back. There was the same intensity that she felt whenever he looked at her, as though he wanted to steal her away and keep her all to himself. His hands were on her back, stroking her and gripping her shoulders and her waist and anything he could reach.

She pushed the sheet down and out of the way so that she could feel even more of him.

And he pulled it back up to her waist, keeping them apart, but gripping her bottom and her legs so that she could feel how hard he was, even through the fabric.

She wrapped her legs around him, tangling in the sheet and rocking, letting the linen rub against them, as he reached to play with her breasts, cupping them with his hands, stroking and pulling at the nipples. And then he caught one of her hands, bringing it to his mouth to suck on the fingers and kiss the knuckles and the palm. At last, he whispered, 'If you would be so kind.' Then he led it down his body, over his chest and stomach, until it rested between his legs under the sheet.

She understood what he wanted, for she had often had to help her husband, before he was able to perform. But Anthony was not in obvious need of help. He was long and hard and ready, and he sucked in his breath when her hand touched him, and gritted his teeth in a smile.

She stroked him, running her hand along the smooth flesh and tightening around it, and he trembled next to her. She kissed his lips and bit his throat, and worked her way down his chest to explore his nipples with her tongue, tasting salt and feeling his gasps as her grasp grew stronger and longer and faster. She ran her other hand over his body, feeling the muscles tighten and his back arch as he grew near to climax and her own body grew wet and heavy, and eager to know his first thrust inside of her.

And when she knew it could not be much longer,

she reached to pull the sheet out of the way so that they could join. But he held fast to it.

Did he mean to come without her, as she had without him the night before? She had thought, the way he looked at her, that he had wanted more from her than this. Was it the woman he said he loved that kept him from completing the act with her? Her stroke faltered.

'Tony?'

'Just a moment, darling.' His words came between groans. 'Just a little while longer.'

'I must ask—'

'After, please. Anything.'

'But I need to know—'

'Constance, I am dying,' he begged. 'Finish what you have started.'

She stilled her hand, holding him in a loose grip, and said, 'Is there some reason that you cannot crawl beneath the sheet and finish yourself?'

He said through gritted teeth, 'I thought that would be obvious. I do not want to get you with child.'

She yanked her hand from his body and rolled away, turning her back to him and wrapping herself in the bed linens. 'Get out.'

He laid a gentle hand on her shoulder, and his voice was unsteady. 'I am sorry to be so selfish. You have needs as well and I should think of my lady before myself. But I have been able to think of nothing but your hand on me for the whole day…'

She shivered in the bed and wrapped the sheet even tighter around herself. 'I can see to my own needs from now on.'

'Constance,' he whispered. 'What is the matter?'

When she tried to speak, it felt as though her throat were full of tears. 'You know what is the matter. How could you say that? I trusted you. And how could you hurt me so? To use such an excuse to avoid making love, when you must know as well as the rest of the world that I have been barren for thirty years. Producing a child will not be at issue. If you have a distaste for me, or for the act, or if there is another woman, can you at least tell me the truth? Do you think me a fool?'

'Constance.' He pulled her to him, so that she could feel him, still hard, and pressing against her from behind. Then he rested his head against her shoulder, so that he might speak in her ear. 'I do not think you foolish. But I think that you have been told for so long that there is a deficiency in you that you believe it yourself. Now, answer me honestly. Have you ever lain with a man, other than your husband?'

'No, of course not. How could you say such a thing?'

'How old was he when you married?'

'He was almost two score.'

'And you were just out of the schoolroom, were you not?'

'Well, yes.'

'And did he have mistresses?'

She never liked to think of such things. But there had been the scent of strange perfume, and the occasional trace of rouge on his cravat, although she wore none.

'Constance?'

'Yes. There were other women.'

'But no rumours of bastards?'

'No.' The thoughts that she had never dared think, when Robert was alive, mingled with the doubts.

'Did you ever have to dismiss a chambermaid for getting herself in trouble? And I do not mean for care-lessness with the silver.'

'No.'

'So your husband had no children when he married you, and in the last fifteen years he lay with several women, without issue. While you were only with him.' He placed a hand negligently on her hip. 'I told you before, Constance, I am not prone to gambling. But I'll wager, if we are careless and lower this sheet, you are liable to find that the problem was not yours, much to your regret.'

Regret? He must be mad. Awareness flooded her. Tony was young and strong and hard. Virile. And he wanted her, as much as she wanted him. If there was a chance, even the slightest chance, that she could ever hold a babe... She yanked the sheet out of his hand and turned to face him, wrapping her legs around his body so that his sex could rest against her.

She kissed him, and rubbed her body against his, urging him to do what she knew he wanted to.

And he muttered, 'You are not thinking clearly, Constance. God knows, I can hardly think at all. Now give me back the sheet before I do something that we may rue later.' But he did not push her away.

'Take me, Tony,' she murmured. 'I do not care. Take me, now.' And she reached between them to guide him into her body.

He took a long breath and stayed her hand. 'I must be mad to stop you. A moment. Please.'

There was a pause as he tried to remember what it was he wanted to say. 'You may not care now. But no child of mine shall be a bastard. If I am right and there is a consequence to this act, do you swear to me that you will tell me, and accept the next time I offer for you?'

'Yes,' she whispered. 'Now, do it.'

Still he waited, and he was trembling with the effort. 'There will be no fuss from you about my low birth, or my chosen profession, no nonsense about not knowing my family or my past. You will marry me without question, and follow where I lead.'

'Yes, Tony,' she panted. 'Yes, now just do it, before it is too late.'

And he rolled over her, thrust into her, shuddered and collapsed.

She held him close and smiled into his shoulder, at the feel of him filling her, the thought of his seed inside her, and the idea that she might not be dead inside after all.

He raised himself up on his arms to look down into her eyes. 'Woman, you are mad to be smiling at me. That was a pathetic effort on my part. I had hoped for so much more from our first true meeting. To leave you satisfied at least. But to so totally lose control of myself…'

'It was fine,' she assured him. 'I am just so glad that we were not too late.'

'Too late for what, sweet?'

'You almost did it without being within me. I had hoped that it would happen this evening. And it would be a shame if I had missed it.'

He was staring at her in a most unusual way. And he muttered, 'You husband was quite a bit older than you. Well, I suppose…'

And then he moved against her, to stroke inside her. 'I think, my darling, that if you thought that was to be an isolated incident, there is yet more to teach you.'

She gasped as he grew hard again and her body tightened in surprise.

He sucked in his breath. 'Do that again, love. Yes, just like that. And again. You are heaven, for I never expected to feel something so good in this life. You did not think I would stop at once, if you let me have you. I am insulted.'

More than once. He was right, there were things she

needed to learn. He was large and he was hard for her again. Her excitement grew at the thought.

He paused. 'Let us try something new.'

She wanted to argue that it was already new to her and quite good enough, when he had rolled so that she was lying on top of him.

She froze in confusion, wondering what he wished her to do next. And she shifted up on to her elbows so she could look at him. And the feeling took her. And she shifted, again. And again. And then she drew her legs up under her, and he grabbed her by the waist and let her do as she would, whispering words of encouragement as she rocked herself to climax upon him. Then he steadied her hips and thrust upward, again and again before his back arched, and he called her name, and then he pulled her down to lie on top of him again.

Their bodies were sweat slicked and chill in the darkness, and she shivered.

He threw the sheet over her back and wrapped his arms around her.

'You were right,' she whispered. 'That was even better.'

'And that was just the beginning,' he promised. 'We can try again, if you let me rest for a few minutes.'

'Minutes?' she asked in surprise.

'Or longer, if you wish.' He paused. 'I had rather hoped to stay the night, if you would allow it. I will be gone before dawn, of course. No one will see me.' He paused again, as though he thought, after what had happened, that she still might have the strength to deny him.

She snuggled into him, turned her face into his shoulder and kissed it. 'Stay as long as you wish.' Then she remembered her fears of the previous night. 'As long as it is safe for you to do so. Barton is not still searching for you, is he?'

'We are both safe from Barton. For a time, at least. He is not stalking me at the moment, and I hope he will have the sense to leave off bothering you, after the beating I gave him.' His arm wrapped protectively around her to pull her closer. 'So we should have several days of peace before Barton feels brave enough to try again. And I mean to spend every moment I can in your arms.'

Chapter Fifteen

Several days later, Tony was up early when Patrick brought him his breakfast tea, his pick working the lock mechanism in his practice safe. Barton's lock would be keyed differently, but it would be good to have the confidence that picking the first lock might give him, and some idea of the total amount of time involved.

And the time it had taken so far was considerable. He had been working on his own lock for several days without success, even though he could work unhindered and get hints from the shape of the key. Stanton was becoming restless. There had been a terse note, reminding Tony of the urgency of the situation, as if he did not know it himself. Much more time and the government would be forced to take action, and the rest of the story would play out in *The Times*, much to the embarrassment of all concerned.

Patrick cleared his throat to announce breakfast.

'Set the cup on the desk, Patrick.'

Patrick was looking over his shoulder.

'You may go.'

'I wouldn't dream of it. This is too interesting to miss.'

'That is my repayment for rescuing you from certain hanging so many years ago. Continued insolence. I had been better off to hire a servant in the ordinary way, than to take a charity case from Newgate.'

'And what would you have learned from this imaginary servant—how to polish your own boots? Have you tried oiling the lock?'

'And it has done me no good, other than to make the pick slip.'

'You could drill the lock out, and gain entry that way.'

'If I wished to announce the theft. I assume that Stanton wanted this done discreetly. And it would take even more time to drill through the steel.'

'Last night, were you attempting this at Barton's home? What methods did you employ? Did he leave you to work in peace, the whole night? For you were gone until almost dawn.'

Tony winced. He had gone to Barton's home and observed the study window for a time, but, seeing light and movement in the room, he had given it up as a bad job. 'He and I have come to an impasse, I fear. I have frightened him enough to keep him away from Constance. But now he will not leave his house, for fear of giving me a chance to enter. It is actually rather annoying, since it will make it difficult for me to finish the job, even if I can manage to open the safe.'

'If you were not with Barton, then where have you been spending your time?'

Tony cleared his throat. 'I spent the evening with the duchess.'

Behind him, Patrick chuckled. 'You have had better luck unlocking her affections than you have had with Barton's safe.'

Tony laid his check against the cool metal of the safe door and grinned. He had meant to visit her briefly the previous evening, and then return to his work. But several hours later, he was too exhausted to rise in any way, begging the woman to leave off tormenting him, assuring her that he had not an ounce of strength left in his body for the things she was suggesting.

And she had smiled at him, and rung for a bottle of champagne.

She had ignored him as he had argued that the wine would do more damage than good. Then she had taken the glass from his hand and drunk deeply. And she'd kissed her way down his body, taking little sips of the wine, and he'd had the strange sensation of bubbles on his skin, along with the kisses.

Then she had disappeared beneath the covers. And suddenly he was not nearly so exhausted as he had

been moments before, and any plan he'd had of returning to Barton's was long forgotten.

He could hear the clink of the china as Patrick
picked up the teacup and began to drink it himself. He
glanced over his shoulder. His valet was balancing his
hip on the corner of his master's desk, and helping
himself to a scone to go with his tea. He glared.

Patrick shrugged. 'The tea is getting cold, and you
would only get butter on your hands if you had a scone.
I will get you more, when you have opened the lock.
So, tell me, does the dowager have a lady's maid?'

'Don't be an idiot. Of course she does. And stop eating my breakfast.'

'Tell me about her.'

'I have been telling you about her for years.' Although he couldn't help but smile at the memory.

'Not the duchess. The maid.'

'She is just an ordinary maid. Not much in evidence, when I am there. Constance generally sends her
to bed.'

'The dowager is a most understanding and generous mistress, to be sure. I look forward to meeting her,
again. And her maid, as well. Whose name is?'

'Susan,' Tony responded.

'And I suppose she is old, pinch-faced, and sour
tempered.'

'She appears to me to be a most pleasant girl of
twenty, blonde, somewhat plump and quite attractive.'

Patrick offered a toast with his teacup. 'To the fair Susan. Now that things are settled, and the duchess knows who you are, I can hope but to spend a happy future, below stairs with a beautiful blonde.'

Tony swallowed and renewed his efforts with the lock. 'Well. About that…'

'You haven't told her. Have you?'

'We have been rather busy.'

Patrick poured another cup of tea. 'In the past week, you have spent more time in her company than you have in all of the previous thirty years.'

'But I would have to have been a fool to have spent it talking, Patrick. Apparently, the late duke was neglectful of his marital duties. And the duchess wishes to make up for lost time. I am happy to oblige, although I am near to exhaustion. Once the novelty of my visits wears off, we will have time to chat about old times. But until that time… Well, I'll be damned.'

The locked turned under his hand, and the door to the safe swung open.

'I have done it.' He stared from the lock to Patrick and back to the lock. 'I have picked a Bramah.'

Patrick stared over his shoulder at the open safe, and patted him on the back. 'Well done, sir. Do you mean to try the challenge lock in the Bramah Company window, next? You could claim the two hundred guineas.'

Tony sat on the edge of the desk. 'I cannot very well tell them it has been done. They'll want to know how I managed it. And then they will change the lock to make it impossible again.' He reached forward to touch the open door, as though he expected it to be an illusion. 'And worse yet, they'll wonder why a gentleman, who is not a locksmith by trade or by hobby, had reason to try.' He laughed to himself. 'I am the man that beat Bramah. But I cannot tell anyone, or I will not be able to use what I have learned.'

Patrick nodded in sympathy. 'But you can use the information now, can't you? Against Barton?'

Tony stared at the open safe. 'I certainly hope so. If the man ever leaves his house, I mean to try.'

Tony leaned against the trunk of the tree that had become his evening home. He had spent three nights, perched like a bird in front of Barton's house, watching the man sit in his study until almost midnight, only to be replaced by a servant, who was left to sleep in the chair by the desk. Tony had returned to Constance's rooms each night, and let her soothe the frustration away, only to see the process repeated again the next night.

Barton must know he was watching. The guard upon the things was obvious enough, and all carried out in plain view of the window. So it was left to him to find a way to force Barton from cover, or the pattern could play out indefinitely.

Tony glanced back at the house, in frustration. To

be so close to the plates, and finally in a position to have another go at the lock, only to be thwarted...

The room was empty.

He stared again. The lights were on, and the room was empty. He shifted his position in the tree to view it from another angle. There was no sign of life in the study.

His pulse quickened.

The front door of the house opened, and Barton appeared on the front step and paused, almost dramatically. He looked in the direction of Tony's tree and made a grand, welcoming gesture towards the house, before signalling to a servant to bring the carriage around.

Tony sat perfectly still, straddling his branch as the carriage accepted its owner and drove away. The bastard had known he was there, and known his location as well. And he was leaving the house in plain sight and daring Tony to enter.

It was a trap, of course. But an irresistible one. Barton knew, and was taunting him.

Tony considered. If he was wise rather than clever, he would head away from the danger, and not towards. But he was tired of sitting in trees and trying to wait the man out. Now or never, then.

He dropped to the ground and made his way stealthily across the grounds to the ornamental drainpipe at the corner of the house that had served as ladder on his last entry. He rattled it, examining the areas nearest the ground for loosened bolts. It seemed secure, and so he began his ascent, working up the first flight, and the next, to the level of the window he sought.

Only to slip rapidly down. He'd dropped almost ten feet, and very nearly lost his grip before regaining his hold.

The bastard had greased the metal. Tony grinned through gritted teeth. If he had been careless, other than merely rash, he might have fallen, as Barton had intended.

He examined the stone front of the house. A more difficult climb, but not impossible. Clinging to the pipe with his legs, he pulled gloves from his pockets to cover the grease on his hands. Then he renewed his grip and reached out with a leg, finding a toe-hold in the stone of the house. And then a hand hold. And so began his ascent again.

It was unlikely that Barton would guess his route and lay another trap, but Tony felt carefully as he went for loosened stones or chiselled mortar. He was progressing nicely, within an arm's length of the ledge beneath the window. He reached, grasped, and felt the pain before his fingers had fully closed on the bricks. When he pulled his hand away it was followed by a shower of broken glass.

He shook his hand to dislodge the shard that had poked through the palm of his glove, thanking God that the leather had taken the majority of the damage, and then reached out to brush the area clear, so that he might proceed.

An excellent effort, Barton. But not quite good enough. He examined the window for traps before opening it. It was mercifully clear and unlatched. Perhaps the next snare waited inside, since Barton did not think the window worthy of his effort. Tony made a quick circuit of the lit room before setting to work on the safe. No servants concealed behind furniture or curtains. And the key had been left on the inside of the door, as though he were invited to lock it, if he wished to work in privacy.

He turned the key in the door, and, as an afterthought, pushed a chair under the door handle as an additional safeguard. Then he set to work on the safe.

Tony tried to ignore the creeping flesh at the back of his neck. There was something wrong. He had expected the traps. But there should have been more of them. Aside from the unpickable nature of the lock, which was proceeding rather nicely, he thought. There had to be something that Barton knew, that he did not. The man would not relinquish the prize so easily, if he thought Tony could make it into the room. There must be something he was not considering, then. The thought nagged at him, as he shifted the pick in his hand to catch the next slider. Barton could not have concealed the plates on his person before leaving. They were not huge, but too large to slip into a coat pocket.

He would not leave something so precious unguarded, would he?

And then the thought hit him. Barton might leave the plates unguarded to go to something he wanted more.

Tony had left Constance. Unprotected.

Even as he thought it, he felt the pick slip home to move the last slider. With a slight turn of his wrist, he opened the lock and the door to the safe swung wide.

He reached into the opening.

There were no plates within.

Chapter Sixteen

Constance was waiting in her sitting room until it was late enough to go to bed. Her life was falling into a familiar pattern, now that Tony was part of it. She would nap in the afternoon, and have dinner, alone. She then sent the servants to bed early and spent the rest of the evening reading before the fire until almost midnight. Then she would find her own way to her room.

Shortly afterwards, her lover would come, and they would pass the hours until dawn.

Tonight, she had chosen Byron to keep her company until bedtime. She smiled and closed her eyes. When she had asked Tony to read to her, he had looked into her eyes and recited the poems from memory.

If she was not careful, she would become quite spoiled by his attentions. When the time came to return to reality, she would remember that Tony's behaviour was an aberration of character, and a sign of the minimal depth of their relationship. Men might spout poetry to their mistresses, but never to their wives.

But it was lovely, all the same. 'So lovely,' she whispered.

'Yes, you are.' When she opened her eyes, Jack Barton was standing in the doorway.

She stood up and backed away, until she felt her shoulders bump the wall behind her. 'How did you get into my home?'

He smiled at her, as always. 'You gave me your key.'

'Only because you forced me to. And Tony got it back for me.'

'Tony.' Barton sniffed in dismissal. 'He is not much of a thief if he does not realise that keys can be copied. I let him take the one, and kept the duplicate, assuming rightly that I might need it later.'

'Get out. I shall ring for the servants.'

'I would not advise that.' Barton pulled a pistol from his pocket, and pointed it in her direction.

'Go ahead and shoot. You would not dare,' she said and started for the bell pull.

'Not you,' he replied. 'But I will shoot the first one through the door, if you ring for help. If you remember my last visit, you know I am capable of it.'

Her hand faltered before it reached the pull.

Barton nodded. 'Very good. You must agree, it is better if we remain alone. And since you have dismissed the staff for the evening, they will not disturb us.'

'But we will not be alone for long,' she threatened. 'I am expecting a guest.'

'Anthony Smythe?' Barton shook his head in disappointment. 'I doubt he will be troubling us again. It was very simple, in the end, to beat your lover. It is a pity that I could not be there to see him fail. But I needed to be away from the house, to lure him in.'

'What do you mean?' Constance felt a chill.

'The minute I was away, I have no doubt that he rushed into the house, ready to search the study. If he made it past the traps I set for him without falling to his death, he is still in for a nasty shock. The safe he has been trying to open for the last several weeks is, to the best of my knowledge, empty. I have never had reason or ability to open it. It was left by the previous owner of the house. For all I know, the man took the key to the grave with him. If he has not found them already, I doubt that your Mr Smythe will have sense to intuit the location of the things he is looking for.

'I fear, darling, that in his initial excitement, he may have forgotten all about you.'

Constance tried not to imagine Tony, dangling unsteadily from a ledge or lying in a broken heap at the base of Barton's house. He had made it into the house. She must believe that he had survived, if she meant to keep her wits about her. 'I doubt he is so easy to beat as all that. He will come to my aid when he realises that you have tricked him.'

'But if your vulnerability occurs to him later, he will come rushing back here, breakneck, to rescue you. He enters your room through the window, does he not?'

She stared at him, keeping her expression a blank.

'Oh, come now. There are no secrets left between us. I have seen the ivy that leads right to your room. I doubt an agile climber could resist such an easy path. Now, where was I?

'I have left him my plans for the evening. When he realises that I mean to have you while he is chasing after nothing, he will come rushing back to this house, to the bedroom, where he expects to find us. I will be waiting…' he gestured with the pistol in his hand '…to rescue you from the intruder, bent on entering your room. One shot, as he is framed in the window. He will die from the bullet, or the fall, or a combination of the two.'

'It will be murder. And I will tell anyone who will listen.'

'I doubt anyone will, Constance. And even if they do, you might think before you speak. We will be in your room, together. There will be no question as to why I am there. It would be better, for you, should the world think that Smythe was attempting to rob you. If it appears you were entertaining two gentlemen, you will be the talk of the town.'

The book of poems slipped from her hands and dropped to the floor.

'And you will want me to be free of prosecution. You will need my protection for quite some time, I think. If I am in jail for murder, or worse, you will gain nothing by it but revenge. Your reputation will be in tatters. You will not see another penny out of your idiot nephew, for he will cut you from the family for the disgrace.

'On the other hand, if I am free, I will take care of you, just as I have always promised. We may have to leave the country, at least for a time. My business is not going quite so well as I'd hoped. But we will have the comfort of each other.'

Constance felt something snap, deep inside her. This was not how her life was to end. She was not some pawn to be passed from man to man and abandoned as they chose. She could not very well sit waiting for a rescue that might never come. Suppose Tony was dead, as Barton hoped. Or worse yet, on his way to her window so that she could watch him shot before her eyes and disgraced as a burglar.

She would not let it happen. If anyone was to be shot tonight, it would not be Tony.

Barton gestured with the gun.

'We will go to your room, and wait.'

'I suppose I have no choice,' she said.

'We have been over this before, Constance.'

'If I submit willingly to you, will you spare Anthony Smythe?'

Barton laughed. 'That offer is no longer available to you. What transpires now is a matter between gentlemen. You need not concern yourself with it.'

'It is not the act of a gentleman to shoot an unsuspecting man.'

He smiled. 'It is plain, Constance, that you are trying to prolong the inevitable. You have no need to be nervous, you know. I have every intention of being a gentle and courteous lover. Fine things should be savoured, not devoured.'

There he went again, referring to her as a thing. Not for very much longer, she hoped. Any minute, Tony would be here to put a stop to it.

Or he would not, and she would have to act for herself.

Barton reached across the table to stroke her hand. 'And you are fine indeed. Your skin is soft, your eyes are bright…'

Her teeth were good, and her coat glossy. Soon he would be extolling her good wind and her ability to take jumps at the gallop. Tony never wasted half so much time on pretty words. And yet she had no doubt that he found her beautiful. She felt the anger in her, rising to push out the fear.

'I will take great pleasure in loving you…'

And what was she to take from the experience? At

least Tony did not blather on about how much he would enjoy being with her, although he clearly did. He seemed most concerned with how she felt about it. This man was obsessed with bedding her, nearly insane with it.

'Come, let me show you.' He rose and offered her his hand, and gestured towards the door with his gun.

She looked at the hand held out to her. Tony might be dead already. And if that was true, there would be no last-minute rescue. But if he was dead, then it did not matter, one way or the other, what happened to her. She no longer cared, so there was nothing to be afraid of.

She looked at Barton. He had seemed so frightening, but he was a pathetic creature who could think no further than the bed in her room. She knew his weakness, and she could exploit it to her advantage.

'Very well.' She took his hand and he escorted her towards the stairs, a pace behind, with the gun in his pocket. She turned as they were halfway up. 'And you intend to be gentle?'

'Of course.'

She allowed a small disappointed sigh to escape her lips.

Behind her, on the steps, she heard the slight hesitation in his step.

She paused again. 'Robert was always very careful, when we were together. I assumed that it was the fault of age. Tony, as well, treated me as though I were made of glass.' She turned to look back at Barton. 'Some day, perhaps I will find someone who is not afraid to give me what I want.' She glanced back at him and saw the avaricious glimmer in his eyes.

'You do not wish me to be gentle?'

'Let me be plain, Jack. You are a cold-blooded brute and I detest you. But perhaps I have had my fill of gentleman lovers. You mean to have me and I cannot stop you. But if you must, then do not bore me with talk of gentleness.' She turned back to him on the stairs and kissed him, biting his lip.

She heard the intake of breath as she released him and watched his eyes go dark. He hurried the last few steps to draw even with her, pushing her back against the wall to kiss her hard in return.

She moaned convincingly back at him, tangling her hand in his hair and running a hand down his spine.

He pulled away again, smiling at her in surprise. And then his gaze turned suspicious. 'If this is a trick, I will make you pay for it.' But she could see in his eyes that he wanted to believe her.

'You mean to make me pay, no matter what, Jack. There is nothing left to threaten me with.' She walked the last few steps to her room, stepped inside and closed the door behind them.

He was on her as soon as the door was shut, shoving her against the wall, his fist in her hair and his mouth on hers. She felt his hands gripping her shoulders and fumbling at the front of her gown for her breasts.

Neither hand held the gun.

She made as if to hold him about the waist, then plunged her hand into his pocket to seize the pistol and point it into his ribs.

It took a moment for him to recognise the feel of the metal barrel in his stomach, and stop molesting her. 'Constance!'

'Step away from me, Jack. And do not make any sudden movements. I do not know much of guns, but I seriously doubt that I will miss you, should I shoot.'

'Yes, Jack. Do step away from her. For if she does not want to shoot you, I most assuredly do.'

Tony's voice startled her so much that she almost dropped the gun.

Seeing her indecision, Barton made a lunge for the weapon only to come up short, as Tony grabbed him by the coat collar and yanked him away from her, and back into the room. Barton tripped and landed hard on the floor, momentarily dazed.

'Constance, if you don't mind?' Tony held out a hand for the gun, and she gingerly handed it to him.

He pointed it at Barton, and confided, 'I really don't know much more about weapons than you do, but I should hate to see you kill him, no matter how much he might deserve it. If either of us must shoot, let it be me.'

'You're all right,' she breathed, leaning back to let the wall support her weight.

He reached over and yanked hard on the bell pull to summon the servants, and glanced apologetically at Constance, before focusing again on Barton. 'I fear, darling, that I cannot keep my presence here a secret. I will need help removing this refuse from your room.

'You will never believe the night I've had. First a greased drainpipe. Then a handful of broken glass. And when at last I get the damn safe open, there is no sign of the plates.' He shook his finger at Barton.

'You thought you had me there, I'll wager. And perhaps, if you were decent to your servants, they'd have bothered to clear the evidence of the true hiding place out of the grate.' He pulled a burned scrap of paper from his pocket, and held it out for Barton to see. 'You burned a book, didn't you? Two, actually. Volumes one and two of *A History of British Currency*.'

He glanced at Constance again. 'That is Jack's idea of wit, darling. Let us be glad you will not have to suffer with it. He ripped the books from their bindings and burned them, then wrapped the plates in the book covers and put them back on the shelves. I have spent countless hours, fiddling with picks to crack that safe, and all for no reason. The plates were in plain sight and I could have left with them at any time.'

There was a sharp knocking at the door and Constance rushed to let the servants enter. Susan entered, in her night clothes, accompanied by...

Constance stared in shock. Tony's valet, Patrick, hair mussed and in his shirtsleeves, had followed her maid into her bedroom.

Even Tony looked surprised.

Patrick shrugged. 'I recognised the pull on the bell rope. You ring as if you are trying to yank it off the wall. Most distinctive, sir.'

'And you happened to be here, by fortunate coincidence?' Tony enquired.

'With you spending so many evenings from home, I had little to occupy my time. And it occurred to me that there might be another who would sympathise with my idleness.'

Susan giggled.

Tony struggled to find an appropriate response, before giving up. 'Well, you will not be idle tonight.' He pointed to Barton on the floor. 'Patrick, I wish this removed. From the room, certainly. From the country, if possible. I understand there are often ships in need of crew and none too particular about where the men come from. Use your initiative.'

Patrick looked at Barton, and back to the maid beside him. And he said softly, to Susan, 'This is the man who hurt you?'

Susan's eyes grew round, and she nodded her head.

Patrick's smile was broad and full of menace. Suddenly, he did not look like a humble manservant, but a large, and very threatening, man. He seized Barton from off the floor and punched him once, hard and in the face. 'No problem, sir.' He dragged the limp body towards the door.

'Breakfast will be late tomorrow, Patrick,' Tony called after him. 'Do not trouble yourself.'

'Very good, sir.'

Susan stepped out of the way and closed the door again.

Tony listened to the sound of Patrick and Barton retreating down the hall, before stepping close and seizing her around the waist. Then he spun her around in his arms, kissed her once, full on the mouth, and threw her on to the bed.

He was alive. Young and strong and safe. And she loved the feel of his hands on her, even as her mind struggled to sort out what had just happened. She pulled herself up to lean upon her elbows, trying to regain decorum. 'Tony, what the devil are you doing?'

He was standing over her with a most curious expression on his face, a mixture of joy and lust. 'Celebrating. You are safe, and Barton is in the soup. And I have done it, Constance. I have picked the unpickable Bramah lock. What say you to that?'

'Thank you?' she said, hesitantly.

'Actions speak louder than words, Constance.' And he climbed into bed after her and threw up her skirts.

'You do not mean…' She reached to smooth her skirts back down.

'Oh, yes, I most certainly do.' He caught her hand, and placed it on the front of his breeches, so she could feel how ready he was. Then he began to undo his buttons.

She had just threatened to shoot a man, after attempting to seduce him, and now, she was going to make passionate love to another. If she looked into the mirror, would she recognise the woman she saw? 'Do not be ridiculous. I cannot. I am still dressed. The door is not locked. I—'

He pushed her down on to the bed, kissing her in a way that left no doubts as to how much he wanted her, and how soon.

'Well, at least take off your boots,' she suggested breathlessly, recognising the old familiar Constance, trying to regain control.

He ignored her.

And the woman that she had become did not care in the slightest. He came into her fast and hard, and she arched as the shock of it ran through every nerve in her body and hummed in her blood. And as he thrust, he told her of things he wanted to do to her, and with her, and for her, each one more scandalous than the last.

And she wanted it all. She wanted his breath on her throat and his voice in her ear, and his body hard inside her for ever. But for now, she wanted him harder and faster, and she told him so over and over again until her breath was a gasp and her voice a sob and her body was trembling with the need for release. And when he demanded it, she came with him, and they collapsed, shaking with weakness, into a tangle on the bed.

He moved against her and she caught her breath in surprise as her body shuddered again, and he rolled away so that he could look into her eyes, reached a hand to her and stroked her to another climax.

And somewhere, deep down, her brain was screaming that this was madness, and it must stop. What had she just promised him? And what could he make her do, when he took her to this state? He knew her body, and he used his knowledge. She was helpless to resist him because it was all too good, and the waves ran through her again as she trembled at his touch.

She looked into his eyes. They were not empty, like Barton's, but full of shadows. He looked into her soul and he knew her. But who was he?

She sat up and looked around her in confusion. She was lying fully dressed in her bed with a strange man, whose boots were leaving mud on the sheets. And he'd just taken her so violently that her body ached, and then soothed the ache away with his hand.

And he'd done it all because she begged him to.

Now, he was undressing her with exquisite care, undoing her gown and removing her stays, pausing to touch and kiss with featherlightness in ways that he knew pleased her. And now he was taking the pins from her hair and letting it down, combing it out with his fingers.

He knew every inch of her. He knew her life and her finances, and her body, all the intimidate details that she'd never dared share with Robert…

Why had she told him? And why had she not told her husband? Who had she become, now that she'd chosen to fall from virtue with such wanton abandon? Because she certainly was no longer herself.

And who was he? What did she know of him, other than that he was a thief, and that he said she could trust him?

And that he loved another.

He was still fully dressed, and she was naked beside him with her hair free around her shoulders. He was smiling his enigmatic smile as he admired her in her vulnerability.

She pulled the sheet around herself before she let him pull her down beside him and love her again.

He looked at her curiously, waiting for her to speak.

'It is truly over, then, with Barton?'

'He would be a fool to remain in the country, even if Patrick allows him to. I will turn the plates over to the Earl of Stanton in the morning, to be destroyed. If Barton reappears, St John will have no trouble hanging him as a traitor. You need never worry about him again.'

He might as well have been speaking nonsense.

'You spoke of the plates before. What are they? And what does St John Radwell have to do with it all?'

Tony pulled away from her, and puzzled for a moment, before saying, 'Ah. Yes. I'd meant to tell you about that. Barton was a counterfeiter. Or wished to be. And St John works for the government, and they wanted the plates back, so he hired me to steal them.'

'So you are not a thief at all.'

'Well, I am still a thief. A very good one. But currently, I steal when I am ordered to, by a higher authority.' He grinned. 'Perhaps I am a humble civil servant. I quite like the idea. It sounds most respectable.'

'Then why did you not tell me?'

He looked evasive. 'Frankly, it had not really occurred to me that there would be a difference. Stealing is stealing, and I have not much concerned myself with the reason. St John does not wish me to discuss our association, since the world knows little of what he does, and to reveal my part in it reveals his.'

'So you are a spy, then.'

He thought about it. 'I suppose you could say that.'

The truth began to dawn on her. 'When I found you here, in this room, you were spying on me. And my best friend's husband sent you. Because he thought I was a traitor. Just like Barton.'

Tony tried to laugh, but it came out sounding small and nervous. 'I soon set him straight on that. The very first night, I told him you were innocent.'

It was some consolation, she supposed, to know that he thought she was innocent, even though he continued to spy upon her. 'And this great secret, which you could not share with me to spare my feelings. Is that the only secret? Or are there other things that you have not told me?'

He looked positively uncomfortable, and had trouble meeting her gaze. 'Well, everyone has secrets, I suppose.'

'But you have more than most, I think. What is it that you are still not telling me, that makes you so evasive now?'

He attempted to laugh again, and failed completely. 'You make it sound very ominous. I swear, I was not attempting to hide things from you.'

'But you have hidden them all the same. I do not like being played for a fool, Tony. Not by my friends, and not by you.'

He flinched at the word 'friends' and then looked her squarely in the eyes. 'I do not think you a fool, nor do I wish to play games with you. But I wish, Constance, that by now you would have looked with your own eyes and known the truth for yourself.'

'So that you did not have to admit to it? What is it, that is so horrible that you cannot speak it out loud? You had the gall to offer me marriage, and yet you cannot manage to be honest with me.'

'Perhaps it is because I knew how you would respond, should I tell you the whole truth. It is quite plain, Constance, that whatever you might pretend, on the subject of love you are as cold hearted as any woman in my experience. It was a hundred times easier for me to steal your heart than it would have been to gain it by honest means. If I came to you and presented my case openly, with the rest of your suitors, you would have dismissed me as unworthy of your time and gone after Endsted and his title.' He was able to laugh again as he mocked her. 'But it excites you if I approach in darkness and you let me take what I want from you.'

Then he touched her skin, and her body responded with a shudder of passion. 'You want what I can give you,' he said, 'but you wish to be free of me when the sun rises, in case there is a better offer. And I let you use me, because, God help me, I cannot resist you.'

'I was using you, was I?' She looked down at her bare body, next to his. 'When you threw me down and took me, just now? Of course, you did manage to get rid of Barton for me. Although you said before that you did not wish to wait for payment, until after the deed was done, I should think, after tonight, that our accounts must be close to even.'

'And now you are trying to tell me that you behaved thus just so that I would help you?' He stared at her in disbelief. She could see the pain in his eyes. 'Why are you doing this, Constance?'

'I do what I must to survive, Tony. I did when I married Robert, and I must continue doing so, now he is gone. I am beautiful, or so everyone tells me. If that is all I bring to a marriage, then I must hold out for the best offer. Soon the beauty will fade, and, if I am not careful, I will be left with nothing.'

'Just as you were when your husband died?' His smile was sardonic. 'A pity. For he seemed such a good choice and it all came to naught.'

'Do not dare to question my marriage, you—'

'Thief? Criminal? Commoner?' He got out of the bed and did up his breeches. 'Guilty on all counts.' He turned and bowed to her, tugging his forelock. 'And now you no longer need my services, am I dismissed, your Grace?'

It was over. His business was completed, and he was leaving, unless she could think of a way to stop him. But she was not sure she wanted him to stay, if she could not trust him to tell her the truth. 'Well, you didn't think it would last for ever, did you?' She heard the quaver in her own voice, and wondered if she needed to speak the words to herself.

'No, actually, I didn't. In my experience, happiness seldom lasts for long. But I thought when we parted, you would not need to convince yourself that you had been coerced. Do you need me to be the villain of the piece? Does it make you feel better to think you had no choice?'

He stepped closer and she shrank from him, pulling the bedclothes up to cover her nakedness.

'Let me tell you the way I remember what happened. I came to your bed because you invited me there. You wanted *me*, your Grace, because you knew what I could do for you, and it had nothing to do with money or deeds. You wanted me to love you as your husband could not.'

Even as he said it, she could feel the need burning inside of her.

'Now you are going to pretend that while you writhed in ecstasy beneath me, it was because I was forcing you to make a noble sacrifice to preserve your reputation for someone more suitable.'

He reached to his throat and ripped off his cravat and threw it to the floor. Then, he opened his shirt and pointed. 'See there? These are the marks of your kisses on my throat. Your nails have raked my back and your hands have held me so tight that my arms are bruised. I've heard every word you've said to me, when we made love. I know what you felt.

'Perhaps there is already another player waiting in the wings. Someone with a title, or money honestly come by. Someone you can introduce to your friends.'

She watched as he stepped towards the door of her room, preparing to walk out, only to check himself, curse, and turn as usual to leave by the window. 'He can be the one to ruin your reputation. For I suspect the next man to share this bed will think nothing of arriving at night and leaving by the front door in the morning for all to see.'

He reached into his jacket and dropped a card on the floor. 'If you need further assistance, go directly to my man of business. There will be funds for you, should you ever need them. What I have is yours to command. You need never speak to me again, so there will be no misunderstanding of my motives. As I told you before, I do not expect payment for acts done in friendship. But do not ever claim again that you need do something against the wishes of your conscience, because of a lack of funds.'

And he walked across the room and stepped out of the window and out of her life.

Chapter Seventeen

Tony woke as the earth tipped out from under him, and he landed face first on the floor of the study.

'Rise and shine, Smythe.' Stanton's voice was disgustingly cheerful as he dropped the wing chair with a crash, next to Tony's prone body.

'What the devil… You bastard!' Light came streaming in the windows as his visitor yanked aside the velvet curtains. The sunlight was blinding, stabbing into his brain, as he tried to focus on the figure in silhouette against the morning sun.

'And a pleasant good morning to you, as well. You missed our regular appointment. Twice. To prevent your missing it a third time, I have come to you.' St John stared down at him in bemusement. 'I have seen better things than you stuck to the bottom of my boot after a night in Whitechapel. And smelled better as well. For God's sake, man, pull yourself together. There is work to be done.'

'I resign.'

'I am not totally sure that that would be permitted. While you have not technically enlisted, I might still find a way to court-martial you. Perhaps not. Thieves in the army are usually flogged or hanged. Do you have a preference?'

'Why don't you just shoot me and get it over with?'

'Very well, then.' And before Tony could process the action, St John produced a pistol and put a bullet into the wall next to him.

Tony rolled to the left, covering his head with his hands as the sound of the shot echoed in his ears. 'What the hell are you doing in my house, firing a weapon? Are you mad? The ball missed my head by inches. You could have killed me.'

St John righted the wing chair and sat in it, arms folded. 'The ball missed you by several feet, just as I intended. I am an excellent shot, especially at such close range. But I am pleased to see you have recovered the will to live.' He gestured to the wreckage of the room. 'And the ball in the woodwork is the least of the problems here. Explain this, please.'

Tony looked at the mess he had made of the room. The mirror was broken, and Patrick had not bothered to replace it. It was just as well, for he had a fair idea of what he must look like after who knew how long without a razor or change of linen. He did not need to see his reflection.

Broken glasses littered the cold fireplace, and empty bottles littered the floor. Patrick had continued to bring the bottles for a while, after refusing him glasses, and hiding the windows behind the curtains so as to remove temptation. And now he refused him brandy, hoping to starve him out. It had made Tony so angry that he'd thrown a small table at the head of his retreating servant.

And missed. He glanced at the chipped plaster of the wall and the pieces of broken table on the floor below it. 'When you came, did I still have a servant to let you in?'

'Yes. Patrick is most concerned about you. He sent me up alone and told me not to turn my back on you if there was anything left for you to throw. Now tell me, what happened to this room?'

'A woman,' Tony said with finality.

'On the contrary, my man, I think it was you who did it.'

'A woman happened to me, you idiot. And I happened to the room.'

'What a relief. I thought it might be serious. Get yourself a bath and a shave and another woman. And then get back to work.'

'There are no other women. None but her,' Tony said sourly.

St John sighed. 'May the good Lord spare me from melodrama. Are we all to suffer for your broken heart? Her Grace the Dowager Duchess of Wellford was miles above you, in case you hadn't noticed. I don't see why—'

'How did you know?' Tony demanded.

'Let me see.' St John tapped his chin. 'Perhaps it is because I am a spy, you moron. I set you to watch her. You were nervous when I suggested it. You have been distraught since the moment the project was completed. And you look like a gaffed flounder whenever I mention her name. As I was saying, the Dowager Duchess? I am most relieved to find that she had no part in any of this. She is a lovely girl. A favourite of my wife's. What I'd have told Esme if I'd had her friend arrested for treason, I cannot say. And they are both quite angry with me for my part in this, although I expect to find forgiveness in time.

'Tony…' his tone became quiet and sympathetic '…Constance is charming, pleasant and totally out of your league. Far be it from me to let the cold light of day into your tragic fancy. While you have enough money to support a wife and a brood of little Smythes in sufficient comfort, I would suggest you choose a woman who is not a renowned beauty, accustomed to a thirty-room mansion and a coronet. Unless you wish to spend the rest of your life tossing furniture against the walls of a darkened room.'

Tony sat on the floor, trying not to notice the shambles he'd made of his life. He'd held on to the dream for so long that it had seemed quite natural, when the moment came, to have Connie fall eagerly into his arms. He'd had no trouble believing what he'd wanted to believe, that there was much more to it than there actually had been. He'd been a glamorous diversion, and an answer to so many of her problems, that she had succumbed to temptation, only to regret it later.

Perhaps, if he had taken time to court her, instead of simply seducing her, she'd have taken the whole thing more seriously. Perhaps not. It was a bit late to un-ring that particular bell.

And now Stanton was staring at him, waiting for a response. If he did not think of her, or the last few weeks, or any of the foolish assumptions he'd had over the last thirteen years… If he could focus on the task immediately in front of him, he would be able to move forwards, and put some space between himself and the whole situation.

He pulled himself up to his feet, leaning on the corner of the mantel. He could feel the brandy still fogging his brain and muffling the sound of his last argument with Constance, as it echoed endlessly in his head. Perhaps, if he had something to do with his time and kept very busy, he could ignore it all together.

Perhaps he would fall off an ivy trellis or out of a window somewhere and never have to think of anything again. But he could not stay locked up in his rooms, alone with the knowledge that the dream that had sustained him for many lonely years was over.

He brushed imaginary dust from his stained shirt, and lifted a stubbled chin to his guest. 'Very well, then. I've made an ass of myself, and you have seen it. But the worst of it is over, I think. If you still wish to employ me, then give me time to bathe, shave and change. And then tell me what you want taken.'

St John smiled as if nothing unusual had occurred. 'Good man.'

'Susan, you know I don't take milk in my tea.'

Her maid looked at her with guilty eyes. 'I thought perhaps, your Grace, you might wish to try something more fortifying. Now that autumn is here, I mean. It wouldn't do to take a chill.'

'Fortifying.' She looked at the tea. It was wretched stuff, but Susan was right. It was probably more nourishing. She took a sip.

Susan added, 'If you are not feeling well, your Grace, there is a lady in Cheapside that sells certain herbs. And when brewed up in a tea, these tend to clear up the sort of malady that you might be coming down with.'

'No!' Her hand went instinctively to cover her belly. She relaxed. 'I am sorry, Susan. I did not mean to shout so. You were right the first time to put milk in my tea. No matter how I might complain, it is good for me. And perhaps an egg and a bit of dry toast. Could you bring it to my room? I do not feel like going downstairs until I am sure that I will not be sick.'

There was no point in pretending any more with Susan, who knew her cycle almost as well as she did herself. She was two months gone with child.

'Very good, your Grace. But…' Susan left the statement open. She dare not ask the question, but she wanted an answer, all the same. Something must be done. They must leave London and retire quietly to the country where she could have the babe in secret. Or she must take the herbs and end it.

'Please, Susan. A little breakfast, perhaps.'

'Very good, your Grace.'

Her maid left the room, and she turned to the window, staring out into the garden. The trellis below her was bare, and she could see that it had been as if she had installed a ladder to her bedroom window. The garden gate and wall were still an easy climb, although the garden had less cover than when it had been in full bloom.

She closed her eyes, trying to imagine him making his way across it. It wouldn't happen, of course. She had seen nothing of him for a month and a half. Even when she had gone out in public, the most she'd heard was someone mentioning that Anthony Smythe had just been in attendance, but had retired early. Or was expected, but seemed to be late.

He was avoiding her. And she could hardly blame him.

Fortunately, other men were not. Endsted had returned, and renewed his attentions with a kind of plodding respectability that rekindled her hopes for the future. And other, more eligible, men were more respectful, now that Barton was no longer warning off suitors and spreading rumours about her.

Of course, in a few short months, everyone would know that the rumours were true. If she wished to marry well, she needed to act quickly to put an end to the pregnancy. It was just as her own mother would have told her to do, had anything stood between her and her goal.

And it was the sensible thing to do, she reminded herself. She had proved her fertility to herself, at least. She could hint to any man who showed serious interest that she had reason to believe the problems getting an heir were her late husband's and not her own. She could find another peer, and resume her status in society. She could have her comfortable old life back. But this time she might have children, as well as a husband.

She wrapped her arms around her stomach. Or she could go to Tony, and never be content again. She would spend her life alternately terrified by his job, and frustrated by his carefree attitude about the risks and his unwillingness to share everything that was in his heart or his mind. She might never have his full heart, and perhaps some day he would leave her to chase the dream woman he longed for. But when he came to her at night, she would have his undivided attention.

And she would not have a family in the future. She would have the baby she'd always wanted. The one that was growing in her now would be warm in her arms in a few months, smiling up at her, with his father's smile. And no matter what might happen, she would love them both with her whole heart, for how could she help but do otherwise?

Susan returned with the tray, setting it gently down upon the bed.

'Thank you, Susan. I am sure that I will feel much better after a little breakfast. And I will not be wanting any herbs.' She looked at her maid. 'I have waited too long for this. No matter what, I will not end it.'

Susan looked at her with pity. The poor abandoned duchess and her bastard. How could she explain that it was only pride keeping her from doing what she had promised?

Pride and the whirlwind of emotions that caught at her, every time she looked at the future. She had thought it would be easier to send him away than to keep him close. But life without him was every bit as hard as life with him had been.

She had told him it was over, and she'd regretted it the moment the words had been out of her mouth. She had finally managed to make him angry. He had shouted so. And his words had been so bitter. It was not, as she had expected, the cavalier agreement that the time had come to part. She had cut him to the heart in one stroke.

She'd cut herself as well. She had stood, frozen, watching him go. Wanting to call him back, even as he stepped through the window.

Every night since, she'd thought of him, burning hot and cold, with desire, or remorse, or longing, or the strange sensations coursing through her body that she had come to know as pregnancy.

She was having his child. Even better, their child. She could no more end it than she would end her own life. To be able to have something so precious, a gift that he had not wanted to give her, for fear that it would ruin her. Even then, he'd cared more for her reputation than he did his own pleasure. He'd left a bit of himself behind for her to keep, after vowing that he would protect her, and the babe, if it came to that.

He had never said he loved her. But did she really need to hear the words, if he would behave thus?

How could she have been so blind? He might not love her with the grand passion she wished, but he cared for her in all the ways that mattered.

She loved him, with a dizzying, soul-wrenching intensity that was nothing like the warm glow she had felt for Robert. And doubted that she could bring herself to marry another, no matter what Tony might feel for her.

Constance reached beneath her pillow for the strip of linen, hidden there. A man's cravat, carefully folded, hidden where she could touch it, when the night was dark and she was feeling most alone. If she could bring herself to admit that she had been wrong, and persuade him to forgive her, she might never be alone again.

'Susan,' she called. 'Lay out my clothes. I am going out.'

Chapter Eighteen

Patrick announced her, and she entered the study more hesitantly than she had the last time she'd needed a favour from him. She was dressed differently as well. Where she had come to seduce before, today she was attired modestly: the low square neck of her bodice filled with a fichu, the skirt of the dress cut so that it revealed nothing of the changes already taking place in her body.

Tony was sitting at his desk, papers spread out in front of him, but he rose as she entered. She thought she detected a rush in the movements, as though he was caught off guard and took a moment to control his actions, before she noticed. 'Your Grace?'

He gestured her to the chair in front of the desk and then seated himself again. 'To what do I owe the pleasure?' There was no trace of irony in his voice. There was no emotion of any kind.

'Do I really need a reason to visit, after what we have known together?'

He looked at her. 'In a word, yes. It has taken me several weeks to recover from our last discussion, and I have no wish to be unnecessarily reminded of it.' He was staring at her body. 'Unless...'

'I have come to say that I am sorry.' She hung her head.

He looked at her with concern. 'Your Grace, you are white as a sheet. A drink, perhaps?' He turned to the decanter on the desk and his glass next to it, and sighed. He finished the contents in a gulp. Then he wiped the rim and poured her a small brandy.

She found it an oddly fastidious gesture, from one who had known her so intimately. She took the glass, sniffed at the brandy, and felt her stomach roll. She set it down untasted. 'I was wrong to leave you with the impression that I viewed your visits as unwelcome, or that I felt them to be a duty or an obligation, or anything that might be construed as a repayment of debt.'

'Thank you,' he said softly. 'That is something, at least.'

'It was just that, with the threats and the stress of the debts, and not knowing how to go on, I was not myself.'

His gaze was flat and sceptical.

'I am normally a most proper and respectable person,' she continued. 'Although you would not know it by my behaviour when alone with you. Had it not been for circumstances, I am sure I would never have behaved as shamelessly as I had, or as abominably as I did in ending it.'

He rose. 'And now you have quite undone any good you did before. If you wish to discount your behaviour with me as an aberration, then it is better we remain apart to avoid disappointment. If we are together again, either you will be horrified by your continued deviance, or I will be crushed by the lack of it. Please leave me, now. Unless...' he stared at her '...there is any other reason for you coming here.'

She was afraid to meet his gaze. 'There is another thing. I know that you made me promise to not trouble you on that account, but I cannot help it. While I am relieved to know that you do not steal for no reason, so much of your life is kept in secret. Have you never considered another career? I knew you would be angry, and that it is hardly a point of pride for me to intercede. But I have gone to my nephew, and enquired after a position for you. He needs a man of business to run his estates and prevent him from being as ninny-hammered as he was when he lost my house. And you are quite the smartest man I know.' She laid the sheet of parchment in front of him.

He glared up at her. 'You were enquiring after honest employment for me?'

'Yes, Tony.'

'Was there anything in our brief interaction that led you to believe that I might welcome a change of career?'

'Well, no, Tony.'

'And did I not specifically request that you never trouble me on the subject, and tell you that I had no intention to change for you or any other?'

She stared at the floor. She had promised. She had sworn to him that it would not matter, and, by asking, she was forswearing herself. She raised her chin to look into his eyes. 'I understand. I am sorry. It was not my place.'

He stared back at her and she felt her lip begin to tremble. She wished she could turn and run, and not say the rest of the words she would have to say, before this could be over. 'Tony.' She tried a small sip of the brandy, but it did nothing to improve her nerves.

He held out a hand for the paperwork. 'Do not look at me so. Give me the paper. I can at least read it, although I suspect you have heard my final answer on the subject.'

He took the papers away from her and sat back down at the desk, feet flat on the floor. Then he removed a pair of reading glasses from the pocket of his coat, brushed them absently against his lapel to clean them, and put them on. He leaned forward, resting his chin on his elbows, tossing his head to get the hair out of his eyes. 'No, no. This will never do. You'll have me counting sheep in the country for your half-witted nephew, so that you can have the comfort of knowing I lead a poor but honest life. It is not going to happen, no matter what your motives.'

And as she stared at him, the memory came flooding back to her. He had done the same in his house, and in hers, in chapel and in the library. She had always seen him thus, from the time he had learned to read, until she had left home and forgotten him. Anywhere that there was something to be read, she was liable to trip over him, polishing his spectacles and muttering over the paper. And some part of her mind assumed, should she go home, he would be there still, sitting under a tree in the garden, conjugating Latin and declaiming in Greek.

The brandy glass slipped from her hand and shattered on the desk. 'Eustace Smith.'

Without looking up he said, 'Connie, if you must insist on breaking the glassware, I'll leave you to explain it to Patrick. And I can assure you that I do not need menial employment, so you can take your offer with you. Or better yet, leave it and I will pass it on to my niece's new husband. Much more in his line, I think. He has a fine head on his shoulders, unlike your nephew the duke, and will soon have the estate put to right.'

'Eustace? It is you, isn't it?' She stood and planted her hands on the desk in front of him. 'Little Eustace Smith who used to live next door to me?'

When he looked up into her eyes, he was smiling, the smile of her lover, Tony Smythe. 'There was nothing little about me, even then.'

She swallowed hard at the memory of him.

'I have always been six months older than you, although you never noticed the fact. You were too busy dangling after my brothers, or the neighbours, or the duke.'

The words wounded her, for it made her feel like a fortune hunter, or, worse yet, the foolish young girl she had been.

'You were most interested in anyone else but me, as I remember it,' he reminded her.

Although the smile hid it, she could hear the pain in his voice, as though the wound was fresh. And perhaps it was, for she had been intimate with him, had loved him, and still not seen him for who he was.

'Oh, Eustace…' the name stuck on her tongue and she forced it out '…I am so sorry. So very sorry, not to have known it was you.'

He looked at her sharply. 'I have never favoured the name Eustace, nor has it favoured me.'

'But…but it is you, isn't it? To see you sitting there with your head in your hands, you are just as I remember you. Why didn't you say something?'

'So that I could listen to you dismiss me as "little Eustace"? Not a memory I needed to renew. Perhaps if you had recognised me. But there seemed to be no risk of that.'

She stared into his face as he peered at her from over his glasses and wondered how she could not have seen it. He looked very like his handsome older brothers.

She blushed to remember that she had been quite taken with the older Smiths. 'You do not wear your glasses any more?'

'I only ever needed them to read, and that was all I ever did, when you knew me last. Now I do so much of my work in the dark, glasses are really quite useless. It is easier to operate by touch.'

She blushed, remembering how good he was in the dark, when operating by touch. 'It was a very long time ago. And you are most different than you were.'

He sighed. 'And you are very much the same as I remember. Every bit as beautiful as when you left home. And still in search of a title. How goes the husband hunt?'

'Better than it had been, now that Barton is out of the way.' Her voice was a little tart. 'I have you to thank, for clearing the way for more honourable men.'

He looked tired. 'I would have removed Barton, in any case. But it pleases me you benefited from it.'

'So when you took the deed for me?'

'I was helping out an old friend.'

'And I am just an old friend to you?'

He looked at her long and hard. 'If that is what you wish. But I suspect that you came here for a matter more personal than friendship. Enough nonsense, Connie. I was right in my surmise, was I not? You were not to blame for the barren union at all.'

She shook her head.

'Have you come to torment me with the knowledge that by removing Barton, I have helped clear the path for some other man? Or do you need me, again? Have you come as you promised to? Come, out with it. What is the truth?'

She nodded. She needed him again, to fix yet another problem. He must be terribly tired of women in distress to look after and change one's plans for. He had just got free of his sisters, and now he would be saddled with her. And when she opened her mouth to speak, she sobbed.

He rose from behind the desk quickly and caught her in his arms. 'I am sorry that I spoiled your plans to catch another peer. I know you do not want me, and that I am not nearly good enough for you.' His voice was rough. 'But if you are carrying my child, I really must insist.' He swallowed, and when he spoke his tone was strong and confident again. 'Let me take care of you.'

'No.'

He stiffened against her.

'I am honoured that you will have me. But I am so sorry, Tony. So very, very sorry. I do not want you to have to take care of me, yet again. It is not fair to you, to never have what you want, but to have your future forced upon you by a foolish woman. Once you have married me, you need hardly take care of me at all. I will not be a bother. And I will do my best to take care of you.' She erupted in a fresh bout of tears.

'There now, do not cry.'

'I cannot help it. I cry at every little thing, I am sick in the morning, tired during the day, restless at night.' She sobbed into the wool of his coat. 'And I was afraid to come here, but afraid to stay away.'

'You have nothing to be afraid of, any more.' He was stroking her hair and holding her tight against him. 'Everything will be all right, if you will just say yes to me. Everything. I promise.'

'You warned me this would happen. But I wanted you, and I wanted a baby as well, no matter the consequences. And then I forgot all about the risks and wanted to feel what I felt whenever I was with you. I did not think what it might be like for the poor baby to have such a fool for a mother, or care that you would not want to marry.'

'When did I ever say that?'

'You said you loved elsewhere. And you would marry me for the sake of the child. I have been in such a marriage, Tony, and do not want another.'

'Were you so unhappy with the duke?' His voice was strange in her ear, shaky and hoarse. 'I always told myself that you were happy, and had what was best for you. And that I needn't concern myself.'

'After a fashion. I was fond of him, and he of me. We did comfortably together. And I did not love him, so it did not hurt so very much when he grew bored with me and visited with other women.'

'My poor darling.' He stroked her hair again.

'Now you will marry me, because you promised to. And I will be happy. I have always wanted children. Always. I will be very happy. And I will be a good mother, and a good wife to you.

'But some day you will say you are going to your club, but you will not come home. And I will lie alone in my bed, knowing that you have gone to her, and because I love you, but you can love only one woman, I fear it will break my heart.' She let loose with a fresh batch of tears.

He wrapped his arms even tighter around her, and waited for the sobbing to abate, passing her his handkerchief. 'You love me that much, do you?'

'Mnnnhmmm.'

'And you sent me away because…'

'It was foolish of me to fall in love with you. I could not keep you, and I could not control myself when you held me in your arms. I only ever felt alive when I was with you. The longer I kept you, the more I wanted you, and the more disgracefully I would behave to keep you with me, and the harder it would be to let you go. And it was already too late.'

The tears were ready to start again, but before they could, he kissed her and, for a moment, she forgot what it was that she was crying about.

'There, now. No more tears. Lay your head on my other shoulder where it is dry and comfortable, for the coat on the right is cried through to the shirt front.' He kissed her temple. 'Better?'

She nodded.

'Then I have a riddle. If I loved one woman my whole life, which is as long as I've known you, but she would look right through me if she saw me on the street, and she is as lovely and as far above me and un-attainable as you are yourself, and I have kept myself apart from matrimony, until now, hoping for a mira-cle, can you not guess the identity of my great undy-ing passion, the love of my life, the woman I would brave oceans and fight lions, and crawl in and out of three-storey windows to steal deeds for?'

She held very still, hoping he would just tell her what she wanted to hear. It couldn't be. But it must be, for he would never tease her so, if it weren't.

'And yet I was terrified to tell you the truth. I could not speak to you when we were children, and I could not speak to you now. There was only ever room in my heart for you, Constance. But if fate had not forced my hand, I might have been fool enough to let you marry someone else.'

She laid her hand on his arm and whispered. 'Do not think of it, again. Now that I have found you, there can be no other man for me, Anthony Smythe.' She fur-rowed her brow. It was not his true name, though she would always think of him thus. She tried again. 'I mean, Eu—'

He winced and covered her mouth with his fingers. 'Connie? Before you speak, let me warn you that it will spoil a lifetime of fantasy if you ever again call me by my given name. I did not take you to bed wishing to make you cry "oh, Eustace" loudly enough for the neighbours to hear.'

He had called her Connie. No one called her Connie any more. Not even Robert. But to her true friends she had always been Connie. She snuggled into the warmth of his shoulder, feeling safe, and it made her smile.

'If we have a boy, I'll hear no nonsense of naming him after his father. My mother fought to defend my brothers from that fate, but when it came to me, she no longer cared to be bothered, and let my father christen me Eustace Anthony after himself.'

'We will name him Anthony,' she murmured. 'After his father. It is a wonderful name. I am quite fond of it.'

'Very good.' He reached behind her knees and scooped her up into his arms. 'And now we will adjourn to the bedroom, where you can tell me that bit again, about how losing me would break your heart. Not that you ever will, of course.

'And perhaps later, we might go to Bond Street and choose a ring fitting worthy of a former duchess.'

'You needn't, really,' she whispered. 'Money is not important. If you truly love me.'

He laughed. 'I know, darling. And I would be only too happy to live on love, if I have you. But what shall

I do with the great stacks of money that I got off Barton? The safe did not contain what I was looking for, but it was full to the top with hundred-pound notes. Why did the fool want to print his own money, when he had a safe full of the stuff?' He shrugged. 'If he did not appreciate his wealth, I saw no reason to let him keep it.'

'You thief,' she said. But she was laughing.

And she raised her face to his, and let him steal another kiss.

Lady Folbroke's Delicious Deception

CHRISTINE MERRILL

To Dr Eugene Swanson and his helpful staff.
Thanks for taking care of my eyes.

Chapter One

While Emily Longesley could say with truth that she did not dislike many people, she had begun to suspect that she hated her husband's cousin Rupert. There was something in the way he looked at the manor when he visited that made her think he wished to measure it for furniture.

It was all the more annoying to know that he was entitled to his feelings of possessiveness. If she remained childless, the title fell to Rupert. And as the years had passed since her husband had abandoned her, Rupert's visits had grown more frequent, more intrusive, and he'd become more generally confident in the eventuality of his inheritance. Lately, he had taken to giving an annoying smirk as he'd asked after the health of her husband, as though he were privy to some bit of information that she was not.

It was even more bothersome to suspect that this

might be the truth. Although her husband's secretary, Hendricks, insisted that the earl was well, he was equally insistent that Adrian had no desire to communicate with her. A visit from him was unlikely. A visit *to* him would be both unwelcome and out of the question. Were they hiding something, or was her husband's dislike of her as transparent as it appeared?

Today, she could stand it no longer. 'Rupert, what is the meaning of that expression on your face? It almost appears that you doubt my word. If you suspect that Adrian is ill, then the least you could do is pretend to be sympathetic.'

Rupert looked at her with a smug grin that seemed to imply he'd caught her at last. 'I do not suspect Folbroke of illness so much as I begin to doubt his existence.'

'What utter fustian. You know perfectly well that he exists, Rupert. You have known him since childhood. You attended our wedding.'

'And that was almost three years ago.' He glanced around him, as though the empty air were some recent discovery. 'I do not see him here, now.'

'Because he resides in London for most of the year.' All of the year, in fact, but it would not help to bring that to the fore.

'None of his friends has seen him there. When Parliament is in session, his seat in the House of Lords is vacant. He does not attend parties or the theatre. And when I visit his rooms, he is just gone out and not expected back.'

'Perhaps he does not wish to see you,' Emily said. If

so, she had found one point of agreement with her absent spouse.

'I do not particularly wish to see him, either,' Rupert said. 'But for the sake of the succession, I demand to see some evidence that the man still breathes.'

'That he still breathes? Of all the ridiculous things you have said, Rupert, I think that this is the worst. You are his closest living relative. And his heir. If the Earl of Folbroke had died, you would have been notified of it immediately.'

'If you chose to tell me.' He was looking at her with a suspicious cat's gaze, as though he was sure, if he stared long enough, she would admit to a body buried beneath the floorboards.

'Of course I would tell you if something had happened to Adrian. What reason would I have to conceal the truth from you?'

'Every reason in the world. Do you think I cannot see how you are left in charge of this property when he is absent? The servants take their orders from you. I have seen the steward and the man of business come to you for their instructions, and caught you poring over the account books as though you would have any idea what to do with them.'

After all the time she had spent reading them, she knew perfectly well what to do with the accounts. And her husband had no problem with her taking them on, even expressing his approval of her management in the few curt communications that had come to her through

Hendricks. 'Since you are not yet the earl, why should it matter to you?'

Rupert's eyes narrowed. 'Because it is unnatural. I do not wish to see my inheritance squandered through the mismanagement of a woman. I have written to Folbroke frequently with my fears. Yet there is no sign of him coming to take control of what is rightfully his. He is here so seldom that he might as well be dead. And perhaps he is, for all you seem to care. You have arranged the running of the place to your own satisfaction, have you not? But if he has passed and you think can maintain a charade that there is a master here, you are sorely mistaken.'

Emily gathered her breath, trying to remain calm in the face of the bombardment. Rupert had always been a bit of a pill, but she had done her best to be kind to him, for the sake of her husband. Her even temper had been wasted on both Adrian and his ridiculous cousin, and her patience had reached its end. 'Your accusations are ridiculous.'

'I think not, madam. The last time I visited his rooms, the servants claimed he was indisposed. But when I forced my way in to search for him, I could find no trace.'

'If you abuse his hospitality and bully his servants, then no wonder he does not wish to see you. Your behaviour is beyond rude. The fact that you have not seen him does not indicate that I have not. How do you think papers of business for this estate are signed? I cannot sign them myself.' Actually, she found her forgeries quite credible. And what could not be forged was passed through to her husband's secretary and then returned to her. Though she knew Hendricks to be as devoted to her husband as he was helpful to her. While there was no proof that these papers were forged as well, she sometimes had her suspicions.

But Rupert had no faith at all. 'On the contrary, I have no doubt that you could and do sign documents. Should a miracle occur, and I receive a letter from your husband, I will have no proof that his hand was the one that wrote it.'

'And I suppose you do not believe me when I say that I have contact with him regularly.'

Her cousin laughed. 'Of course I do not. I think it is a ruse to keep me from what is rightfully mine.'

His surety in the emptiness of her marriage had pushed her temper to the breaking point. 'This estate is not yours. None of it. It belongs to Adrian Longesley, the current Earl of Folbroke. And after him, to his son.'

Rupert laughed again. 'And when are we likely to see an heir from your invisible husband?'

The idea struck suddenly, and she could not help but express it. 'Quite possibly in eight months. Although it is just as likely to be a girl. But Adrian assures me that in his family the first child is almost always male.'

This seemed to deflate Rupert, who sputtered his next answer. 'You are…are…'

'Increasing. Yes.' Now that the first lie was out, it emboldened her to continue in it. 'I did not mean to be so unladylike to broach the subject of my condition, but since you insist on trying me with baseless suspicions, I have no choice. And I would think carefully, were I you, to speak what is probably in your mind and hint that it is not my husband's child at all. If I hear so much as a breath of that, I will tell Adrian how you speak to me when he is away. And he will think nothing of family connections and run you through for spreading salacious rumours about me. He was in the army, you know. He is still a crack shot, and a dab hand with a sword. And very sensitive of my feelings. He would not wish me to be hurt.' The last was the biggest lie of all. But what did it matter, next to her imaginary baby?

Rupert's face was white mottled with red, and his lips twitched as though she had pushed him so close to apoplexy that his speech had failed. Finally, he managed, 'If this is true, which I sincerely doubt it is, then I hardly know what to say of it.'

Emily smiled, turning his sly looks back upon him. 'Why, my dear cousin Rupert, that is simplicity itself. The only thing you must say to me is "Congratulations." And then, "Farewell." Women in my condition tire easily. And, alas, I have no more strength to socialise with you.' She gripped him by the hand in a way that might appear fond were it not so forceful, and gave a forward tug, propelling him past her to the doorway of the salon and allowing his momentum to carry him out into the hall. When he was clear of the door, she shut it quickly behind him and leaned her shoulders against the panel, as though that were all it would take to block out any further visits.

It had been bad enough, at the beginning of the interview, when she had feared that she would have to produce her wayward husband. But now she would be expected to produce both him and an infant—and get Adrian to agree that he had fathered the child, whether he had, or not.

Or not. Now there was an interesting possibility. At the moment, she had no admirers to encourage in so passionate a way. And while she did not think herself unattractive, she suspected that there were some things that even the loyal Hendricks would not do in the name of maintaining the status quo.

But if Adrian had any interest in her continued fidelity, than he had best get himself home at least long enough to prove his good health, if not his virility. She had not heard a word from him in almost a year. Although the servants swore that they had seen him, they did it with the sort of worried expressions that told her something was seriously amiss. And they followed their avowals with equally worried assurances, similar to Hendricks's, that there was no need for her to go to London to see for herself. In fact, that would be the worst possible thing for her to do.

It was a woman, she suspected. They were trying to shield her from the fact that her husband had taken up permanent residence with someone else. He was willing to let his own wife and the chance at a family go hang for a mistress and a brood of bastards.

She tried to tell herself she was being both ridiculous and overly dramatic. Most men had arrangements of some kind or other, and wives who were content to ignore them. But as months had turned to years, and he paid no attention at all to her, it grew harder to pretend that she did not care.

And at the moment, her problems were concerned less with what he might have done, and more with what he had not. While it was difficult to be the object of such a total rejection, it became untenable when it damaged her ability to stay in her own home. In her three years of residence here, she had come to think of Folbroke Manor as rightfully hers. And if the fool she had married was declared dead because he could not be bothered to appear, she would have to yield it to that oaf, Rupert.

It would result in inconvenience and bother to all concerned.

Emily glanced at the desk in the corner, and thought of composing a sternly worded letter on the subject. But this matter was far too urgent and too personal to risk exposing it to another's eyes. If, as she expected, Hendricks read all of my lord's mail, she did not wish him to know that she had resorted to requesting sexual congress in writing.

And it would be even more embarrassing if the answer came in someone else's hand, or not at all. Or worse yet, in the negative.

All things considered, it would be far better to make a sudden appearance in London, camp out in Adrian's rooms, and await his return. Once the servants saw that she was in earnest, they would accede to her perfectly logical demand for an audience with her own husband.

When she saw him, she would tell him that either he must get her with child, or tell the odious Rupert that he still breathed so that the man would leave her alone.

Then they could go back about their business of leading separate lives. And he could pretend she didn't exist, just as he obviously wished to.

Chapter Two

For the first time in ages, Emily was in the same city as Adrian Longesley. Scant miles apart—possibly even less than that. Even now, he might be in residence behind the closed door, just in front of her.

Emily fought down the wave of terror that the prospect aroused in her, placing her palm flat against the rain-spattered window glass of the carriage, willing herself to feel as cool as it did. The nearness to Adrian was a palpable thing, like a tug on a string tied to something vital, deep inside her. Although she had felt it for most of her life, she had learned to ignore it. But it grew stronger as the carriage had reached the outskirts of London, an annoying tightness in her chest, as though she could not quite manage to catch a full breath.

With that lack of breath would come the weakening of her voice, the quiet tone and the tendency to squeak without warning. And, worst of all, it would be impossible to talk to him. When she tried to speak, she would stammer things out, repeating herself or pausing inappropriately in the middle of a thought, only to have the words rush out in a jumble. Even if she could manage to stay silent, there would be the blushing, and the inability to meet his gaze.

And since she was sure that he felt no answering pull on this magical bond between them, her behaviour would irritate him. He would think her an idiot, just as he had from the first moment they'd married. And he would dismiss her again, before she could explain herself.

When dealing with Adrian, she found it much easier to express herself with written communication. When she had the time to compose her thoughts, and the ability to toss any false starts and missteps into the fire, she had no troubles making her point.

And in that she was the very opposite of her husband. He had been clear enough, when he'd bothered to speak to her. But the few letters she'd received were terse, full of cross hatching, and in a hand so rough as to be practically illegible. She suspected it was drink that caused it. While easy to decipher, the latest ones came with a brief preamble, explaining that my lord was indisposed and had dictated the following to Hendricks.

She glanced at her reflection in the watery glass. She had improved with age. Her skin had cleared. Her hair was better dressed. Despite her rustication, she took care to outfit herself in the latest styles. While she had never been a pretty girl, she counted herself a handsome woman. Although she did not agree with it, it flattered her that the word *beauty* had been applied by others. She had also been assured that her company was charming, and her conversation intelligent.

But to the one man she'd always longed to impress, she could not manage to behave as anything other than David Eston's troublesome little sister. She was sure that it was only out of loyalty to his friend and family that Adrian had been willing to saddle himself with such a dull and graceless creature.

Before her, her own image dissolved as the coachman opened the door and put down the step for her, holding an umbrella over her head as he rushed her to the door, knocking for her.

The door opened and her husband's butler greeted her with an open mouth and a breathless, 'My Lady Folbroke.'

'No need to announce me, Abbott. If you can find someone to take my cloak, I will make myself comfortable in the salon.'

When no footman appeared to help her, she untied the neck and stepped forwards out of the garment, letting it drop from her shoulders.

Abbott reached forwards, hurrying to catch it before it struck the floor. 'Of course, my lady. But my Lord Folbroke—'

'Is not expecting me,' she finished for him.

At the end of the hallway, her husband's secretary appeared, took one look at her, and then glanced behind him as though he wished, like a rabbit meeting a fox, to dart back under cover.

'Hello, Hendricks.' She smiled in a way that was both warm and firm, and pushed past the butler, bearing down on him.

'Lady Folbroke.' Hendricks looked quietly horrified to see her and repeated, 'You were not expected.'

'Of course not, Hendricks. Had he expected me, my darling Adrian would have been shooting in Scotland. Or on the Continent. Anywhere but sharing London with me.' She tried a light laugh to show how unimportant it was to her, and failed dismally. She ignored the strange, sharp feeling in her stomach and the ache in her heart that came from knowing she was not really wanted.

The secretary had the courtesy to look shamed by it, but made no effort to deny what she had said.

'I suppose it is too much to hope that he is here at the moment.'

'No, my lady. He is out.'

'That is the same story you give to his cousin Rupert, who has been tormenting me endlessly on the subject of Adrian's whereabouts. I have had enough of it, Hendricks.' She stopped to breathe, for while her tone had sufficient volume, she did not want it creeping into shrillness. Then she continued. 'My husband must accept that, if he cannot deal with his heir, he will have to deal with me. It is unfair of him to avoid us both. And while I am quite willing to shoulder the responsibility of land, tenants, crops and several hundred-odd sheep while Adrian gallivants about the city, the added burden of Rupert is simply too much, Hendricks. It is the last straw to this camel.'

'I see, Lady Folbroke.' Hendricks had replaced his hunted look with an expression of neutral courtesy, as though he hoped that his silence would still her questions.

'My husband is still in the city?' She gave the man a critical look.

He squirmed and nodded.

She nodded in reply. 'And how long might it be until he returns here?'

The secretary gave a helpless shrug.

'Honesty, Hendricks. You know more than you are saying, I am sure. All I require of you is a simple answer. I intend to wait as long as is needed, in either case. But it would be nice to know if I should request a light meal, or send for my trunks and prepare for an extended stay.'

'I do not know, Lady Folbroke.' There was a kind of hopelessness in the statement that made her almost believe the man.

'Surely he must tell you his plans when he goes out.'

'When he bothers to make them,' the secretary said, revealing a bitterness that smacked of honesty. 'If he sets an agenda, he rarely keeps to it. Sometimes he is gone for hours. And other times days.'

'Then he must be letting rooms elsewhere.'

'This may be true. But I do not know where, for I have never visited them. And when he returns?' Hendricks shook his head, clearly worried.

'I suppose he is foxed.' She gave a disgusted sigh. It was no less than she feared about him, but the confirmation did nothing to improve her mood.

'If that were all. He is…' Hendricks struggled to find a phrase that would not give up a confidence. 'Not well. Unhealthy, my lady. I doubt he eats. Or sleeps. When he can bring himself to come home after one of these excursions, he collapses for days at a time. I fear he will do himself an injury through self-neglect.'

'His father was around the same age when he lost his life, was he not?'

'Yes, my lady. A riding accident.'

It was gently put, as was everything Hendricks said. The man was a master of understatement. But she remembered the circumstances quite well, for the severity of the last earl's injuries had been the talk of the neighbourhood. Adrian's father had been the worse for drink, and riding hell for leather through the woods, taking jumps that other men would not have risked while sane and sober. The fall had killed both man and horse in a way that was neither quick nor painless.

Her brother had said nothing of his friend's reaction when the accident had occurred. But she could remember clearly the solemn darkness of the young man on the neighbouring estate, and the way it had both frightened and intrigued her. 'Perhaps it preys upon his mind. And all the more reason that I should be here to put a stop to it.'

The secretary looked both doubtful and hopeful, as though he could not decide where his loyalty might lie.

'Summon the coachman who took him when he departed, so that we might learn his destination. If we can find his normal haunts, then I will search them until I find him.'

'You cannot,' Hendricks leaned forwards, and she knew the situation must be serious for the taciturn man was clearly alarmed.

'I mean to do it, all the same.'

The man stared into her eyes, as though to gauge the strength of her resolve. Then he sighed. 'I will accompany you.'

'That is hardly necessary.'

Hendricks squared his shoulders, doing his best to look formidable. 'I am sorry, Lady Folbroke, but I must insist. If you mean to continue on this unadvisable course of action, than I cannot leave you to do it alone.'

'And who gives you the right to question me?'

'Lord Folbroke himself. He has been quite clear to me in his instructions, with regards to you. I am to assist you in all things, trust your judgement and obey you as I would him. But first and foremost, he trusts me to keep you from harm.'

The sentiment brought her up short. After a year of silence on his part, it had never occurred to her that her husband thought of her at all. And certainly not for a sufficiently protracted time as to concern himself with her safety. 'He worries about me?'

'Of course, my lady. He asks after you each time I return from Derbyshire. Normally, I assure him there is no reason to be concerned. But in this case?' He shook his head.

Emily dismissed the momentary feeling of warmth

at the picture of Adrian asking about her. 'If my welfare is his foremost desire, perhaps he could have seen fit to share it with me. Or he could make an effort to stay out of low haunts himself. Then it would not be necessary for me to seek him in a place he did not want me to go.'

Hendricks was frowning at the twisted logic of her statement, trying to find a rebuttal, so she allowed him no more time. She turned to the butler. 'Abbott, have the carriage brought around. Mr Hendricks and I will be going out. We will be returning with Lord Folbroke.'

She glared at Hendricks. 'Whether he likes it or not.'

'You are sure this is the place?' The building before her gave every indication of being just what it was: a villainous hole that was well below the genteel debauchery she'd expected.

'Yes, my lady,' Hendricks said, with a grim smile. 'Of late, the servants bring him here. He finds his own way home.'

She sighed. There was a sign swinging above the battered door that appeared to be a woman of limited virtue, and even more limited clothing. 'What is it called, then?'

'The Whore's Left…' Hendricks coughed as though he could not bring himself to finish the name.

'Is it a brothel?' She peered out the window at the grimy glass panes in front of her, trying not to show the curiosity she felt.

'No, my lady. A public house.'

'I see.' It was nothing like the rather conservative inn

in their village. But things were very different in London, she was sure. 'Very well, then. Wait in the carriage.'

'I most certainly will not.' It was a moment before the secretary realised how completely he'd overstepped his bounds in his effort to protect her. Then he said more softly, 'I have been through doors like that one, and seen the clientele inside. It is a dangerous place for Lord Folbroke and even more so for a woman alone.'

'I do not mean to be there long enough to experience risk. If he is there, he will think the same as you, and though he might choose the place for his own entertainment, he will be forced to escort me out of it. But I do not mean to leave without him.' She set her chin in the way she did, to let the Derbyshire servants know that she was brooking no more nonsense, and saw the secretary weaken before her.

'If you find him, he might not be willing to go.' Again there was a delicate pause as he searched for a way around her orders. 'You might need my help.'

It was perfectly true. She had no reason to believe that her husband would listen to her entreaties, if he would not answer her correspondence. 'Would you remove him by force, if needed?'

Hendricks paused again. To take her side when in the presence of her husband would seem close to mutiny. He had been Adrian's aide-de-camp in the army, and had the fierce loyalty of a soldier to a superior officer to match his dedication to a friend and employer. But then he said, as though the confession was a thing he did not want to share, 'If the instruction came from you, and it was meant for his own good, I would do it. There are reasons for his aberrant behaviour, which you will understand soon enough. But if he is no longer able to act in his own best interests, then someone must do it for him.'

Emily touched Hendricks's shoulder to reassure him. 'Do not fear for your position. I promise you will come to no harm for doing what is right. But we must be agreed on this before we begin. I will ask him to come. And if he does not, you must help me remove him.'

'Very well.' He nodded. 'Let us do the thing quickly, now that we are decided. The situation cannot stand as it does much longer.'

They walked through the door together, Hendricks close at her shoulder. And Emily stepped back into him as she took in the room before her. The sound of drunkenness hit her first: laughing, fighting and ribald song. And then the smell—urine and vomit added to the smoke from a blocked chimney and burned meat to make the room even more unpleasant. She had expected to find Adrian in some normal gaming hell where the play was deep and the women were not ladies. Or perhaps a whorehouse where the play was of a different sort entirely. But she had assumed it would be the sort of place where lords went, when they sought to amuse themselves outside polite society.

There was no sign of even the lowest members of their set in evidence. This was a rough place full of even rougher men who had come to enjoy their vices with no care for the law of God or man.

Hendricks put his hand on her shoulder. 'We will take a table in the corner, out of the way of this mob. And I will enquire after him for you.' He led her to the corner, and a barmaid brought two mugs to the table with a sneer on her face. Emily glanced into hers to see that it was already filled. She smelled juniper.

Hastings placed a hand over her glass. 'The strength of the gin will not make up for the dirtiness of the glass.' He tossed a coin on the table. As the barmaid reached for it, he caught her by the wrist. 'The Earl of Folbroke. Do you know him? Is he here?' The girl shook her head, but he did not release her. 'Do you know an Adrian Longesley?'

'Addy?' She gave a single nod, and he let go of her arm, but his action had drawn the eyes of others.

The men who rose from the nearest table were hulking brutes, looking for any reason to fight. 'Here now, stranger. You have a dollymop of your own, do you not?' The one who spoke gave Emily a toothless leer.

'Aye,' said another. 'If you wish to share our Molly, then you must share as well.' Behind her, a man leaned close, and she inched her chair away.

'Now, see here.' Hendricks's gaze was steely, and his shoulders broad. Though she thought him timid when compared to Adrian, he had been a captain in the army, and she had no doubt that he would defend her honour to the best of his considerable abilities. But with so many against him, she doubted that his strength would do them much good.

And as she feared, when Hendricks started to rise, a fist to his jaw knocked him back into the chair.

She gave a little shriek of alarm as one of the men crowding the table reached for her. This had been a dreadful mistake. The place was horrible, the men were horrible, and what was likely to happen now would be the fault of her own stupidity. Even if her husband was here, she doubted she wanted to see him. If he were part of the crowd around her, he was most likely beyond redemption.

And then, as she gave another cry of alarm, a hand reached out through the press of bodies around her chair, seized her by the arm and pulled her forwards until she was crushed against the body of her rescuer.

Chapter Three

'Can't you see that she does not wish your company?' A silver-headed cane shot out, rapping one man upon the head and another across the knuckles. The men who were struck gave sharp cries of pain, and grumbled as their fellows laughed at their distress.

Emily wrapped her arms about the waist of the man who held her to keep from swooning with relief. She recognised the voice of her husband, and was more gratified to be close to him than she had been at any time since the day of their marriage.

'And you think she wants you instead?' a man called. There was a chorus of laughter from around the room.

'How can she not?' Adrian called back. 'I am the only gentleman amongst you.'

More laughter in response.

'And she is clearly a lady of discerning taste, if she has the sense enough to reject you.'

There was yet more laughter to this, and she could not decide if it was directed to Adrian, or to the fact that she had been called a lady.

There was a pause, as she wondered if he meant to answer the insults to her with anything more than jests. Then he turned her to face him.

He had changed, of course, but not so much that she could not recognise him. His coat was of good quality, but ragged and dirty. His neckcloth was stained and his dark brown hair needed combing. But he still had shockingly blue eyes, though they gave her little more than a sidelong glance. And there was the roguish smile that he shared with other women more often than he did with her. His body was just as strong and solid as it had ever been, so muscular that she felt dwarfed against him as he held her close. Frightened of being crushed, and yet still protected.

She could feel her nerve failing now that he was close, and the growing desire to sink into him, soaking in the warmth of his body as though immersed in the bath. What was around them did not matter. She was with Adrian. She would be all right.

And then he kissed her. On the mouth.

The suddenness of it shocked her. She had expected a distant greeting, and his customary slight frown, as though, even as he was saying hello, he was thinking of ways to say goodbye.

But he was kissing her. They were really kissing. And it was like nothing she had experienced before. He tasted of gin and tobacco, smelled of sweat, and his cheeks were rough with several days' beard growth. It was a sensory onslaught: a strange combination of the pleasant and the unpleasant. Joyful. Abandoned. And wet.

His kisses of the past had been unmemorable. Reserved. Flavourless and without texture. And much as she had wanted to feel otherwise, she had not liked them very much. He had been so careful to give no offence that he could not have enjoyed them either. Even in consummation, he had set himself apart from her, allowing no loss of self-control.

But today, in a crowded tavern, without asking her leave or showing a care to the men watching them, he devoured her mouth as he might a piece of late-summer fruit, giving a low *hmmm* of approval at the ripeness, the juiciness. He clutched her bottom through her skirts, and eased a leg between her parting thighs, giving her a small bounce there, to make sure that he had shaken her to the core.

And for a moment she forgot her anger with him and her fear. All the feelings of hurt and betrayal disappeared, along with the shyness she felt when she was with him. After all this time, he had decided he loved her. He wanted her. And if she could have him back, just like this, everything would be all right.

Then he pulled away and whispered in her ear, 'Here now, love. Nothing to be frightened of. Let us leave these brigands behind. Come and sit on my lap.'

'I beg your pardon.' The happy thoughts froze in her head, and cold logic returned to its proper place. The request was odd, and delivered in a way that showed a strange lack of feeling for his friend and servant, Hendricks, struggling back to consciousness in the chair in front of him.

Adrian gave her another small hug and a quick kiss on the lips to coax her. 'You may help me with my cards tonight. There will be a shiny sovereign for you, if you are good.' He said it as if he were talking to a stranger. There was no trace of recognition in that voice. No hint that this was to be a shared joke, or a lark or that he was trying to protect her from the ruffians by hiding her identity.

Was he honestly so drunk that he did not know her?

'Help you with your cards?' she said. The last haze of desire cleared from her mind. If he did not claim her as wife, then just who had he thought he'd been kissing? 'I should think you could manage them without my help, just as you normally do, my lord.'

The censure in her voice did not seem to register. 'You would be surprised, my dear.' He was whispering in her ear. 'It seems I need more help by the day.' He kissed her on the side of the head, as though to confirm to the others that he was whispering endearments, and then said more loudly, 'Since we are to be fast friends, you may call me Adrian.' And then he pulled her away from the crowd, stumbling back towards a gaming table on the other side of the room.

Emily struggled against him, trying to catch her breath long enough to argue that this behaviour was an insult worse than any she had yet borne. But he conquered her easily and sat down on a chair with his back to the wall, drawing her into his lap. And all the time he continued to kiss the side of her face and her neck, as though he could not get enough of the contact.

The feel of his lips, hot on her skin, made her anger seem distant and unimportant. If he could not overcome this sudden desire to touch her, then why should she? His body knew her, even if his mind did not. She arched her back and pressed her cheek against his lips, vowing that while they had differences to settle, surely it could wait a while longer...

And then he whispered in a calm voice, unaffected by the nearness of her, 'They will deal a hand to me, and you must read the pips on the cards into my ear. Pretend it is merely affection, just as I have done to you. Help me to know the cards that are played. And as I promised, you shall have your sovereign.'

'Pretend?' Was that all this was to him?

'Shh,' he whispered, lips still against her jaw. 'A guinea, then.'

Her anger returned. He was nothing more than she believed him to be: a drunken reprobate who could think no further than his own pleasure. And she was a fool who could not conquer the fantasies she had created around him, no matter how many times he showed his true face to her.

And with the anger came curiosity. He still did not know her. But it seemed his seduction was just as much a sham for the stranger he thought he held. He seemed to care more for the cards than he had for the kisses. And if that was true, his actions made no sense at all to her.

So she did just as he had requested, hoping the motive would become clear with time. He held her close as the hands were dealt, and she whispered a description of the play into his ear.

Emily watched the men across the table from her, certain that they must have some idea of what was going on, for they kept their eyes on her, and their hands tilted carefully towards them, as though fearing that she might be attempting to read what was concealed there.

But her husband did not seem to notice the fact, nor care what the others might hold. He greeted each new hand with a vacuous and unfocused smile, head tilted slightly to one side so that he might concentrate on the words she whispered in his ear.

As she watched, she began to suspect that it was not his smile that was unfocused. It was the look in his eyes. He looked not on her, or the cards before him—not even the men across the table. It was as though he were peering through the space around him, a little to the left, at some spot near the floor, expecting an invisible door would open a view to another place entirely. Was he drunk, or was it something far worse?

Despite his strange behaviour, his mind was still sharp. After a single recitation of information, he had no trouble keeping his hand straight, nor with bidding or points. He won more than he lost. And then he ran his hands once over the winnings heaped in front of him, conscious of any move to cheat him out of what should rightfully come to his side of the table, reaching for his cane and tapping it sharply on the floor to emphasise his disapproval, if what he found was not to his liking.

She saw the wary look that the men around them gave to that stick and its heavy silver head, and the speed with which they put an end to any mischief when Adrian reached for it. They seemed to view it and her husband not with fear, but with a sort of grudging respect, as though experience had taught them he was an opponent who would not be easily bested.

After a time, Adrian seemed to tire of play, shifting her on his lap as though he grew restless. 'Enough, gentlemen,' he said with a smile, pulling the money before him to the edge of the table and into a purse he removed from his coat. He gave a theatrical yawn and turned his head to hers again and said, 'I am of a mind to retire for the evening.' And then, 'If you would be so kind as to accompany me, I will give you the coin I promised.'

He pocketed the purse and his hand went back to her waist, and then up, stroking the underside of her breast through the fabric of her dress.

She gave a little yelp of alarm, embarrassed by his forwardness, and slapped his fingers away. 'Please do not do that.'

The men around them laughed, and she kept her eyes firmly on the table, not wanting to see what Hendricks thought of this public affront upon her person.

Nor did she wish him to see the flush of excitement on her cheeks. Though she did not want to feel anything from it, her husband's touch was arousing her. It was probably just as well that he did not know her. If he had, he would have stood up, spoken politely and taken her by the arm instead of the waist. Then he would have rushed her back to the country so that her presence in London would not have spoiled his fun.

Instead, she could feel the hardness beneath her bottom, and the way her denial of him had made his response more urgent. He buried his face in the hollow of her throat, inhaling deeply and licking once at her collarbone. 'I cannot help my reaction. You smell wonderful.'

'And you do not.' She shook him off, sitting up straighter, angered by his weakness and her own.

Adrian gave a sharp laugh, and it was honest mirth, as though he had not expected to be matched in wit by a doxy. He gave a sniff at his coat, as though gauging his own unpleasantness. 'Once I get out of these clothes, you will find I am not so bad.'

Although she doubted the fact, she nodded. It would be better to hold her temper for just a little while, for there was much that needed to be said, and she had no wish to do it in front of this rough audience. If she could get him to leave the place willingly, it would achieve her ends, and would be easier for both of them when difficult revelations had to be made.

He cocked his head to the side, not acknowledging her agreement, and so she said, 'Of course, Adrian. Lead the way.'

He pushed her bottom and slid her out of his lap, then stood and reached for his stick. And she noticed with a grim certainty that he did not lean upon the cane for sup-

port, nor swagger with it, as though it was a mere ornament. Instead, he used it to part the crowd around the
table, letting it tap idly along the ground as he walked.
And instead of going towards the front door and freedom, he walked farther into the tavern, towards the stairs
at the back of the room.

Emily pulled on his sleeve and said through clenched
teeth, 'My lord, did you not wish to leave this place?'

He took her arm, pulling her along with him. 'I have
let space here. It is easier, after a long night of play.' He
kissed her again, thrusting his tongue once deep into her
mouth, until her mind went blank. 'And much closer.'
When they reached the steps he put his hand on the rail,
sheltering her body between his and the wall. As they
started to climb, she turned back to Hendricks, who still
sat by the door, giving him a helpless look and hoping
that he had some wisdom or explanation to offer.

Instead, he gave a small shrug in answer, as though
to tell her that this was her plan, not his. He would wait
upon her orders to decide the next action.

So she shook her head and held up a staying hand,
hoping that he would understand that she meant to follow
Adrian, at least for now. There was no point in explaining
her identity to him in this crush. It would be embarrassing enough when they were alone.

It was then she saw a body breaking from the throng
below, running for the stairs. An angry loser from the
gaming table had waited until Adrian's back was turned
and was coming after them, his arm raised in threat.

Her husband cocked his head at the sound of running

footsteps on the treads behind them; without a word, he switched his stick to his other hand, turned and brought the thing down on the head of his adversary. Then he gave a shove backwards with it, knocking the other man off balance and sending him down the stairs.

'Idiot,' he muttered. 'I shall take my play elsewhere, if this is how they wish to behave here. What he thought to accomplish by that, I have no idea. He should know damn well that I am blind, not deaf.'

Chapter Four

'Blind?' She should not have been surprised, for it had been obvious as she'd sat with him that he could not read the cards in his hand, nor recognise his own wife, though she sat in his lap.

He smiled, not the least bit bothered by it. 'Not totally. Not yet, at least. I can see shapes. And light and dark. And enough of you to know that you are a more attractive companion than that blighter I just knocked down the stairs. But I fear that cards are quite beyond my scope.'

'But how?'

'You are a curious one, aren't you?' He climbed the rest of the stairs with her, opening the door at their head and leading her down the gloomy corridor behind it. 'It is a family condition, aggravated by a war injury. There was a flash, you see. And I was too close. Without that, I might have lasted a good long time with these tired old eyes. A lifetime, perhaps. Or perhaps not. Not all the men of my family have the problem. I understand that it can take some time before the world begins to go dark.'

'But I never knew.' And his family had lived beside hers for generations.

'A blind man?' He smiled, and turned suddenly, pushing her against the wall and pinning her hands above her head with his ebony walking stick. Then he kissed her again, more ardently than he had at any point in their brief time together. His lips were on her mouth, her cheeks, her chin, her throat. And she felt the delicious loss of control she'd felt when he kissed her below stairs, and nothing had mattered but the moment they were sharing. He sagged against her so that he could suck and bite at the tops of her breasts, where they were exposed above the neckline of her gown, as though he could not wait a moment longer to bare them, and take the nipples between his lips. It made her moan in frustration, arching her back, struggling against the wood that held her in place and kept her from giving herself to him. It did not matter that he could not see who he was kissing. It was Adrian, and he wanted her. And, at last, she would have him the way she'd always imagined, the way she had wanted him for as long as she'd known the reason for kissing.

He gave a slight buck of his hips so she could feel what their kisses had done to him. And she felt her own wet heat rising in response at the memories of hardness and length and welcome penetration, and the panting eagerness to be so possessed.

And then he said in a voice that was not nearly flustered enough, 'It is only the eyes that are the problem. The rest of me is quite healthy, I assure you. Once we snuff the candles, you will find me much like any other man.'

Like any other man? For her, there had never been another. But what was happening to him was so common he was barely affected by it. Her eyes flew open and she stared past his shoulder, aware of their shabby surroundings and remembering the reason that she had come looking for him. He had treated her abominably since the day they had married. And now, after a few kisses she had forgotten it all, willing to be used in a public hallway like one of his whores. 'Let go of me. This instant. Release my arms, you beast, or I shall scream to bring down the roof.' She struggled against his lips, against his body and against the stick that stayed her hands.

He stepped back and lowered his cane, a slight puzzled frown upon his face. 'Are you sure? There is a private room just down the hall. The door locks, and only I have the key. We will be all alone, with no fear of interruption.' He paused, and then his lips twitched into a coaxing smile. 'I can give you the guinea I promised. There is more than enough from the table tonight. You should know for you saw it. I can tell money well enough, one coin from another,' he assured hurriedly, as though assuming this might be the problem. 'They feel differently in weight and size. And as for the rest of it?' He stepped close again. And when she did not pull away he dipped his head and began to kiss her again, slowly working his way down her throat to settle on the hollow of her shoulder. Then he moved just enough so his lips were no longer touching her, then spoke and let his breath do the teasing. 'I have been assured that the reliance on other senses has made me an unusually observant lover. I particularly value touch in these moments, and use it to good advantage. And taste.' He licked with just the lip of his tongue, as though he were sampling her flavour.

Emily gave another dizzy shudder; she could swear that she felt that single lick to the very core of her body, making her imagine he was kissing her in a place that was most unlikely and very improper. And she wondered, would he be shocked if she suggested such a thing?

Or had he been doing that, and worse? He had been assured of his prowess, had he? *Assured by whom?* She buried her fingers in his hair, trying to pull him away, focusing on the last three years, the doubt, the loneliness, the anger. Had he been going blind, even from the first? Had he known when they married? Had he hurried to marry a foolish woman who was oblivious to his disability?

And what had he been doing since he left her?

Adrian gave a small grunt of pain from the tugging on his hair and lifted his face as if to gaze at her, but in the same sidelong way he looked at everything that told her he could not really see. 'The coin I offered is still yours, for services rendered at the gaming table. But now that we are above—' he gave a small shrug '—if you do not think it sufficient, I am open to discussion on the subject.'

She balled her fist and gave him a clout upon the ear. 'I am not a whore, you cloth-brained drunkard. And even if I was, I would not lie with you for all the money in the world.'

The blow did not faze him at all. And the insults made him laugh. But he released her with a bow. 'Then I apologise for my mistake, though I can hardly be blamed for it. If you are not a whore, then what are you doing in a place such as this?'

It was a fair question, and even she did not know the whole answer to it. At last she said, 'I was searching for someone.' She stared at him, willing him to recognise her. 'For my husband.'

'And I assume, since you are alone here with me that you did not find him?'

'No, I did not.' For the man before her, although right in appearance, was as far away from the man she'd thought she married as was possible. A little bit of her anger gave way to disappointment. And then she felt the growing heat of embarrassment. If he was already amused, how hard would he laugh to realise that he had wasted kisses on his own wife?

'I should have recognised that you were a lady of breeding earlier by the tone of your voice.' He sighed, and tapped his forehead with the head of his cane. 'Perhaps the gin has finally addled my brains. But when you came upstairs with me, I was under the impression...'

He cleared his throat and grinned, allowing her to fill in the rest.

'You might not be able to see where you gamble, but I have the misfortune of two good eyes. I foolishly blundered into a place that was not safe for me. You came to my rescue, and I thought that, unlike the other men here, if I got you alone it would be possible to reason with you. Which I am doing, now.' Though he could not appreciate the fact, she reached to straighten her hair and clothing, trying to erase the signs of her earlier compliance.

'Well. Never mind what I assumed.' He gave another little clearing of the throat. 'The less spoken of that the better. I was wrong, and I am sorry if I have given offence. If there is a way I can be of assistance, then, please, tell me.' It was as if, with a few sentences, he thought to regain his honour and pretend the last few minutes had not occurred.

Emily did not know whether to be angry, or impressed by the transformation. From beneath them, she could hear the men in the tavern growing louder, angrier and possibly more dangerous. Perhaps now was not the best time to tell her husband what she thought of his behaviour, and his quick about-face turn on the subject of her virtue. 'If you wish to help me, then take me away from here. It is a bad place, full of violent, drunken men. Is there some back stairway that we can use to escape?'

He shook his head. 'The only way out is to go back the way we came.'

'You allowed us to be trapped upstairs?' This was certainly not the sharp military strategy she had expected from a former officer of his Majesty's army. 'Whatever were you thinking to take a room here? You might be able to fight them tonight, but some day the ruffians you gamble with will catch you unawares and make an end to you.'

He shrugged and fumbled to pat her on the arm. 'Of course, my dear. I fully expect that to be the truth.'

She stared at him in amazement, and then realised that her shocked expression was useless as a way to covey her emotions. 'Then why are you here?'

'Because soon, the last of my vision will go, and I will be of no use to the world. Better to go out doing things that I enjoy, than to put a bullet in my head at the first sign of trouble. That is the way, in my family. My father died on horseback.' He grinned. 'Or just off it, actually. A snapped spine and a crushed body. But he loved to ride. And up till the end, he was sailing over jumps that he could no longer see. My grandfather was a crack shot. Until the day he missed, at least.' He grinned as though it were a point of admiration. 'Killed in a duel. Over a woman, of course.'

And hadn't that been what she had always known about her husband and his family? But her brother had assured her that Adrian was *wild like all the Folbrokes. But with a good heart, Emily. A very good heart.*

'And you?'

'I am a soldier,' he added. 'And well used to drinking and gaming in rough company. If the night ends in a scrap? I like nothing better. When the odds are bad, it gets the blood flowing in the veins.' He seemed to swell a little at the thought as though readying himself for battle.

'And now, because of your foolish desire for self-destruction, I will end my night at the mercy of the gang below.'

He stilled, and then something in him straightened, as though he could cast off the inebriate as easily as throwing off his coat. And for a moment, in the dark, he was the dashing young man who had gone off to war, only to return and break her heart. Then he smiled. It was the old smile, too, unclouded by gin or lust. Brave. Beautiful. And a little sad. 'Have I not proved to you already that I am still capable of taking care of myself, and you as well? Or is another demonstration in order?'

Although he could not see, he looked at her with such intensity that the pain inside her did not seem to matter. There was something in that gaze and that smile that said any action he might take was likely to be a great adventure, and that it would be his pleasure to share it with her. It made her heart flutter in the way it used to, before he had married her, and before she had learned what a mistake it was all likely to be.

'Perhaps it would be better if we wait in the room you mentioned, until it is safe to depart.' She could hear her nerve failing again, and her voice becoming weak. The old hesitant Emily was returning with her husband's gain in sobriety.

He laughed. 'I have done nothing yet to earn such intimacy from you, pleasant though the offer might be. But if you stay just behind me as we descend, I can get you to safety. Hang on to my coat tails and leave my hands free, for I may need to fight.'

'But you cannot see,' she said plaintively.

'I do not need to. I know the way out. And I intend to hit anyone who stands between me and the door. Those that mean us no harm will have the sense to get out of the way.'

Emily had no answer for this, having no experience with fighting one's way out of a tavern. So she took his coat tail in her hands, and followed close behind him down the stairs. As they breached the upper landing, she could tell from the sounds below them that the crowd had grown worse. There was more chanting, a raucous edge to the singing, the scuffling of boots and fists, and breaking furniture.

Adrian paused, listening. 'What do you see before you? Quickly, love.'

'Two men are fighting on a table to the right.'

'Very good.' He continued down the stairs, hugging the wall as he worked his way towards the door. As the fight spilled off the table and into his path, he struck out with the cane, just as he'd said he would. The first blow was a glancing one, causing the man in front of him to yelp and cringe back.

But the second man surged forwards as though willing to fight both his supposed enemy and any other that might stand against him. Adrian forced the stick forwards quickly, jabbing into the man's midsection.

The drunkard retched, and then flailed out, trying to strike. Adrian brought the stick down upon the man's back so hard that, for a moment, Emily feared the wood had cracked.

He stepped over the man's prone body, reaching back to steady her. But the momentary distraction over her safety was enough to make him jeopardise his own. Out of the corner of her eye, she caught the flash of a raised hand, and saw the man that had accosted them on the stairs throw a bottle up and out from the throng in the middle of the room.

Before she could get out a warning, Adrian had been struck, and was staggering backwards, clutching his temple. His body went limp in her arms as she tried to catch him.

Chapter Five

Then there was a flash toward the ceiling and the sound of a warning shot. Her husband's secretary appeared out of nowhere to pull Adrian forwards again, and off her. In his usual quiet way, Hendricks said, 'I apologise for not intervening until this delicate juncture. But I am sure that my lord would have preferred it thus. And now I think it best that we make a retreat while we are able.' He pressed a second pistol into her hand. 'I doubt this will be necessary now that I have frightened them. But it is better to be over-prepared.'

He pushed her husband back against the wall for a moment, and then slung the limp body over his shoulder, staggering towards the door to the street.

Emily held the pistol in front of her, hoping that she did not look as frightened by it as she felt. But it appeared to be effective. The man who'd hit Adrian had been preparing to strike again. At the sight of the gun he took a large step back, his anger dissolving into submission.

Hendricks lurched through the door and towards the waiting coach. When he saw them, the coachman rushed forwards to help his unconscious master up and into the carriage.

As they set off, poor Adrian remained slumped against the squabs, rendered insensible by the combination of violence and gin. It was not until they were nearly back to his rooms that he surged suddenly back to consciousness, throwing a hand out as though searching the air in front of him. 'Hendricks?'

'Yes, my lord.'

'There was a woman in the tavern with me. I was trying to help her.'

'She is safe, sir.'

He relaxed back into the seat, with a sigh of relief and a grimace of pain. 'Very good.'

Once they arrived at the flat, she followed behind as the men helped him up the stairs. She noted the looks of alarm on the faces of his servants as they saw her appear from behind him. Clearly, the jig was up and they expected punishment from her for concealing the state of things, or from Adrian for revealing them.

As she passed them, she shot them glares that would warn them to silence.

Hendricks gave her a helpless shrug, opening the bedroom door and putting his arm around the shoulders of his employer. 'The valet will help him from here, mmm—ma'am.' He struggled a moment to choose an honourific, as though remembering that he apparently did not know the name of the woman who had come home with them. 'I will find someone to see you home.'

When she was sure that her husband would see the shadow of her head, she nodded in approval. Then she backed from the room and shut the door.

'Hendricks,' she kept her voice low, so that it would not carry to the bedroom, but used a tone of command that had served her well when dealing with employees who thought, even for a moment, that they owed more loyalty to her husband than to the woman standing in front of them.

'My lady.' She saw his spine stiffen instantly to full obedience.

She glared at him. 'You did not tell me.'

'That he was blind? I thought you knew.'

She was his wife. She should have known that about him, if nothing else. But what was one more regret on a very long list? But now, Hendricks mocked her ignorance.

Then, as a sop to her feelings, he said, 'The servants are not allowed to discuss Lord Folbroke's indisposition. He pretends it does not matter. Often it does not. But he acts as if the careless things he does pose no greater risk to him. He is very wrong.'

She had to agree, for it was quite obviously true. 'Between the drink, and the loss of vision, he did not know me.'

'Yes, my lady.' Hendricks did not seem surprised. But

she felt some gratification to see that he looked ashamed of his part in the state of things.

'It will save us both embarrassment if that is the way this night remains. You will inform the servants that, no matter what they might think they have seen, he was brought home by a stranger. Is that clear?'

'Yes, Lady Folbroke.'

'When I have had time to think on this, I will have some words with him. But it must wait until my husband's mind has cleared itself of blue ruin.'

The secretary's reserve broke. 'While I have no doubt that you will achieve the first half of the statement, the last may be beyond all of our control.' Then, as though he could mitigate the forwardness of the statement, he added, 'My lady.' And then he gave her a desperate look as though it pained him to betray the confidence. 'He is seldom sober any more. Even during the day. We who have served him for most of his life are at our wits' end as to what can be done.'

Emily thought of the man in the other room, reeking of gin. Was it really so different than what she had feared? In her heart, she had been sure that she would find him drunk. But she had mistaken the reason. She reached out to touch the arm of the man beside her. 'How long has he been like this?'

'The whole of the last month, certainly.' He tapped his forehead. 'It is the eyes, my lady. As they fail him, he loses all hope. My lord's valet has heard him laugh and say that it will not be a problem for long. We fear he means to do something desperate. And we do not know how to stop him.'

She closed her own eyes and took a deep breath, telling herself that this was an estate matter, nothing more. Her heart was no longer involved in it. She must remember her reasons for coming to find him, and that they had nothing to do with a reconciliation or delivering scolds about his scandalous conduct.

But no matter how she felt about his treatment of her, she could not very well allow him to kill himself.

'My husband has taken the notion that this is for the best. I can see, as plainly as you can, that this is nonsense. He is not thinking clearly, and I will not allow him to do himself an injury. At least not until he can present a better reason than the minor problem he has.'

Or until I am sure that my own place is secure.

If he was truly resolved to end his life, she doubted that there was anything to be done. She was little better than a stranger to him. What would he care what she thought? She hardened her heart against the desperation and panic that she was feeling. 'My orders stand, just as they are. You and the other servants are forbidden from speaking of my efforts to find Adrian, or my return with him this evening. Let him think me a stranger.' Then she pushed past the secretary and went into her husband's room.

The valet looked terrified by her sudden appearance, and she held up a hand as a sign of caution. Then she looked down at the man on the bed who was now dressed in a nightshirt, and sporting a makeshift bandage on his temple. 'Before I left, I wished to assure myself that you are all right.'

At the sound of her voice he looked pained that she had found him helpless. There was a lost look in his blank blue eyes that made him seem smaller than she knew him to be. 'It should not be your job to see to my safety. As a gentleman, I should have been able to take care of you.'

'You succeeded,' she said. 'You fought well. We were within a few feet of the door when you were struck down. And that was by an unfair blow. A sighted man could not have done better and would have ended just as you did.'

There was a ghost of his old, rakish smile, as he tried to joke away his embarrassment. 'My talents do not end there, my dear.' He patted the bed at his side. 'If you wish to come closer, I would be happy to demonstrate.'

'That will not be necessary.' She paused long enough to see the slightest crease of disappointment form on his forehead. 'I prefer my companions to be washed and shaved And not soaked in gin. However...'

She leaned in to give him a peck on the forehead as a farewell reward. But as she did so, she realised that the token kiss would be everything he feared about his future. What she had intended as comfort would seem a sexless and maternal gesture, a cruel dismissal to the man who had fought to protect her.

So she pushed back upon his chest, forcing him into the pillows, and kissed him properly on the mouth. His lips opened in surprise, and she threw caution to the winds and slipped her tongue between them, stroking the inside of his mouth as he had done to hers. She felt the same rush of excitement she had felt in the tavern, and the desire to be closer still. And the feeling that she had felt often, over the last few years: that something was missing from her well-ordered life—and that, perhaps, it was Adrian Longesley.

Then she ended the kiss and turned to leave.

'Wait.' He caught her wrist.

'I must go.'

'You cannot. Not after that.'

She gave a little laugh. 'Neither can I stay.'

'Meet me again.' He ran his other hand through his hair in exasperation and his words were hurried, as though he was trying to think of anything that might tempt her to stay. 'So that I might assure myself of your safety, when I am not indisposed.' His smile was back again. 'You will like me better when I have had time to wash, dress and shave.'

'Will I have to go to a brothel to find you? Or merely a gaming hell?' She shook her head, and remembered that he would not see her refusal, then said, 'I think not.'

'Why not here? Tomorrow morning.'

'You expect me to come to a man's rooms, in daylight and unescorted.'

His face fell. 'Your reputation. I had forgotten.'

'Thank you very much for your belated concern.'

He winced as though it were a physical effort to stumble through the courtesies she deserved. 'If there were somewhere that we could talk, in privacy and discretion…'

Emily sighed, as though she were not sure of the wisdom of her actions and then let herself be persuaded. 'I will send you a letter, and you will come to me when it is convenient.'

He released her hand, letting his fingers drag down the length of it until he touched only her fingertips. 'I look forward to your communication.'

She was glad that he could not clearly see her. Had he not been blind, he would know that her cheeks were crimson and that the expression on her face was not the sly smile of a courtesan, but goggle-eyed amazement. Her husband looked forward to meeting with *her*. Before she could spoil the moment by saying something inappropriate, she turned and left.

It was not until she was in the carriage, on the way back to her brother's town house, that she allowed herself to collapse, then glared across the coach at Hendricks. 'How long have you known?'

'From the first. It came on gradually, after we left Portugal. He insisted that I tell you nothing. And although you and I have had reason to work together, he is, first and foremost, my employer. I must obey his wishes before yours.'

'I see.' Therefore, Hendricks was not to be trusted. She felt a cold chill at the loss of one she had trusted almost as a brother since the day she'd married Adrian. But if he could keep hidden a fact this momentous, then there was no telling what other secrets he'd hidden from her. 'So you meant to take the man's pay and allow him to destroy himself, when a word to me might have prevented it?'

Hendricks was embarrassed almost to the point of pain. 'I did not think it my place.'

'Then you had best reassess your position.' She took the stern, almost manly tone she used with him to indicate that she spoke for her husband and that disobedience was out of the question.

'Of course, my lady.'

She had cowed him, and it made her feel better, more in control than she had since the moment she had realised that she must see Adrian again.

But on the inside, she was unsure whether to laugh or to cry. It had finally happened, just as she'd dreamed of it, since she was a girl. Tonight, the man she loved had looked at her with desire, hung upon her every word and clung to her fingertips as though parting with her was an agony.

Of course, he was drunk, blind and did not know who she was. And the whole thing had happened so long after it should have that the point was moot. It had been nothing more than a girlish fantasy to have the dashing Earl of Folbroke dote on her like a love-struck fool. But then, she had thought that wedding him would mean something other than the sterile arrangement it was. Time had proven to her that he had no feelings for her, or he'd have been home long before now. 'I suspect the reason he found me so appealing is because he thought me married to someone else.'

'Lady Folbroke!' It was an exclamation of shock at her candour, but not one of denial. She feared it was a sign that Hendricks knew her husband only too well. She would return in the morning, when he was sober, and tell him what she thought of this nonsense. Disability was no excuse for the way he'd behaved. If he was not careful, he was likely to kill himself. Where would that leave her?

And if Adrian died, then she might never know...

Tomorrow, he would be hoping for a clandestine meeting, where they could be alone to talk. Ha. When she saw him next, she would talk aplenty. She would tell him what an idiot he was for not knowing her, and for thinking that his good looks and easy manner would be enough to make her forget his abandonment and let him bed her.

A delicious thrill went through her at the thought of being bedded, and she stifled it. It seemed there was no end to her foolishness over the man. She had known from the first that he was a rake. That knowledge should have provided some insulation against his charm. But his kisses made her wonder what it might be like, should he turn his full attention to winning her, even for a few hours.

And it might be the only way to get an heir by him. That was what she had wanted, above all. It was her reason for coming to London.

Emily stared at Hendricks, eyes narrowing and chin

set to remind him that she was the Countess of Folbroke, and not some silly schoolgirl. She deserved his respect every bit as much as her wayward husband. 'Adrian is sorely mistaken if he thinks to keep me in darkness about events any longer. And you are as big a fool as he, for helping him this long. I will not condone his drinking, or support this lunatic notion he has that being struck down in a common brawl is the way to meet his Maker on his own terms. But if a liaison with another man's wife is what he desires, then I see no reason not to give it to him.'

She smiled and watched Hendricks draw away from her in alarm. 'And how do you mean to do that?'

'I mean to return to my brother and do nothing at all. But you will have a busy day tomorrow, Mr Hendricks. I wish you to engage a flat for me while I am in London. Something simple, small. *A pied-à-terre.* Decoration does not matter, since my guest will not see it. I will need staff as well. Choose what is necessary from our household, or hire if you must, but I will have no gossip. They will speak not so much as a word to identify themselves to Lord Folbroke, or I will sack the lot of them. Is that understood?'

'Yes, my lady.' Clearly, the actions were not understood at all. Judging by the look on his face, he found them to be incomprehensible. But he knew better than to cross her, and that was enough.

'When that is completed, and not before, you will take a note to my husband. And you will give him no indication of my involvement in it, or I swear, Mr Hendricks, that no matter what my husband might say in the matter, you will be seeking other employment before the sun sets. Is that clear?'

'Yes, Lady Folbroke.' There was a trace of awe in his tone. But she also recognised the relief in it, as though he understood that, if she were allowed to take the reins, they would all be the better for it. His obedience was gratifying, and yet strangely disappointing. She was tired of being surrounded by men that presented no real challenge to her authority.

But she suspected that she would be regretting the lack of just that by tomorrow evening. It made her tremble when she thought of the kiss Adrian had given her, and the kiss she had given him in return. She had never felt such power in her life and yet utterly in the thrall of another. The man she'd kissed had wanted to be seduced by her as much as he'd wanted to take her. And, for a moment, she had wanted the same.

Tomorrow, on neutral ground, they would meet. She would invite. He would accept. She would feign *naïveté*. He would suggest. She would protest. He would cajole. She would be persuaded. The conclusion might be inevitable, but for a time there would be a battle of wits and wills leading to both a complete surrender and an equally complete victory. If handled correctly, there would be ecstasy, satisfaction and sweet, sweet revenge.

Across from her in the carriage, Hendricks looked quite unsettled by the latest turn of events. But with regard to Adrian, Emily had never felt so confident in her life. As soon as all things were in place, she would go about the tawdry, ridiculous and strangely exhilarating process of ensnaring her own husband.

Chapter Six

Adrian Longesley awoke the next day with the same nagging, drunkard's headache he had grown accustomed to. A morning would come soon enough when he did not wake at all. In comparison, it would be a welcome relief. But today, he was alive and conscious, and feeling the worse for a lump on his forehead. If he had been coshed from behind, he'd have felt better about the injury. But to be hit from the front with a blow that had seemed to come from nowhere proved how far his abilities had diminished. He sighed into the pillow, waiting for the rolling of the room to subside enough so that he might sit up.

The nausea would probably be worse if he could see the movement. Even without that particular sense, he was sure that he could feel the rocking, as though he were making a rough crossing to France. But he was still in his own bedchamber, and could smell a breakfast he had no appetite for.

The woman.

He had been a drunken fool to think he'd be lucky enough to rescue her twice from the place he'd found her. If his carelessness had allowed her to fall into the hands of the men there...

He lurched upright in panic, and then regretted it, before remembering the end of the evening. He had a hazy recollection of her voice on the carriage ride home, along with that of Hendricks. His man must have found him in time, saved the girl and helped them to return here.

It pained him further that he had needed rescuing at all. If he had fallen to a place where he could no longer care for himself and put innocents around him at risk, then it might be time to seek a sudden end to things and stop dawdling about, waiting for nature to take its course. But last night had not been the time. The strange woman had needed him, if only for a short time. If the intervention of Hendricks had assured her safety, then his own pride could survive the damage of needing assistance.

She had claimed to be well bred, and gentle, though she certainly hadn't been wise. A wise woman would never come to such a place. Maybe what she'd said was true, and she'd actually been looking for her husband. Sad for her, if that was the sort of place she might find him. While Adrian shared it, it was nothing to be proud of. But at least he had the small comfort of knowing that his wife had never seen it.

The stranger had refused him, when they'd been alone. So it was not a visit brought on by a secret desire to slum for the novelty of it. And then she had followed him back to his house. She had been in this very bed-chamber, though not for long enough. He remembered her assurances that he had fought well for her, and the tiniest hint of awe in her sceptical voice.

She had been tart in manner and in kisses. And scent as well, for he could swear that the smell of lemons still clung to his skin where she had touched him. What a woman she had been. If his memory could be trusted, he'd have been happy to have more of her company. The round, soft way she had felt in his lap, and the tingling friction of her tongue in his mouth. The pleasant weight of her breasts brushing his arm as she bent over his bed. And a kiss that hinted of more to come.

He laughed. Another meeting was unlikely, and per-haps impossible. She had promised, of course, to get him to release her hand. But she had not given him name or direction and had called him rough company. He rubbed at the stubble on his chin. She was probably right.

His valet must have heard him stirring, for Adrian could hear his entrance, and smell the morning cup of tea that he put on the bedside table and the soap that he carried as he went to the basin to prepare the water for washing and shaving. There was another set of footsteps, the scrape of curtain rings, and the sudden bright blur as the sun streamed into his bedroom. 'Hendricks,' he said, 'you are a beast. The least you could do is allow a man to adjust slowly to the morning.'

'Afternoon, my lord,' Hendricks responded politely. 'It is almost one o'clock.'

'And all the same to me. You know the hour I came home, and the condition I was in, for you brought me.' A thought occurred to him. 'And how did you come to do that? When I left here, I was alone.'

There was an awkward shifting of weight and clearing of throat. 'I came searching for you, my lord. While you were out, Lady Folbroke visited to inform you that she is staying in London. She was quite insistent to know your whereabouts. And I thought it best...'

'I see.' His wife had come to town before. And each time he had managed to avoid her. But it was damned awkward, after the events of last night, to think her so close. He reached for the miniature of Emily in its usual evening resting place on the table by the bed, fingering it idly.

'You had been out for some time, already,' Hendricks continued. 'The servants were concerned.'

The voice in Adrian's head snapped that it was no one's business what he did with his time. Their concern was nothing more than thinly veiled pity, and the suspicion that he could not be trusted to take care of himself. He held his temper. If one had been carried insensible out of a gin mill, it hardly gave one the right to argue that one was fine on one's own.

Instead, he said, 'Thank them for their concern, and thank you as well for your timely intervention. It was appreciated. I will try to be more careful in the future.'

In truth, he would be nothing of the kind. But there was no point in rubbing the man's nose in the fact.

And then, to make it appear an afterthought, he came back to the matter that concerned him most. 'But you said Emily is in town. Did you enquire as to the reason for the visit?'

'She did not say, my lord.' There was a nervous rustling of the papers in Hendricks's hands.

'You saw to the transfer of funds to the working accounts that we discussed after your last visit north?'

'Yes, my lord. Lady Folbroke inspected the damage from the spring storms, and repairs on the cottages are already underway.'

'I don't suppose it is that, then,' he said, trying not to be apprehensive. The efficiency of his wife was almost legendary. Hendricks had read the report she had written, explaining in detail the extent of the damage, her plans for repair and the budget she envisioned. The signature she'd required from him was little more than a courtesy on her part, to make him feel he was involved in the running of his lands.

But if she had come to London, and more importantly, come looking for him, the matter was likely to be of a much more personal nature. He remarked, as casually as possible, 'How is she?'

There was such a pause that he wondered if she was not well, or if there were something that they did not wish him to know. And then Hendricks said, 'She seemed well.'

'Emily has been on my mind often of late.' It was

probably the guilt. For he could swear that the scent of lemons still lingered in the room so strongly he feared Hendricks must smell it as well. 'Is there anything at all that she requires? More money, perhaps.'

'I am certain, if she required it, she would write herself a cheque from the household accounts.'

'Oh. Clothing, then. Does she shop frequently? I know my mother did. Perhaps she has come to town for that.'

'She has never complained of a lack,' he replied, as though the subject were tiresome and devoid of interest to him.

'Jewellery, then. She has received nothing since our wedding.'

'If you are interested, perhaps you should ask her yourself.' Hendricks said this sharply, as though despite his patient nature, he was growing frustrated by the endless questions.

'And did she mention whether she'd be likely to visit me again?' The question filled him with both hope and dread, as it always did. For though he would most like to see her again—as though that were even possible—he was not eager to hear what she would say if she learned the truth.

'I think she made some mention of setting up housekeeping here in London.' But Hendricks sounded more than unsure. He sounded as though he were keeping a secret from him. Possibly at his wife's request.

'Does she visit anyone else that you know of?' As if he had any right to be jealous, after all this time. But it would make perfect sense if she had found someone to entertain her in his absence. It had been three years. In the time since he'd left she would have blossomed to the prime of womanhood.

'Not that I know of, my lord. But she did mention your cousin Rupert.'

'Hmm.' He took a sip of his tea, trying to appear non-committal. Some would think it mercenary of her. But there was a kind of sense in it, he supposed, if she transferred her interests to the next Earl of Folbroke. When he was gone, she could keep her title, and her home as well. 'But Rupert...' he said, unable to keep from voicing his distaste of the man. 'I know he is family. But I had hoped she would have better taste.'

If he had eyes as strong as his fists, there would be no question of interference from his cousin in that corner. Even blind, he had a mind to give the man a thrashing, next time he came round to the flat. While he might forgive his wife an infidelity, crediting the fault to his own neglect of her, it would not do to let Rupert think she was part of the entail. She deserved better.

Not that she is likely to get it from you...

'It is not as if she shares the details of her personal life with the servants,' Hendricks interrupted his reverie. Was that meant as a prod to his conscience for asking questions that only he himself could learn the answers to?

Surely by now Hendricks must have guessed his real reasons for curiosity, and the utter impossibility of talking to Emily himself. 'It is none of my business either, I am sure. I have no real claim on her.'

'Other than marriage,' Hendricks pointed out in a dry tone.

'Since I have made no effort to be a good husband to her, it seems hypocritical to expect her continued loyalty to me. And if she has a reason to visit me again? If you could give me advance notice of the visit, I would be grateful. It would be better, if a meeting cannot be avoided, that it be prepared for.' On both sides. She deserved warning as well. He was in no condition, either physical or mental, to meet with her now.

'Very good, my lord.' Adrian could sense a lessening of the tension in the man beside the bed at the mention of even a possibility of a meeting. Acting as a go-between for them had been hard on his friend.

But now Hendricks was shifting again, as though there was some fresh problem. 'Is there some other news that brings you here?' he asked.

'The post has come,' Hendricks said, without expression.

'If I have slept past noon, I would hope it has. Is there something you wish to read to me?'

'A letter. It has no address, and the wax was unmarked. I took the liberty…'

'Of course.' Adrian waved away his concerns. 'Since I cannot see the words, my correspondence is as an open book to you. Please read the contents.' He set down his tea, took a piece of toast from the rack and waited.

Hendricks cleared his throat and read with obvious discomfort, 'I wish to thank you for your assistance on the previous evening. If you would honour me with your presence for dinner, take the carriage I will send to your rooms at eight o'clock tonight.'

Adrian waited for more, but no words came. 'It is not signed?'

'Nor is there a salutation.'

'Give it here. I wish to examine it.' He set his breakfast aside and took the paper, running his fingers over it, wishing that he could feel the meaning in the words. There was no indication that they would be dining alone, but neither was there a sign that others would be present.

'And there is no clue as to the identity of the sender? No address? A mark of some sort?' Although he'd have felt a seal or an embossed monogram with his own fingers.

'No, sir. I assumed you knew the identity of the woman.'

Adrian raised the paper to his nose. There was the slightly acrid smell of fresh ink, and a hint of lemon perfume. Had she rubbed the paper against her body, or merely touched it to the perfume bottle to send this part of the message?

He smiled. And did she know how she would make him wonder on the fact? He preferred to think of the paper held against those soft breasts, close to her quickly beating heart.

'About that...' What a blatant display of poor character that he had not even learned her name. It gave him no comfort to show Hendricks how low he had sunk, for the man was more than just a servant to him, after years together in the army, and Adrian's growing dependence

on him since the injury. But as Hendricks's devotion to
Lady Folbroke had grown, Adrian had come to suspect
that the man's loyalties were more than usually torn.

'There was no time for a formal introduction last
night. I had only just met her a few moments before you
arrived. And, as I'm sure you could see, the situation was
quite hectic.' He paused for a moment to let his secretary
make what he could of that, and then said, 'But you saw
her, did you not? What was she like?'

He heard Hendricks shift uneasily again. He had
never before required the poor man to help with a liaison. It must prick at his scruples to be forced to betray
the countess. But Adrian's curiosity about the woman
would not be denied. 'Was she attractive?' he suggested.

'Very,' admitted Hendricks.

'Describe her.'

'Dark blond hair, short and dressed in curls. Grey
eyes, a determined chin.'

Determined. He could believe that about her. Last
night, she'd shown fortitude and a direct way of speaking
that proved she was not easily impressed by fine words.
He could feel the attraction for her, crackling on his skin
like the air before a storm. 'And?' he prompted, eager to
know more.

'She was expensively dressed.'

'And when you returned her to her home, where was
it? It was you that escorted her, was it not?'

Hendricks shifted again. 'She made me swear, on my
honour, not to give further information about her identity

or her direction. You have a claim upon my honesty, of course. You are my employer…'

Adrian sighed. 'But I would not use that claim to make you break your word to a lady.'

'Thank you, my lord.'

'And I expect she will divulge what she wishes me to know, if I go to her tonight.'

He heard another uncomfortable shifting.

'And I will not expect you to be further involved in this, Hendricks, other than to help me with the reading of any correspondence. I understand that you are a valuable aid to Emily, as well as myself. I will not force you into a position more difficult than the one you already occupy.'

'Thank you, my lord.'

'This evening, I will take the carriage when it arrives, and whatever thanks the woman wishes to give me. I suspect that will be the end of it. You will hear no more of it.'

'Very good, my lord.' But Hendricks's voice sounded annoyingly doubtful.

Chapter Seven

At a tap on his shoulder, Adrian lifted his chin to make it easier for the valet to shave him for the second time that day. He did not like the feelings of helplessness that the process of dressing raised in him. They were ridiculous, of course. He had stood for it his entire life. And it was done just the same as it had been, when his eyes had been good. But now that he could not see to do it himself, he sometimes had the childish urge to slap the helping hands away.

He focused on the letter in his hand to calm his nerves. When the mysterious woman in the tavern had refused him, it was because of what she could see, and not what he could. She had thought him slovenly and commented on his drunkenness. It had made him regret the numbing effects of gin for the first time in ages. She was right, of course. If he valued her company, he would need a clear head to appreciate it, just as she wished for a lucid partner.

To show his respect on their second meeting, he must be immaculate. It was not a condition he was likely to achieve by himself, and he should be grateful for what his servant could do. He rubbed a hand along his own finished jaw. Perfectly smooth. He stood to accept the shirt, the cravat and the coat, and the final brushing of hair and garments, before his man announced him finished.

Then he walked the three paces to the doorway, stopped and turned back, setting the letter aside and picking up the miniature of Emily to drop it in its usual place in his coat pocket. It would serve as a reminder, should the attractiveness of his companion make him forget where his true heart and duty were promised. Tonight would be an enjoyable evening. But nothing more than that.

He travelled out of his room, took the ten paces through the sitting room, through the front door, and down the four steps to the street.

He could hear the carriage waiting in front of him, smell leather and horses, and see the dim shape of it, clearer at the edges, but fading to impenetrable blackness at the centre. The touches of vision that still remained were almost more maddening than nothing would be, for it gave the futile hope that the picture might suddenly clear if he blinked, or that a slight turn of the head and shift of the eyes would make it easier to see what lay in the fringes.

He calmed himself. It was only when he did not chase clarity that he could use what sight he had. A groom stepped forwards to help him, and this time he shook off the assistance, feeling along the open door in front of him to find the strap, searching with his toe for the step that had been placed, and then up and into the seat. The man closed the door and signalled to the driver, and they were off.

To pass the time he counted turns, imagining the map of the city. Not too far from his own home. This would put him in Piccadilly. And then, past. They travelled for a short time more, and then the carriage stopped, the door opened, and he could hear the step being put down for him again. The same groom that had been ready to help him up offered no hand this time, but murmured, 'A little to your left, my lord. Very good', allowing him to navigate on his own. When he had gained the street, the man said, 'The door you want is straight in front of you. Two scant paces. Then five stairs with a railing on your right. The knocker is a ring, set in a lion's mouth.'

'Thank you.' He must remember to compliment his hostess on the astuteness of her servants. With a few simple actions, this man had relieved the trepidation Adrian often felt in strange surroundings. Following the directions, he made his way to the door and knocked upon it.

It appeared the footman was prepared as well, describing the passage as they walked down it, opening the door to the sitting room and informing him of the locations of the furniture so that he did not have to fumble his way to the couch. He could feel the fire in front of him, but before he sat down he paused. The air smelled of lemons. Did her scent linger in the room? No. He could hear her breathing, if he listened for it. He turned in the direction of the sound. 'Did you mean to trick me into rudeness? You are standing in the corner, aren't you?'

She gave a small laugh and he enjoyed the prettiness of the sound. 'I did not think it necessary to have a butler announce you. We are meeting in secret, are we not?'

He walked towards her, praying that the confidence of the movement would not be spoiled by unseen furniture. 'If you wish it.'

'I think I would prefer it that way, Adrian.'

He started, and then laughed at his own foolishness. 'I gave you my first name last night, didn't I? And got nothing in return for it, as I remember. Perhaps a full introduction on my part will encourage you to reveal more.'

'That is not necessary, Lord Folbroke,' she said. 'Even without your telling me, I recognised you last night. And you would recognise me, should you still have your sight.'

'Would I, now?' He paused to rack his brains, trying to place the sound of that voice with a name, or at least a face. But when none appeared, he shrugged apologetically. 'I am embarrassed to admit that I do not know you, even now. And I hope you do not mean to punish me by keeping the secret.'

'I am afraid I must. Should I give you any clue to

my identity, you would know me immediately. And this evening will end quite differently than I wish it to.'

'And how do you wish it to end?' he coaxed.

'In my bed.'

'Really?' He had not expected her to be so very blunt about a thing that they both knew to be true. 'And if you were to tell me your name?'

'Then it would be a significant stumbling block to that. It might give you reason to be angry with me, or to discover a distaste or a hesitance that you do not have now. It would change everything.'

So she was likely the wife of some friend of his. And she thought him honourable enough not to cuckold a chum. 'Perhaps that is true.' Or perhaps it wasn't. His character did not bear close scrutiny at this time.

She sighed. 'I would much prefer to have you think me a stranger, and to kiss me as you did last night, as though you had no thought for anything but the moment, and for me. As though you enjoyed it.'

'I did enjoy it,' he said. 'And apparently so did you if you are willing to go to such great lengths to do it again.'

'It was very nice,' she said politely. 'And unlike anything I have previously experienced.'

Should he discover that she was the wife of an old friend, he might be unwilling to continue. But he would have to hunt the man down and give him a lecture on the care and tending of his lady. Considering the state of his own marriage, the idea that he would give advice to anyone was laughable.

'It pains me to hear you say such. There was nothing

so unusual in the way I kissed you. You have been sorely neglected. And I would be honoured to rectify such a grievous error, if you will allow me to. Lips as sweet as yours are made to be kissed hard and often.'

She gave a loud sigh that ended in a little squeak of annoyance, as though she had thought herself too sensible to be swayed by his words. 'Not quite yet, I think. We should eat. Dinner has been laid for us in the next room and I would not wish it to get cold.'

'Allow me.' He took her hand in the crook of his arm, wondering what he was meant to do next. Pride was all well and good, but what did it save him, if he did not know where to lead her?

She sensed his dilemma. 'The door is in front of you. And a little to the right.'

'Thank you.' He walked forwards, and she let him guide her. He half wished that they'd cross the threshold and find themselves in a bedroom. Then he could rid himself of the tension that was building in him. But, no. He could smell a meal somewhere nearby. She showed no hesitation, so he walked forwards into the blur in front of him, putting his hand out nonchalantly to feel for the table that he was sure must lay before them.

There it was. His fingers touched the corner and a linen cloth. He led her to what he hoped was an acceptable chair and worked his way to the other side, finding his seat and taking it and running his hand over the plate in front of him to familiarise himself with the setting.

Now the tension in him was of an entirely different sort. Suppose he spilled his wine, or dropped the meat into his lap without noticing? Suppose, dear God, she served him soup? If he made a fool of himself, he might never have the chance to know her better.

Adrian listened for the approach of the servant, and sniffed the food he was served. Was it fish? Or perhaps lamb. There was rosemary there, he was sure. And fresh peas, for there was the smell of mint. Problematic, for they would roll across the plate, if he was not careful. Better to flatten them with the fork than to chase them about the plate.

There was a faint laugh from the other side of the table, and his head snapped up. 'What is it?'

'You are glaring at your plate as though it is an enemy. And you seem to have forgotten me entirely. I am trying to decide whether to be amused or insulted by it.'

'I apologise. It is just that, meals can be a difficult time for me.'

'Do you require assistance?'

'That will not be necessary.' It humiliated him to display his weakness so clearly, and he longed to end the game they were playing and lie with her. Once their bodies touched, she could see how little this mattered.

But she had ignored him, for he could hear her drawing her chair closer to his. 'I said I did not need your help.' His tone was sharper than he had intended.

But it did not seem to bother her, for her response was placid enough. 'That is a pity. For it might be quite pleasant for both of us.'

He started as she touched his mouth with her finger,

resting the tip on the centre of his lower lip, almost as though it were a kiss.

He touched his tongue to it and tasted wine. She had dipped her finger into the glass.

He reached out, very carefully, to his own glass, dipping a finger in the contents, and then following the sound of her voice to try to touch her lip.

She laughed again, catching his hand and bringing it the last few inches to her mouth to kiss it clean. At the touch of her tongue, his own mouth went so dry he could hardly speak.

'You see?' she whispered. 'It might not be so bad to accept my help.'

'But I would not want to grow used to being hand fed, no matter how attractive the hands might be.'

She laughed. 'My hands might be ugly for all you know. And my face as well.'

He pulled his hand away from her lips, clasping her fingers in his. Then he turned it over, stroking the fingers, rubbing his thumb along the palm, over the back, circling the wrist. The fingers were long, the nails short, the skin soft. He held it to his cheek. 'The hand is lovely, as is the woman. You will never convince me otherwise.'

She sighed in response and he could feel her lean towards him as the pressure of her hand increased. 'You flatter, sir. But you do it well.'

'And you tempt. I am utterly captivated.' Which was not so much flattery as truth. He was hard for her, and they had not even begun to eat. But while he could not change his body's reaction, control of the evening was returning to him, and with it, he relaxed and focused on his ultimate goal. 'Before we go further, am I to be your only company tonight?'

'Of course.' She seemed surprised that he would ask. Surely that was a good sign.

'Then I take it that you still have not found your husband? Or have you found him, and are punishing him for leading you into last night's danger?'

She gave a little hiss of surprise and snatched her hand away. 'I did not betray my husband. It was he who left me. I have not seen him in some time. And I suspect he would make sport of my search for him, just as you do.'

'I am sorry. I did not mean to remind you of unhappiness. I only wished to ascertain that we would be alone for the whole evening.' To cover the awkward moment, he went back to his meal. As unobtrusively as possible, he touched the food on his plate to learn its location, then wiped his fingers on the napkin and reached for a knife to cut the chop he had found. He could hear the scrape of her cutlery as she began to eat as well.

Then she spoke. 'We need have no fear of interruption. This is not actually my home. It was let so that I might entertain in private. And tonight I am expecting no one else.'

So she had ample funds, and took scrupulous care of her reputation. He could not help trying to guess her identity from the clues she was giving him. 'Have you brought many admirers here?'

'There have been no others. Only you.'

His pulse quickened.

'Do not think that I have not had offers,' she added, as though she did not wish him to think her unworthy of masculine attention. 'But they know that I am married. And that I will not allow them to do the things they hint at when they are alone with me.'

'And yet you invited me here?' He smiled at her. 'I am truly flattered. What is the reason for my good fortune?'

'You are different.'

The way she said that word felt wonderful and strange, as though she thought it a good thing to be unlike one's fellows. Perhaps it was, if it attracted such a woman to him. 'I spend much of my time wishing I were not. But you seem to deem it an advantage.'

'I am not talking about your sight.'

'What then?'

'You are more handsome than the others, for one thing. And more brave.' Her voice still had the solid, matter-of-fact quality of the previous evening, but he could almost feel the warmth of her blush on his own skin.

'And what would make you think that?'

'The way you protected me last night. I doubt that the men who normally seek me out would have the courage to do that with two good eyes. But you did not think twice.'

'Which proves me a foolish drunkard, more than a hero.'

'I think it may be possible to be both.'

And he felt the little puff of pride, along with the

desire coursing in his blood. 'And you wish to reward me for my gallantry with dinner?'

'I told you before that it was more than that. I invited you here because you seemed to desire me. But I was not sure, when you were sober, that you would wish to come. I thought it would be better, should I be wrong, to enjoy a nice meal, than to sit alone, *en deshabille,* waiting for a man who did not want me.' The need in her voice was evident, though she'd tried to disguise it with a light tone. Without thinking, Adrian reached out for her, almost knocking over his water goblet in the process. She steadied it effortlessly, meeting his hand with hers on the stem of the glass.

'I think I have had quite enough to eat,' he said, guiding the glass to his lips for a sip of water before kissing the fingers that rested beside his on the goblet. 'If I had known that you were dressed to seduce me when I entered, I doubt we would have made it as far as the table.' He put down the glass again and stood. Then he took a step closer to her, listening to see if she moved away.

There was a faint hitch in her breathing as she rose. 'I had not expected it to be so easy to trap you. Should I take it as a compliment? Or is it that you are none too particular about your conquests?'

Was that bitterness he heard? 'Are you angry with me for coming when summoned?'

'Perhaps I am angry at myself for doing the summoning.' There was another pause. 'Or perhaps, now that the moment grows close, I cannot maintain a facade of sophistication. While I might wish to pretend otherwise, to be with you like this frightens me.'

There was that hint of vulnerability in her voice again, and it drew him to her in a way that was very different than the simple lust of the night before. He closed the distance between them and put his arms around her body, feeling her stiffen, and then relax. 'Do not feel the need to play the coquette to hold my interest. Or to continue with the act, should you change your mind. I wish to know you just as you are. And I wish to give you pleasure.' And for a moment, he took comfort at how good it felt to have something to offer her, and to know that the night might be about more than his needs.

'Of course,' she said. 'The bedchamber is on the other side of the sitting room. If you wish to retire there, I do not mind...' Her body tensed again.

'There is no need to rush,' he assured her, stroking her shoulder. 'You were quite right to think that I desired you. I have been on tenterhooks the whole day, fearing that I misunderstood your offer. And if I seemed to rush through my meal, it was not because I wanted to be elsewhere. I worried that I would do something laughable, or give you a distaste of me.'

'By dining with me?' she said. 'What a strange notion. I would never find you laughable, unless you sought to amuse me. And I'm sure that when you upset me, it will have little to do with your table manners.'

'When I upset you? You seem most sure of the fact, madam.'

'Of course. You will have your way with me—and then be off. That is your intention, is it not?'

And what could he say to that? For that had been his intention exactly.

'But I am hoping that, after all of your bragging last night, that the experience is sufficient to assuage some of the pain of your departure.'

What had her bastard of a husband done to her that she was so eager to be used, and yet so convinced that she could not hold his interest for more than a night? It put him in mind to prove her wrong. 'But suppose that was not my intention at all?'

She seemed to shrink, as though she wished to evaporate, even as he held her close. Then she said softly, with none of the confidence he'd grown used to, 'Have I done something wrong?'

'On the contrary. You are more right than I ever imagined. Why do you ask?'

'If you do not want me...'

'Of course I want you, my darling. But things have more flavour if we take the time to savour them. Is there a couch by the fire where we might take our wine and sit for a time?' He could feel her taking a breath, ready to object. So he reached carefully and found the tip of her nose with his finger. 'Do not worry. When the time is right, I mean to take you to bed.' From there, he touched her chin with the same finger, guiding himself to her face until her lips met his. The briefest kiss was a taste of heaven, just as it had been the previous night. 'As a matter of fact, I doubt I will be able to help myself.'

He kissed her again, slowly. Her mouth tasted of wine. He ran his knuckles over the curve of her shoulder, and felt the smooth fabric of her clothing. 'What are you wearing? I think it is a dark colour. And it feels like silk. But beyond that...'

'It is but a robe. Blue silk.'

'Describe the colour. Is it like the sea? A robin's egg?'

She thought for a moment. 'I think it could be called sapphire.'

'And what do you wear under it?'

He heard her swallow nervously. 'My nightdress.'

Adrian wrapped his arms more tightly about her, stroking her body lightly, so as to satisfy his curiosity without arousing her. He felt no stays or petticoats. And he damned his eyes for their betrayal. He would not have been able to take food had he known that on the other side of the table there had been only a few layers of fabric between him and the softness of this woman's body.

She was straining on tiptoe to match his height, kissing his ear with little licks of her tongue. He could feel each touch of it to the soles of his feet. 'Let us sit,' he whispered again. 'Show me where to go.'

She slipped out of his arms and took him by the hand to lead him into the fog of the room, through a doorway, towards the glow of a fire. She sat him down on the grey blob before it, which turned out to be some kind of sofa, and he pushed her gently back against the arm of it. 'Before I kiss you again, I would like to touch you.' He wondered if it sounded strange to her. But there was so much he still did not know about her. It would not have mattered what she looked like if his intent had been to leave before the dawn. But with this woman? Somehow everything was different.

He could feel the hesitation as she tried to decipher the request. And then she said, 'Where?'

He laughed. 'Everywhere. But let us begin at the beginning, shall we?' He reached out a tentative finger to touch her hair.

Curls, just as Hendricks had said. Although he'd thought he enjoyed long hair on a woman, the texture was interesting. He could feel the carefully styled ringlets at the side, the pins that held them in place, and the way they revealed the smoothness of her neck. He dipped his head close and found the place at its base where scent had been dabbed, inhaling deeply and touching the point with his tongue.

She gave a little jump of surprise.

He ran his fingers along the place his lips had touched, finding the tendons, the hollows, feeling movement as she swallowed. It was a lovely, long neck and he wondered if the complexion was pale or a dusky gold.

Her chin was well shaped, with a firmness that hinted at stubbornness. She'd proven that already, so it was no real surprise. And there was her mouth. He smiled, remembering the taste of it. High cheekbones, a dimple, a raised brow. He smoothed it, feeling the tiny wrinkle of confusion on the forehead and the beat of a pulse in her temple. Her eyes were closed. He brushed them with his thumb, feeling the long lashes lying upon her cheeks. When they were open, he was sure that the look in those eyes would be probing, discerning, intelligent. But she would look like a child when she slept, gentled and at peace.

'Did you discover what you wished to know?' He heard another faint twinge of doubt in her voice, as though she feared that she had been found wanting on close inspection.

'You are beautiful. Just as I knew you would be.'

He could feel the heat in her cheeks, the little puff of exhaled breath, and the way her body relaxed beside his, knowing he approved of her.

Then he cupped his hand at the back of her neck, and brought her lips to his to take them as they opened to speak. Her tongue touched his eagerly, and she put her hands on his shoulders, holding him in place as though she suspected, at any moment, that he would regain his senses and reject her.

He took her mouth with deep greedy strokes of his tongue, letting his hands roam lightly over her body, feeling the heat of her through the fabric. Then he found the tie of her robe and reached beneath it, tugging her night-dress upwards until he caught the hem, pulling it until it rested even with her nipples and left her lower body sheathed in nothing but smooth blue silk. He stroked her side through the robe, moving the fabric against her until she gasped with pleasure and fought to free herself from her clothing.

He laughed, rubbing the rougher cloth of the dress against her nipples, dipping his mouth to the bare undersides of the exposed slopes beneath it, kissing the peachskin softness of them, licking up to the place where they puckered with excitement.

Her struggling ceased and she went still, waiting for the moment when he would uncover her. When he did not move, she arched her back and moaned, and he pulled the fabric aside suddenly and feasted upon her, drawing them in turn into his mouth, sucking hard, squeezing them with his hand.

'Adrian.' Her voice was tortured, desperate. 'Adrian, finish quickly.'

'I am just beginning, my love.'

'But I fear… I think I am ill…I feel so strange…' The words came out in a series of gasps.

And he wondered—could it be that a married woman might still be a virgin to her own pleasure? He released her breasts, slowing his attack to let her calm. 'You will be fine, darling. But you must trust me to know what is best for you. Now help me remove your gown.' He kissed her on the mouth again as he reached to untie the belt. She struggled out of the sleeves, and between them they pushed the cotton nightrail over her head and to the floor.

'Now lie back upon the silk. Relax. There is a place on your body as wondrous as the pearl in an oyster. And I mean to touch you there until you submit to me.' He sank his fingers into the warmth between her legs, deeper between the folds of her to find the spot that he knew would drive her mad. With his other hand, he found the belt of the robe and its silk tasseled ends, drawing one up her belly to dangle it back and forth over her breasts.

She was sobbing now, shaking as though she would fight against the release. So he slowed his hand, resting the pad of his thumb against her as he let his fingers sink deep inside her. She was hot, tight and wet, and he would go there himself soon. And as he stroked he felt an answering throb in his loins to match the one against his hand as her body gave up the last of her control to him.

'Adrian,' she cried louder than his pounding heartbeat, 'I am yours.' He could feel her, collapsed on her back before him, legs spread wide around his hand, ready to be taken.

He had thought to take her to bed, to carry her if he could. But it was quite impossible, for he could not stand to wait. He curled his fingers inside her and made her shudder again as he fumbled with the buttons on his trousers, and then in his pocket for the sheath he carried.

She froze, and then he felt her scrambling, crablike, away from his touch. 'What is that?'

He reached for her again. 'I do not expect you have ever seen such a thing. It is called a French letter.'

'And what is its intended purpose?' she asked.

He wanted to groan to her that there was no time for questions, and to put the thing on and ram himself home. But he struggled through the roar of desire in his head to be patient for the sake of her innocence. 'One might call it a preventative. It can be worn by the man during the physical act of love.'

'And just what do you seek to prevent?' she said, distant and cold.

He gritted his teeth to keep his temper and lust in check. 'Several things. Disease, for example.'

'You think I have an illness?' She struggled off the sofa and he heard a wine glass clink against the side table before tumbling to the carpet.

'Of course not. You are a lady, and have limited experience with such things. But by my recent behaviour, I can hardly be called a gentleman. And it is better, if one cannot see, to be more careful than usual, when one decides to…' He let the sentence hang open.

'I found you yesterday, dead drunk in a gin mill, brawling with navvies. And now you wish me to believe that you care so much for your own health, and the health of your women, that you would bother with such a thing?' The innocence was gone now, replaced by the tart, demanding tone that he had heard yesterday.

'Better a quick death in a fight than a slow death of the pox.' He patted his knee, inviting her back on to his lap.

'Get out,' she muttered, stepping even farther away.

'Does it really bother you so?' He stuffed the thing back in his pocket, wondering if it were possible to make her forget it again.

'Perhaps it bothers me to think of you consorting with who knows whom. And then coming to me, treating me as a nothing, just as you have always done. Leave me immediately,' she said more loudly.

'Darling…' he gave a diminishing laugh, as though it would be so easy to reduce the pain of what she was doing to him by her delay '…it is for the best, really.

You are married, and so am I. We do not wish to risk an accident of another sort. Suppose you were to get with child?'

'Of course we would not want that.' Her voice was well on the way to being shrewish now. 'Why would anyone wish to get a child on me? It is good that you cannot see, I am sure, for you would find me so repellent that you would run from me, after only a few days.'

'That is not it at all,' he muttered, his desire for her dying in annoyance with her foolish need for reassurance. 'I am sure that you are most beautiful, as I have already said.'

'Liar,' she said, and the word ended in a sob. 'Liar. Get out. Go away. Do not touch me.' She pulled the silk robe around her body with a swish to make sure that he heard.

'You were quite willing enough to have me touch you a few minutes ago. I do not understand your sudden change of heart.'

'Well, I understand quite enough for both of us. You refuse to lie with me in a normal manner. And so I refuse to lie with you at all.' She stomped her foot hard enough for him to feel the vibrations of the floor through his boot soles. 'Get out.'

He stood, doing up his buttons, wanting to storm out the door and to the street, to take the first carriage he could find far away from this place, so that he would never have to see her again.

And then he barked his shin on the little table beside the couch, and remembered that he could not see her at all. Nor could he remember the way to the door. He was wilting with shame now, red faced, limp and weak and helpless in the presence of a woman he desired. 'I am sorry. But I will not...I cannot...'

'Of course you could. If you thought, even for a moment, about what damage you have done to those who care for you...'

'No. It is not that at all.' What she was saying made no sense, and had nothing to do with the confusion he was suffering. 'Believe me, at this moment, I want nothing more than to leave this place and forget this evening as soon as I am able.'

Then he held his hand out in resignation. 'But I will need someone to give me my stick and find my coat and hat, for I cannot. Then you will need to call a servant to lead me to a carriage, unless you mean to turn me helpless into the street. Or maybe you wish to laugh at my struggles.' A thought occurred to him. 'Perhaps that was your game all along. Does it amuse you to see me in such a state over you, and then reject me, knowing how easy it will be to escape?'

'Of course,' she bit back. 'Because everything that happens is about you and your pride and what people will think. For a few moments tonight, I was foolish enough to think that you were not the most selfish man in the world.' She pushed him on the shoulder to spin his body a quarter-turn. 'The door is in front of you. Straight forwards. Go.'

She did not say another word to him, but walked at his side until he was in the entrance hall. Was she ashamed at her outburst, or as disgusted by his weakness as he was? In either case, he knew she did not want him enough to relent, for she went to the bell to ring for aid.

As they waited in silence for a servant to come and lead him out, he felt carefully over buttons, arranging his clothes as best he could, double and triple checking to be sure he had not done up his trousers crooked, so that it was not obvious to all that he had left in haste from an assignation. When he was sure he would not shame himself further, he said, 'And now you know why I am so careful not to spread my seed. This curse that has rendered me helpless came to me because my father, and his before him, had no compunctions about breeding. I have no intention of making the same mistake, leaving my son a useless joke of a man. It is the reason I fled my own marriage. And it is why I will not join unhindered with you. I am sorry if that displeases you, but it is a fact of life, and cannot be changed. Good evening to you, madam.'

Chapter Eight

Emily waited until she was sure that her husband was well on his way before moving from the doorway. As it was, she hoped he had not known that she watched him climb into the carriage to make sure he got to it safely. He was not a child. He did not need her help. And it would hurt him even more if she showed a final lack of confidence.

There was some relief in knowing that she had had her trunks moved to the bedroom of this apartment. At least she would not be forced to creep back to the Eston town house and risk revealing to her brother David the depths of her foolishness.

But she felt she must share some small part of the truth with someone if she was to keep from going mad. So she signalled the footman who had just helped Adrian out the door that she wished to speak with Mr Hendricks, and to go with haste to the rooms to retrieve him, before Lord Folbroke had returned to them.

Then she went to her bedchamber and summoned her maid, requesting that all evidence of her tryst with Adrian be removed from the sitting room and that she be dressed in a way more appropriate for a visitor.

But a part of her, newly awake and alive, did not want to dress. It wanted to recline upon the bed and revel in the touch of silk on skin, and the memory of her husband's hands on her body.

This had been both the best and the worst night of her life. For most of it, he had been everything she had imagined he could be. Gentle one moment, forceful the next. But ever aware of her needs, eager to please her before he took pleasure.

And the pleasure he had given… She hugged her arms close to her body, feeling the silk shift over her aching breasts. Lord have mercy upon her, she still wanted him. Her skin was hot from his touches, and her body cried out that she had been a fool to let pride stand in the way of a more complete union between them.

Until he had produced his little sheath, she had all but forgotten how his neglect had hurt her, or how far she was from forgiving him. She had not thought further than the immediate need for intimate contact with his body, unhindered passion, and for even the smallest possibility that she might bear his child.

That was what she had come here for, after all. And once the idea had planted itself in her mind, it had grown there, not unlike the baby she was seeking. If she could not have Adrian, then perhaps she could have some small part of him to raise and to love.

But now it appeared that this had been the precise reason he had left her. In his present state of mind, even if he went back to Derbyshire for a time to appease his cousin, he would refuse to touch her. He would die recklessly as his father had and leave her alone, just as she feared.

Even pretending that she was not his wife—it had not been as she had expected. She'd imagined the separation to be a personal thing. He was avoiding her in particular, but giving himself with abandon, body and soul, to any other woman that struck his fancy. In anonymity, she might have some share in what others had received from him. But it seemed the act was only a gratification of a physical urge, and that there had never been trust from his side at all. He kept himself apart both from her and any other woman he might lie with.

A footman tapped upon her door to signal that Hendricks awaited her in the sitting room. Her maid, Hannah, gave a final tug upon the sash to her dress and pronounced her respectable, and she went to greet the secretary. But entering the sitting room brought on a flood of embarrassing memories and she hurried to take a seat upon the couch before the fire, gesturing him to a chair opposite.

'My lady?' From the way he looked at her, she wondered if some clue remained in the room or about her person that might indicate what had gone little more than an hour before. He watched her too closely as she entered, lingering on her dress, her body and her face in a way that was most inappropriate.

'You wish to know what occurred, I suppose?' she said, trying not to let her failure be too obvious.

'Of course not.' The poor man must have realised that he had been staring. He looked away quickly and then went quite pink, probably afraid that he had been dragged out of bed to receive some all-too-personal revelation on her part.

'You have nothing to fear.' Emily scowled back at him. 'The evening was without incident.'

'Without...' He looked back at her and pushed his spectacles up the bridge of his nose as he sometimes did when surprised. But behind the lenses, his eyes narrowed as though he doubted her word.

'Well, very nearly,' she said, trying to find an appropriate way to explain. 'The situation is much more complicated than I feared. When I came to London, I had assumed for years that Adrian had a distaste of me, and that that was why he abandoned me in the country. Since I knew he did not like me, I thought there was little future for us, beyond the arrangement we have come to. One cannot change one's nature, after all.

'But our estrangement is not about me at all. He avoids me because he actively seeks to die without issue. He thinks by doing so, and letting Rupert take the title, that he can stamp out the weakness in his family...which is utter nonsense. But it means that I am the last woman in the world he wishes to know.'

'But his idea is not without merit,' Hendricks said

sensibly. 'It is logical that he would want a healthy heir, and to believe that his own child might share his problems.'

She glared at him. 'I do not care to hear about the logic. I am sure, if we get out the family history and examine it, we will see some of the earls from this very line lived long and successful lives, fully sighted to their last day. As have many of the second sons and daughters. And it is quite possible, if we examine Rupert's branch of the family, that we will find similar problems with blindness there. His own father was nearly sightless upon death, was he not?'

Hendricks nodded. 'But nothing was made of it, because he was not Folbroke.'

'Then Adrian's plans are quite—Lord forgive me the expression—short sighted. It is only a medical anomaly that has caused the weakness in the last three earls, and not some dire curse upon the heir to Folbroke.'

'The line would need new blood entirely to solve the problem,' Hendricks admitted.

'How democratic,' she said drily. 'Next you will suggest that I be bred like a mare to someone healthy, for the good of the succession.' She shuddered in revulsion. 'I believe I should have some choice in the matter. And like it or not, I choose the husband I already have. Perhaps Adrian thinks our marriage was forced upon him. But from the first moment I can remember, I have wanted no other man, nor is that likely to change now that I have seen his situation.' She sat up straight and reached into a pocket for a handkerchief to wipe away the mote that was making her eyes tear. 'We do not always want the person who is best for us, I am afraid.'

'The poets never claim that the path of true love is an easy one,' Hendricks added in a dejected tone.

'No poetry was necessary to prove that for myself tonight.'

'Then you told him who you were?'

'I most certainly did not,' she said, and was annoyed to notice the hole in her own logic. Her current understanding of her husband did not negate her previous one. While he had been most attentive to her when he thought her a stranger, he had not mentioned his feelings for his wife at all. 'Things were difficult enough, without bringing my identity into the conversation. If he'd known I was his wife, we'd have...' she shrugged, embarrassed '...we'd have got much less close to the thing he was avoiding than we already have.'

Hendricks was looking at her with a kind of horrified curiosity. She had spoken too much, she was sure. With a hurried wave of her hand, as though she could wipe the words from the air, she said, 'I am sure, if I'd told him who I was, he'd have been quite angry at being tricked. It would be better, I think, to wait until I can find some other way to explain. And a time when he is in an exceptionally good mood.' And let Hendricks wonder as much as he liked what might cause an improvement in her husband's disposition.

She went on. 'But tonight, he left angry. And it was my fault. We argued over...something. And when I turned him out, I had forgotten that he could not see to find his own way to the door. To see him standing there, proud, and yet helpless?' And now, when she raised her handkerchief, she could not deny that it was to wipe away a tear. 'He needs me.'

'That he does, my lady.' Hendricks seemed to relax in his seat, like a man who had found a patch of solid ground after getting lost in a bog.

'I need you to deliver another letter to him, similar to the one you did this morning. Lord knows if he will welcome it, for I am sure he is very cross after the way I behaved tonight. But I mean to try again, tomorrow night, to gain his trust.'

When Adrian awoke the next morning, the lack of headache made the feelings of regret more sharp. He had come back to his rooms, ready to rave at Hendricks about the vagaries of the female mind. But the man, who seemed to have no life at all outside of his work, had chosen that evening to be away from the house.

And then he'd thought to find a bottle and a more sensible woman. Liquor would lift his spirits and a whore would not refuse the predilections of any man with the money to buy her time. In fact, the ladies of that profession were often somewhat relieved that a client would take the time to protect himself.

But a gentlewoman would have no such understanding. To her it was a grave insult to even mention such a thing. To imply that she was not clean enough, and to do it to a woman that had already felt the sting of rejection?

Any frustration that he felt after tonight was his own

fault. And his own discomfort was probably a deserved punishment for leading the woman to believe he was worthy of her, and then leaving her disappointed and insulted. In the end, he had called for a single glass of brandy and taken it with him to his own large and empty bed.

This morning, the rattle of the curtains came as usual, but the daylight following it seemed more of a gradual glow than a rush of fire. 'Hendricks.'

'Yes, my lord.'

'It is still morning, is it not?'

'Half past ten. You retired early.'

'Earlier than you, it seems.'

'Yes, my lord.' His secretary showed no interest in sharing his activities of the previous evening, and Adrian regretted the loss of the easy camaraderie they'd shared while fighting together in Portugal. At one time, they'd have gone out together, or shared the stories of their exploits over breakfast the next morning.

'Lady Folbroke required my services.'

And that was the true reason for the breach, more than their inequality of rank, or his growing helplessness. And for a moment, Adrian wondered if there was a reason for the timing of the visit. When better to go to her, than when one could be sure that her husband would be occupied elsewhere? 'She is well, I trust.'

'When I left her, yes.'

Did that imply that she was the better for Hendricks's company? They would make a handsome couple, similar in colouring and disposition, taciturn but intelligent.

And yet the idea disturbed him, and he rushed to replace the image of them together that formed in his mind. 'I congratulate you on your success. Would that my own evening had gone as well. It seems I am no longer fit company for a lady, for I could not manage a few hours in the presence of one without offering insult.'

Hendricks requested no details, nor did he offer to correct any misconceptions about his own activities. Adrian heard the nervous rattling of the morning paper against the post. 'Do you wish me to read the news, my lord? Or shall I begin with the mail?'

'The mail, I think.' If he did not intend to attend Parliament when it was in session, then hearing the news of the day only made him feel helpless.

'There is only one letter here. And it is similar to the one you received yesterday.'

'Similar in what way?' He doubted it would be in content, after the way they had parted.

'In handwriting, and lack of a return direction. The wax is the same, but unmarked. I have not opened it.' Hendricks gave a delicate pause. 'I thought it better to wait upon your instructions.'

The embarrassment from last evening was still fresh, and a part of him wanted to throw the missive in the fire, unread. What would she have sent, so soon after parting from him? An angry diatribe? A curt dismissal? Florid words of love or a description of their activities on the couch were unlikely. But they would be particularly awkward today, delivered in Hendricks's pleasant baritone as Adrian tried not to imagine the man doing similar things with his Emily.

He steeled his nerves and said, as casually as possible, 'Best read it, I suppose, for the sake of curiosity if nothing else.'

There was a crackling of paper as the wax seal was released, and Hendricks unfolded the note.

'I am sorry. If you would accept this apology, return tonight.'

So even after last night, she still wanted to see him. He felt both relief and shame that she should think she was the one who needed to apologise—and damned lucky that he would have a chance to set her straight.

But was it worth the risk of another rejection? If she meant to toy with him, then so be it. Even after the disasters of the previous two nights, he felt a singing in his blood at the thought that he might kiss her again, and that she might let him take more liberties than he had as yet achieved.

He grinned up at his secretary, who said benignly, 'Will there be a reply?'

The things he wished to say to her came and passed in a rush, as he realised that they would need to be filtered through poor Hendricks, who would be feeling as uncomfortable as he. He had never before forced the man into a position of writing a billet-doux, nor would he today. 'Normally, I would wish to send something immediately. But she has given no address. And after several hours in her company, I still have no idea what to call her, for she would not even give me her first name. If she wishes to shroud herself in mystery, I have no objection. But for punishment, she may wait in ignorance of my feelings until I see her tonight.'

Chapter Nine

Emily paced the front hall of the rented flat, unable to contain her agitation at the thought of the evening's meeting. She had waited nervously for some response from her husband. In the afternoon there had come a hurried note, directly from Hendricks, that she could expect a visit that evening. But there had been no mention of Adrian's reaction, whether he was angry, elated or indifferent.

She was both relieved and annoyed by this. While it was flattering to think that her rejection had not dampened his interest, she could not manage to forget that her husband thought he was rushing to a stranger with the intention of betraying his wife.

But then she remembered the feelings she had experienced on the previous evening. The things he had done to her were so different than his behaviour during the first week of their marriage that she could hardly believe he was the same person. If a revelation of her identity meant that they would be returning to the country for a life of such sterile conjugation, she much preferred being the mysterious object of his infidelity.

Promptly at eight, there was a knock on the door. Before the servant could arrive, she had opened it herself, and pulled Adrian into the hall with her.

At first he resisted, unwilling to be helped. But then he recognised her touch and submitted to her, fumbling to help with the closing of the door once he was through.

Before she could speak, he had seized her, the cane in his left hand bracing vertically along her spine as he kissed her. It was long and hard and unyielding, holding her body against his as he reached between them to unbutton his top coat with his right hand. With the open coat shielding them from observation, he began a careful examination of her dress with his fingers. 'A dinner gown tonight, my dear? Afraid to risk the night-dress again, I see. But what is this, here amongst the net and beads?' His hand cupped her breast. 'You have not bothered with stays. That is a welcome thing to a sight-less man. I can read your response to my arrival with a touch.'

'You are terribly forward,' she said, but made no effort to remove his hand from her body as it brushed against her sensitive nipple.

'I am,' he admitted. 'And I had meant this evening to put you at your ease with my good manners. Already, I have failed.'

'It does not matter. I am happy that you returned. And for last night, I am sorry.'

His fingers left her breast and unerringly found her lips, and he laid one against them to stop the apology. 'It is I who must apologise. I was the one who offered insult. I treated you as I would treat someone who meant nothing to me.'

'Which is how it should be. You barely know me.'

'Now, perhaps. But I would like to know you better.' His head bowed to rest against hers, forehead to forehead. 'You could not understand my reasons for behaving as I did. And I gave you no reason to try. I thought only of my own needs, which were urgent, and offered no explanation for it.'

'It is all right. It does not matter.'

'It does. I hurt you. I made you feel that you are not worthy of love. But that is not the case.'

Emily laid a hand on the front of his vest, over his heart, and he clasped it there. They stood for a time, just like that, as though it had been ages since they had been together, and not hours. And for her, it had been. For how could a few evenings fill the void created by three years apart?

And as she thought of their marriage, she could feel the old breathlessness coming back, the terror of doing something wrong in his presence and spoiling this sudden intimacy. At last, she murmured into his lapel, 'Supper?'

Adrian groaned in frustration and tightened his arms upon her. 'Might it be possible to take light refreshment, and to sit before the fire? And I truly mean that we will talk tonight before anything else occurs between us. But you needn't keep me at arm's length across a table to ensure my good behaviour.'

It surprised her to find him as intimidated by a formal meal as she was in talking to him. 'Very well. I will have the servants lay something simple for us, if that is what you wish. Come.'

She led him to the couch, and arranged for a tray of cold meats and bread to be brought to them, along with wine and fruit. And then she sat down beside him, and offered him a grape. 'Do not think for a moment to deny me the pleasure of helping you.'

'If it means that you will sit close beside me and let me kiss the crumbs from your fingertips? Then of course.' He took the fruit from her hand, and said with a full mouth, 'And while I eat, you will tell me about your husband.'

'And…why would I do that?' She hurriedly offered him more food, wishing that there were a way to get him to the table again so that they could be equally uncomfortable.

He smiled back at her and wiped the corner of his mouth with a napkin. 'I will admit, there is an allure in an anonymous coupling. And a decided lack of guilt at parting from a stranger. But it has been a long time since I have been willing to play the fool for a woman. When I left here, I wanted to be angry, to blame you for all of it, and dismiss the incident from my mind. But I have brooded on it for most of last night and the better part of today as well. I want to know the meaning of your words.'

'What did I say that you did not understand?' She took a fortifying sip of wine.

'You seemed more offended that I feared to get you with child than you were with the implication that I might think you poxed. You may tell me that I have no right to enquire, but it makes me wonder at your motives in lying with me, and fear that you are seeking something other than pleasure. If you cannot give me a suitable explanation, than I must leave you.' He took her hand, and squeezed it. 'But I very much want to stay.'

Emily leaned back in her seat and took another sip of wine. It was as good a time as any to explain to him, she supposed. 'To make you understand, I must tell you about my marriage. My husband and I were together for but a brief time. And while we resided under the same roof, he barely spoke to me. As a matter of fact, he seemed to avoid my company.'

He gave a grunt of dismissal. 'I cannot believe it.'

'In his defence, I barely had the nerve to speak in his presence. I was quite in awe of him.'

'This surprises me,' he said. 'You seemed fearless when I first met you. You have a direct and intelligent manner of speaking that is most refreshing.'

'Thank you.' She coloured. For while the compliment was delivered unawares, it was welcome.

He traced a finger along her cheek. 'Of course, were I married to you, conversation would have been the last thing on my mind.'

'Oh, really. And what would be the first?'

'Getting you to bed, of course. Just as it was when I met you.'

'Then you are obviously not the man I married,' she said, 'for on the three times he visited my room—'

Adrian's brow furrowed. 'Three times?'

'Yes.'

He laughed. 'You mean in the first night, of course.'

She grimaced. He did not even recognise himself in the quite obvious clue she had given him. 'I mean in total. I remember it distinctly. How many women can, after several years of marriage, remember the exact number of conjugal visits and count them on less than a hand?'

'That is an abomination.'

'I quite agree.' And she hoped that the frosty tone in her voice might bring some mote of recollection from the man at her side.

'And these visits…' he cleared his throat as though to stifle a laugh '…were they in any way memorable?'

'I remember each instant, for they were my first and only experiences of that sort.'

'And how would you describe them?'

Her timidity forgotten, she finished her wine in a gulp and said, 'In a word? Disappointing.'

He seemed taken aback by this. 'Was he not gentle with you? Did he give no thought to your inexperience?'

'On the contrary. He proceeded with gentleness and all due care.'

'Then what was the problem?'

Emily almost growled in frustration, for it was clear that he had no memory at all of what had been the most important week of her life. 'He made it plain that he did not enjoy my company. My deflowering was done with martial efficiency, at a tempo that might have been more appropriate for a march than a frolic. And then he had returned to his rooms, without another word.'

Adrian gave a snort, before managing to master himself again. 'You know little of the army, if you think that men in the, uh, heat of battle...' And then, as though he remembered that he was speaking to a lady, he stopped 'Well, then. Never mind. But you are right in thinking that such restraint could not have been pleasant for him. And did you tell him, the next day, of your dissatisfaction with his performance?'

'How could I? I was innocent of the subject. For all I knew, it was the same for all. I had been watching him for years, and dreaming of how it might be. And the waking truth was not at all as I expected. But when one can barely bring oneself to discuss the weather with the man to whom one is wed, how is one to explain that one had hoped, in the marriage bed, for something more?'

'I see.' He laid a hand on hers, in comfort.

'And the next night was the same. And then the next.' She was almost shaking with rage at the memory of it, and the returning shame. 'And then, it seemed he gave our marriage up as a bad job. When evening arrived, a servant informed me that he would be dining with friends, and that I was not to expect his company. And shortly thereafter, he removed to London and has not returned.'

His hand reached up to brush her cheek again, and she shied away, trying to hide the tears of shame that had come unbidden at the recitation.

'And all this time you thought it was somehow your fault?'

'What else could I think? And when you came to me, with that…thing? Is there something wrong with me, that a man I want does not wish to touch me as he should?'

Adrian laughed. 'It does no credit to my gender, but I assure you that there is little that a man cannot stomach when his appetite is good. I can find nothing about you so far that would lead me to believe you capable of inducing such a reaction. I might say, after last night's intimate inspection of you, that you are sweetly formed and temptation itself. You had reduced me to such a state when you turned me out that even with two good eyes I doubt I could have found the door.'

'Really?'

'If the man you married was sane and whole, he would have responded differently.'

'If he was whole,' she repeated.

Adrian nodded. 'Therefore, we must assume that the fault lies on his side. For myself, I would suspect impotence.'

She coughed on a bit of bread, and hurried to pour herself another glass of wine. 'Really?'

He nodded again. 'An inability to perform effectively, no matter how tempted. And he left before you might notice that he had given all he could. It is either that, or a penchant for other men.'

'Oh, I seriously doubt that,' she said, relieved that he could not see her smile.

'It is not unheard of, you know. When you find him in London, it is quite possible that you will discover his relationship with one of his friends is...unusually close.'

'I see.'

'But in either case, it has nothing to do with you, or your attractiveness to members of the opposite gender.'

'You think that is it?'

'I have no doubt. You married a fool, too ashamed to admit a flaw in his own person. And it has caused you grief.'

'When it is put to me thus, I think that is a very accurate assessment of the situation. Thank you for your opinion.' For, although she did not think him a fool, *per se,* the rest of the sentence was true enough.

But the Adrian that sat beside her now did not seem likely to repeat the mistakes he had made in the past. He took the glass from her hands and set it aside. Then he trailed his fingers along the skin of her arms, tracing the line of her shoulder and neck. It made her feel sleek, graceful, desired. 'Think of it no more.' He kissed her shoulder.

'Sometimes I find it hard to think of anything else,' she admitted. 'When I am alone at night.'

'And unsatisfied,' he whispered. 'It is a condition that is easily remedied. Allow me.'

'Allow you what?' She pulled away from him, somewhat surprised by the husky tone of his voice.

'Allow me to prove to you, as I did last night, that there is nothing wrong with you. And that the disappointment you experienced at the hands of your idiot husband need not be repeated.'

'Oh.' The word came out of her, part sigh and part moan, for his lips were on her throat, nuzzling at the place where her heart's blood beat. 'But last night, you said you could not lie with me without using that thing you brought. And I do not think I would like that at all.' For while she wished to have his baby, suddenly, she wished even more to feel her husband inside of her, unsheathed, and as besotted with her as he seemed tonight.

He paused his kisses and looked into her face, his eyes sightless, but still searching to reach her, to make her understand. 'If that one thing is so important to you, then I do not think it is possible for me to give you what you desire. There is only one woman on earth that could command such an intimacy from me. If I deny it of her and tell myself that it is done for her own good, but I give myself freely to another, I will sacrifice the last scrap of honour I have left.' Without thinking, he touched the pocket of his coat, in a place just over his heart.

'What were you reaching for, just now?' she asked.

'Nothing. It is foolishness, really. And certainly not the time...'

Emily ignored his protests, slipped her hand into his pocket and withdrew a battered miniature, no bigger than a locket. She'd remembered sitting for it when she was sixteen. She'd been quite miserable at the time, having just recovered from influenza.

'It is my wife, Emily,' he said softly.

Without thinking, she responded, 'It is not a very good likeness', forgetting that there was no way she could know. Then added, 'Those paintings never are.'

He smiled and took it back from her, opening the cover and running a thumb over the ivory that it was painted on. 'Perhaps not. But it hardly matters, for it has been some time since I've seen it clearly. Still, I like to look on it.' He held it in front of him as though pretending he could see it, then passed it to her.

The question of a likeness was no longer a matter. In the place he had touched it, he had rubbed the paint away from the ivory, smearing her eyes and leaving only a white smudge in the place where her lips might be.

'She was a sweet girl,' he said, smiling and reaching out to take it back. 'And from what I am told, she has grown into a fine woman.'

'You do not know?'

'It has been several years since I've seen her, and she has adjusted to my absence. She handles the business of the estate as well, if not better than I would. I sign what papers are needed when she sends them to me, of course. But her decisions are sound, and I have had no reason to question them. My holdings profit from her wisdom.'

'You treat her no better than your man of business, then?'

'Hardly,' he said. 'Our families were old friends, and

when we married, we had been betrothed for ages, promised to each other almost in the cradle. I had no problems with it, at first. But then I learned the fate of my father, and my grandfather before him.' He gave a wry shrug. 'It was clear that there could be no normal marriage between us. But it hardly seemed fair to her to cry off. I was by far the best offer the girl was likely to have.'

'Bloody cheek,' she murmured.

'But true, none the less. The title is an old one. The house and lands are enough to tempt any woman. By the time I wed her, she was nearly on the shelf. I had hoped that my neglect of her would put her off me. But she'd waited patiently for me to come back from the army when she could just as well have been at Almack's on the hunt for a better man.'

'Or you might have married her sooner,' she pointed out. 'Instead of risking your title by buying a commission.'

'True enough,' he agreed. 'The army is a better choice for a second son. It is dangerous for an heir to go into battle. My cousin Rupert was ecstatic, of course.' When she did not ask, he added, 'He is next in line for Folbroke.'

She responded with an 'I see' to hide her lack of ignorance on the subject. 'And are you pleased that he will succeed you? Is he worthy of it?'

Adrian frowned. 'He is my nearest male relative. It does not matter whether he is worthy or not.'

'Then you think he is not, or you would have answered in the affirmative without hesitation,' she said.

'He is not blind,' Adrian said, as though that answered all. 'And if desire for an earldom is an indicator of worthiness, then he has more worth than I possess. He wants the place more than I ever did. For my part, I expected Napoleon would finish me off before I had to admit the truth to Emily. Once gone, it would be no concern of mine. I would die gloriously and never have to face the future. Instead, a muzzle flash blinded me, and I was sent home. The surgeon told me that the damage to my eyes was a temporary thing, but I knew better.'

'And did you explain any of this to your precious Emily?'

He shook his head. 'I am a coward, and there is your proof of it. I counted her brother as a close friend and comrade, and even he does not know.'

'There is comfort in that, I suppose.' For she doubted she could have survived the shame if David had kept the secret from her as Hendricks had.

'And I have made sure that she will want for nothing, during my life or after it,' he said, as though it would justify his neglect. 'She is my countess, with all the comforts and freedoms that the title allows her. She has free access to the accounts, and she may spend them as she sees fit. All that I have, outside of the entail, is deeded to her, secure in trust.'

'And you think that will be enough to satisfy her, as she waits your return, never knowing what has happened?'

'I doubt she misses me so very much. It has come to my attention that she means to take a lover.'

'And who would tell you such an awful thing?' Since she had only recently learned that he cared at all, it had never occurred to her that her husband might have developed an exaggerated view of her love life.

'Hendricks, my secretary. He is the man who helped you from the tavern two nights ago. He makes frequent trips between us and acts as my eyes and ears at Folbroke Manor. When he comes to town, I question the poor man quite mercilessly about her.' He laughed sadly. 'Recently, it has grown increasingly difficult for him to recount her behaviour. He does not speak of it, of course, but he has a penchant for her as well. And I would not be surprised if she returned his affections.'

'Certainly not!' While Hendricks was not unattractive, the idea that she would choose him over Adrian was so ridiculous that she could hardly stand to hear it.

'Oh, yes, my dear. One does not need eyes to see something like that. When I can get him to speak about her?' Adrian shrugged. 'I can tell that the respect in which he holds her is something more than what one would normally find in a servant. I force him to sit with me, share a brandy to loosen his tongue and tell me of her exploits. And through him, I have come to believe that I have quite the cleverest wife a man could wish for.'

'Except that you think her unfaithful to you.'

Emily could see a muscle tightening in his jaw, as though the matter bothered him more than he was willing to admit. 'I merely have realistic expectations of her. I abandoned her. And I have no intention of ever returning. If I deserved her fidelity, I would be with her this evening. But I will not saddle her with the care of an invalid. Nor do I wish to live at her side as an affectionate brother, leaving her untouched to spare her the risk of bearing my ill-formed whelps.'

'But have you not considered? If you continue in this way, your heir is likely to be sired by another man.'

'Do you think I have not realised the fact?' He bit out the words, sharp and cold. 'If she chooses her lovers with the care that she takes with the rest of my business, the child will be strong and sighted. But if I were to get her with child, there is no telling what might happen. And it would leave her stuck with the care of me. She might as well have two infants for all the use I am likely to be in a few short years.' He laughed mirthlessly. 'Would you like to go and tell her that she must wipe my chin when the spoon cannot find my mouth? Or put me in leading strings so that I can find my own bedchamber?'

'I have watched you, and it is not as bad as all that,' she snapped back. 'You manage quite well on your own, when you are in familiar surroundings.'

'But I have no evidence that she will adjust as well as you have when faced with my disability. You have been unusually understanding, and our arrangement, pleasant though I hope it is for you, is a temporary one. But she should not be put through the bother of a lifetime with me.' He closed the locket and put the picture back into his pocket.

'Nor, apparently, should she be put to the bother of asking her what she wishes.'

'It is what I wish that concerns me,' he said. 'I do not

wish my heir to be blind, nor my wife to look on me with pity, knowing how easy it is to hide the truth from a husband who cannot see her.'

'You do not trust her to be honest.' And, in truth, she was not.

'I would much rather she cuckold me when I am not present than when I am.' He laughed again. 'Either way, I cannot see it.'

'You are horrible.'

'One more proof that my wife is better off without me.'

Adrian was laughing at her, and at their marriage. 'And have you thought, even for a moment, how she might feel to be abandoned, with no explanation? She blamed herself.' She wiped the first stray tear from her eyes with her sleeve, reminding herself that it was unladylike and childish, and that there was no way to know what his wife thought. So she added, 'Or so I would expect.'

He was watching her intently. Or rather he was listening. She could tell by the little cock of his head that he had noticed her stifled sob. 'You are thinking of your own marriage again, aren't you?'

'Perhaps.'

'And I promised that I would give you no reason.' He gathered her close and kissed her upon the forehead, and then the cheek. And then the mouth again, his tongue moving against hers slow and soothing and then faster, as though he meant to tease her back to happiness. He whispered against her lips, 'Let me take the hurt away.'

She could not tell any more who he spoke to. Did he

mean to make her forget? Or did he need to be free of his darling Emily, who, even now, could be lying in the arms of his most trusted friend?

It did not matter. She wanted the same thing he did: for the pain she had carried for so long to go away, and to feel needed and wanted by the one who held her. 'Yes,' she whispered back.

'If you allow me into your bed tonight, I will prove to you that it is possible to meet both my needs and yours. You will have much pleasure and no regrets tomorrow, I promise.'

Emily put her arms around his neck and clung to him, caring for nothing but the feel of his body, close to hers after so long. 'As long as we can be together, that is enough.'

Chapter Ten

'Adrian, please. No more. It is almost dawn and I swear I am exhausted.' Emily laughed, for she had never thought to speak those words, and certainly not to her husband.

'Are you sure, minx?' His hand stole between her legs again, cupping her sex under his palm. 'Although you have left me too weak for another go, I do not think it is possible for a woman to grow too tired for this. Let us see, shall we?'

And it seemed she would know soon enough, for his fingers moved upon her again, as they had so many times since she had led him to her bed.

He had not allowed her to undress him, for he'd claimed that when changing without a valet, he preferred his clothes laid out in a way that ensured he could find them again.

She had watched in eager anticipation as he revealed

without shame the body she had only glimpsed before. The years had not changed him, and she was glad of it. He was as muscular as she remembered, large and strong in ways that made her tremble to the core to look on him.

He had come to her side, kneeling on the edge of her bed and peeled her gown away from her as easily as he had the night before, kissing her face and her body, then toppling her back on to the mattress, his nakedness blending with hers in a tangle of arms and legs and fingers and tongues. He had licked and stroked her to ecstasy more times than she could remember, and spent himself in her hands, between her breasts, and between her thighs, touching her sex with his in a way that was very close to heaven. And then they had slept together, through the night, skin to skin, so close and familiar that they might have been sharing one body.

But not close enough. As he touched her now and dipped inside of her with the tip of his finger, she imagined him entering her, taking her as she had always wanted. She pressed herself against his hand, urging him deeper and remembering the size of him resting heavy in her hands the night before. 'You are bigger than that,' she whispered. And then she gasped, for he had slipped another finger, spreading them inside of her, stretching and moving faster and faster. And she discovered that she was not too tired after all, losing herself all over again in the miraculous maelstrom that she had come to expect from his lovemaking.

'There, my darling,' he said with a smile. 'Admit I was right. Your body wakes at my touch.'

Emily put her arms around his neck and kissed him for what must have been the hundredth time that night. 'And now it would like to sleep at your touch as well. The fire is dying and the sun is rising, but it is still several hours until breakfast. And perhaps the servants would welcome the quiet.' For he had reminded her frequently that he could not see her response, and that it pleased him to hear her cry out.

But now he kissed her gently upon the cheek and disentangled her arms from his neck. 'I had not realised it was so late. You must have your rest.'

She reached out for him, but he had already turned from her, feeling along the edge of the bed and then taking the three steps from the corner that would lead him to the chair with his clothes. 'You are leaving me?' She sat up enough to see the clock upon the mantel. 'It is just past four,' she admitted, with a yawn. 'You can have no other commitments at this hour. Must you go?'

He chuckled. 'If I am honest with myself, probably not. When you know me, you will see that I am the most idle of creatures. I sleep the days away, and my evenings are spent much as you saw the first one.' He pulled on his shirt, tied his cravat in a rough knot, and came back to her, reaching to find her, and kissing her outstretched hand. 'But since I am a wastrel and a rake, it would be better for your reputation if I were not seen leaving this place after breakfast, satisfied by more than a hearty meal.'

She sighed, for perhaps now was the right time to tell him that it did not matter in the slightest. But while they had shared a bed for hours, and done more together than she had ever expected, he had not succumbed enough to do the deed. Nor would he be likely to, if she made him angry.

When she did not answer he said, 'Have you fallen back to sleep?'

'I am merely hoping that if I do not agree, you will not leave.' Because this was how it was supposed to be. How it should have been from the first. The two of them together, sharing the night and greeting the dawn.

'I must go, so that I might return again. And before then, I must have a change of linen and a shave, if you wish me to be the presentable man you want, and not the base ruffian you found me.' He released her hand and returned to the business of dressing. Then he said, casually, as though he did not wish to presume the invitation, 'If you are not busy, of course. And if you desire more of my company. My nights are not empty, but they are not so full that I would not be willing to dedicate them to you.'

He probably meant, if she rejected him, to slip back to the place she had found him, and his inevitable doom. 'No.' She climbed out of the bed to come to his side.

'You refuse me?'

'I refuse to allow you to fill your evenings with anything but me,' she said, twining her arms about him and kissing him again. 'I will meet with you again, as often as you like, night or day, it does not matter to me. I have but one condition.'

He smiled and hugged her. 'I am yours to command.'

'For the duration of our acquaintance, you must not frequent gaming hells or taverns or any other low haunts like the one I found you in. While you may not think yourself worthy of better company, I do not find it flattering to be lumped in with such as that.'

Adrian gave a small laugh, and for a moment she was sure that he would tell her in no uncertain terms that their short acquaintance gave her no right to dictate terms to him. And then he said, 'Well played, madam. In three days, you have succeeded in doing what my friends and family have attempted for years. Of course, they might have had more success in reforming me had they the bait you offer. If you wish me to, I will leave off my vices, for a time, in exchange for the pleasure of your company.'

'And there must be no more talk of seeking an end to your life or dying young by misadventure. You must assure me that whatever happens between us, you will die in bed, at an advanced age.'

'I can hardly be expected to guarantee my own longevity.'

'But you can safeguard what time you have for my sake.' She ran a finger along his chest before buttoning his vest over it. 'I will brook no talk of doom, nor do I wish you threatening to step in front of a dray horse, should I do something that displeases you.' She kissed his chin, nestling her naked body against him and feeling his spirit weaken as his body grew hard.

He groaned and pushed her away, firmly back on her own two feet. 'None of that, then. If I mean to leave you, I will not be able, should you begin again.'

'I will not let you go until you promise. I could not bear it, I swear.'

He leaned against a bedpost, grunting as he pulled on his boots. But he was smiling. 'Very well. To remain secure in your affections, I will do as you ask. Now tell me where to find a bell pull so that I might summon a ride home.'

When she offered to help him, he kissed her firmly on the lips, leading her back to the bed. 'You need not rise. I will find my own way, with some small amount of help. And I dare say your servants must grow used to it. I expect they will see me often from now on.'

Adrian reached his own doorstep without a stumble, handing his coat and stick to a waiting footman. This morning, it was almost a relief to be unable to read the expression on the man's face. If he could see, he was sure that he would find the servant smirking at the master for coming in with the dawn with a smile on his face and smelling of a woman's cologne.

He inhaled deeply. *Lemons, again.* His mouth watered at the thought of her. Or perhaps it was because he had barely eaten. He would have a wash, a shave and a hearty breakfast.

Adrian went to his room and pulled back the curtains, seeing the glow of the rising sun, and felt the first warmth hit his face as his valet came to prepare him for the day.

When Hendricks came to him, several hours later, he swore he could hear the man's shocked intake of breath at finding him upright and taking eggs and kippers at the little table beside the window.

'Come in, Hendricks.' He made a welcoming gesture in the general direction of the door and indicated the chair on the other side of the table. 'Bring the post and *The Times* and help yourself to a cup of tea. And try to contain your astonishment. I swear, I heard your jaw drop as you crossed the threshold.'

'You must admit that it is unusual for me to find you awake, my lord.'

'I am sober as well. And fully dressed. Of course, what I mean to do with all the extra time, I have no idea. I suspect I have put my valet to a great deal of bother, only to spoil my cravat by napping through the afternoon. But what can be done?'

'You are in a better mood today, I see.' His secretary was using his typically mild-mannered voice, but there was a hint of something in it that almost seemed like censure.

'And what if I am?'

'It is rare enough to be worthy of comment. The last time I greeted you cheerfully before noon, you threw a bookend at me.'

'I apologise.' He had been suffering that day from the headache that sometimes accompanied his troubles. Or, if he was more honest with himself, he had been suffering the after-effects of the gin. In either case, it had been no reason to take it out on Hendricks. 'If you felt then as I do today, then I had no right to spoil the mood.' He reached for his tea, and felt Hendricks stay his hand.

'Excuse me, my lord. It has been incorrectly prepared for you. Someone has put lemon in it this morning.'

Adrian grinned. 'And two sugars. Tart, and yet very sweet. Just as I requested it. Never mind the post. I doubt there is anything in it that I care about. But if you could read me the news of the day, I would be most grateful.'

Chapter Eleven

The vigour with which Adrian had started the day had faded by noon. He might have stood the fatigue if there had been a way to occupy himself. But with no word from Emily or his mysterious new lover, there was nothing in the mail that required his attention. And although the news was interesting, it gave him the familiar feeling of restlessness to hear it. If he refused his chance to be involved with the making of laws, he had no real need to keep abreast of current events. He soon grew frustrated with the paper and waved his secretary away.

When Hendricks was gone, Adrian roamed his small rooms like a lost soul. He requested an early lunch, which he promptly regretted, for the food lay heavy in his stomach. Then he went back to his bedchamber, and lay down upon the bed, closing his eyes and falling into an uneasy doze.

He dreamed of *her*, of course. And in those dreams,

he could see her and call her by name. When they had lain together, near exhausted from love-making, he had asked her what she wished to be called, if she would not give him her name.

She had laughed and said, 'Anything you like. Or nothing at all. While I appreciate endearments, I have learned to live without them.'

And it had angered him. For while some women could turn petulant if not given jewels, the woman at his side deserved to be showered with words of love, and yet had been forced to manage with none.

But then she had said, 'But I do seem to enjoy attention that is physical in nature.'

'Do you, now?' He laughed again and moved to touch her, eager to give her what she hinted at. And a name for her had popped easily into his mind. He pushed it away, remembering that though he might imagine what he liked as they made love, he must guard his tongue. She knew too much already about his life and marriage to call her by the name that was always close to his thoughts. It would be an insult to what they shared

But in his sleep he was loving a woman that was a perfect blend of what he had and what he wanted. Though it should have been the happiest of dreams, and one that he wanted never to end, he could not shake the feeling that the happiness would not last.

And then, at the penultimate moment of his fantasy, there was the sound of something heavy moving in the hall. And of men, grunting under the weight of it, and muffled curses as someone banged an arm or pinched a finger.

Adrian rose and stalked across his room, opening the door with such force that it would have slammed against the wall had it not met with an obstruction. 'What the devil is going on out here? Do you not realise that I am trying to sleep?'

'My lord, if you will excuse us, there is a delivery.' They were trying to manoeuvre something past him, towards the sitting room. 'We were instructed to place it in the corner, by the window.'

'Not by me you weren't,' he said, and heard the footman take an involuntary step back and the burden bumping against the walls in a way that must have scratched the paper from them.

'It is from… She said you would not mind.' There was a tiny stammer at the beginning of the sentence, as though they were unsure how to broach the rest of it.

'She?' There could be only one she that would be so motivated. Whatever it was was probably offered as a 'thank you' for their extremely active night. He should accept it in the spirit it was given, no matter what it might be. 'Well, if she insists that it must go in my sitting room, who am I to argue?' *Other than the owner of the room, of course.*

'Very good, my lord. If you would stand back, just for a moment?' From the sound of his voice, Parker, the footman, was fading under the weight of the thing he carried, but made no move to proceed without his master's permission. The man had made the mistake, when first he'd arrived, of trying to touch Adrian and move him manually out of the way of a delivery. But he had learned with the sharp rap of a cane on his knuckles to keep his distance and allow my lord his space.

Adrian raised his hands and stepped back to give them room to pass.

There was more grunting, and the sound of the two footmen manoeuvring a piece of furniture, followed by the instructions to a third man to 'Get the stool as well'.

When things settled down, Adrian folded his arms and demanded, 'What is it?'

'A pianoforte, my lord.'

'A what?'

'A pianoforte. She said that we might have some difficulty with it, but that it was the smallest one she could find.'

Adrian waved his hands as they began to repeat. 'Never mind. I heard you the first time. But what the hell am I supposed to do with the thing? The woman must be mad—take it away, immediately.'

'There is a message, my lord.' Hendricks spoke from the doorway, for doubtless there was little space left in the room for him.

'Really. Well, then? Speak.'

'She said you would likely object to it. And to inform you, when you did, that you needed something to occupy your days, since idle hands are the Devil's tools.' Hendricks sounded faintly amused, as he could afford to do, being well out of reach of my lord's cane.

Adrian glared into the sitting room, then followed in

the wake of the servants and the unwanted gift. His lady had been happy enough with the Devil's tools when he'd left her. Perhaps she was afraid that he would use them on another, if she did not fill every minute of his life. 'And I suppose, if I send it away…'

'The note says she will find something larger, since simple presents do not seem to entertain you.'

He imagined her voice, framing those words with a hint of disapproval. 'If her man is still waiting, tell him that I will be by this evening to deliver my thanks in person. I would go now, but there is a large piece of furniture blocking my way to the door.'

'Very good, my lord.'

The men cleared away, leaving him alone with his present. And it was as though he could sense the interloper in the room, without even approaching it. He could feel the faint vibrations of the strings inside, for they still hummed with the recent disturbance.

He walked towards it, bumping into the corner and hearing the hollow rap of his cane against its body, running his hand along the side and hoping that she had not wasted money on some gold, heavily ornamented monster of an instrument. It felt simple enough. Rectangular, and with the slightly sticky feel of varnish rather than paint.

So she thought he should keep busy. Clearly, she did not understand what it meant to be a gentleman. His status in society removed the whole point of an occupation. He was not supposed to make work for himself. And many of the things that might have kept him entertained were quite lost to him, now that his eyes were gone. Even gaming had lost its lure. He could no longer read the cards without help, and his need to touch the face of the dice, to feel the spots and assure himself of the roll, was often taken as cheating by his opponents.

He sat down on the bench and laid his hands on the ivory keys, depressing one to hear the tone of it, and depressing his spirit as well. It would need continual tuning, of course. These things always did. But was he expected to know by listening whether it was right or wrong?

He walked his fingers up a scale and sighed, already bored with it in a few short notes. He laboriously picked out a folksong, and then a familiar hymn. The tunes were thin, and he was sure that a talented musician would be searching for seconds and thirds, and chords, finding harmonious combinations by trial and error.

What had he taken from the few music lessons of his youth? Damn little. While his mother had thought it a good idea to give him some understanding of the arts, his father had thought it a waste of time. The clock on the mantel chimed a quarter past the hour. It was just as it had been when he was a boy. He had been sitting at the instrument for only a few moments, and already he was stiff, bored and aching to leave it behind.

'A visitor to see you, my lord.' Abbott had entered with the announcement, and Adrian looked up with eagerness, forgetting for a moment that he had not accepted a guest in months as his condition had deteriorated.

'Mr Eston.'

'Damn and hell.' Emily's brother, and the last man on the planet he wished to see. 'Put him off. Any excuse you like, I do not care.'

'He will not be denied. He says that he means to wait in the entry until he meets with you, either coming or going.'

It sounded very like his old friend David, who in comparison to Adrian had both the patience and morals of a saint. 'Give me a moment, and then show him in.'

When he heard the door close, he hurried across the room to the brandy decanter, filling a glass with such speed that he spilled some on his sleeve. Even better. The smell of the liquor burned in his nostrils, making an attempt at the appearance of drunkenness more obvious. For good measure he dipped his fingers into the glass and sprinkled more of it onto his coat then took a mouthful and swished it about a bit before swallowing. Then he went back to sprawl in a chair by the fireplace with the decanter in one hand and the half-empty glass in the other, barking his shin against the piano bench on the way, then sitting down again just as the door opened.

He looked up as though the hulking shadow in the doorway seemed the least bit familiar, and raised his glass in salute. 'David, it has been so long.'

'Over a year,' his brother-in-law grunted at him.

'And what brings you to London?'

'I have come to fetch you home.'

'Why, my dear sir, I am home.' He waved the glass to encompass the room, spilling more of the contents in the process. 'Please, avail yourself of my hospitality. A drink, perhaps?'

'It is just gone noon, Adrian,' David said with disgust. 'Far too early for brandy.'

'But this is a special occasion, is it not? We have established that you do not visit often. To see you now is a cause for celebration.' To see him at all would be more of a miracle. But for now, his unfocused gaze and unwillingness to meet his friend's eye would be blamed on a guilty nature and the glass in his hand.

Eston grunted again, and he did not need eyes to guess the expression of distaste on the man's face. 'You celebrate too often, as it is.'

'There is much reason to make merry, for London is a fine town.'

'But not so fine that you would bring my sister to it.'

'I did not think she would enjoy it. You said often enough, before we married, that she was a simple girl.'

'She is a woman, now. And she is here in town.' David paused to give significance to the next words. 'But she is not staying with me.'

Adrian gave an uneasy laugh. 'Is that so?'

'She has taken rooms, and refuses to tell me where. I assume that she is using them to receive someone that she does not want me to meet.'

'I do not mind her coming to town. Nor have I forbidden her from socialising. There is money enough to take lodgings of her own, should she choose to. And there is hardly space enough here, should she want to come to me.'

'If there is money enough to maintain two residences,' David said with irritation, 'then there is also money enough to get a town house large enough to share.'

'But would that allow her the privacy she seeks?' Adrian said with mock innocence.

David made a noise of exasperation. 'Why should it matter to you? She is your wife and should not require more privacy than you wish to give her.'

Adrian took a swig of his brandy, and waved his other hand, as if the concept were too much for his addled brain. 'Well then, we are in agreement. I wish to allow her as much privacy as she wants, and to allow myself the same.'

'So it does not bother you that she has taken a lover?'

There would be no way of avoiding the truth if David insisted on sharing it with him. Adrian poured himself another brandy and drank deep, pretending that he cared for nothing but the spirit, ignoring the tightening in his guts. 'And who might that be?'

'I do not know his name,' David said. 'But I ran into her today, shopping on Bond Street. And it was obvious what she has been doing with the days she has been absent from my lodging. She positively glowed.'

'I am encouraged by her continued good health,' Adrian said absently, feeling both relieved and discouraged by the sketchy information.

'It is not health I am referring to, you drunken ninny,' David snapped back, all patience gone. 'I have never seen my sister looking thus. She has been with a man.'

Adrian sipped his drink, looking down into it as

though he could see it. 'And I have been with a woman. I can hardly blame her, David. You know we are estranged.'

'But I do not know the reason for the separation.'

He took another drink from his glass. 'Perhaps not. But it is no business of yours. It is a matter between my wife and myself.'

'And now it is a matter between you and me. You have made no effort to be a husband to her, and now she is likely to shame herself and you with a public affair.'

'With my blessing,' Adrian said, gritting his teeth.

David swore. And then the shifting shadows seemed to indicate him stepping closer, towering over Adrian as he sat by the fire. 'You have been with Emily for three years, and it is clear that you do not mean to get her with child or show her even the slightest modicum of respect. If she looks elsewhere for affection, it is quite possible that your heir will be illegitimate, and then all will know you for a fool, and my sister for a whore.'

Adrian stared into the faint orange glow that marked the ashes from the previous night's fire. 'I think there is little doubt already that I am a fool. And as for her reputation?' He shrugged. 'She is my wife. Any child of hers will be my heir, no matter who his father might be.'

'Are you saying you cannot stir yourself sufficiently to care for Emily that you would be with her long enough to ensure the parentage of your children? If you had so little regard for her, then why did you marry her?'

Adrian drank again. 'Perhaps I never for a moment

wanted her. But I saw no way out of it. My future was sewn up tight by my parents and by yours, before I had any say in it. I am willing to abide by my obligations. But it is a bit much to expect me to do it with a light heart.'

'You selfish bastard,' David said with disgust. 'I remember you of old, Adrian. And I thought you near to fearless. Now, you are telling me that you lacked the nerve to stand up to a slip of a girl and trapped her in a sham of a marriage rather than set her free to find the love she deserved.'

'It is not as though she gained nothing by marrying me,' he muttered. 'She has the land.'

'You have the land,' David reminded him. 'And she has the running of it.'

'And a fine job she does,' he nodded, smiling. 'In reward, I have given her the freedom to find love where she likes. That is what you wished for her, did you not?'

'But it is not what she wishes,' David insisted. 'She adores you, Adrian. At least, she did when you wed her.'

'She gave no sign of it, at the time,' he answered. Not that he had made any great effort to discern the feelings of the woman he had married. But suppose there had been some affection there that he had been too thick to notice? The tiny portrait in his pocket seemed to grow heavier at the thought.

'I know her, even better than I know you. She was too shy to say so, but she was overjoyed at the match. And at the time, she had great hopes that you would learn to love her as well. Emily wanted more than what you have given her.' Now David spoke more gently. 'When I press her about the estrangement, she claims to value her freedom. But I can see the look in her eyes. She wants a husband and children more than your estate. And though she might settle for any man willing to show her affection, her heart is not involved. There is a chance, if you return to her now, that it is not too late. Her *tendre* for you could be rekindled.'

Dear God, no. 'And what would make you think that I had any desire for such?' It was the last thing he needed to hear, now of all times. Sometimes it seemed that his only source of consolation was that his death would be a relief to her. But suppose it was otherwise?

'Perhaps I think you should care less about what you desire, and stop behaving like some stupid young buck, fresh from the classroom and eager to indulge every whim. Go back to your wife before she sinks as low as you have and cares for naught but meeting her own needs.'

'Now see here,' Adrian snapped back, feeling the beginnings of a cloud over his thoughts from the brandy he had bolted. 'What I do or do not do with your sister is no affair of yours. The only reason it bothers you, I think, is because you had some designs on my land yourself. See it as an extension of your own park, do you? Hunting and fishing and riding on my property as though you own it. You must think that I will go the way of my short-lived ancestors, and that when I am gone, you will twist my heir around your little finger.' He laughed and took another gulp, letting his imagination run wild. 'That'll be much harder to do if the whole thing passes to some cousin, won't it? If there is no heir, your sister will be put off to dower, and your plans will all be for naught.' It was a disgusting picture. And he wondered if there was any truth in it.

David cursed and knocked the glass from his hand onto the hearth. 'It is only affection for Emily that keeps me from calling you out.'

'And I might say the same. If any other man had dared to come into my study to tell me how to organise my life and my marriage, I'd have run him through.'

He could almost hear David's eyes narrow. 'You needn't fear that in the future, Adrian. All who once claimed you as a friend are gone, driven off by your shameful behaviour. But if they still existed, they would also tell you that you are a sot and a wastrel and they are embarrassed to know you. You lose yourself in liquor and whores, intent on destroying yourself like your father and grandfather did before you, little heeding the pain you heap on your wife and friends. I rue the day that a union of our families was suggested. I do not need access to your land, and will keep within the boundaries of my own estate, if the thought of my trespassing bothers you so. From now on, I will live as a stranger to you.'

'At last! He means to leave me alone!' Adrian hoped that volume would make up for the lack of true feeling in the dismissal.

'And it is a shame, Adrian, for I once thought of you almost as a brother. I welcomed the connection between us and hoped that a wedding would bring you happiness, moderate your character and be a benefit to Emily. I have proved myself a bigger fool than you are for putting my trust in you.'

His childhood friend spoke with such disappointment that he almost admitted the truth. But what good would that do? The man would be just as angry that poor Emily had been tricked into such an ill-fated match. 'You must have known,' Adrian said softly, 'that there was a chance that you were wrong. That blood might tell, and I would be no better than the rest of my family.'

'But I knew you. Or thought I did. And I was sure, at one time, that you had a heart to be touched. I am beginning to suspect that it is not the case.'

Adrian hid his confusion in a cold laugh that he knew would enrage his guest. 'Then you are learning me right, after all these years,' he said looking up at the hazy spectre of his oldest friend, looming over him.

'Very well, then. The interview is at an end, as is the last of our friendship. You have treated my sister abominably. You have scorned my efforts to intervene. What is likely to occur from all this will be entirely on your head.'

And even without sight, Adrian could chart David's passage out of the rooms by the slamming of the doors.

Chapter Twelve

'Hendricks!' Adrian bellowed. If the man was still in, there would be no way for him to escape the sound of his master's voice.

'My lord?' His response was so prompt that Adrian wondered if the secretary had been listening at the door.

'I was just forced to undergo an excruciating fifteen minutes with Eston. Am I mistaken, Hendricks, or do I pay you to prevent such things?'

'I am sorry, my lord.'

If he wished to be rational, he would admit that it had been the distraction of the piano delivery that had left the doors open and allowed the guest to enter, not any carelessness on Hendricks's part. But the excess of spirits was making him irritable, as was the disapproving sniff that Hendricks gave at the spilled brandy. Adrian set the decanter aside. 'To avert questions about my behaviour, I let him think me drunk. I have most likely ruined this coat by dousing myself with liquor. But he felt the need to tell me that my wife has taken a lover. What do you know of the situation?'

'Nothing, my lord.' But the man said 'nothing' with such a lack of conviction that he might as well have said everything.

'Really. But you have seen her recently, I trust?'

'Yes, my lord. This morning.'

'And how did she look, when you last spoke with her?'

'Well.'

'Is that all, Hendricks? For her brother implied that she was looking, perhaps, too well.'

Adrian's comment should have been incomprehensible. But Hendricks seemed to understand it perfectly. 'I did not notice anything unusual about her, my lord.' It was a pitiful attempt to hide the truth.

'And where was she, when last you saw her?'

Hendricks paused, as though he could not seem to remember his story, and said, 'At her brother's town house, my lord.'

'How strange. For she has not been in residence there for several days.'

Hendricks sighed. 'At her rooms, my lord.'

'So you have seen them, then?' He resisted the desire to add the word *Aha*. 'I suppose you have been there several times.'

'Yes, my lord.' He sounded glum now, as though any good spirits that the lady might have gained through his visits were not shared.

As an afterthought, Adrian asked, 'As I remember it, Hendricks, you wear spectacles, do you not?'

'Yes, my lord,' said Hendricks, clearly baffled as to what this had to do with anything.

And there went his hopes that the next Earl of Folbroke would be unencumbered by difficulties with vision. Still, some sight was better than none. 'Her brother David seemed most concerned at the damage to her reputation, should it be known that she is setting up housekeeping with a man. If she wished some space of her own, it is a shame that she has not seen fit to ask her husband for permission.'

'Did you expect her to? It has been long since you have spoken to her—she no doubt assumed that you would not care.' Hendricks had answered a trifle too quickly with this, and altered his tone to be less censorious before adding, 'If you wish to see her today, I could arrange it for you.'

'It merely surprises me that she has not sought me out. If she cannot visit her own husband when she is scant miles from him, then it gives credence to her brother's theory.'

'She did visit you, my lord, on the day she arrived in town. As you remember, I came to fetch you.'

And pulled me from another woman's arms and dragged me home, insensible. Touché, *Hendricks,* touché. 'Since she did not return, I did not think the matter was important.'

'Perhaps it is because she has been spurned and avoided for such a long time that she has no more desire to try.' His secretary's voice was sharp and scolding. And there could be no questioning his meaning. 'At this point in time, perhaps it is up to you to seek her.'

'Do you presume to tell me how to handle my marriage?'

'Of course not, my lord.' But the tone said just the opposite.

'You might as well do it, for it seems quite a popular activity this week.' He gave a vague gesture towards the writing desk. 'Draft a letter to Emily. I will see her this evening at six. Do it quick, man, before I sober sufficiently from Eston's visit to realise what a mistake I am making.'

'See her, my lord? Do you wish me to explain the unlikelihood of that? For I believe your condition still a mystery to her.'

For a moment he *had* forgotten. Damn that strange woman for getting under his skin and making him think, even for an instant, that his life could be ordinary.

'No. Emily has no clue. Unless you have told her.'

'You forbade me.' It was a comfort to hear the resignation, and the resolution, in that sentence and the lack of even a fraction of a second's hesitation. Whatever else he might be doing, it was plain that Hendricks followed some of his instructions to the letter, no matter how unwise he thought them.

Adrian shook his head. 'After all this time, there are no simple words to describe to her what has happened, or to explain why I hid the truth. It will be easier when we are face to face to explain things, so that there can be no mistaking. It is not as if my lack will come as a severe shock to her. I am not disfigured in any way, am I?' He touched his own face, suddenly unsure. Perhaps time had made him an ogre, and the servants were too kind to remark on it.

'No, sir.'

'Then I will explain to her, once she arrives. It is time, I think, that there be some truth between us.'

'Very good, my lord.'

'Mr Eston, my lady.'

When the footman announced her brother, Emily was enjoying what she'd thought was a well-earned cup of tea. With her morning's shopping and calls, she had taken what she'd hoped were the first steps to sorting out her husband's problems. Or perhaps they were steps towards encouraging him to do so, for she doubted there would be any change in his character without full co-operation from the man himself.

But since no one knew of her location, she had not expected visitors other than Hendricks. And she certainly had not expected to see her brother. 'David?' Thinking of the confrontation she expected from him, his name came out of her mouth in a breathless whimper that made her sound guiltier than she was over her behaviour. 'What are you doing here?' There, she noted with some relief. The strength returned to her when she turned the challenge back to him.

'I have come to see what you are doing here, and who you are doing it with.' Her brother signalled the footman for another cup and sat in the chair opposite her. His presence was so commanding that she thought for a moment that he had invited her to the room to explain herself.

'It is not necessary for you to watch over me. Nor is it your place,' she reminded him. 'I am both grown and married.'

'If you can call what you share with Adrian a marriage,' he responded.

'Says the man who is the same age as my husband, but has no wife of his own.'

The mention of this seemed to make him uncomfortable, so he turned the argument hurriedly back to her. 'It is your husband I wish to speak of, and not my nonexistent wife. I have been to see Adrian, since you have not.'

'That was not necessary.'

'I feel it was,' he said, looking around him at her rooms. 'I saw you this morning, shopping in Bond Street.'

'I remember,' she said coolly. 'I greeted you, did I not?'

'But you were behaving strangely. Secretively. There is but one reason that I can think of to explain such behaviour.'

'Oh, I seriously doubt that,' she said. Emily could feel herself begin to blush, which would make her look even more guilty. But there was little to be done to stifle the sudden and rather graphic memories of what she had been up to in the days since she had moved from her brother's house.

'You have taken up with some man.' He was staring at her clothing, which was too casual to accept any but a lover, and the flush of her skin. And God forbid that he should look in the bedroom, for he might see the sheets, still rumpled from last night's activities.

She took another sip of tea to hide her confusion. 'Hardly, David.'

'And you have rented rooms so that the meetings could be done in secret.'

'Not much of a secret, clearly, since you have followed me to them. Was that how you found me?' But he had clearly not looked too closely into the matter, if he had not identified the man in question.

He showed no sign of noticing her censor. 'I questioned my coachman, since you seem intent on using my vehicle as your own. And he admitted taking your baggage to this place. But we are not discussing my behaviour. It is yours that is in question. I waited outside this morning. And in the dim light, I saw someone creeping away from here. He was in the carriage and away before I could get a look at him.'

'Oh, David,' she said, wincing with embarrassment at this further complication of her plans. 'Why now? You have not given a thought to my behaviour in years. It is not as if I did not have admirers before.'

'But you were not serious about them. And even if you were, that was in the country. It was not as if anyone was likely to notice you there.'

So she had been out of sight and out of mind to him as well, had she? 'I suspect it was easier for you, when

I remained there. But you could not expect me to avoid London for ever, could you?'

'Perhaps not. But I expected that when you returned to town, you would be circumspect in your behaviour. If you cannot manage your reputation, you will come home immediately.'

'I will not.' She thought for a moment. 'And just where do you mean to take me, if I must come home? Not to your house, certainly. I have not lived under that roof since I married.'

'But perhaps you should, if you mean to disgrace the family.'

'I am no longer a member of your family. But if Adrian has a problem, after all this time, then he should be the one to come here, and drag me back to the country.'

'We both know that he will not,' her brother replied with disgust. 'If he exercised the discipline necessary in his own house, then the job would not fall to me. And if you did not go to such lengths to make absence easy for him, he might be forced to return home and see to his business.'

'Then why do you not go to the source of the problem and talk to him? Why do you think it necessary to harass me over the state my marriage?'

'I have been to him,' her brother ground out through gritted teeth. 'I took what I learned to Folbroke, just now. He was already drunk, though it was barely noon. And he showed no interest in my company, nor your presence in town.'

Drinking again? She frowned. Adrian had seemed sober enough when they had been together the previous evening. She had hoped that problem, at least, was in abatement. 'And that was your only fault with him?' For there was a significant matter that her brother had not mentioned.

'Other than his damned stubbornness and bad temper. He barely looked at me the whole time I was there. As though, if he ignored me, he would not have to answer to me.'

'I see.' Her poor brother would be even angrier than she had been when he learned of the trick. 'I expect he liked your interference no better than I do.'

'Is it truly interference to wish that my oldest friend and my dear sister would find happiness with each other, instead of behaving in ways that are a scandal?'

Emily thought of the things that had occurred in these rooms, which, while exciting, were probably some of the least scandalous things her husband had done since their marriage. 'Perhaps we shall. Perhaps I have my own plans to rectify the breach. You must trust that I can manage this. You are not married, and cannot understand what goes on between a husband and wife, even when they are not happy.' She thought for a moment, and smiled. 'Especially when they are not happy. Although it might not seem so, I find that I am quite capable of managing Adrian, now that I have set my mind to try.'

Her brother shook his head. 'You had best manage this quickly, then, for my patience with his behaviour is nearing an end. If you cannot bring him home with you, by God, I will drag him back home by the ear. I cannot stand by any longer and watch him destroy himself, Emily. I simply cannot.'

She could see, by the look in her brother's eyes, that his interference came not from a desire to control, but sincere pain at the way his friend was likely to end. She gave him a pat on the hand. 'Trust me. A little longer. It will be all right. You will see.'

There was the sound of yet another guest, and Hendricks walked into the room, unannounced, as though he were perfectly at home there.

And Emily saw the narrowing of David's eyes, as he came to a conclusion that was not evident to her. 'Mr Hendricks?'

'Mr Eston.' There was a similar narrowing of Hendricks's eyes behind his glasses, as though he answered some unspoken challenge. Then he looked to her. 'My lady, I bring a letter from your husband.'

'Do you, now?' David said, as though he assumed there was some ruse in play.

'I believe he wrote it at your suggestion, sir,' Hendricks said innocently.

'And you were able to deliver it here so quickly without stopping first to find Emily at my town house.'

'Oh, really, David,' she said. 'Mr Hendricks knows the location because he helped me to let it. And if there is a letter from Adrian, you must assume that we are more *simpatico* than you know. Now, if you will excuse me, I wish to read the thing in private.'

'Very well, then.' He shot Hendricks another suspicious look. 'But if I do not hear of a meeting between the two of you within a week, I will go back to Adrian, and tell him what I have seen here. I suspect he will find it of interest.'

When he had left, Emily looked down at the paper in her hand, thoroughly annoyed with her brother for spoiling what she hoped might be a pleasant read. And then she noticed that it was addressed to Emily, and written in the hand of his secretary. She glared back at Hendricks. 'So my lord finally summons me, does he?'

'Yes, Lady Folbroke. And he asked after you. He seemed most interested in your status, and rather ashamed of the length of time since he has last seen you and the fact that he has hidden his blindness.'

She sniffed. 'The pangs of a guilty conscience, more like.'

'He had just received a visit from your brother, and was concerned about the reason you removed from the Eston town house. Mr Eston thinks a gentleman is involved.'

'Too rightly. And with your sudden arrival here, he has concluded that the gentleman is you. What nonsense.'

There was a long pause as Hendricks tried to decide how to respond to his change in status from servant to Lothario. 'Of course, my lady.'

'And my husband's response to this rumour?'

Hendricks held out the letter to her again.

'I see that. And that it is written in your hand. What, in your opinion, was his reaction to rumours of my infidelity?'

'In my opinion?' repeated Hendricks, as though he wished to make it clear that he did not speak for her husband. 'He is jealous, my lady.'

She felt a brief moment of triumph, followed by annoyance. 'So what is sauce for the gander is not sauce for the goose.' She tapped the letter with her nail. 'And has he set an agenda for this meeting?'

'He means to tell you of his problems.'

'And I already know of them. What is meant to come after this grand revelation?'

'I think he means to come to some understanding between you.'

She tossed the paper on to the fire. 'In which I am more discreet and he does not change at all. If that is the case, then I hardly need to stir myself, for I am having no part of that.' She smiled at Hendricks, trying not to look as smug as she felt. 'I am enjoying myself far too much to stop now. And if the thought of my happiness without him causes him discomfort, then all the better.'

'Do you wish to send him a message to that effect?'

'No.' For some reason, Adrian's sudden need to see her had angered her to the point where she could hardly speak, probably because she had worked hard and long to quash any hope that it would ever happen. 'There is no message. If he asks, tell him I have refused. Since he has waited years to summon me, he should not be surprised to find me otherwise engaged on the night he is ready to unburden his soul.'

'Very good.' Hendricks frowned at her as though he did not mean it.

And he was right. It was not good. Her behaviour was foolish and childish. It should have been welcome news to find that he worried about her, pined after her and had worn the paint from her picture through constant handling of it. Instead, it reminded her of all the time that had been wasted. She resented being the afterthought to her husband's infidelities, almost as much as she enjoyed receiving the attention from them. She sighed. 'I am sorry, Hendricks, that I cannot make this easier upon him. His wife is quite out of patience with him. But I will wait upon him here, tonight, as I have done before. Perhaps he will be more free with his thoughts to his lover.'

Chapter Thirteen

Adrian arrived at her rooms that evening, so full of anger and indignation that he did not need to speak to show his mood. It was there in the set of his back, the tightness of his gait, and the staccato rapping of his cane against the parquetry floor. After a moment's hesitation, she went up on tiptoes to kiss him, and he responded with a perfunctory peck upon the cheek.

Then he brushed off her advance as though he could not be bothered with it, tucking his cane under his arm so that he could tug the gloves off his hands, then tossed them into his hat with unusual force.

Emily stepped away. 'I thought, after this morning, that I would receive a better greeting than this. What is the matter?'

'It has been a trying day,' he said with a glare, tapping about the hall to feel the bench beside him and landing the hat on it with a flick of his wrist. 'When I am home,

I prefer peace and quiet, uninterrupted by changes or surprises. But today it was impossible. Someone had taken it upon themselves to give me a pianoforte.'

'Do you like it?' she asked, although she could see by his expression what the answer was likely to be.

'Have I given you any reason to think that I would?'

'You had said that you were idle most days. And I thought, if you had something to occupy the daytime hours, then at night you would not need to go out.'

He closed his eyes and gave the frustrated sigh of a man pushed beyond the edge of his temper. 'Did I not promise you last night that I would not carouse?'

'While we were together, yes. But I am concerned that, once we are parted, you will forget your promise.'

'Once we are parted?' He raised an eyebrow. 'Have you grown tired of my company so soon?'

'It is not that at all,' she said.

'Or perhaps, after only a day or two, you think you have some claim on me, that you would reorder my life to suit you?'

'A single gift is hardly an attempt to reorder your life,' she said.

'And a large gift it is. A large gift placed in a small space. When you know me better, you will find that I do not like the furniture rearranged once I have taught myself the lay of it. And your pianoforte presents more of an obstacle than an opportunity.'

'That is because you have not tried it, I am sure,' she said. 'You do not need your eyes to play it. Once you learn the scales, you will find that you can make music with your eyes open or closed.'

'So it is a gift of charity to the poor blind man, is it?'

'Only if you choose to see it so,' she coaxed. 'Some people quite enjoy playing an instrument.'

'I had quite enough of it, as a boy.'

'You took lessons, then?' For she did not remember hearing of them.

'One or two. And then, in one of my father's rare shows of sense, he fired the music master and freed me from the duty of it. He bought me a fine jumper, instead.' He smiled as though he were remembering. 'And a beautiful beast it was. He could take a fence as easy as walking, and went over the stone walls at the bottom of the yard as though we were flying.'

'But you cannot do such as that any longer,' she said.

'Thank you for reminding me,' he answered. 'Neither can I shoot, for it would be a torture to the animals I hunted, more than a sport. From my father and grandfather I learned the dangers of pretending to be a gentleman—I no longer bother to try. And without your help, I have lasted longer as a rogue than either of them.'

She put her hand on his arm. 'You might think I am showing a lack of faith in your abilities, but we both know that it is a matter of luck and not skill that has brought you some of the way. It is not that I have a claim on you, so much as I would not wish the fate you seek on anyone.'

'And I have no desire to be led about on a pony, as though I am an infant. Nor do I wish to spend the rest of my life in the parlour, playing scales. Next you will be encouraging me to weave baskets or make buttons. Or maybe I can learn needlework, like an old lady. I swear, you are as bad as those meddling souls that incarcerate the sightless and train them like dogs.'

'Hardly,' she said. 'And I have been to the blind school here, if that is what you mean. It is not so bad.'

His eyes narrowed. 'It is not a school, my dear. Call it by its right name. The Blind Asylum at Southwark.'

'It is called an asylum only because it is meant as a place of safety.'

'Is that what you think? For I went there as well, while I could still see the place. And to me, it seemed as though it was meant to keep the sighted safe from the presence of those of us who are less fortunate.'

'The children there are clean and well cared for.'

'And taught to do simple trades as befits their intelligence, and their station in life.' He sneered at her. 'They are not taught to read and write and study. They are made useful, and the training is done by men almost as common as they are themselves. My father would have ended his life before getting me, if he had thought that this was the only future that waited.'

'And I am sure he is much more proud to think you gambled and drank and whored your life away, rather than finding some valuable way to occupy your time.' His stubbornness infuriated her. But it was not without cause. Adrian had been a vigorous youth. And one by one, the things that gave him pleasure were becoming impossible. 'If you do not like the pianoforte, then you need not play it,' she said, in a soothing voice. 'I will send someone to remove it tomorrow and that will be the end of it.'

But she could tell by his expression that he was not mollified. She put her arms around his neck and added, 'If that is all that is bothering you.'

'It is not,' he snapped. And then muttered, 'But the rest is no concern of yours.'

'I see.' She gave an audible sigh to let him know that she was pouting, surprised at her desire to try feminine wiles that she was sure must be long withered from disuse.

'It was just that the damned instrument was followed by a visit from my brother-in-law, come to trouble me about my wife's misbehaviour.'

'And of course it annoyed you,' she said with sympathy, stroking his arm. 'It was rather pointless of him to bother you, since you do not care how your wife behaves.'

His head snapped up, as though he had been struck. 'Do not dare to presume what I feel about the woman I married.'

'I presume nothing,' she said with a little laugh of surprise. 'You told me how you felt not twenty-four hours ago. That it did not bother you what she did, and that you had no claim on her fidelity.'

'But that was before she took up publicly with another,' he answered. 'And to think that I trusted the man. It upsets me that he can lie to my face. And it upsets me even more that he does not do a better job of it. I might not be able to see my hand before my eyes, but I can see through him like a piece of tissue.'

'And who might he be?' she asked, for it was clear that Adrian had formed an opinion.

'Hendricks, of course.'

The idea was so ludicrous that she laughed out loud. 'Are you still going on about him? I have met the man, and it hardly seems likely.'

'Oh, I am almost sure of it. He has admitted knowing of her lodgings, and visiting her there. And he is quite clearly uncomfortable around me, as though he is afraid of being caught in some secret.'

'And have you asked your wife what she has to say on the matter?'

'I would have asked, had I been able to persuade her to visit me. I requested her presence this evening and she ignored me.'

'So that is it,' she said. 'You are angry with her and everyone around you must take the blame for it. But you take no part of the fault for yourself, of course.'

'I?' He disentangled her arms from his neck.

'If you had spoken honestly to her before now, she might not have chosen another. And you would be telling her of your displeasure, not some woman that you barely know.'

'That is not true at all,' he argued. 'In my experience, I am doing nothing so unusual. Few men speak to their wives. When they wish to discuss things of importance to them, they seek the company of other men.'

'And when they wish to unburden their souls?' she pressed.

'Then they go to their mistresses. When a woman is paid to do as she is told, she is less likely to disagree. A wife, though she might swear at the altar to be obedient, seldom is. Emily has proven thus. And I would have thought her the most tractable female on the planet. Until today.' He stared up at the ceiling with a furrow in his brow, as though, for all his fine talk, he had never really believed her capable of leaving him.

'And suppose you find yourself with a woman who owes you no obedience at all?' She reached up to touch his face, putting a hand to his forehead and smoothing the lines with her fingers.

'Then I would have a mind to show her a new use for her pianoforte.' He kissed her palm.

'Do you mean to invite her to your home, so that you might play a duet?' she teased.

'More likely I would be inclined to bend her over the stool for her impudence, and love her until she was more agreeable.' His voice was husky, and he pulled her close, kissing her hard until his anger began to dissipate.

She opened her mouth, and let him convince her, marvelling at how little effort it took him to arouse her. A word or two, a kiss, a touch. And she wanted to be his. She pulled away, slow, almost drowsy, and murmured back at him. 'You presume too much, my lord. Do you think you can force all women to submit to your every wish?'

'Not all women,' he whispered back. 'Just you.

Because you do not want chaste duets in the drawing room any more than I want to play a pianoforte. We are physical creatures, you and I. Not made to sit tamely to the side while the rest of the world dances.'

Emily had never thought of herself in that way before. But it was true. She was happier walking his land, visiting cottages and farms, meeting the stock and the people than she would have been sitting with her needlework in the drawing room, waiting for her husband to favour her with a visit. And when he talked to her, rough and low as he was doing now, she felt like a sybarite. The things he suggested made her flush with eagerness and not embarrassment. Instead, she focused her mind on more innocent pursuits. 'If there is music, you would rather dance than play, my lord?'

He considered. 'I have never tried. There has been scant little music in my life, these last few years.' He swept her into his arms as though he heard a waltz and spun her once, bumping her into a chair.

She felt him hesitate, gripped his hand tighter and said, 'A moment, please.' Then she released him, righted the furniture and pulled him into the doorway of the salon. 'Now try again.'

He began more slowly this time, and they took a few steps without incident. 'I will lead,' he said, 'but you must guide me.' He turned her again.

They were nearing a table now. 'Left. No. Right.' The turning had confused her for a moment, and they moved past it, rocking the china ornaments upon it, but not breaking them. 'Now straight back for a bit. And turn again, another right. And there is a circuit of the room.'

He gave her a final flourish and her silk skirts sighed about her legs, and then settled.

Adrian nodded, as though satisfied with their success, and then dismissed it as unimportant. 'Of course, there is no orchestra to keep the beat. And we did not have to navigate a room full of people.'

'Dancers with all their sight cannot manage as well as you have done. It seems I cannot escape a rout without crushed toes and bumped elbows And I am sure you would find a dance, with lines and patterns, to be easier. A drunken idiot can manage the Sir Roger de Coverley.'

'Thank you for your confidence in me,' he murmured sarcastically. 'But dancing in a crowded room would not be quite so pleasant as holding my partner close like this when we are alone.' He had her now, in his arms, swaying as though he still heard a tune. But they were far too close to be waltzing, their bodies rubbing together until she could feel them both becoming aroused.

'I do not think what we are doing now can be called dancing,' she said a little breathlessly, brushing her breasts against the front of his coat and feeling the roughness of the net bodice against her nipples.

'What would you call it, then?' he asked. His hands bunched in her skirt, pressing their hips together, but his lips brushed lightly against hers.

'I think you are trying to seduce me again.'

One of his hands found the pocket slit in the side of

her skirt, and reached inside to press his palm against the bare skin of her leg. 'Am I likely to be successful?'

She rubbed her cheek against his. 'I think you might be.' She swayed against him, letting him urge her closer, slipping one of her legs between his and drawing her foot up the inside of his calf. He caught her leg between his, tightening his muscles, and she felt the now-familiar rush of feeling, knowing he was close to her, knowing what would come next between them.

She rubbed herself against him with a little moan, and he pushed her back against the edge of a desk, getting some distance between their bodies to put a hand down the loose bodice of her gown. 'You are a most welcoming woman, my dear. Bare under your dress again tonight. I think, if I had a mind to, you would let me take you here.'

'Yes,' she said with a groan, thinking how wonderful it would be if he would lose control.

'I could just hoist up your skirt…'

'Yes…' He was kissing her, short sharp bites on her lips, down her throat.

'Undo a few buttons…'

'Yes…' One hand, tight upon her breast, the other in her skirt, squeezing her leg.

'And I could be inside of you, before anyone was the wiser.' He was holding her body a tantalising inch from his. And she pressed herself down onto his thigh.

'Show me,' she whispered back and pushed her hands between the buttons of his vest, searching to touch skin and not clothing.

'Wait.' He laughed. 'Wait. There is time. We do not need to rush. Let me take you into the bedroom.'

But if they took their time, he would be careful. And while it would be wonderful, it would not be what she truly wanted. 'No. Here, now. Quickly.' She kissed him, deep and wet, pushing her tongue into his mouth, sucking his back into hers.

And for a moment, he stopped resisting her and pulled her hips forwards, wrapping a hand around them to lock her sex to his, grinding against her through their clothing. She wrapped her arms around his neck, lifting herself onto her toes, making it easier to join with him.

Then he pulled his lips from hers and gave a shaky sigh. 'No, my sweet. Let us go lie down and treat each other properly.'

'And suppose I do not wish you to be proper?' she said. 'Suppose I wish you to be rough with me, and finish with me quickly and carelessly, in a public room, because you cannot stand to wait?' She ran her leg up between his thighs until she could feel his manhood and pressed hard against it, rubbing her knee against him until he groaned.

Then he unwrapped her arms from his body, trying to part them. 'You do not understand,' he said. 'It is not that you do not tempt me.'

'Then give me what I want,' she demanded and lifted her own skirt to bare herself, pressing her naked sex against the front of his trousers, so close to him that she wanted to weep with frustration.

Without thinking, he swore and his mouth covered

hers again, and his hand fumbled to open his trousers, pushing the cloth away until they were skin to skin. He parted from her, just enough to mutter, 'Lean back, just a bit.' And now he was resting between her legs, rubbing himself gently against her and peppering her lips with desperate little kisses. 'Just for a moment. Just a taste of you. I will be careful. I promise.'

She smiled, trembling, waiting for the delicious shock of sensation that would soon come. 'You do not have to be careful with me. Never with me. I am yours, Adrian. I love you.'

And then it was over. He jerked away from her so fast that it was as though she had burned him, hurrying to do up his buttons although he was still obviously in need of her. 'I think, my dear, that we had best take supper. Suddenly, I find myself in need of a cooling drink.'

Emily held out a hand to him, remembering too late that he could not see it. But neither could he see her crimson cheeks, or the beginnings of tears. Then she smoothed her skirt back into place and wrapped her arms around herself as a shield against his rejection. 'Do you really? Do you think I will forget my feelings for you? Or do you wish to distract yourself?'

'Both, perhaps.' He looked older than he had a few minutes ago. His face was serious and lined with stress, and his posture stiff and unnatural, as though he was guarding himself from her as well. 'I do not think you understand what you are saying to me, and I do not mean to take advantage of a generosity that is based on lies and suppositions, no matter how pleasant they might be. You do not love me. You cannot.'

'I do,' she cried. 'Do not think to tell me the contents of my heart, just because you wish it to be other than it is.'

'We have known each other for only a few days. And what there has been between us is not love. It is something else entirely.'

'Perhaps that is how it is for you,' she said, 'but I have known you for ever. And for as long as that, I have loved you.'

He had nothing to say to that, and stood a little bit apart from her with a strange, lost look on his face, as though he feared that any direction he might move would be misinterpreted by her, as his other actions had been.

She wanted to gather him close, to kiss his sightless eyes, and to tell him he had no reason to deny her or her love. There was nothing more natural in the world than for him to give in to the temptation and join with her. Her heart ached for it—just as her body ached for the child that he refused to give her.

She took deep, slow breaths, willing the passion in her to subside, leaving cold emptiness in its wake. For a few moments, it had been as if the barriers he kept between them had fallen. He had returned to her, was with her, body and soul. And for that time, no matter what he might claim now, he had been ready not just to make love, but to love her without fear of the future.

But now he was gone again. Hiding from his wife. Hiding from his lover. And even though they shared the same room, she felt lonelier than she had a week ago, when he had seemed as distant from her as a ship on the horizon.

Though it did not matter how she looked, she put on a false smile and said, 'You are right. There is a supper laid for us in the dining room. Let me take your arm, that you might lead me to it.' She put her hand in the crook of his elbow and gave him the direction he needed so that he might walk her to the table. They seated themselves and ate in near silence, with only the occasional nervous comment from him about the tenderness of the vegetables, and his gratitude to the cook for doing such a thorough job of boning the salmon.

When it looked as though he was ready to give a lengthy oration on the dessert, Emily cut him off. 'I am sorry if I upset you.'

'You did nothing of the kind,' he assured her, a little too quickly.

'Of course I did. And I would understand if you did not want to stay with me tonight.'

'Of course I wish to stay,' he said, reaching across the table to grasp her hand, 'but I do not know if it is wise.' And then he squeezed her fingers. 'But I do not know if I want to be wise, if it means losing my time with you.'

'That is a comfort. I promise not to say it again. You needn't worry.' *It.* As though she felt some objectionable thing that needed to be hidden.

'Actually, I would prefer that you are honest with me. It is most refreshing to find a woman who speaks frankly.'

'Thank you,' she said, hating herself for the lies, wanting to scream the truth in his face. *I am your wife. Your Emily.*

Love me.

'It is just that I do not want you to raise your hopes about what can be between us in the end. It is not that I do not…have feelings for you. Strong feelings,' he amended. There was a wistful quality in his voice, as though he were staring through a shop window at something he could not have. 'You are a friend and confidante. Someone I trust implicitly and who trusts me in return. If that is the true definition of a lover, then that is what you are to me. And that is what I wish to be for you.'

Emily stared down into her plate, thinking of how it had been in Derbyshire. Then, such pretty words would have sent her heart racing. He felt strongly for her. He wanted her. She was something like a lover to him. Why could she not be satisfied? Why was that not enough?

Without releasing her hand, he stood, drawing her up with him. From memory, he led the way from the table to the bedroom. He took the time to arrange his clothes as he removed them, but took no such care with hers, opening the buttons at the back of her gown and letting it fall to the floor at her feet. He lifted her out of it and set her upon the bed with a kiss on the lips before sliding his body down hers, taking her breasts with long slow licks, smoothing his hands over her ribs and settling himself between her legs to kiss there, tenderly, worshipfully.

She closed her eyes and gave herself over to his ministrations, the tug of teeth, the gentle probing of fingers, the tentative invasions of his tongue. And she told herself that it was greedy of her to want more when he was giving her something that felt so good. And she knew, from the previous times he'd done it, that what he was doing had the strength to rend her soul from her body and send it crashing back to earth again.

The final pleasure was slow in coming. And when it came, she wept.

Chapter Fourteen

The sun was well up by the time Adrian awakened. He did nothing to acknowledge it for his lover was still sleeping on his arm. The night had been as glorious as the night before, and parts of the night before that. As exciting as the fight in the tavern. And probably almost as dangerous.

I love you.

When she had said it, along with the abject terror it had raised in him had been the ghostly echo of a response in his own heart—how could something as perfect as the time they spent together not have some deeper feeling in it? He smoothed a hand over her curls and she nuzzled him in her sleep.

If she had said nothing, he'd have ignored his intentions and taken her up against the wall in the salon, trusting that she would tell him if they were not alone—he could not have heard a servant's footstep had he tried, his heart had been beating so loudly. Apparently, there was madness in what he felt for her as well.

And then she had said the words, and he'd stopped himself, too near the brink. He'd taken her to dinner, then he'd taken her to bed. And he'd loved her in all the ways he could until he was sure that she had forgotten.

But her pillow was wet with tears. And in her sleep, she had whimpered like a lost child.

She stirred; he ran a soothing hand over her back, wishing that she would sleep again. It felt good to be here and he did not want to go. She rolled off his arm to free it, and he could feel her and see the shadow as she propped herself up on her elbows in the pillows. 'You are not going to run away from me in the dawn?'

'I am afraid it is too late for that already. But I must go soon.'

'Then stay a while longer,' she said. 'Give me time to wash and dress. I will go with you and see you home.'

He frowned. 'There is no need to help me. I am quite capable of managing a carriage ride, you know.'

'Of course you are, Adrian.' She rose from the bed, and opened the window curtains without waiting for a servant, letting the light stream in on them. 'But it is a beautiful morning. And to walk in the park, for just a little while, would be delightful.'

'You should not go out without escort,' he said absently, wondering if she meant to take a maid with them as well.

'I will have you.'

'You will not.'

'Just a short outing together. In sunlight.'

'Do you wish for me to ride in Rotten Row?' he snapped, wishing that he had not just revealed the fear he felt when he thought of so public a place. 'I suspect that would be most amusing for all concerned.'

'Of course I do not wish you to ride. If you mean to break your neck, then I pray you, find another way. You cannot trust a horse to do the deed without undo suffering. To me especially, for I would not wish to watch.'

And now she had made him laugh, against his better judgement.

'But there is nothing wrong with your legs, is there?' She had come back to the bed and her fingers were stroking them, with faint touches meant to raise the hairs and tease the nerves to restlessness.

He pulled away from her and sat up, dangling his feet off the edge of her bed. 'No.'

'How long has it been since you have enjoyed a simple walk in the park? You prowl the streets at night, of course. But it would be nice to feel the sun on one's face.' She crawled after him, putting her arms about his waist and giving a little squeeze. 'For both of us.'

She was right, of course. It must be difficult for her to meet only at night. While the secrecy was necessary, it must make her feel as though he was ashamed of her company. And he knew how sensitive she still was on the subject of her worth. 'It is not just a matter of revealing ourselves, my dear. I have not made my condition publicly known. And while it is possible to disguise it in familiar territory and for short periods of time, should I be seen blundering into a tree in Hyde Park, I suspect that the world will be too soon completely aware.'

'I am suggesting nothing of the kind,' she argued. 'It is not fashionable there until late in the afternoon. If we go now, no one will be about. We could keep our stroll short, on a path that is straight and level and far away from Kings Road. If you take my arm, you might lead me, and I will inform you of any obstacles, just as we do here. It will be most uneventful.'

'And not particularly interesting. If you wish to spend the day with me, I can think of better uses for your time.' He leaned against her, feeling her breasts pressing into his back, and her breath upon his neck.

'If a morning outing bores you, then you need have nothing to fear from it,' she responded tartly.

'Fear? I faced Napoleon's army without flinching. I do not avoid the park because I am afraid.' *Terrified* was more the word.

'Of course you are not. But I do not see why you cannot give me what I ask, when it is such a small thing.'

'It is because it's so small that I see no value in it.' He reached behind him to touch her face. 'Perhaps I could buy you a trinket. Some fobs for those lovely ears…'

'And how would I explain them to my friends? Would I tell them that my husband had given me a gift?' Now it was her turn to laugh bitterly. 'They will assume that I am unfaithful far more quickly from that than if they see me taking the air with a male acquaintance.'

She was glib this morning, and as frank as she had been from the first. But last night she had said she loved him. And he was pretending she had said nothing, and treating her little better than a whore, kept for one purpose, and plied with jewellery to avert a sulk. He shamed himself with his behaviour more than he ever could by groping his way around Hyde Park.

As if she could sense his weakening, she said, more softly, 'We will not be out for long. And tonight, for your reward, you can do as you like with me.' She was kissing his back now, and spreading her hands in his lap over his manhood, perfectly still as though waiting for his instructions. 'But for now? You owe me this, at least.'

Because you will not love me. That was what she meant, he was sure. And he wondered if this would be the first of many such bargains: pouts and capitulations that would lead to arguments, bitterness and regrets. If it was, it was likely the beginning of the end for them. The scales that had been so delicately balanced would never be right again. Last night, words had been spoken and they could not be unsaid.

But he did not want to give her up. Not yet. It was too soon. And although he had not intended to feel anything, ever again, she made him happy. He captured her hands before she could arouse him, and turned his face to kiss her, then pretended to consider. 'To do as I like with you? That is an offer I have no power to resist. Even without it, I will go. I need no other reason but that it pleases you. Now if you mean for me to leave this room in daylight, you had best let me dress before I change my mind and take you back to bed.'

Emily could see, from the moment they left the carriage, that the trip had been a good idea. She allowed the

coachman to help her down, and then took her husband's
arm as he waited on the ground for her. Adrian's face
was tipped towards the sunlight; he was staring up into
the canopy of leaves above them as though he had never
seen such a wonderful thing.

Without knowing it, she would never have guessed
that the sense of wonder had less to do with the fine day
than his inability to see the trees with any clarity.

He looked down and to the side again, as he always
did, tipping the brim of his hat a bit to provide more
shade. 'There are tinted glasses they gave me, after the
injury on the battlefield, to shield my eyes against the
glare of the sun. Perhaps I shall find them again, for
occasions like this.'

'You mean to go out with me again?'

He sighed. 'With or without you. Someday, rumour
of my condition is bound to get out. There will be no
point in hiding in my rooms when it does.'

It was the first she had heard of him planning for
anything but his premature death. She stifled the surprise
she felt, fearing that an acknowledgement of it might
scare the idea from his head.

But he did not seem to notice his own change in attitude, and touched his own eyes thoughtfully. 'It might
make it easier to manage in sunlight, with what vision I
have left. And disguise any unfortunate staring on my
part. I would not want to be thought rude.'

'An interesting sentiment, coming from the man I met
a few days ago,' she answered.

He laughed again. 'No gentleman wishes to be met by

a lady in such surroundings as you found me. It makes it too difficult to pretend to any gentility at a later date. Come, let us take a turn around the park, so that I might prove I have manners.'

She gave his elbow a little squeeze. 'The path is just to the left. And straight on. There is no one in sight.'

'There never is, my dear.'

She cringed at her own insensitivity. 'I am sorry.'

'Why ever for? You did not strike me blind with your beauty,' he said, taking her hand and raising it to his lips for a salute. 'Nor do I begrudge you your vision.'

She relaxed a little as he put her hand back on his arm. 'Sometimes, I am still unsure how to behave around you. You have been angry enough to destroy your life over this, you know. It does not bespeak a man content in his disability.'

'Perhaps not. But today, things are different.' He took a deep breath. 'It is much harder to be bitter when the sun is shining and the roses are in bloom.'

'You can smell them?'

'You cannot?'

Emily paused and sniffed. Of course she could. But she had been far too focused on the delicate colour of them to notice the fragrance. She let him walk her closer to the bank of carefully tended flowers. 'They are beautiful,' she said.

'There was a fine garden of them at my home in Derbyshire. York and Lancaster and white damask, with boxwood hedges. I wonder if it is still there.'

Yes. We will walk in it yet this summer, my love. 'I

would expect so,' she said. 'A country home is nothing without a rose garden.'

'Describe these to me.'

'Red, pink, yellow.' It was quite inadequate to his needs, she was sure. 'The red has a touch of purple in it. And shadows. Like velvet in candlelight.'

He reached out a hand, and she put it on a bloom. 'The texture is velvet as well. Feel.'

She touched them, too, and found that he was right, then moved to the next bush. 'And these,' she said, 'are apple roses. Big and pink, and the velvet is more in the leaves than the flowers. And here are your damasks.'

He gave a nod of approval. 'As there should be.' And then he cocked his head. 'And there is a lark.'

She glanced around her. 'Where? I do not see him.'

He pointed, unerringly, towards a tree on their left. When she looked closely, she thought she saw a flash of feathers in the leaves. 'Poor confused fellow,' he said. 'It is past nesting season. Unusual to hear that particular song so late in the year.'

'They have different songs?'

'They speak to each other, just as we do.' He smiled, listening again. 'That is a male, looking for a mate.'

There was an answering warble, in a tree on the right. 'And there she is.' He sighed. 'He has found her after all. Well done, sir.' And, almost absently, he patted her arm.

She smiled up at him, happy to be in her rightful place, on the arm of the handsome Earl of Folbroke, even if it was just for an hour. She had never noticed the park to be so full of life before. But Adrian was quick to discover things that she had not noticed and to point them out to her as they passed. The few people that they met as they walked smiled and nodded, taking no more notice of her husband than they would have in any other passer-by.

She could feel him tense each time, as though fearing a response. And each time, when none came, he relaxed a bit more. 'There are more people here than you promised,' he said absently.

'I might have lied a bit in calling it empty. But it is not crowded. And not as bad as you feared, I am sure,' she said. 'I see no one that I recognise. And the people that are out take no notice of us, walking together. There is nothing so unique in your behaviour as to incite comment from a casual observer. In truth, we are a most unexceptional pair.'

He chuckled. 'My pride is well checked, madam. I have made an appearance in public and the sky did not fall. In fact, no one noticed. If they thought anything about me, I am sure they whisper at what a lucky fellow I am, to be taking the air with such a beauty.'

'You are in excellent spirits today.'

Adrian looked up, and around him, as though he could still see his surroundings. 'It is a beautiful day, is it not? You were right for forcing me into the sunlight, my dear. It has been far too long.'

'It has,' she said softly back to him. 'And I have another gift for you, if you will accept it from me.'

'It is not another piano, is it? Or perhaps some other musical instrument? Are you about to pull a trumpet from your reticule and force me to blow it and scare away the birds?'

'Nothing so great as that, I assure you.'

He smiled down at his feet. 'And it is not your own sweet person that you offer. Although if you were to suggest that we nip behind a rosebush for a kiss, I would not deny you.'

She gave him the mildest of rebukes, nudging his arm with her shoulder 'Not that, either.'

'Then I have no idea what you are about. But since we are in public when you offer it, I assume you are unsure of my reaction. Here you know I do not wish to call attention to myself, and will have little choice to accept, with grace, whatever you offer me.' There was a sardonic twist to his lip. 'Out with it. You are making me apprehensive.'

She reached into her reticule, digging for the card she had found. 'Can you read French?'

He gave her a dubious grin. 'Madam, I thought I made it plain enough the night we met that reading of any kind is quite beyond me.'

She responded with a sniff so that he might know of her annoyance, and said, 'You are being difficult with me again. And I am not being clear enough with you. For that, I apologise. I should have more rightly said, before your difficulty overtook you, did you learn to read the French language?'

It was his turn to huff impatiently at her. 'Of course I did. Despite what you might think, after finding me in such low estates, I was brought up properly and well educated. It might have been easier had I not been. One cannot miss what one has never known.'

'But you were fluent?'

'Better in Greek and Latin. But, yes, I managed tolerably well in French. I could understand and be understood. But I fail to see how that matters.'

Emily thrust the stiff sheet of paperboard into one of his hands, and placed the fingers of his other on the raised letters there. 'See what you can make of this.'

He frowned as he dragged his fingers over the surface, moving too quickly to interpret the patterns. 'What is it?' he whispered.

'A poem. The author was a Frenchman, and a scholar. And blind,' she added. 'From what I have been able to gather on the subject, the French people seem much more enlightened in the education of those with your problem. There are quite interesting experiments in place for the teaching of mathematics, geography and even reading and writing. But much of the work is all in French, and I have not…'

He held the card loosely, not even trying to examine it. 'And if you have not noticed, my love, we are currently at war with France.'

'But we will not be for ever. Once we have conquered Napoleon, there will be peace between our countries. I am sure of it. And then, perhaps, we might go to Paris.'

'And perhaps they will have established a language for me, and perhaps I shall learn it. And we will live together, in a little flat on the banks of the Seine, and forget our spouses and our common English troubles.

And I will write French poems to you.' He handed it back to her.

'Perhaps we shall.' She took the card and turned to him, forcing it into the pocket where he kept her picture. 'Although I understand the impossibility of some of what you are saying, is it really such a strange idea that you might be able to better yourself, or to live very much as other men do?'

He sighed, as though tired of arguing with her. 'You do not understand.'

'But I am trying to,' she said, 'which is more than your family taught you to do. When faced with the same challenge, your father and grandfather gave up. And they taught you to do the same.' She held his arm again, wrapping her fingers tightly around the crook of his elbow. 'But you are not like them. You are so much more than they were. And you will not know, until you have tried for yourself, what you are capable of. If you do not see that, then you are crippled with something far worse than blindness. You suffer from a lack of vision.'

Adrian stood still, as unresponsive as a mannequin. For a moment, she hoped that he was thinking about her words. And then he said in a gruff, irritable voice, 'Are you quite finished? Or do you have other opinions that you wish to share with me?'

'That is enough for the morning, I think.' She let out her held breath slowly, hoping that he did not notice, but was sure that he had, for he could read her like a book.

'I quite agree. I think it is time for me to escort you back to the carriage, if you will tell me where it is.'

She was in no mood to help him, fairly sure that he knew perfectly well where to go and was only feigning a need for instruction. 'The carriage has not moved since we left it. Take us back the way we came.'

There was a miniscule pause as he retraced his steps in his mind. Then he turned and led her back down the path that they had walked, feeling along the grassy edge of it with his stick to help him find the way.

They went along without incident, not speaking. She forced herself to stay relaxed at his side, praying that there would be no familiar faces amongst the few strollers there. She had half hoped, when they stood happily by the roses, that they would see some members of their set and engage them in a brief conversation, to gently reveal her true identity to her husband. But after the fresh start they had made this morning, she had overstepped herself. The distance born between them last night was growing. And if she could not find a way to stop it, she would lose him. She doubted it would be a pleasant experience for anyone should he be hailed by a friend and forced, without warning, to explain his condition.

They were within steps of the carriage, now, and she knew by the relaxing of the muscles in his arm that he knew it as well. While they walked, she had felt him tensing as he listened for clues, alert to any change, but now he had heard the jingle of the harnesses, and the chatter of the driver and grooms, silencing to attention as they drew near. He'd released her arm, putting a protective hand upon her back as she moved to step up and into it, when a call came from behind him.

'Alms!'

Adrian froze for a moment, as though the single word had the power to control him. Then he turned back, his head tracking to find the source.

'Alms for a blind beggar! Alms!' There was a woman beside the entrance to the park, probably hoping to catch some member of the *ton* on their way in or out. She stared towards them with eyes clouded milk-white, with no idea who she accosted, other than that they had sufficient funds to afford a carriage and should be able to spare a few pennies for her. When she shook the cup in her hand, it gave off the pathetic rattle of an unsuccessful morning.

Emily could feel the fingers on her back sliding away, as her husband turned, forgetting why he touched her. And she turned with him, taking her foot off the step and waving the groom away. She caught at Adrian, her fingers tightening on his arm, and he reached up with his other hand to grip them. It was not the gentle and reassuring touch she had grown accustomed to, but a rigid, claw-like reflex.

She tugged at his arm, trying to get him to move. 'Come, Adrian. We can go back to the carriage, if you like.'

Then his grip began to relax again, and he led her towards the woman, and not away. 'Tell me what you see. Spare no detail.'

'She is an old woman,' Emily said. 'Her clothes are

clean and in good repair, but they are simple. There are worn patches at the elbows, and the lace at the throat will not see many more washings. Her eyes were blue, but are obscured by pearls. Cataracts, I think they are sometimes called. I doubt she has been blind her whole life.'

As she spoke, the woman before them stood mute, accepting the scrutiny as though she had given up being anything more than an object of pity. And then her hand tightened on her cup and she gave it another little shake.

'Is this an accurate description?' he said. When he got no response, he fumbled to touch the beggar on the arm.

The woman started and shook his hand away, unsure of the reason for contact and frightened by it.

'I need to ask, because I am blind as well,' he said, in a soft and reassuring voice.

'Yes, sir.' The old woman gave a relieved smile.

'My lord,' Adrian corrected absently, reaching in his pocket for his purse. 'I am the Earl of Folbroke.'

The woman dropped into a curtsy.

And feeling the movement in her arm, he dipped his head in response to the gesture of respect. 'What brings you to this, old mother? Do you have no one to care for you?'

'My husband is dead,' she said. Her accent was not refined, but neither was it coarse. 'And my son is gone off to war. For a time, he sent money. But it has been long since I've heard anything. And I fear...' She stopped, as though she did not wish to think of what news was likely to come.

'It might mean nothing,' he assured her. 'I served as well. It is not always easy to get word home. But perhaps I can discover something. Today, I am busy. But tomorrow, you will come to my rooms in Jermyn Street. I will tell the servants to look out for you. And I will take your information and see if anything can be done with it.'

'Thank you, my lord.' The woman was near to breathless with shock, already. But when she heard him drop a coin into the cup, it was clear that she could tell the difference between gold and copper by the sound. Her surprised mouth closed, and widened in a smile. 'Thank you, my lord,' she said with more emphasis.

'Until tomorrow,' he said, and turned away from her, signalling the coachman for assistance with a whistle and a tap of his cane.

They rode in silence toward his rooms, until she could stand it no longer. 'That was a wonderful thing you did for her.'

'Soldiers have enough to worry about on the battlefield, without coming home to find that their mothers are begging in the streets,' he said, as though that was the only thing that concerned him. And then, as an afterthought, added, 'What I did was not enough. If there is a way to find honest employment for her, it will be done.'

There was a lump rising in her throat as they pulled to a stop before the building that housed his rooms. And as he rose to exit, she touched his arm to make him pause.

He turned his head, waiting for some word from her.

'I know you do not want to hear it. But I cannot help but speak,' she said. 'I love you, Adrian Longesley.'

He swallowed. Then he said, 'Thank you.' And then he left her, tapping his way to the steps of his door.

Chapter Fifteen

Thank you.

What an idiotic thing to say to a woman who had just bared her soul to him. But what else could he say to her? The response she wanted was not the one he wished to give her. And anything else seemed inadequate.

'Hendricks!' Adrian handed his hat and gloves to the footman and went directly to his room, hearing the secretary fall into step behind him.

'My lord?' Hendricks said, the words muffled by what was probably a mouthful of his breakfast.

'What time is it?'

'Half past eight. Very early for you, my lord.' This seemed to be not a reproof, but as an apology for his own lack of preparation.

'Very early for any coherence, you mean. Well, prepare to be surprised. Not only am I sober, but I have slept, breakfasted and gone for a walk.'

There was a little cough from behind him, as Hendricks inhaled a toast crumb from the shock.

Adrian smiled to himself. 'I am getting ahead of you today, it seems. Go, finish your breakfast. Or, if you wish, bring it to my room, along with the paper. You are welcome to use the table by the window, if you wish. The breeze this morning is particularly nice. And the view, from what I can gather, is quite pleasant.'

'Thank you, my lord.'

His valet had preceded him and was waiting in the bedroom to take his coat, making every effort not to appear as flat footed as Hendricks. As it slid from his shoulders, Adrian reached, as he always did, for the miniature in the breast pocket.

His fingers brushed something unexpected. It was a moment before he remembered the bit of card that had been forced on him in the park.

He balled his fist in frustration, then quickly relaxed it so as not to crush the paper. He had not handled that well. He should not have laughed at her attempts to help him, or snapped. It would be all his loss if she left him after one of those outbursts of temper.

Especially when fate had then demonstrated just how small his problems were in comparison to others. Perhaps his lover was wrong and he had reached the end of his usefulness. Perhaps he would spend the rest of his life sitting in the window, listening to the world pass by. But at least he would not be forced to spend it on a corner with a tin cup.

The image in his mind of such a common thing, a

future in Paris, or anywhere else, with his lover sprawled close to him on a *chaise* while they drank wine and read poetry to each other, had been sharp and painful. The idea that there could be any permanence in what they had seemed as unattainable as if she'd told him they would fly to the moon.

As he sat to be shaved, he fingered the card in his hands, tracing the rows of pinpricks with his nail. If he'd simply attempted to read the thing while she was there, she'd have seen how hopeless it was, and she'd have given up bothering him with it.

Or he'd have proved her right. His pride must be a very fragile thing, if he feared success as much as failure. He ran his fingers over the surface of the card, noting that the bumps were set in patches, and the patches in rows. And when he forced himself to move very slowly, he could begin to make out letters.

She was right. It seemed to be in French. He chuckled, as he began to understand the words, wondering if she had attempted them herself. How hard could it have been to read them, if one was able to make out the embossing on the page?

"'Love is both blind itself and makes all blind whom it rules,'" he read aloud, and heard the valet grunt in irritation and give a stern warning of 'my lord' against sudden movement while at the mercy of a man with a razor.

Adrian smiled cautiously to prevent injury and thought of the woman who had given him the card. It was very like her to choose these as the first words he had read in months. For a moment, he thought it might be Shakespeare, and nothing more than an ironic choice on her part. But she had been wrong about the contents being poetry. It seemed that the man was not a poet at all, but a Latin scholar, and a blind one as well.

He traced his fingers over the letters again, faster this time, as they grew more fluent with the feel of what he found there. Still not as fast as if he could read. But it felt good to recognise the ideas forming under his hand. The writer had called blindness a divine good, rather than a human ill. The idea made Adrian smirk, causing another groan from his valet. If the Almighty had smitten the Folbrokes in an attempt to make them divine messengers of goodness, then God must be blind as well. Choosing such an unworthy lot did not bespeak much for His taste in servants.

And yet...

'Hendricks.'

'Lord Folbroke.' His secretary, who had settled at the little table by the window, answered in a voice clear of any obstruction.

'Can you recall—has there ever been a Member of Parliament who was struck blind?'

'Of course, my lord.'

Adrian leaned forwards hopefully, only to hear, 'You, my lord. And your father, of course. And grandfather.'

'No, you ninny. Someone from another family.'

'None that I know of, my lord. But certainly it is not impossible. There are those that are lame, aren't there?'

'And deaf, as well. And probably without sense,'

Adrian added. 'For how else can we justify the decisions that are made by them?'

'I can look into it, if you wish. But I suspect that they
would have little choice but to make accommodations
for...any peer that was so inconvenienced.'

Good old Hendricks. He had been about to say *you*—
and had taken care to stop himself, lest he be guilty of
putting words in my lord's mouth. 'Please, do. And let me
know what you discover. I have another task for you as
well. I need to speak with someone in the Horse Guards
to see if there is anything to be done about locating the
fate of a soldier. I met the man's mother in the park
today...'

'In the park,' Hendricks parroted, as though he could
not quite believe what he had heard.

'Just outside of it, actually. Circumstances had
reduced her to begging in the street. And I said that
I would attempt to help her, if she came to my rooms
tomorrow.'

'A beggar is coming here, my lord?'

'Yes, Hendricks. A blind beggar. She is the mother of
a soldier.'

'I see, my lord.'

'And whether the news is good or bad, if some sort
of pension could be arranged for her...'

'Consider it done, my lord.' Hendricks set down his
cup and rose from his chair, ready to begin his errands.
'Is there anything else?' The last was said as though he
assumed dismissal was imminent.

'Actually, there is.' As the secretary neared him,

Adrian passed him the card he had been holding. 'What do you make of this?'

'It is a lecture by Jean Passcrat, my lord.'

'I am aware of that, Hendricks. Because I read it.'

'My lord.' The exclamation was so surprised that Adrian suspected it was a hushed prayer and not meant for him at all.

'You can see how the letters are raised up. I can feel them, Hendricks. It is a laborious process, to read these pinpricks, but not impossible. And it occurs to me that there might be a stationer or a printer who could do something similar. They have the raised lead type already in their possession.'

Hendricks thought for a moment. 'That is backwards, to make the impression on the page.'

'But if they could make a mould, somehow. Or if special letters were struck that were the right way round.' Adrian drummed his fingers on his knee, imagining all the ways that such a system could be applied. And suddenly he felt eager to be up and doing something. 'It would be expensive, I suppose. But I have the money.'

'You do indeed, my lord.' Hendricks sounded relieved, now. And happy.

'And if it can be done for me, then I see no reason why other reading materials cannot be made. Perhaps the Southwark Asylum could take some on. I know they do not think it is their place to educate the residents, but I beg to differ on the subject.'

'And who would know better than you, my lord? You have a very personal interest in the subject.'

'Which would put me in an excellent position to become a patron of that institution, I am sure. The combination of money and influence could be instrumental in making a long-lasting change in the place.'

'Of course, for the residents to feel the full benefits of your assistance, a considerable amount of time might need to be devoted to the subject,' Hendricks cautioned.

Time. And when had he not had enough of it? Days stretched on before him, and the rush to dull the ennui had been at the base of so many of his diversions. Adrian smiled. 'It seems to me, Hendricks, that of all the mad endeavours of my family, in three generations, the support of a charity has not been on the list. By the traditional standards of the house of Folbroke, I shall be behaving quite recklessly should I rush in any direction other than my own doom.'

'Very true, my lord.' There was definite amusement in the voice of his servant. 'You could very well be the wildest of your family, if you mean to squander your estate in philanthropy.'

'It would give me a chance to appreciate your dry wit, Hendricks. It is a quality I have missed in our recent interactions.'

'Of late you have given me little reason for mirth, Lord Folbroke.'

'Change is in the air, Hendricks. I am my old self, again, after a very long time.'

'So it would seem, my lord.'

'Can you not manage, after all the time in my service, to call me Adrian? Or Folbroke, at least.'

'No, my lord.' But the title was given with affection, and so he allowed it to pass. Hendricks cleared his throat. 'But if I might take the liberty of informing Lady Folbroke of your improved mood, she might be most gratified.'

Adrian felt the return of the old panic at the realisation that Emily would get wind of his plans, should they be carried too far before he had explained himself. 'That must wait until I have had a chance to speak to her myself. But you think she would approve?'

'Yes, my lord. She still enquires after you regularly. And she has been concerned by your silence.'

'But she did not respond to my summons.'

'If I might be so bold, my lord, as to offer advice?'

'Of course.'

'I believe it was the manner, and not the man, she objected to.'

Adrian sighed. 'I have made so many mistakes with the poor girl I hardly know where to begin to rectify them.'

'She has not been a poor girl for some time, my lord.' And there again was that strange sense of admiration that he heard sometimes when Hendricks spoke to him of his wife. And he remembered that the reconciliation he imagined might not be welcomed by his friend.

'It is my own punishment that I was not there to see Emily blossom into the woman she has become. Too proud to watch her with half my sight. And now I cannot see her at all.' He sighed. 'Thank you for taking care of her, Hendricks.'

'I? I have done nothing, my lord.'

'I suspect that is not true.' And what did he expect the man to say? Nothing he wanted to hear. But Adrian could not seem to leave the subject alone.

Hendricks said, after some thought, 'For the most, she takes care of herself. I do very little but to follow her wishes. But I am sure, if you speak to her for yourself, you will find her eager to listen.'

'Perhaps I shall.' And his nerve failed him again. 'But not today. Today, I think I shall go out for lunch.'

'Out, my lord?' He could almost hear Hendricks's brain, ticking through the possibilities, trying to decide where he would be drawn so early in the day. And whether there would be a way from dissuading him from whatever fresh folly he had discovered. For though the morning had been full of promise, Adrian had given his poor friend no reason to believe that his good intentions would last to the afternoon.

When Hendricks could not come up with the answer on his own, he responded, 'When I have completed the tasks you set for me, I will accompany you.'

'Will you, now? And did I ask for a companion, Mr Hendricks?'

'No, my lord.'

'Then you needn't stir yourself. What I do, I must do for myself. You are not a member, after all.'

'Not a member? What the devil…?' For a moment, Hendricks was completely lost. And his subservience slipped, revealing the man underneath.

Adrian reached out into the open air, until he could

find the secretary's arm and give it a reassuring pat. 'Do not concern yourself, man. I am not an infant. I will manage well enough on my own for a few hours in broad daylight. Now, call for the carriage. And tell the cook I will not be home for supper.'

White's.

It was the very bastion of the sort of gentlemanly society that he had denied himself in the months since his sight had utterly failed. He had forgotten how peaceful it was, compared to the taverns he had been frequenting, and the sense of belonging and entitlement that a membership carried with it. It was a place where eccentricity was ignored. If a man had the blunt and the connections to be invited through the front door, then even aberrant behaviour might be deemed, if not creditable, at least not worthy of comment.

And when comment could no longer be restrained, then someone would most likely get out the betting book. Adrian grinned in anticipation.

'Lord Folbroke. May I help you with your hat and coat?'

'You can help me with several things,' he said, turning to the servant and placing his hand on the man's arm. 'It has been some time since I have been here. Have the arrangements changed at all?'

'My lord?' The footman seemed surprised, and a little confused at the question.

'It is my eyes, you see.' He passed his own hand in front of his face, to indicate the imperviousness of them.

'Not as blind as a bat, perhaps. But near enough.' *Blind.* Saying the word aloud felt good, as though it had been trapped on his tongue for an age, waiting to be shaken off. 'Take my hat and gloves. But my stick must remain with me.' Then he added, 'And I would appreciate a brief description of the room and its occupants.'

Once he was aware of what was required, the servant was totally amenable to the task, and not the least bit shocked or embarrassed by the request. He explained, *sotto voce,* who and what were to be found on the other side of the threshold. Then he said, 'Will there be anything else, my lord?'

'A drink, perhaps. Whatever the others are enjoying. You may bring it to me, once I have found a seat. And please announce yourself when you do so, for I might not hear you approach.' Then he turned back to the difficult task of re-entering society.

He stood for just a moment, taking a deep breath of the familiarly stuffy air. It was a trifle too hot in the room for him. But hadn't it always been so? He could smell alcohol and tobacco. But not the foul stuff he'd grown accustomed to. The smell of quality was as sharp as the ink on a fresh pound note.

'Folbroke!' There was a cry of welcome at the sight of him, followed by the sudden silence as his old friends realised that something had changed.

'Anneslea?' He started forwards, towards the voice of his old friend Harry and forgot himself, stumbling into a table and almost upsetting a game of cards. He apologised to the gentlemen in front of him, and turned to go around, only to feel Harry seize him by the arm and draw him forwards.

'Folbroke. Adrian. It has been almost a year since I have seen you. Where have you been?' And then a quieter, and more worried, 'And what has happened? Come. Sit. Talk.'

He smiled and shrugged, allowing the help of friendship. 'I have not been very good company, I am afraid.' Anneslea pressed him to a chair, and almost instantly the servant returned with a glass of wine. Adrian took a sip to steady his nerves. Suddenly, speaking a few simple words seemed more fearsome than a cavalry charge. 'My eyes failed me.'

'You are…?'

'Blind.' He said it again, and again there came a small lightening of spirit. 'It has been all downhill since that flash burn in Salamanca.'

Harry gripped his arm. 'There is no hope for recovery?'

Adrian patted his hand. 'The eyes in my family are no damned good at all, I'm afraid. The same thing happened to my father. I had hoped to dodge the condition. But it appears I am not to be spared.'

There was the pause he'd expected. Then Anneslea burst forth with a relieved laugh. 'Better to find you blind than foxed before noon. When I saw you running into the furniture, I feared I'd have to take you home and put you to bed.'

The men around him laughed as well, and for a change he laughed with them, at his own folly.

'Folbroke?'

Adrian offered a silent prayer for strength. 'Rupert. How good to see you.'

'But you just said, you cannot see me.'

Some things had not changed. He still enjoyed the company at White's—except for the days when his cousin was present. 'I was speaking metaphorically, Rupert.' *As I was when I said it was good to see you.* 'Although you are not visible to me—' *and that is a blessing* '—you can see that I have no trouble recognising you by your voice.'

'Your other faculties are not impaired?' Rupert sounded almost hopeful to be proven wrong. Could the man not pretend, even for an instant, that he was not waiting in the wings to snatch the title away?

'No, Rupert,' he said as patiently as possible. 'You will find that I am still quite sharp. And since my brief period of reclusion is nearing its end, I will be returning to my usual haunts, and my place in the Parliament.'

'And I suppose Lady Folbroke spoke the truth as well?'

About what? he wondered. And then decided to give his wife the benefit of the doubt. 'Of course. She would have no reason to lie, would she?'

'I suppose not. But then, congratulations are in order,' Rupert said glumly.

'Congratulations, old man?' Anneslea addressed this to him. 'You come to me with your dead eyes, and nothing but bad news. But your wife spreads the glad tidings, I suppose. What is it that we are celebrating?'

Not a clue. 'I will let Rupert tell you, since he is obviously eager to share what he has learned.'

Rupert gave a sigh, sounding as far from eager as it was possible to be. 'It seems that there will be a new heir to Folbroke, by Easter.'

Chapter Sixteen

When Hendricks came to her that afternoon with news of his errands, Emily could barely contain her excitement. It seemed the blind beggar had done more in the space of a few moments than she had managed in a week. 'He saw himself in her, I am sure. And has been reminded of the advantages of his rank. Thank you so much, for helping to lead him the rest of the way.' She leaned forward and clutched Hendricks by the arm, as he sat taking tea with her, so overcome with emotion at the thought of a brighter future that she thought she would burst from happiness.

At her touch, Hendricks gave a start that rattled his saucer, and glanced down at her hand as though he did not know quite what to do about it. 'You give yourself too little credit, Lady Folbroke. It is your devotion to him that made the difference.'

'And did he say anything of me?' she asked hopefully.

'Emily, that is. His wife.' And she began to realise the extent of her confusion. It was as if she was two people, and unsure which of them would deserve Adrian's attention.

'I asked if I should go to you with this news. And he acknowledged that you would need to hear of it sooner, rather than later, and that he wished to speak to you himself. You will have some contact from him in the next day or so. I am sure of it.'

'That is good,' she said, closing her eyes in a silent prayer of thanks.

'Perhaps his outing this afternoon will shed more light upon his plans.'

'An outing?' This was news, but she could not tell whether it was good or bad. 'Did he say where he was going? Or when he might return? And who accompanied him?' She peppered Hendricks with questions, until the poor man held up a hand to stop her.

'He would not tell me, nor would he accept my escort. He left word that he would not be dining at home. But I assume he means to return long enough to dress and then visit you here, this evening. Beyond that, I know no more than you.'

'That leaves me nothing to do but wait,' she said, getting up to pace the room. 'I did not give two thoughts to the risks he was taking, for all the time he was gone. I just assumed that he would be well.'

'And he managed well without your help,' Hendricks reminded her.

'It is not as if I do not trust him to take care of himself,' she said, trying to convince herself that it was a fact. 'But now that I have seen him, and know how reckless he can be—' she looked desperately at Hendricks '—what shall I do? What shall I do if he does not come back?' When she had come to London, she had been worried about household economies and the loss of her freedom. But now the thought consumed her that, if she should never see him again, it would mean that he would never know who she was, or how she felt for him.

Hendricks stared down into his teacup. 'Lord Folbroke would be most annoyed with me should I leave you to worry over nothing. You need have no fear for yourself, for even if the worst should occur, you are not without friends. You will not be alone, Emily. You shall never be alone.'

'But I have no thought for myself,' she said, going to look out the window in the vain hope that she would see his carriage pass by. 'It is only he that I care about. He is at the centre of all my happiness. And now that I have found him again, I must keep him safe and healthy, and happy as well. Just as he was this morning.'

'Then you must trust him,' Hendricks said. 'In a few hours, all will be right again. You will see.'

At a little before eight o'clock, she heard the sound of Adrian's step in the hall and his call for a servant to take his hat and gloves. She rushed past the footman, dismissing the servant so that she could tend to him herself, running into his arms and pressing a kiss upon his lips.

Tonight, though well dressed, Adrian was not his usual, immaculate self. His cravat was tied loosely, his brown hair was mussed, and there was colour in his cheeks as though he had just come back from a ride, or some other strenuous pursuit. He gave a laugh when he recognised the feel of her, and gathered her close in a kiss so hungry that it bordered on violence.

He tasted of brandy, and salt as well. She felt a strange wetness upon her own lips. When she managed to push him clear so she could wipe it away, there was red on her fingers. She reached out gently to touch his mouth, and he flinched and batted her hand away. 'There is a cut on your lip.'

It was odd. For instead of the reaction she had been expecting, of a curse or another wince of pain, he ran a finger tentatively across the wound and grinned at her, wolfish and wicked. 'So there is.'

She reached into her sleeve and withdrew a handkerchief, wetting it the tip of her tongue and reaching up to dab away the blood.

He pulled her close again, lifting her so that her toes barely touched the ground and gave a growl. 'Kiss it better?'

'I do not want to hurt you.'

''Tis a pity that the man who hit me did not feel the same. Of course, I'd pegged him good by the time he landed this on me. So I suppose I had it coming.' Her husband was still grinning, blue eyes sparkling with an emotion that she had not seen before. And he kissed her again, as he had on that first night, as though he could not wait to take her to bed and did not care who knew it.

'You were fighting?' The words and the kiss sent her thoughts rushing back to the man he had been when she'd found him. She sniffed his breath again. 'You have been drinking, haven't you?'

'And what if I have?' He kissed her throat, fondling her body through the gown she wore.

She pushed at his hands, trying to catch her breath. 'You promised me that there would be no more of that. You are too valuable to me to squander yourself. I was beside myself with worry over you.'

He paused, leaning his face against her hair. 'Really, madam, you cannot expect me to place my calendar totally in your hands, no matter how lovely those hands might be. My life is still my own, is it not?' But somehow, he did not sound particularly happy with his freedom.

'Of course it is,' she assured him. 'You know I have no claim on you. But no matter what happens between us, it is very important to me to know you are safe and well.'

He leaned against her for a moment, as though his day had exhausted his strength. 'And I thank you for it. It is good to know that someone cares. And you need have no fear of my condition. I gained it as any proper gentleman should. I went to White's for luncheon.'

'You went out again? And without me?' She could not control the little shriek of delight she gave and threw her arms about his neck.

He gave her a pat upon the shoulder and shrugged as though the sudden change was nothing unusual. 'I could not very well take you to my club, darling. No ladies allowed. Not even wives, thank God.' The last was uttered under his breath, so quiet that she barely heard it. And then he continued, as if he had said nothing. 'My taking lunch there should not be such an uncommon thing to you. I am still a member, in good standing. Anneslea was there, as was his brother-in-law, Tremaine. Good to see them again, after all this time. Anneslea asked about the eyes, of course.'

'And you told them?' She leaned away from him, staring into his face.

'Unlike some problems, my condition is rather hard to conceal.' He looked past her, not even pretending to see. Then he gave another non-committal shrug, as though his mind had moved on to other, far more important matters than the one thing that had consumed him for months.

She hugged him again and kissed him on his sore lip. 'But what of this?'

'After we got the niceties out of the way, there were others who were eager to share the news of the day with me. Some of which was quite surprising. It seems I have much reason to celebrate. My cousin Rupert was there...' He frowned again, pinching his lips tight together until the cut went white.

That might explain his strange mood. She doubted he had wanted to reveal himself so soon to his family.

And she knew from experience that Rupert had a way of ruining even the happiest of days.

Adrian seemed about to say something, and then smiled again, and went on with his story. 'In the course of the afternoon, the bottle was passed around. We got to talking about what was possible for a blind man to accomplish. And then, someone got out the betting book.' He gave another shrug, as though to minimise the foolishness of it. But it was coupled with a satisfied grin. 'Some of the fellows and I went off to Gentleman Jackson's for a bit of pugilism, as any proper gentleman of the *ton* might. Blindfolds for both men. Since I have the advantage of some sight, it would be hardly fair for me to go without. When equally blinded, it seems that I can manage two out of three opponents. A healthy average, I think. I proved quite good at finding my mark. If I can stay out of reach of the first few blows, I can hear the other fellow breathing like a bellows, and take aim upon the source of the sound. I am not as fast as I used to be, and my form was sadly lacking after this extended period of inactivity. But they could not fault my enthusiasm. Although it was a shame that the man I wanted to stand up with was not there to share the moment...'

'You boxed?' She did not know whether to laugh or scold him.

'Just a little harmless sparring. No anger behind it.' But the glittering of his eyes and the set of his jaw made her wonder at the truth of that. 'It was a shame that dear Rupert was too big a coward to share the ring. I dare say, after today's demonstration, he will not think me a helpless invalid, and will know to shut his mouth and keep his distance.'

And wasn't that what she had wanted all along? She gave him another enthusiastic kiss.

'You are glad that Anneslea split my lip?'

'I am glad that you left the house in daylight, and spent time in the company of true friends.' She stretched to kiss both of his damaged eyes. 'And that you told them.'

Adrian pressed his lips on the top of the head. 'It is your fault, you know, with your continual prodding that I do something with my life. And you were right. It was time. A little past time, I think.' And then he kissed her on the mouth. But although it started as a gentle kiss of thanks, it soon became something different.

His hat and gloves fell to the floor, and he gave them a kick that sent them across the hall, clear of their feet. Then his empty hands found her body, moving from her shoulders down her back, crushing her breasts to the front of his coat so he could feel them, and lower until she could feel the first stirrings of his erection pressing against her belly. Though his injured lips were soft on hers, his tongue moved in her mouth, rough and hungry. The brandied taste of it made her drunk with answering desire.

It would take little seducing to gain her ends tonight. He would make love to her, if she asked him to. For there was no sense of playfulness in his kiss, only the demand for swift release.

And as her body readied itself to succumb, her mind

whispered that more had changed than this. In the new world he was creating, there would be no place for secrets. And no way to hide his mystery lover from his friends, or his illness from his wife. Now that he had moved into the light, he was poised on the brink of yet another decision. And there was a chance that she might lose him for ever, if she did not talk soon and tell him everything. She broke from the kiss and freed herself from his grasp, then grabbed his arm and tugged. 'Come. You may tell me all about your plans, over dinner.'

'I have already eaten,' he said, pulling her back and running his hands over her bare arms.

'A glass of wine, then.'

He kissed her again, and said, 'You know what I want. And it is not food or wine. Do not deny me.' With one hand, he locked her hips to his, and with the other he pushed her breasts high, until they strained at the neckline of her bodice. Then he gave a yank on the fabric that covered them. She heard a button pop and her dress gaped. And he bent her back over his arm, and took her nipples in his mouth by turn, sucking hard upon them, biting them, leaving the exposed breast marked with his kisses, plain to see by anyone who might wander into the entranceway of the flat.

He was holding her so tightly that she had no breath to resist him. But the helplessness felt right. This was her husband, after all. And he was so overcome with desire for her that she doubted he'd have heard an objection, had she made one.

And then he paused, raising his head from her aching breasts. 'Last night, and this morning, when you said—'

'Let us pretend I said nothing.' She answered hurriedly, for she did not want him to stop again. 'Do not punish me for what I feel.'

'I do not mean to punish you. I only wish to be sure that your feelings have not changed.'

'They will never change,' she swore, panting, eager for him to resume. 'No matter what might happen between us, I will be steadfast.'

He seemed to flinch a little at this, as though he had hoped for some other answer. 'Good,' he said. 'Because otherwise, I would not...' And then it did not seem to matter, for he was kissing her again, undoing fastenings, pushing her dress farther down her body until he could stroke the tops of her hips above the fabric as he nibbled her shoulders. 'Say whatever you like. Nothing stands between us.'

She gasped, and said, 'I love you.'

He made no effort to answer with a similar sentiment. Instead, he said, 'Show me.' Then he pulled her, as sure as if he could see the way, through the sitting room and towards her bed.

She closed the door behind them. And before it was shut, he had pushed her gown to the floor and was tearing at his cravat to loosen the knot. When he tossed the fabric away and reached for the buttons of his vest, she stayed his hand. 'You will not be able to find things again, if you are so careless.'

He gave a strange laugh. 'Tonight, I am quite past caring.'

She stepped clear of her own clothing and kissed his bare throat. 'Then let me. I have watched you, these last nights. I will lay them out, just as you have. There will be no mistakes. But do not deny me the pleasure of undressing you.'

He gave a chuckle that was half sigh. Then he stood still, his arms a little apart from his body, as though he were standing for a valet. She felt a tremor go through his body at the first touch of her hands.

First, she took his coat, feeling the weight of her own picture and the purse in his pockets, and set it on the back of the chair. And then the waistcoat, and the cravat that she'd picked from the floor, one on top the other, folded and draped over the coat.

She paused to touch him. Broad shoulders, straight back, trim waist—she had seen him in bed, and touched every inch of him. But it had never been like this, with his body half-hidden by clothing. She pressed her lips to the opening at the throat of his shirt, spreading her fingers over the linen, feeling. Then she pushed the cloth out of the way and kissed his chest.

'You are a most interesting valet, madam,' he said, stroking her body before cupping his hand to the back of her neck and urging her to take his nipple into her mouth. 'A man could grow used to this.'

And she thought the same. He made her feel safe and cared for, even as he allowed her to care for him. And it was good to feel the hair on his chest brushing against her cheek, a hint of softness over muscles that were strong and sure. She stripped the shirt over his head, shook the wrinkles from it and laid it carefully with the cravat, then went back to him, rubbing her hands over his bare chest, before pushing him the few steps back to sit on the bed behind him. She sat on the floor to pull off his boots and stockings, stroking his calves, working her way up his legs and undoing buttons, pulling trousers aside and finding him fully awake to her touch.

She set the rest of his clothing by the chair. Then she went to the night table and doused the last candle so that they could lie in darkness.

As she did, he called out to her in surprise.

'Does it bother you to have no light?' she asked.

He reached to take her hand as she climbed up on to the bed with him. 'You will think me foolish, but I have a fear of the dark, when it comes on me suddenly. I am never sure if the last of my sight is leaving without warning, or it is merely a guttering candle.' He gave a nervous laugh. 'With the lights extinguished, we are both equally blind, are we not?'

'Yes,' she said, surprised that she had not thought of it. 'It will teach me to use my hands to find my way, as you do.'

'In darkness, we could be anyone. We could imagine anything. Fulfil our darkest wishes,' he whispered. 'And no one will see.' He kissed, long and hard, full of need, holding her so tight against his body as he did it that she could scarcely breathe. It was another proof of how easily he could dominate her, should he choose, and it made her shudder with anticipation. Then he relaxed back upon the bed to prove how utterly she had tamed him, giving her leave to explore him further, waiting to see what she would do with the freedom.

She straddled his legs, squeezing his thighs between hers and leaning forwards over him so that she could touch the muscles of his chest with her breasts. She could tell by his breathing that the faint touches of her nipples against his skin were as arousing to him as they were to her. He reached for them, pulling her breasts up and cupping them in his hands so that he could take them into his mouth again, rubbing them against the front of his teeth and nipping suddenly, then releasing them to blow them dry with his breath until they felt tight and cool.

She sat up and slid away from him again, running her hands down his abdomen, settling them upon his member and stroking it from base to tip, holding it against the skin of her belly in a way she knew he liked.

He let her work over him for a few moments before bringing his own hands down his body to meet hers, grasping her around the crease at the top of her thighs until his thumbs met between her legs, stroking her. 'Slowly,' he cautioned, while speeding up his own hands. 'Let me last. I want to enjoy you the whole of the night.' His hands came around her body, grasping her bottom. 'Slide forwards. Onto me. I want to be in you.'

She glanced at the chair across the darkened room, thinking one last time of the sheath in his pocket. 'Did you want…?'

'Do not think of it,' he commanded, as though he could guess her thoughts. Then he pulled her hips up his body so that he could rub himself against the wetness between her legs. 'This will be better. If you still wish it.'

'Yes,' she answered, guiding him even closer to where he belonged. She bent forwards and kissed him and rose up on her knees so she could touch herself with the tip of him, as though that were a kiss as well. Then she eased forwards, just an inch, and felt the beginnings of satisfaction as he began to slip inside.

'So good,' he whispered. 'But I want more.' He reached behind her again, trapping her hips and forcing her suddenly down and on to him in one quick, smooth stroke, until he filled her completely. 'There.'

She gasped in shock. She had forgotten how big he felt, resting inside her. And this sudden entrance was nothing like the cautious way he had thrust when he had last done this. Then he had seemed afraid to frighten her.

But tonight there was none of that. Before she could catch her breath, he was moving under her, into her. His hips rose and fell, bucking and grinding against hers as he sought release, making her tremble with excitement at the ease with which he controlled her body.

He slowed for a moment, seeming ready to withdraw. So she pressed against him again, guiding him farther, letting him slide deeper into her until she was sure that he would not change his mind. 'You did not want this from me, Adrian. What has changed?'

He groaned, but did not pull away. 'Am I hurting you?'

'No. It is so good. I want it.'

'Then nothing has changed. Say the words you said to me last night.'

'I love you, Adrian.' She tried to give an answering thrust, but he held her in place against his body. 'Take me. Please, Adrian, make love to me.'

'Yes. Again.' He sank into her, sighing in satisfaction. He was stroking slowly now, in and out of her, making her forget that it could be any way else.

'I love you.'

Then he slowed even more, skin sliding against skin, his hands on her back, moving to clutch her so that he could push with more force. She leaned forwards to lie on top of him. Suddenly, he rolled with her, over and onto her.

She dug her fingers into him, raking his back, afraid that he was trying to escape, and terrified that he would not finish what he had started.

And he laughed at her, as wicked as he had been that first night, straddling her as she had him and pumping hard into her until she lay breathless under him. She was close, so very close now, and he knew it. And he stopped to touch her face.

She nipped at his fingers, begging him to finish her, and he felt her eagerness and pulled his hand away and left her body.

She reached for him, flailing in desperation, and he grabbed her hands and rolled her onto her side. 'No, my darling,' he murmured. 'I will give you what you want, soon enough. You promised this morning that I would have whatever I liked from you. There are other ways to join. And tonight, I mean to try as many as I can.' He was entering her again, from behind, pushing up and down, and pressing hard against places inside her body that had barely felt him before. His hands were on her breasts now, circling the nipples as he thrust, his lips on her ear. 'Does this please you?' he growled, holding her tight.

'Yes,' she gasped, totally possessed by him, totally in his power.

'I am going to make you mine, soon,' he said close to her ear. 'And then I will do it again. And again. I will love you until there is nothing left in you but need of me. And then I will love you again.' He thrust harder and her climax began at the thought of having his seed inside her. And as she relaxed, satisfied that he would finally be hers, his hand came down to press between her legs and rub against her special place. He moved his thumb there in little flicks, keeping time with his thrusts until she broke again and again, mindless and helpless, shaking in his arms, crying his name.

And he felt her surrender and followed her, releasing deep inside her with a cry of 'Emily'.

The joy of it shot through her in a final spasm. He knew her. In this most intimate moment, without sight or words, he had recognised her.

Then he groaned and pulled away, shuddering and covering his face with his arm, as though he could hide himself from her by the act.

She rolled to lie close to him, wrapping an arm around

his waist and pulling at his hand until she could see the faint glitter of his eyes in the moonlight as he stared, sightless, towards the ceiling.

At last he spoke. 'I am sorry. I did not think. But I have saved myself for her for too long.'

'Your wife?' she asked softly.

'When I could not stand to be alone, and availed myself of the services of some nameless woman or other, it was her I imagined. Always her.'

He reached out to touch her hair. 'This week has been different, I swear it. But tonight, when it should have been no one but you, I used what you felt for me. I lied and pretended to be what you wanted me to be. And while I did it, I thought of her. I did not mean to say that name. You are precious to me. It would not have been thus, were you not. And I do not wish to hurt you.'

'It is all right,' she said, trying to gain understanding of what had just happened. The man beside her was racked with guilt over feeling just what she wanted him to feel for the woman he had left behind. She rolled even closer to lean over him and put her hands on his face, kissing his eyes and his lips, and whispering words of love. 'It is all right. It changes nothing between us. I understand. She is with you, even as my husband is never far from my thoughts.'

'She is in London. She will hear of my visit to White's. She will hear about my eyes.'

'Rumours, perhaps,' she answered. 'But it will be better if she hears the rest of it from you.'

'And I have heard things as well,' he whispered. 'But

not rumours. More truth than I ever wanted to know.' He pulled her down on top of him, into his arms, crushing her cheek to his chest and she could feel the pain in him in the vibrations as he spoke. 'She came to me, on the day we met. And I was not there for her. It would have been so much easier, had I been there when she needed me. And I failed her, because of my selfishness. It must not happen again.'

'Your words do you credit,' she said, glad that he could not see the smile on her face, for there was no way she could have explained it.

He must have caught some trace of her mood, for he said, a little puzzled, 'You understand what this will mean to us?' His voice was sad, but resolute. 'This cannot go on. I must go home to her.'

'I knew that what we shared could not last, as did you.' She gathered his hand to her mouth and kissed it lightly, in the dark, glad that he could not know how happy she felt. 'And I know that you love her. You cannot see it, of course. But on the day you showed me her picture, I knew. You have worn the paint away from the continual touching of it. You want to be with her. You know it is true.'

He gave a weak laugh. 'More than I understood. More than I ever believed possible. I can deny it no longer. The woman is my home, and all I could have hoped for, had my life been different. I wronged her horribly by keeping the truth from her. And I have waited too long. Things have been lost that can never be regained.'

'You will not know for sure until you speak to her,' she urged.

'I know it, true enough,' he said. 'About some things, there is nothing more that can be done. And now, I must make the best of what I have left.'

She touched his face again, wishing she could soothe his worries away and tell him how little the blindness mattered. 'It will be all right. But you must go to her.'

He laughed again. 'It is most unusual to accept advice from one's mistress on what to do about the deep and unrequited feelings one might bear for one's wife.'

'Your feelings are not unrequited.'

'How can you know?'

'Because I know you. And as I love you, so will she. If you let her.'

He pulled his hand away and wrapped his arms around her again, holding her close to him as though he were afraid to lose her. 'And then, what will become of you?'

'I will find my husband again, just as I planned to from the first.'

'He left you.'

'And yet I have never stopped loving him.'

He held her even tighter. 'I know it is wrong. And that I cannot have you. But I envy him even a portion of your affection, just as I long to be elsewhere. I am selfish and stupid, and I want to stay with you.'

'It feels so good to hear those words from you. No matter what happens, I will remember them always. But you know what we must do.' She kissed him then, letting the warmth of his love sink into her bones.

'This could not last for ever,' he whispered.

'Perhaps, in a way, it shall,' she whispered back. 'We are happy now. And we shall be happy again. I am sure of it. But you need to do this one thing, to make it all right.'

Chapter Seventeen

When Adrian arrived back at his rooms it was well past breakfast, and he made no attempt to disguise his entry from Hendricks. The man was at the desk in the small sitting room, giving disapprovingly sharp rattles to the paper as he read, as though he could pretend that he had not been checking the clock and waiting for milord to come back from his whore.

Let him wait, said the irritable voice in Adrian's head. *What right does he have to complain about your behaviour, if he has been using your absence to put horns on you?* Had it been just yesterday morning that he had convinced himself that the man was guiltless, and that David was clearly mistaken about Emily's behaviour?

He struggled to calm himself, as he had lying awake in his lover's arms. It did not matter what had happened, now that it was too late to change anything. The best he could hope for was to contain the damage. He could hardly blame Hendricks for loving the woman he wanted. And if she had true feelings in return, his attempting to slaughter Emily's lover might break her heart. And nothing he did now would make him any less a cuckold.

He stared in the direction of the rattling paper and said in his most bland voice, 'If you will give me a few moments to prepare myself, then I will be ready for the post and the paper.'

'Very good, my lord.'

As the valet helped him to change, he could hear the sniff of disapproval at the condition of his cravat, and the ease with which the man had noticed that it had been tied by hands other than Adrian's.

On any other day, he would have found it amusing. But today, a part of him wished that he could tell the man to take the razor and slice it up the back. After today, there was a chance that it was the only evidence he would have of the touch of *her* hands, anywhere in his life.

And his valet might as well follow the act by slitting his throat. He had lain there, after they had spoken of the future. And much as his mind had wanted to begin again, and to love her until he forgot what was to come, his body had found it impossible. He had done nothing but let her hold him. He had dozed as their last hours together ticked away, waiting to see the hazy glow of sunlight that was still allowed him.

And when he'd awakened enough to listen, he could tell by her breathing that she slept soundly, as though she had no fears. Perhaps her feelings had not been as she'd claimed. Faced with their inevitable parting, it had not caused so much as a bad dream for her. And when the sun was fully up, she'd woken, washed and dressed him, and sent him out of her life with a hearty breakfast and a kiss upon the cheek.

Halfway through his shave, Hendricks came into the room and went to the little table, bringing a cup of tea and lemon and forcing it into his hand.

Much as he wanted it, he said, 'Pour this out and bring me another. Just the tea. No sugar. No lemon.' Perhaps some day, when he felt himself starting to forget her. But not today.

'Very good, my lord.'

Hendricks returned shortly with the corrected cup, and drew up a chair and his little writing desk, and began reading the mail. And Adrian allowed the ordinariness of it soothe his mind, pretending that nothing had changed between them.

After dispensing with a tailor's bill and an invitation to a ball that Adrian had set aside as a possible peace offering to Emily, Hendricks said, 'The next is from your cousin Rupert.'

Adrian took a sip from his cup. 'Must we?'

'Hmm.' There was a pause as Hendricks scanned the letter. 'If you will trust my opinion, my lord? No. It is more of the same, really. He saw you yesterday?'

'At White's,' Adrian affirmed.

'He wishes to see you again.'

'How unfortunate for him.'

'There is the matter of your wife…'

'My response is the same as always,' Adrian snapped. 'Throw it on the fire.'

'Very good, my lord.'

And for the first time, Adrian wondered how much of his mail was read properly, and how much Hendricks had chosen to censor. For there was a chance that each letter he had received from Rupert had been full of warnings that his secretary had not seen fit to convey. 'Hendricks.'

'My lord?'

Adrian reached into the pocket in his coat, and held out the locket containing the miniature. 'Describe this to me.'

'It is Lady Folbroke, my Lord,' said the man, puzzled.

'But what does it look like?'

'It is done on ivory. In the painting, she is younger. Sixteen, perhaps. Her hair is longer and darker than it is now. Her face not so full.'

'And the quality of the work?'

'It does not do her justice, my lord.'

'I see.' And he had been displaying the ruined picture to the man for who knew how long, with no mention of it, with no clue that things were not as he thought they were.

'I mean to write to her, today.'

'Will you be needing my help, my lord?'

'No. This is something I must do for myself.' *Then I shall hope that you are not so far gone in love for her that you do not deliver the letter. For I know we are rivals for her affection, even if you do not admit it.*

There was a rattle as Hendricks opened the desk drawer and got out the little frame that Adrian some-times used to help him in his rare correspondence, with the notches to space the letters and the little bar on the paper so he could write a straight line. He arranged the pen and ink, explaining the location of each item as he placed them. Then he stood back to allow Adrian the seat.

'A few minutes' privacy, please, Mr Hendricks.' God knew, the composing of the thing would be hard enough without having to concern himself with other eyes than his catching sight of the letter.

'Very good, my lord.'

When he was sure that the valet and secretary had left him alone in the room, he put pen to ink, and hoped for the best.

Dear Emily,

Now he was lost as to what he must say next. He got the little miniature back out of his pocket, rubbed his finger across the face of it again and set it next to the letter. It did not matter what was truly there. For a little while longer, he must believe in what he wanted to see.

Almost without thinking, he picked it up and touched it again. It had been years since he'd seen Emily. And now that she was lost to him, he regretted not having looked at her more when he'd had the chance.

He dipped his pen again.

How are you faring in London?

No, that would not do. She would look at the line and think that if her welfare concerned him, he should have come and seen for himself long before now. Hendricks had said she'd thrown the last letter into the fire, just as he had the note from Rupert.

But he could not very well lead with a demand that she reveal the identity of her lover. Or a description of the events that had made his contacting her necessary. There had to be some preamble, some words that she would want to hear that would make her read more than a line or two.

And so he wrote the words that he knew she most deserved to hear.

I am sorry. Sorry for so many things that I hardly know where to start. But you have felt the sting of my neglect, and could give me a beginning, if I asked. Was it worse that I abandoned you? Or that I married you at all in the slipshod, neglectful way that I did, never asking your opinion in the matter, or taking the time to know your mind on the subject? I am sure that rumours of my disgraceful behaviour in London have reached you. Too many of those rumours are true. And I am sorry for the shame that they might have caused you.

And for burdening you with the responsibility of my property and all that it entails, I am equally sorry. If it gave you pleasure, then I am glad of it. But if it caused you pain or worry to take on the part of a man while receiving none of the privileges, then I am sorry for that as well.

He paused to wet his pen again. How could he tell her the rest?

I wish to assure you that none of what has happened between us is any fault of yours. In many ways, you are a better wife than I deserved.

All perfectly true, if a trifle understated.

The fault lies with me.

I am blind.
Say it, he commanded himself, as though he could order his hand to move and write the words. *Just say it. No dancing about.*
There are certain impediments to our marriage.

No, that was not right. It sounded as if he had another wife.
Problems.

And that was too small. She was well aware that there were problems, unless she was as blind as he.

I am unable to be the husband that you deserve.

And that made him sound impotent. He cast another paper to the floor. He began again.

I have been hiding from you the cause of our
ration. I find that I am unable to explain the

difficulty, and my conscience can no longer bear the weight of the secret. Were I to come into your presence, it would be plain enough. And so, my dear, I think it is time that we talked. If you are as bothered by this prolonged separation as I am, then I would have you come to my rooms this evening to discuss it. And if you are not, then I will plead all the harder that you grant me an hour of your time. If you cast this on the fire, as you did the last missive, know that I will not relent until we have spoken.

I think I have guessed the reason for your recent visit, and there are things that must be settled between us before any more time passes. For my part, I wish to begin again and start fresh as though the last years that passed have never occurred.

If you do not, I can hardly blame you. If another has captured your affection, then I am glad for him and will regret my folly for waiting too long and losing the chance for happiness between us.

Either way, if you come to me tonight, you need have no fear of reproach. You will find me a humbled man, willing to take any course of action that puts your happiness ahead of my own. With my most heartfelt respect…

His pen hovered for a moment and added, 'and love', before signing his name. After the last week, it would be a lie to say that she had all his love. But she held the place closest to his heart.

And now, he began the other letter that he knew he must write. He scribbled the words hurriedly, not caring how they would look, just wishing to be done with it before he changed his mind, or said something he might regret. Then he blotted the ink, and fumbled for the wax and seal as he waited for it to cool. He addressed only one paper with a name and called for Hendricks, handing his secretary the two letters.

'One to my lover. If you do not know by now how to reach her, then wait for evening and send this back in the carriage I know she will send. And the other...' he moved the second letter carefully to the side '...to Emily.' He smiled. 'And careful not to confuse the two. That would be rather embarrassing.'

From the silence from the man, and his rather abrupt movement in reaching for the papers, Adrian could feel the disapproval crackling in the air.

'I know you think less of me because of my behaviour towards Emily, Hendricks.'

'I have no opinion on the matter, my lord.'

'Nonsense. If you weren't so damned polite, you'd have told me so to my face, long before now.'

There was another telling silence, rather than the quick denial of an honest man.

'If it is any consolation to you, there will be no more of this after today. I have chosen in a way that will do credit to my family and to myself.'

'Very well, my lord.' Hendricks was a good man. But he could not manage to sound pleased by this either, managing to say too much, in no words at all.

'But while I have much to be ashamed of, and much to apologise for, I cannot feel guilty for what has happened. Although I have tried to do so, I simply cannot. The woman I have been with has loved me. Truly, and for myself. Not the title, but the man and all his flaws. It is not something I have experienced before. It was a wonderful thing, Hendricks.'

'I would not know, sir.'

Adrian bit his tongue to hide his surprise. Was it possible that he had misunderstood the reason for the man's hesitance when speaking of Emily? Or perhaps it was that she did not return his feelings for her. If so, there was hope for him, though it might come at the expense of his friend.

But then, who was the source of the rumours about her?

And here was another unexpected gift from his lover. The sudden ability to feel sorry for someone other than himself. 'That is truly a pity, Hendricks. I hope, for your sake, that your circumstances change. Love, whether given or received, is transformative, in and of itself.'

And then he sat back in the desk, knowing that there was little for him to do but wait.

Chapter Eighteen

Emily sipped her morning chocolate, stretching luxuriously under the silk wrapper she wore. Lord, but she was stiff. And it made her blush to think of the reason for those sore muscles. Her darling Adrian had loved her quite enthusiastically.

And he had loved his wife as well. Her heart had ached afterwards almost as much as her body did now, to see him curled against her, broken by his betrayal of both the women he imagined were a part of his life. And she had wanted to reveal herself to him, to ease his suffering.

But a small part of her had cautioned her to stay silent. And as she thought about it, that bit had grown, reminding her that he was not the only one to suffer for his actions. Her misery had lasted for nearly the whole time she had known him. And his could last a day more. At least until his repentance bore fruit, and he made some kind of overture to the woman he had promised before God to cherish.

There was a knock at the door, and her maid informed her that Mr Hendricks was waiting in the sitting room with news for her. Emily gave a quick glance in the mirror to be sure that the robe she wore was decent enough to receive company, tightened the belt under her breasts and went out to greet her husband's secretary.

He held two sealed papers out to her and said, 'He has written to you. In both your guises. I was instructed to be sure not to confuse the letters, to take the first one immediately to his wife, and that if I did not know the direction to you here, to send this with the coach that would come for him in the evening.'

'I see.' So whatever he had to say, he meant to speak first to his wife on the matter. Emily weighed the two pieces of paper in her hand, trying to guess the contents without opening them, and nodded absently to Hendricks, directing him to await her replies.

Did it really matter which she opened first? For if she had read the situation correctly, they would be two sides of the coin. She must trust, now that she had met the man, that the pair of them were not full of lies.

She cracked the seal on the one that bore no name, and read.

My love.

It is with difficulty that I pen these words to you. More than the usual difficulty, of course.

So he had taken the time to joke with her? The news must be bad, indeed.

But it seems some things are better written, for they prevent me from avoiding what could be an unpleasant truth.

In this, she was very much in sympathy.

I have taken your suggestion, and written to Emily, in hopes of resolving the difficulties in our marriage. After last night, I proved to both of us that I cannot leave the spectre of her between us any longer. And I know that you will understand when I say I have no desire to hurt you, any more than I did my poor wife.

Obviously. Her eyes rushed down the uneven lines on the page.

And know also that I would not have had the nerve to face this, had it not been for the time spent in your arms. It has brought about a change in me. A change for the better.

She smiled, thinking how nice it was that he would say so.

This evening, should my wife desire it, I will return home to face what future there is for me, and you will see me no more. I beg you, my darling, understand that I would not leave you were it my choice. For this time we have spent together has been some of the happiest of my life. The past days with you have been closer to perfection than any man deserves. And thus, I fear, they cannot last.

Your words of love were not unwelcome. And though I wish I could say otherwise, I hold honour too dear to reciprocate them. My first obligation must be to the woman I married, and I can no longer fulfil it from a distance, any more than your husband can for you.

Emily had his duty. Which was all well and good. But love would be better.

If my wife rejects me, which I fear is quite possible, then I will write to you immediately and you will know that my heart has no claim on it. It is yours to command, should you still wish it. Half of it is already yours, and always will be.

But whether we be together or parted, Emily has the other half. And the better portion, for it was the one I gave first.

She stopped reading for a moment, and looked at the other letter, wondering if it was half as sweet. Then she returned to the one in her hand.

If I had known you three years ago, I like to think that things might have been different and that I would be at your side today. But if you have the love for me that you claim to, I pray you, wish me well in this most difficult decision and let me go. I must try to make my Emily happy, just as I wish you all the happiness in the world.

For ever yours, Adrian.

Without thinking, she clutched the paper to her lips and kissed it. Then she tore the seal on the next letter, and read what he had to say to his wife.

It was cautious. Polite. And shorter. And when she got to the line about his being humbled, she almost laughed aloud. Even in humbleness, he was more proud than any two other men.

But his willingness to put her pleasure before his own? She thought of how he had treated her when he took her to bed. He had proven that he could do that so often that it made her blush to think about it.

She kissed the second letter as well. Fondly at first. And then touching her tongue quickly to the paper and thinking of how it would be, tonight, when she came to him in his own bed. A marriage bed. Just as it ought to have been between them all along.

Was this not the best of both worlds? She was his lover, and had half his heart for the asking. And she was his wife as well, and commanded his honour and loyalty, along with the rest of his love. He would be her faithful servant, if she wished to take him back. And though he came to her with head bowed, she would make sure that he lost nothing by it. They would both gain by his homecoming.

Once they got past the surprise he would get on learning her identity.

Emily smiled to herself and dismissed it. Surely that would be as nothing. It would set his mind to rest to realise that the woman he loved and the woman he had married were one and the same.

From his place in front of her, Hendricks cleared his throat, reminding her that she was not alone. 'Well?'

She smiled up at him. 'He has chosen me. *Me.* Emily.'

The man at her side looked confused, as though he did not see a distinction. 'Was there ever any doubt?'

'Surprisingly, there was. And now I must go to him, and explain the meaning of his choice, as gently as possible.'

'I suppose you will expect me to come along in this, to support you when it goes wrong.' Hendricks was glaring at her. His tone was sharp, as though he had any right to question her activities.

'I do not expect you to make the explanation for me, if that is what you fear,' she said back, equally annoyed. 'It is my husband who leaves you to write his messages for him, not I.'

'While you have never made me write them, you have had no qualms in making me carry them,' he reminded her. 'You have forced me to lie to a man who is not just my employer, but an old friend.'

'As he forced you to lie to me,' she said.

'But he did it in an effort to protect you,' Hendricks answered. 'Can you say the same?'

'What makes you think you can question me on my

marriage? After all this time, neither of you has cared to inform me of the truth. If I choose to keep a secret for a matter of days, you have no right to scold me.'

'I do not do it to scold,' he said, more softly, 'but because I know Folbroke and his pride. He will think you did what you did to amuse yourself with his ignorance.'

'And now, after all this time, I do not know if I care,' she admitted. 'If what I have done annoys him? Then it will pay him back for the hurt I suffered, all the time he has been away. When he did not know me, and I told him the truth of our marriage, he did not recognise that, any more than he did me. He thought my husband's treatment of me was unfair. And he had admitted the same of his treatment to his wife.'

'Then you must realise that he has suffered as well,' Hendricks said.

She spread her arms wide, to encompass the problem. 'And tonight, he will apologise for it. And I will apologize for tricking him. And then the matter will be settled.'

Hendricks laughed. 'You really think it will be that easy. And have you thought what you will do if he does not forgive you? He might well cast you off for this. And if he does, he will be in far worse shape than you found him in.'

'It will not come to that,' she insisted, but suddenly felt a doubt.

'If it does, he will not last long. You will have taken his hope from him. It might be more merciful of you to leave him with that than to bring him a truth that comes too late.'

What good would it do her to leave him his fantasy, and destroy any hope she had that they would ever be together? And what would become of her, if she could not have him?

Then she remembered Adrian's suspicions about his secretary's interest in the unobtainable Emily. And she said the words that she was sure both dreaded, but that needed to be spoken. For if there was any truth in what her husband took as a fact, than she must settle it now, once and for all. 'Mr Hendricks, if there is something else you have to say on your hopes for my future, then you had best say it, and clear the air between us. But before you do, know that I decided on the matter from the first moment I laid eyes on Adrian Longesley, many years ago and long before I met you. Nothing said by another is likely to change me on the subject at this late date.'

She waited in dread that Hendricks might speak what he was really thinking and thus ruin their friendship and any chance of his continued employment. There was a pause that was longer than simple circumspection. And then, he said nothing more than a curt, 'I understand that, my lady. And I have nothing to say.' And for a moment, she could see that he smouldered with frustration and a range of other emotions inappropriate to his station. Then they submerged beneath the surface again, leaving him the placid and efficient secretary she had grown to depend on. 'I will accompany you this evening to assure

Lord Folbroke that there is no hidden motivation to your actions, and that all was done in his best interest. But I suspect that although he may say he loves you both, it might not extend to an easy forgiveness to all of us who have had a part in this attempt at reconciliation.'

As the afternoon changed to evening, Adrian paced the floor of his sitting room, wondering if he had done the right thing. After a few false moves, he had learned to correct his course to avoid the pianoforte that still blocked the corner. And he wondered—would he ever have to explain the thing? Or would Emily take it as a given that it had come with the rooms? Perhaps she would expect him to show some interest in playing it, just as its giver had done.

If she did, he would admit his ignorance, but would submit meekly to lessons, if they were necessary to keep the peace. And if, each time he touched the keys, he thought of someone else?

It would be better if he did not think of the thing at all, and suggest they remove to Derbsyshire. It would give them a chance to discuss their differences in private, and he would be far from temptation. And if necessary, it would disguise the length of Emily's confinement.

He squeezed his eyes tightly shut, realising that it made no difference. His progress across the room was unaffected, and it did nothing to shut out the pictures in his mind of his wife growing big with another man's child. One did not need eyes to see one's thoughts.

But he had told himself for over a year that this was

likely to happen, and that it would not bother him. Now he must survive the future he'd created with as much grace as he could manage. Tonight could not be about recriminations. He had promised something quite different in his letter.

And had that been the correct course of action? Perhaps it would have been better to go to her, rather than expecting her to come to him? It would have shown more respect.

And that would have left him fumbling his way through Eston's town house, demonstrating the worst of his condition before he had a chance to speak to her. Or, worse yet, he'd have discovered she was at her rooms.

'Hendricks?'

'He has not yet returned, my lord,' said the footman who had come into the room to bring his afternoon tea.

Now Adrian imagined his secretary and his wife in the process of a tearful parting, spending a languid afternoon alone in each other's arms.

He sat and took a sip of tea, scalding his tongue and focusing on the real pain instead of the imagined one. He must not doubt his choices, now that they had been made. Here, in his own home, he could show to best advantage that he was not the helpless invalid she might fear him to be. He had told his man to take care with his dressing, that everything about him must be just so, clean and unrumpled. And he had not taken so much as a drop of wine with his noon meal, that there would be no evidence of excess in his diet. He would hold himself with a posture worthy of a dress parade, so that, in the first glance she had of him after so much time, she would think him strong, capable and worthy.

Yet he knew them to be superficial changes that might not be enough. Perhaps it would be better if he were not alone for this. He was blind. And he had not told her. There was no way to excuse that.

He called out to the footman, 'Parker, I wish to see Mr David Eston. Send someone to his rooms and request his presence, tonight, a little before seven. Explain to him that his sister will be visiting me. And that we may require his assistance in a delicate matter.' Her brother could act as a buffer between them and escort Emily home, should the worst occur and she rejected him.

But if she was truly in a delicate condition, it was unfair of him to expect her to weather this alone.

Chapter Nineteen

That night, Emily twisted nervously upon the handkerchief in her hands as they came into her husband's lodgings. Hendricks glanced at her and then at the footman, waving aside an announcement of their entrance. Then he threw himself down on a bench by the front door as though he suspected the need for a hasty retreat and gestured towards the sitting-room door. 'He will be there, waiting for you,' he said in a surly voice. 'I am staying here. Call if you need me.' He glared up at the footman, as though daring the man to find anything odd about the situation and said, 'Parker, bring me a brandy. A large one.' And then he stared at the opposite wall as though he had arrived alone and unwelcome in the home of strangers.

Emily walked down the hall and away from him, hesitating on the threshold of the room where she knew her husband waited.

But the pause had been without purpose, for she could not have turned and left unnoticed. Adrian's head lifted eagerly at the faint scuffling of her slippers. 'Emily?' He listened for the clock. 'You are early.' He stood at her approach and her heart nearly stopped at the look on his face and the way he reached out to the doorway, welcoming her through it. He was wearing a coat of midnight-blue wool that lay smooth over his broad shoulders. Black trousers covered his well-shaped legs without a wrinkle. His cravat was a Mathematical and starched to an almost painful formality, and his boots gleamed in the candlelight as though his valet had made it a life's mission to show her the reflection of her entrance back into her husband's life.

It was a stark contrast to the casual handsomeness that he normally showed her. He had wished to look his best when they finally met.

And then he seemed to lift his face and scent the air. There was a growing look of alarm in his blank eyes. He had recognised her even before she spoke.

'Adrian?' she said softly.

His hand dropped and his smile faltered, becoming a frown. 'I am sorry. I was not expecting…'

'Perhaps you were.'

They both paused then, trying to decide who should speak next. She closed the distance between them, coming behind his desk to lay her hands on his face in reassurance. He closed his fingers over hers and felt the ring she had taken from her jewellery case for the occasion.

'Your wedding ring,' he said.

'It belonged to your mother,' she reminded him. 'I have not been wearing it for some time. It is quite heavy. And I found the continual reminder…difficult.' Then she brushed his fingers over her own features so there could be no doubt that he knew her for who she was. 'There is something I must explain to you.'

'I expect there is.' His voice was as crisp and tight as his cravat.

'Our first meeting was not by chance. I sought you out.'

'I know that,' he said. 'But I did not know that you had found me.' He pulled his hand from her grasp and away from her face.

'Mr Hendricks warned me that I would not like what I found.'

'Hendricks.' Adrian gave her a cool smile. 'Why am I not surprised that he was involved in this?'

'But I insisted he take me to you. I did not know how horrible the place was, and when you rescued me…'

'Lucky for you that I did, my lady,' he said. 'To go there demonstrated no care for your virtue or your safety.'

It had not bothered him so much when he had thought her another man's wife. But perhaps she deserved his scorn. 'I was wrong. I know that now, and will not make the same mistake again. But you saved me from my own foolishness. And you were so heroic. And when you kissed me? It was just as I'd always imagined it could be.'

He pulled her close to him suddenly, and the contact was more frightening than comforting. 'And now you will tell me that you have spent our time apart, dreaming of the taste of my lips. Please spare me the poetry, for there is much more to this story, I am sure.'

She turned her head away from his sightless stare. For the first time since she'd found him, it was unsettling her. 'I wanted to be with you. But there was so much wrong.'

'Finally. We come to the meat of it,' he said.

'What if you laughed at me? What if you rejected me, once you knew?'

He pushed her away from him, and turned away from her to face the fire. 'And in an unguarded moment, I told you that such a rejection was unlikely. That I suspected already, and would forgive you anything. Why did you not tell me the truth then?'

She struggled to remember what he had said that might have been a cue to a revelation, and could think of not one thing that mattered more than any other. 'I did not tell you because I did not want what we were doing to end. It had not yet been as it was last night.'

'But now that I have planted my seed in you, you have nothing to fear. You know there is no chance I will cast you off, now that you might carry my heir.'

'Adrian,' she said, disappointed, 'that is not what I meant at all.'

'Then perhaps you should explain again. For I fail to see any other logical explanation for your behaviour.'

There was a commotion from the hall. The sound of Hendricks's voice raised in protest, and the curt dismissal of someone who had no intention of listening to him. Parker's voice was raised as well, so that he could be heard over the din and making his usual offers of assistance and announcement.

'Emily.' Her brother burst into the room, staring at the two of them together. 'It is about time that you have come to your senses. When I heard that you were invited here tonight, I was afraid I would have to drag you to the meeting. Or do you think that this is the result of your plans to sort your affairs?'

'David. What are you doing here?'

Adrian said, more to the fireplace than to them, 'I invited him because I feared that the shock of discovering my condition might unsettle your delicate nerves.'

'Your condition?' David strode across the room to her husband and seized him by the shoulder, passing a hand in front of his face. 'Adrian, what is this I hear about you from Anneslea? It is a joke, is it not, for I saw you just last week.'

'But I did not see you,' Adrian responded, laughing bitterly, and slapped his hand away. 'I have enough sight left to know that you are waggling your fingers in front of my eyes, trying to catch me in a trick. I can see the shadow of them. But that is all. Now stop it, or I will find sight enough to thrash you for the impudence of it.'

'And you let me stand here yammering at you the other day and said nothing about a problem. You let me think you were drunk. Or were you drunk? I no longer know what to believe out of you.' She could see the anger and confusion clouding David's face, and held up a warning hand, hoping that he would not muddy the situation any more than it already was.

'You can safely believe that I did not tell you, because it was none of your damned business. Any of it,' her husband snapped. Then he pushed David away and walked back to her, grabbing her by the arm and pulling her to his side. A hand came up to her face, and his head cocked to the side as he traced the lines of her, as though trying to replace this image with the one he held in his mind. His other hand released her, reaching for the miniature, as though there were some way left to compare the two.

'Then you shouldn't have invited me into the middle of things tonight,' David shouted at the back of his head. 'And you.' Her brother stared at her, almost shaking with rage. 'It was him, all along, wasn't it? I do not know which is worse—that you do not admit to the world that you are together again, or that you could not at least admit it to me.'

Adrian smiled at her. And his expression was so cold and heartless that she was glad he could not see her fear. 'Oh, I think there is much more that needs to be confessed, if you wish to know the whole of the story, isn't there, Emily?'

'Certainly not.' Surely he did not expect her to tell her own brother the most intimate details of the last few days.

'You could at least assure David that he was right in his assumptions about your entertaining another gentleman under our very noses.'

'I beg your pardon?' Where had he gotten such ideas?

Adrian looked at her brother. 'Your little sister has led me a merry dance, David. She tricked me into thinking she was another woman, rather than admitting from the first that she was my wife. She would not even give me a name, because she said I would know her in an instant, should she give me the smallest clue to her identity.' He laughed. 'And I have been dangling after her for days like a lovesick idiot, racked with guilt at my betrayal of my wife and the depths of feeling I had developed for this supposed stranger.'

David was staring at her, his anger stifled by bafflement. 'Why would you do such a foolish thing, Emily? Would not the truth have been simpler?'

'Oh, I think the answer is obvious,' Adrian announced. 'She came to London to trick me into bed, hoping that she could hide the evidence of her infidelity. And when she realised that I could not see, she found it good sport to trick me with lies. I hope that you have gotten sufficient amusement from our time together. For I certainly have.'

She gasped in fury at the thought that he might refer to the things they had done together, even in such an oblique way. 'Of course, Adrian. Because why would I not find it amusing that my husband had been so long away from me that he did not even know me? Or to have evidence of your frequent infidelity thrust in my face?'

'My infidelity?' he shouted back. 'At least you did not have to drink endless toasts to celebrate the results of it, as I did for you at White's.'

'I have no idea what you are talking about,' she said, angry, but still confused.

'When, exactly, am I to expect the heir you seem to have got for me? Or is the date of delivery to be as much of a surprise as the parentage?'

'I say…' David sputtered, ready, once again, to come to her defence. 'Emily, are you…?'

'Oh, hush,' she said, glaring at him. 'If you have nothing constructive to add, then please refrain from speaking.' She turned to Adrian and said, 'I did not tell you the truth because it was apparent, almost from the first day we married, that you wished no part of me.'

'If my treatment bothered you, then you could have spared yourself the trip to London and written me on the matter. If you had explained your dissatisfaction, we might have discussed the matter like adults.'

She could feel him growing distant again, as though it were possible at this late date to go back to the way they had been. 'If you had bothered to answer my letters at all. Or told me the whole truth when you did. I had to come to London to see you, to learn about the loss of your sight.'

'And when you did, you thought it would be easy to trick a blind fool into thinking he'd got you with child so that you would not have to explain yourself.'

'I have done nothing that needs an explanation. But if you wish to think of yourself as a fool,' she said, 'then far be it from me to change your mind. It is clear enough to me that you are little hampered by your condition, when you want something. It is only when you do not get your way that you insist on reminding people of it. If I turned to childish subterfuge, it was in response to my adversary.'

'I am your adversary now, am I?' He smiled again, as though satisfied that he understood the situation at last. 'On second thought, it is well that you came to see me, so that I could know the way of things. It seems that my idealised view of my little country wife was quite naïve. You run the estate because I allow it, and now you have arranged for my successor. And in all the recent foolishness, I have forgotten how well the arrangement suits me. I will return to my diversions, and you may return to Derbyshire with your bastard, secure in the knowledge that I will offer no objections.' He turned to go into his bedroom and her brother made to go after him.

She placed a hand on David's arm and pushed him firmly out of the way. 'I am dismissed again, am I? And I suppose I should not be the least bit surprised by it. It is just as I suspected, from the first. Once you knew who I was, you would want nothing to do with me.'

He turned back to her. 'I do not want anything to do with a woman who would use my blindness to her own advantage against me.'

'To my advantage?' She laughed. 'And what advantage did I gain that I was not entitled to? In exchange for having you treat me as one might normally treat a wife, I have made every attempt to improve your character. I dare say the man I found was a drunken, suicidal wreck, too steeped in self-pity to be worthy of his estate, his title or the woman he'd married. And now, after the fine promises you made in the last day, you plan a return to that state. By all means, if it pleases you, make yourself as miserable as you do your wife and friends.'

His blank eyes glittered; for a moment, he looked as disappointed by the idea as she was. But then he regained control and stared through her, speaking as though he did not know or care if she was still in the room. 'This interview is at an end. I find further communication between us to be both unnecessary and unwelcome. If it is absolutely required, we will communicate through an intermediary.' He turned to walk back into his room. Then he turned back suddenly and said, 'And for the love of God, woman, choose someone other than Hendricks to carry your messages. Allow me that, at least.' Then he turned again and disappeared behind the slammed door.

Emily reached for her brother's arm before the trembling began, for the outpouring of emotion had made her almost physically weak. 'Take me home, David. I wish to go home.'

She did not have the heart to tell him that his obvious rage at her husband was totally lost on the man, who had not seen the dark scowls he was receiving from his own friend. He was helping her through the front door now, to his carriage.

And for a moment she thought she heard the sound she longed for. A call from the open door behind her, the sound of contrite footsteps hurrying down the tiles of the entry hall. A sign that her husband wanted her, now that he knew who she was.

But there was nothing. Only Hendricks, standing framed in the open doorway.

She turned away from him, far too confused to seek his comfort. Instead, she leaned upon her brother's arm with her whole weight, letting him lead her the rest of the way to her seat. When they were safely inside the carriage, she thought about allowing herself the luxury of tears. But they would only reveal what she suspected her brother already knew: how deeply Adrian's latest rejection had hurt her.

David was staring out of the back window in the direction of Adrian's flat, as though he could not quite believe how suddenly and totally wrong the evening had been. Then, he turned to her, accusing her with his eyes. 'You could at least have told me about the child.'

'There is no child,' she snapped.

'Then why did he think there was?'

'Possibly because my own brother came to warn him about my affair.' She hoped he did not expect some sort of absolution for all the trouble his meddling had caused her.

'I am sorry. I did not know.'

She said, 'You could not be expected to. The circumstances were…unusual. But in future, when I request you not to intervene, I would appreciate your co-operation.' Then she remembered the comment about his afternoon at his club. 'And I think it was Rupert who misled him about my supposed pregnancy. You only added fuel to the fire.'

Her brother fell silent for a time, and then said, 'Perhaps, once he has had time to think, he will relent and come to you.'

'Or perhaps not. He is a very proud man. And I have hurt him.'

'He is afraid of exposure.'

'He is no coward,' she argued.

'Of course not,' her brother said in a voice dripping with sarcasm. 'He merely hid a problem from us, for our own good. He feared the family would remove the title from him.' And then he added more thoughtfully, 'There is a chance we could do it, you know. He has been behaving little better than a madman, shirking his responsibilities, risking life and limb. Perhaps we could arrange an annulment, if this is a family condition. If you had been together, then the children—'

'No,' she snapped back. 'There is nothing wrong with his mind. It is only his eyes.' She glared at her brother, daring him to oppose her. 'You were quick enough to marry me off to him when he was your friend. And still content when he left me. You cannot just grab me back, three years down the road, because you fear that he is likely to leave me childless and lose the entail.'

'It is not that at all, Emily.' David groaned in frustration. 'Why must everyone expect the worst from me? Can you truly be happy with him, in his condition? He will be helpless, and you will need to care for him, just as you would a child.'

'You know nothing of him, and what he can do,' she said hotly. 'He is quite capable, when he has a mind to be. As sharp as he ever was. And if he needs my help?'

She lifted her chin. 'I have been waiting for the chance to be his helpmeet for some time. And if there is to be a baby, there can be no question of it being anyone's but his.'

Her brother raised his hands in front of him, in a gesture of helplessness, as though afraid to ask for further explanation. 'I swear, it all grows more confusing, the longer you explain it to me.'

'It is very simple. All that I have done, I've done out of love for Adrian. And I think, given the time, he will realise that he feels the same for me.'

David looked at her doubtfully. 'Very well. If a reconciliation with him is what you wish, then I hope you succeed in it. But after today's interview, it appears that Adrian is just as stubborn as he ever was at avoiding his marriage to you.'

And remembering what she had told herself on coming to London, she should be satisfied with the results of the visit. She had been with him, in the way a wife should be with a husband. She had assured herself that he was indeed alive, and Rupert had been assured of his well-being. She had ascertained the reason for his absence. If he continued to remain apart from her, she would at least know why. And in the end she had managed to speak clearly to him and to make him well aware of her displeasure at the separation.

She had succeeded in all the things she'd set out to do.

And done the one thing she had never meant to. She had fallen truly in love with her husband.

Chapter Twenty

When his guests had left him, Adrian stormed back to his sitting room, still furious with the way he had been tricked. Emily had known him from the first moment. And had taunted him with the knowledge the whole time they had been together. How she must have laughed, to hold that from him, just out of reach.

The servants had known as well, for they had known her when she'd brought him home from the tavern. And Hendricks had been complicit in the elaborate scheme, for she could not have managed it without his help. Everyone surrounding him had kept mum on the truth, smirking as he mooned over his own wife, pitying him for the poor blind fool he was.

If they had the time to laugh, then perhaps they did not have enough to occupy their time. He swept a hand across his desk in the corner, sending pen, inkwell and writing frame all to the floor in a heap. He pulled down the books on the shelves as well, useless things that they were now that he could not see them. He upended the piano stool, and wishing he had discovered enough about the instrument to destroy the thing so that it would never trouble him with memories again. He slammed the lid down over the keys, and his fingers touched the decanter of brandy that had been set on top of it. To a man who did not play, such a thing was little better than a makeshift table.

His fingers closed around the neck of the bottle and he imagined the sound of shattering crystal, and the sight of the brandy, running in fine rivulets down the wall, or dripping amongst the piano strings, and the pungent scent of the spilled liquor...

Then he stopped. It would be better to drink the stuff than to waste a chance at oblivion. No need for a glass...

His arm froze with the bottle halfway to his mouth, and he held it there. How much of the last year had he spent just that way? Blundering about, breaking things and drinking. Time drifting by, and him neither knowing nor caring how it passed. How long had it been since he had given up even trying to care?

His Emily had been waiting at home for him, doing her best. She had said as much, hadn't she, when she'd told him about her marriage? How she worried that it had been her fault he'd left. And how frightened she had been at first that he would reject her again. She had been sure that if he ever really knew her, it would be all over between them. He had made it his mission to prove otherwise.

In the end, she had been right. The moment he had learned her identity, he'd sent her away.

She had been quite accepting of his truth when she had learnt it. He had assured her that there was nothing on earth his wife could do to lose his trust, for the fault of their parting had been his, and his alone.

Still holding the brandy, he stooped to the floor, fumbling to pick up the books around his feet. How much damage had he done in his rush to destroy what he could not appreciate? The wreckage around him was the result of another selfish act on his part. Just one of many in the last few years.

But when had he ever learned to be otherwise? He thought of how angry he had been with his father's foolish disregard for the future of the family. And how angry his father had been, when talking of Grandfather. All of them angry at fate for the hand that they had been dealt.

But while Emily might be cross with him for his treatment of her, she worked to change the things that made her unhappy and made the best of the rest.

She accepted him.

He took a deep breath and walked through the debris to the door, opening it suddenly on the shadow waiting in the hall.

'Hendricks.'

'Yes, milord.' It was not the usual calm tone of his old friend, but the clipped words of a man simmering with rage.

Adrian cleared his throat, wishing he could call back

any of the last fifteen minutes. 'It seems I have had an embarrassing display of temper.'

'I can see that.'

'It will not happen again.'

'Not to me, at least. I am giving my notice.'

For a moment, he felt the same as he had when his eyes started to fail him. As though everything he'd taken for granted had slipped away. 'You can't be serious.'

'I am always serious, sir. You comment often on my lack of humour.'

'It was never an issue, when we met,' Adrian reminded him. 'On the Peninsula, you were quite good company.'

'And you never used to be such a damned fool.' The blow seemed to come from nowhere as Hendricks kicked the brandy bottle from his hand. It hit the floor with a thump, and Adrian could hear the glug of the liquid spilling from it, and the smell of it soaking into the rug.

'Perhaps not.' Adrian stood, straightening to full height and taking a step forwards, knowing that whether he saw it or not, he still towered over his friend. It would not be wise to let him think he could strike twice. 'But then I did not have to worry about you lying to me to cement your position with my wife. You have known of this charade from the beginning, haven't you?'

'Of course. Because I am not blind.' Hendricks had added the last to goad him, he was sure.

'I can think of only one reason that you would go along with such nonsense. Rupert told me, yesterday, that Emily was with child.'

Hendricks gave a hiss of surprise, and stifled an oath.

'And I assume that the child is yours, and that you rushed her to London so that she might lie with me as well and there would be some assumption of legitimacy.' Adrian laughed. 'Why you would think such a thing might work, I have no idea. I do not need my eyesight to count to nine.'

Hendricks swore aloud now, as Adrian had not heard him do since their days in the army. 'You really are an idiot, Folbroke. And it amazes me that I had not noticed it before now. Do you wish to hear how I found your wife, when I went to her today?'

'The truth from you would be a welcome change,' Adrian snapped back.

'Very well, then. When I saw her this morning, she was nothing like that silly picture you carry of her. The miniature that you have worn to the bone with your fondling is of a rather plain, ordinary young girl. But the woman I saw today was fresh from bed, and wearing nothing but a blue silk wrapper. She had tied it tight under her breasts in a way that left little to the imagination. And as she sat, the skirt slipped open and I could see her ankles, and the slope of her bare calf.'

Adrian's hand clenched, wishing that he had the bottle again so that he could strike out at the voice and shut the man's mouth for good.

'She took the letters you sent her, and read both of them in quick succession. She sighed over them. She kissed them. She all but made love to the paper while I stood there like an idiot, admiring her body and wishing that just once she might give me an instruction that did not involve running back to you. But nothing has changed. In regards to men other than the Earl of Folbroke, she is every bit as blind as you are to her.'

'So you know nothing about this supposed child?'

There was a long pause, as though the next words were difficult. 'She has been faithful to you. From the moment you married. I would stake my life on it. There is no way she can be pregnant.'

'But at White's, Rupert said—'

Hendricks cut him off. 'If you had used the brains you used to have, you would consider the source of the rumour, and remember that your cousin is an even bigger fool than you.'

To the trained ear of someone who had no choice but to listen, there was as much emotion in the last speech as there had been in the first. Regret, frustration and jealousy of a husband so unworthy of the devotion he had received from his beautiful wife.

Adrian knew the feelings, for he had felt them himself when he'd thought of Emily.

'You are right,' Adrian said at last. 'If there is any truth at all, or any explanation that can be made, I should have asked her for it, rather than trusting the man who wants nothing more than to ensure that I do not have a child. And I think I understand your reasons for leaving me as well.' For how awkward would it be if Adrian apologised to his wife and they all went back to Derbyshire together. The two of them, living side by side in the same house, both loving the same woman? And all the worse for Hendricks, forced to witness their happiness, and to know that though Adrian was his equal in ability and his inferior in temperament, he had the superior rank, and the unwavering love of his countess.

He put the thoughts of Emily aside for the moment and said, 'You will have letters of reference, of course. And anything you might need.'

'I have already written them.'

Adrian laughed. 'I expected no less from you. You are damned efficient, when you set about to do something.' He stepped over the bottle on the floor and gripped the man by the hand. 'I trust that I was effusive in my praise of you. And generous in my severance?'

'Of course, my lord.'

'I expected nothing less of me. You have been invaluable as an aide. And you shall always be welcome in my house, as a guest, should you ever wish to return there.'

'I do not think I will be back for some time,' Hendricks said. 'If things go as I expect, you will be too busy for company, at least until after the new year.'

'Next year, then. The fishing is good in the run at Folbroke. You still fancy trout, do you not?'

'I do indeed, my lord.'

'Then you must be sure that the money I give to you in parting is enough so that you might live comfortably on it for twelve months and then visit me as a man of leisure before taking another post. I will not take no for an answer.'

'Of course, my lord.' It would have felt deuced odd to touch the man's face, after all these years. But suddenly, as though there had been a change between them, it was hard to read any truth in Hendricks's words. Adrian had heard the worry and frustration plain in the man's voice for so long that the sudden absence of it was like a void in the room. It had been foolish of him to think that there could ever be mockery or cruel deception. 'Hendricks, I am sorry. I understand that I have not been an easy master…'

'Lord Folbroke. There is no need—'

He held up a hand to forestall the man's excuses. 'It is true. But there will be no more nonsense after today. If you mean to leave me in the hands of my good wife, I will be an amiable man and not trouble her unnecessarily.'

'Very good, my lord.' There was blessed relief in the man's voice, as though he had given him compensation beyond money in that one little plan.

'Of course, I shall have to square things away again, after the mess I've just made of this interview.' He dropped out the statement in the most offhand way possible, as though the entire staff had not heard the argument that had just ensued. 'Eston has taken her back to his town house, I assume?'

'I believe so, sir. I could send for her, if you wish.'

'No, that is quite all right. I will go to her.'

'I will have the carriage brought round.'

'No.' An idea had suddenly occurred to him. 'It is less than a mile from here. And the night is clear, is it not?'

'Yes, my lord.'

'Then I shall walk.'

'I will have a footman accompany you.'

Adrian stood and reached out to grip his old friend's arm. 'If you mean to leave me to my own devices, then I will have to learn to do without you.' Although damned if he knew how. 'The streets are not crowded. And I remember the way. I will go alone.'

'Very good, sir.' There was only a trace of doubt in Hendricks's voice, which Adrian took to mean that he was not suggesting something beyond the realm of possibility. It was something he had never tried, of course. But his sight was unlikely to get any better. It was high time he learned to navigate the city. They walked together into the front hall, and instead of Parker coming to aid him, he felt the familiar hands of Hendricks helping him into his topcoat and handing him his hat and gloves. Then the door opened, and he sent Adrian on his way with a pat on the back.

And almost as an afterthought, there came from behind him a soft, 'Take care of her, Adrian.'

'I mean to, John.' Then he walked down the steps to the pavement and set out into what might as well have been a wilderness, for all he knew of it.

Chapter Twenty-One

Four steps down, to the street. He felt the edge of the kerb with his cane and stepped a little back from it. And now, a left. It would be two roads down in this direction, he remembered, before turning onto the busier street ahead. He listened closely as he set out, to gauge his surroundings. It was more difficult in darkness than it might have been in the light, for he could not use the rays of the sun to set a direction.

But for this first trip, it was better to be out when the way was not so crowded. He heard a single walker on the other side of the street from him, and remembered that he would have to be cautious of footpads and cutpurses. Though the areas he travelled were good ones, not all that ventured out after dark could be trusted.

He tapped ahead of him with his stick, to make sure there were no obstacles, and set out at a pace that was slower than normal, but still little different from a stroll. He almost stumbled, as the pavement gave way in another kerb. But then he caught himself and stood, looking both ways for changes in the shadows that obscured his sight, and listening for the sound of horses' hooves and the rattle of carts or carriages.

When he was sure there was nothing, he made sure his course was straight, stepped forwards, and made an uneventful crossing, gaining the opposite side. He proceeded for a little while longer in the same fashion, before everything began to go wrong.

He could hear the increase of traffic around him as the way became busier. While most passers-by gave him a safe space to walk in, he was occasionally jostled and forced to adjust his pace to those around him. The changes in speed made it harder to keep a straight course, and the corner seemed to come much sooner than he expected. Had he passed two or three streets?

Suddenly, he felt a hand, light as a moth's touch, on the pocket that held his purse.

He caught the tiny wrist easily in the fingers of his left hand. 'Here, you. What are you about?'

'Please, sir. I didn't mean nothing.' A child. A girl? No. A boy. He was sure of it; though the wrist he held was bony, it did not feel delicate, and the sleeve that it jutted from was rough wool.

'You just choose to walk with your hand in my pocket, then? No more of this nonsense, boy. You meant to have my purse. And now the Runners shall have you.'

'Please, sir…' there was the loud, wet sniff of a child

who was near tears and with a perpetual cold '...I didn't mean any harm. And I was hungry.'

'And I am blind, not stupid. And certainly not as insensate as you expected. I am much harder to sneak up upon, because I pay better attention to small things such as you.' He gave a frustrated sigh to persuade the boy that he was serious in his intent, but not without sympathy. Then he said, 'If you want to avoid the law, then you had best prove your worth. I am walking to St James's Square. Do you know the way?'

'Yes, sir. Of course.'

'Then take my hand and lead me the rest of the distance. Keep a sharp eye out and steer me clear of any pickpockets. And I will know if you lead me wrong, so do not try it, or it will be off to the Runners with you.' Then he pretended to soften. 'But if you lead me right, there will be a shilling for you, and a nice dinner.' And at the sound of another sniff, he added, 'And a clean handkerchief.'

'Yes, sir.'

He felt a small hand creep into his, and a tug, as the boy turned him, and set off at a brisk pace in the other direction. After a while, he could tell that the boy was honest, for the sounds around him and the echoes off the buildings of the square changed to something more like he had expected.

It annoyed him that, in his first outing, he had proved himself unable to find a house he had visited hundreds of times. Perhaps that meant that he was as helpless as he feared, a useless invalid that would only be a burden to his wife.

Or perhaps it proved that he would manage as best he could, under the circumstances. In any case, it had been better than hiding in his bedroom. Even having accepted aid, he felt an unaccustomed sense of power.

The boy read off the numbers to him as they passed, and then led him up to the door he specified. 'Here we are, sir.' The boy was hesitating as though afraid to lift the knocker.

For a moment, Adrian hesitated as well, then mounted the step and fumbled and then grabbed the ring, giving a sharp rap against the wood. 'Very good.'

'Lord Folbroke?' The butler's greeting was unsure, for it had been a long time since he'd visited. And if the servants' gossip here was as effective as it was in his own home, the whole household must be buzzing since the return of his wife and her brother.

Adrian gave a nod of affirmation and held out his hat, hoping that the man could understand the nature of his difficulty by the vagueness of his gaze. 'And an associate,' he said, gesturing down to the boy with his other hand. 'Could someone take this young man to the kitchen and feed him? And give him the shilling I have promised him.' He glanced down in the general direction of the child and heard another sniff. 'And wipe his nose.'

Then he reached out, and found the boy's shoulder, giving it a pat. 'And you, lad. If you are interested in honest work, some might be found for you in my house.' If he meant to walk the city in future, a guide would not go amiss. And he suspected a child of the streets should know them better than most.

'Yes, sir,' the boy answered.

'Yes, my lord,' Adrian corrected. 'Now get some dinner into yourself and wait until I can figure what is to be done with you.'

Then he turned back, looking down the entrance hall of his brother-in-law's home and trying to remember what he could of the arrangement. The butler stood behind him, still awaiting an explanation. 'Is my wife in residence?' he asked. 'I wish to speak with her.'

He suspected the man had nodded, for there was no immediate answer, so he tipped his head and prompted, 'I am sorry, I could not hear that.'

The man cleared his throat. 'Yes, my lord. If you would wait in the salon...'

Adrian felt the touch on his arm, and shrugged it away. 'If you would describe the way to me, I prefer to walk under my own power.' The man gave him instructions, and Adrian reached out with his stick to tap the way into the sitting room.

As he crossed the threshold, he heard a gasp from the left, on the other side of the hall. Higher than it should be. There were stairs, certainly. And a woman in soft slippers, running down them with short light steps.

'Adrian.' Her voice was breathless and girlish, as he had remembered it, as though she could not quite overcome the awe she felt, and her pace was that of his eager young bride.

But now, before she reached him, she slowed herself

so he would not think her too tractable, and changed her tone. 'Adrian.' In a few paces she had changed from the girl he'd left to the woman who had come to London for him. She was still angry with him. And pretending to be quite unimpressed with his arrival.

'You notice I have come to you.' He held his arms wide for her, hoping that she would step into them.

'It is about time,' she said. 'According to David, you never visit him here any more, though it is not far, and the way is not unknown to your coachman. Not an onerous journey at all. Hardly worthy of comment.'

He stepped a little closer to inhale her scent. *Lemons*. His mouth watered for her. 'I did not request a coach. The night is clear, the breeze fresh. And so I walked.'

He thought he heard a faint gasp of surprise.

'I very nearly got lost along the way. But there was a boy in the street, trying to pick my pocket. And so I caught him, and forced him to help me.'

Now he could imagine the little quirk of her mouth, as though she said the next stern words through half a smile. 'That was very resourceful of you. There is no shame, you know, admitting that you need help from time to time. Nor should a minor setback on the journey keep you from taking it.'

'Trying to teach me independence, are you?'

'I think you do not need teaching in that. It is dependence that you fear.'

'True enough.' It had made him resist her for far too long. 'It was wrong of you to lie to me, you know. I felt quite foolish, to think I had been seducing my own wife.'

And now he had wrong footed it, for that sounded like she was not worth the effort.

The smile was gone from her voice. 'If you had not kept the truth from me in the first place, then I would not have needed to lie to you. And I doubt you'd have bothered to seduce me at all, had you known who I was. If the first week of our marriage was any indication of our future, you'd have grown bored and left me by now.' Her voice was smaller, and with the breathless lack of confidence that he remembered from the girl he had married. Then there was the tiniest sniff, as though she might have a tear in her eye at the thought, but it was stifled and replaced with the firmer resolve of the new Emily. 'And I would have found a less tame lover to satisfy me.'

Damn the woman. He had forgotten her assessment of his abilities, in the early days of their union. And she had chosen to remind him of it, in a common hallway where anyone might hear. He stepped the rest of the way into the salon and pulled her in after him, closing the door so that they could be alone together. Then he let the heat of anger spread lower in him, to change to another kind of heat entirely. 'Or you would have learned to speak aloud what you wished from me, so that you were sure I understood. I am blind, you know, and need an understanding woman.' He tried to sound pitiful.

But she was having none of it. 'Your eyes were good enough when we married, and yet you were blind to my charms.'

'Which are considerable,' he added. 'Given a little

time, I'd have discovered them. It is far more likely that I would have crept away to London by now just to get some rest.' He leaned closer to her, so that he could whisper into her ear, 'I swear, after only a week in your company, I am exhausted by your appetites.'

'Exhausted already?' She was definitely smiling again. 'I thought it was just getting interesting. But, of course, you had already begun to think of another while you bedded me. Some paragon of innocence and common sense named Emily who is most unlike me.' She caught him by the lapel and fumbled in his coat pocket to be sure that the locket was still where he always carried it. 'And she is most unattractive, to judge by this likeness.'

He gripped her wrist to stay her hand. 'She is a goddess.'

'Your picture of her is spoiled.'

'And yet I am loathe to part with it. It got me through Talavera unscathed, and many other battles after that one. I do not need to see it, for I carried it halfway across Portugal and I memorised every line.'

'Really.' There was a quiet awe in her voice as she softened to him, and he knew he had won. 'But I am not the girl in the picture any more. I have changed, Adrian.'

He eased the locket from her hand, and replaced it in his pocket, marvelling that he had not known her from the first. 'Not as much as you think. You were beautiful then, and you are beautiful now. Emily,' he said, enjoying the sound of the word on his lips and the little cooing noise she made when he named her. 'Emily.' His body tightened in anticipation, just knowing she was with him after so long. 'Have I ever told you how completely I love you?'

'I don't believe you have.' She leaned against him until his shoulders bumped against the door behind them.

'I expect you will hear it frequently, now that I have returned to you.' He kissed her gently, marvelling at how right it felt, holding her close, enjoying the warmth of her body, the now familiar curves of it, and the smell of her hair, and wondering why he had been foolish enough to deny himself.

And then he remembered what she had said to him on the night that they had spoken of their marriages. 'Three times?'

'I beg your pardon?'

'You told me that your husband had made love to you only three times, before leaving you.'

'Yes, Adrian,' she said, giving an impatient little stamp of her foot. 'Of course, the number is greater after this week. Now it is four. Or perhaps four and a half. I am not sure how to count some of the things that have happened.'

'But still. Three times.' He shook his head in amazement. 'I could swear it was more.'

'And you would be wrong. It was only three.' She pressed her body tight to his. 'Now you are treating me so politely that it makes me wonder if I must force you to tend to your obligations.'

'My obligations?' he asked.

'To your wife,' she said significantly. And she slipped

her hands beneath his vest, spreading her fingers over his ribs, then tugging at the tails of his shirt. She was eager for him again. And he remembered what Hendricks had said, and did his best not to wonder at the reason for it.

He stayed her hands. 'Before we continue. When I went to White's yesterday, I chanced to meet Rupert.'

'How unfortunate for you,' she responded. 'But it explains the nonsense you were ranting at me a few hours ago. Your cousin has been harassing me endlessly in Derbyshire over your absence. You had been away so long that he had begun to doubt your existence.' She went up on her toes to kiss him, catching his lower lip in her teeth and nibbling upon it.

'Rupert is a blockhead,' he muttered around the kiss, wondering if he cared one way or the other for the truth. If she meant to distract him from it, she was doing a damn fine job, for her hands had started to move again, reaching for the buttons of his trousers. 'The next time he visits, I will box his ears and send him on his way. As I wished I could have yesterday. He was quick to offer me congratulations on the impending birth. I assured him that you told the truth, of course. And that I was very happy. As I am, of course.' He felt her shoulders begin to shake and feared that tears were imminent. He reached up to wipe them from her cheek and his hand felt nothing but her soft, kissable skin. 'What the devil? You are laughing at me. What do you find so amusing about this?'

'That you insist on being so noble about my poor unwanted child.' Her hands left his body, and he heard the rustle of her skirts and felt the hems brushing his fingers as she drew them up to her waist, then pressed his hands against her belly to prove to him that it was soft, flat and empty. 'Have you not touched me here often enough to find the truth?'

'I was not paying attention,' he said. Nor was he now. He was too busy feeling the bottom of her stays, the tops of her stockings, and all the delicious flesh in between. He ran a finger under the bow in her garter. 'This is new.'

A silk-clad leg twined about his to help her balance as she kissed his throat. 'Your darling Emily is a virtuous lady and does not go naked beneath her gown. But there are limits to my propriety. Your tiresome cousin would not stop bothering me about his plans for the estate when he was Folbroke. So to put him off, I told him I was pregnant with your child and he had been cut out of the succession.'

'You little liar. Do you know what agonies I went through, thinking you loved another?'

'I suspect I do. For I have felt them every day that we have been parted.'

He winced, imagining the pain of the last day, magnified by weeks and months and years, and then pulled her close to him for a kiss that was not nearly enough to expiate it. But it seemed to help, for she purred in satisfaction against the skin of his throat. 'Tell me, when you discovered this supposed truth about my infidelity, did you rush your mistress's bed so that you might vent your frustrations?'

'Perhaps,' he admitted.

'Then I hope that we might go back to my rooms to be alone, and that you are similarly frustrated tonight.'

He remembered their lovemaking of the previous night, and her eager response to it, after her lies to Rupert. 'And when my cousin came back in nine months with a christening gift, where were you planning to get a baby?'

'From you, of course. I came to London to seduce you.'

They were the last words he had thought to hear from his wife. Not unwelcome, of course. Merely unexpected. In response, his pulse increased and his mind filled with possibilities.

'And do not tell me that you do not want a child, for I will not hear of it. Sighted or blind, it will not matter, as long as he has a strong father to show him the way.'

'You think that, do you?' He could not help smiling at the prospect. For a child who had such a mother could not help but grow right.

'And his brothers and sisters as well.'

'Brothers and sisters?'

'You do not know it,' she assured him, 'but brothers, when they are not cutting up one's peace, are a great comfort.'

'We do not have one, yet, and you are already planning a family.'

'And I am quite tired of planning,' she whispered. 'Now that you have taught me what it means to act on the desire.'

He gave a weary sigh, as though it was a burden to

please her and to hide how perfectly wicked he found her plan, now that he had grown used to it. 'You are a most trying woman, my Lady Folbroke. If that is all that will please you, then I am tired of fighting you on it. Take me, and get it over with.'

'As you wish, my lord.' And she was reaching for his buttons again. He grabbed for her wrists. He had not expected that she would take him seriously and now things were getting quite out of hand.

'Emily.' That had been a mistake. For while the feeling of her hands was making him hard, speaking that beloved name nearly made him lose control. 'Can you not wait until I might take you to bed?'

She tugged at the end of his cravat with her teeth. 'I have waited three years, Adrian.' She pulled her hands up until she could kiss his fingers, sucking the tips of them into her mouth. He released her hands, trying not to imagine the lurid things that he wished to do with the mother of those future children.

He would act on them, in time. Soon, he reminded himself, firmly. Very soon. Just not now. He had a lifetime with her. Surely he could wait a few minutes, until they could go to her rooms. Or his. He withdrew his fingers and ran them over her face, tracing her smile, her cheeks, her jaw, in a chaste examination of each feature. How could he not have known this face? It should have been as familiar to him as his own. 'You are so lovely,' he said, trying to fill the void of neglect he had created with a more worthy emotion than lust. 'If you mean to take the locket from me, then I must find something else to carry, so that I can share your beauty with others while I enjoy it myself. Will you sit for a cameo?'

She stepped with her little slipper-covered feet onto his boots to make it easier to kiss him. 'What a clever idea.'

'It is, isn't it?' He smiled and ran a finger down her cheek. 'Something Greek, I think. I see you posed as Athena.'

'Aphrodite,' she offered, 'with bare shoulders.'

He ran his fingers lower, touching her throat. 'And bare there as well. And here.' His fingers touched her skirt, still raised and crushed between them, and remembered the treasures exposed beneath it. 'Perhaps an artfully arranged drape,' he conceded, stroking diagonally across her body until his hand rested on her bare hip.

'And you could touch me, whenever you liked,' she encouraged. And her hands slipped lower again.

'This is madness,' he said, without much conviction. 'Stop it this instant.'

'Why?' she whispered.

'Because we are in a salon and not a bedroom. It is not respectful of your brother. It is not proper.' He tried to think of other reasons. But as she exposed him, stroked him and eased him between her legs, he did nothing to stop her.

'And I am your wife and not your lover,' she said, stopping herself. In her voice, he heard the hesitance and resignation that had been there on their first nights together.

She was soft, warm and willing. And he was harder

than he'd ever been for her. The contact with her body made every nerve in him tingle with eagerness. The air was full of the scent of lemons, and he was wasting time with propriety. 'You are both,' he said. 'Wife and lover. Let me prove it to you.' Then he leaned back against the door, shifted his weight, bent his knees, found her body and lost himself.

The next minutes were a blur. His hand behind her knee. Her leg wrapped around his hip. His hand on her breast. Her mouth on his, kissing as though she could suck the life from him. And their bodies meeting, over and over in subtle, silent thrusts so as not to summon the servants or alert his childhood friend to the delightful debauchery taking place in his home. And all the while, the thought echoing in his head was that most men would give two good eyes for the opportunity to have a woman like this, even for a single night.

But the lascivious creature panting out her climax in his ear was his wife. His Emily. Emily. Emily. And he finished in her with a soul-wrenching shudder, and a single rattle of the door that they rested against. As their bodies calmed, he held her, amazed.

Behind them, the door rattled, and bounced against his shoulders as though someone was attempting to open it. 'What the devil?'

'David,' Adrian said, remembering why he had resisted this interlude. 'A moment, please.'

'Folbroke?' There was a moment of suspicious silence. 'And I suppose my sister is in there with you.'

He smiled, and said, 'My wife. Yes.'

'We are working out our differences,' Emily said, with the smallest sway of her hips before she parted from him and let her skirts fall back into place with a rustle.

'But must you do it in the salon?' David muttered from the hall.

His wife was giggling into his lapel and smoothing his clothing back into place as he said, 'My apologies for the momentary lapse of judgement, Eston. It was...' he rolled his eyes towards heaven for the benefit of Emily '...unavoidable. In a moment, we will be retiring to Emily's rooms, and will bother you no further.'

'But perhaps you might join us for dinner,' Emily offered.

'Later in the week,' Adrian added.

'Several days from now,' she corrected.

From the other side of the door, there was a disgusted snort and the sound of retreating footsteps. Emily burst into another fit of giggling, then she was reaching for him again.

This time he stopped her, ignoring her pouts and the demands of his own body. 'Lady Folbroke, your behaviour is disgraceful.' And then he whispered in her ear, 'And I was a fool to have run from you.'

'Yes, you were,' she agreed. 'But you are my fool, and you will not get away from me again.'

'Quite true.' He grinned. 'Thanks to you, I think I will be the first in a long line of Folbrokes to die in his bed.'

* * * * *

MILLS & BOON®

Want to get more from Mills & Boon?

Here's what's available to you if you join the exclusive **Mills & Boon eBook Club** today:

✦ *Convenience – choose your books each month*
✦ *Exclusive – receive your books a month before anywhere else*
✦ *Flexibility – change your subscription at any time*
✦ *Variety – gain access to eBook-only series*
✦ *Value – subscriptions from just £1.99 a month*

So visit **www.millsandboon.co.uk/esubs** today to be a part of this exclusive eBook Club!

MILLS & BOON®

Why shop at millsandboon.co.uk?

Each year, thousands of romance readers find their perfect read at millsandboon.co.uk. That's because we're passionate about bringing you the very best romantic fiction. Here are some of the advantages of shopping at www.millsandboon.co.uk:

* **Get new books first**—you'll be able to buy your favourite books one month before they hit the shops

* **Get exclusive discounts**—you'll also be able to buy our specially created monthly collections, with up to 50% off the RRP

* **Find your favourite authors**—latest news, interviews and new releases for all your favourite authors and series on our website, plus ideas for what to try next

* **Join in**—once you've bought your favourite books, don't forget to register with us to rate, review and join in the discussions

Visit **www.millsandboon.co.uk**
for all this and more today!